Katharine Donelson

Rodger Latimer's Mistake

A Novel

Katharine Donelson

Rodger Latimer's Mistake
A Novel

ISBN/EAN: 9783337026158

Printed in Europe, USA, Canada, Australia, Japan

Cover: Foto ©Andreas Hilbeck / pixelio.de

More available books at **www.hansebooks.com**

RODGER LATIMER'S MISTAKE

RODGER LATIMER'S MISTAKE

A NOVEL

BY

KATHARINE DONELSON

CHICAGO

LAIRD & LEE, PUBLISHERS

Entered according to Act of Congress, in the year 1891,
By KATHARINE DONALDSON,
in the Office of the Librarian of Congress at Washington.
ALL RIGHTS RESERVED.

*The heart which, like a staff, was one
For mine to lean and rest upon,
The strongest on the longest day
With steadfast love—"*
     This book is
        Affectionately Dedicated

RODGER LATIMER'S MISTAKE

CHAPTER I.

It was a summer evening in the last week of August of
188—. The inhabitants of the suburban university town
of Edgewood, situated on the lake shore, within ten miles
of the city of Clinton, had closed their doors and windows
against the dense fog, that with the setting of the sun,
had rolled down the lake from the north, and enveloped
the village. The fog was so heavy that within an hour
after it had settled upon the numberless shade trees of the
town, they were dripping as though in a rain, and the
sidewalks below were wet. The lamps at the street
corners could be seen but a short distance, and then only
as small circles of luminous fog. The houses loomed up
indistinctly and ghost-like, on either side of the wide
streets. In some, no light at all could be seen, in others
the lamps from within, cast their rays through the trans-
lucent mist, increasing the spectral aspect of the dismal
night. On a side street, some three squares from the
university buildings, stood the house of Professor McVey.
There was no fence around his place, and a broad gravel
walk led up to the four steps, that ascended to the piazza
that ran across the two front rooms, and the hall, and
down the south side of the old-fashioned, square, wooden
house, that was painted white, and had old-fashioned
green blinds to its windows. A large hammock full of
pillows, hung across one end of the piazza, and near it
was grouped three red lawn chairs, a weather-beaten
steamer chair, and a rustic lounge. The hall was dimly
lighted, but from the room on the right, which was Pro-

fessor McVey's study, there came through the yellow silk sash curtains, that covered the lower half of the two front windows, a glowing light that indicated warmth and cheerfulness within. The room was occupied by Professor McVey, who sat in front of a blazing wood fire, his legs stretched straight out, so that his feet might rest upon the wicker wood basket that stood at the corner of the fireplace; and a young girl of twenty, the only child of this sixty-five year old man, and a young man sitting on a sofa beside the fire, who was gazing at the girl, as she leaned over the back of her father's chair, to kiss the head she held between her arms, that were placed each side of her father's neck, and crossed below his chin. This girl was small, delicate, and graceful, dressed in black silk, the waist of which was made without sleeves, and was cut with a low, square neck. Over the black silk, was worn a black lace overdress, the sleeves of which covered the white, plump arms. The square neck was trimmed with a lace edging, that was held together below the throat by a slender golden oar, that was won by the girl a few weeks before in a feminine rowing match. Her only ornament was a bunch of goldenrod, that was thrust into her belt, and lay close against the waist in front. It was a beautiful face that leaned down close beside the old man's cheek; the eyes were large and dark blue, with long lashes, several shades darker than the light brown hair that was arranged in fluffy short curls across the forehead, and in a loose knot low on the back of the head.

"Well, papa," said Margaret McVey, as she pressed one of her cheeks against her father's thin face, "why can't you come home earlier to-morrow; didn't we have a pleasant ride to-day?"

"Yes, my darling, it was very pleasant, but sufficiently long, I think."

"Not half long enough for me," said Margaret as she placed her head on the other side of her father's, and kissed his cheek. The old man lay as in a trance, with closed eyes, as his daughter gently stroked his side whiskers and chin, kissed the top of his bald head, and then again rested her cheek against his. "You dear papa, I do believe you are getting old," she continued, "you don't like to ride as well as you used to, and Doctor Kean says riding is the best thing in the world for you. No, I won't let you go until I kiss you good-night." And she clasped her hands tightly across her father's throat, as though to hold him fast, which appeared to be an unnecessary precaution, for the father looked as though time itself would be too short for his resting under those little loving hands.

"You know," pursued Margaret, "that you said you would do just as I wished you to, during vacation, and you must not shut yourself up in that close college library so much. We will drive to-morrow if you wish, but we must be out of doors two hours; will you do that, papa?"

"Yes, yes darling; I will not go over to the college at all after luncheon if you do not think it best."

"That would be lovely! Good-night, papa." And again the soft warm cheek pressed the thin cold one.

"Good-night, my child." But the flaxen curls rested quietly against the gray beard. How happy is tired age in its quiet submission to loving youth! For a few minutes there was silence in the room, the eyes of the young man sitting on the sofa were full of unwonted tenderness, as they rested on the face of the gentle girl, pressed close, as though in brooding care, to the wan face of the old man. As the clock on the mantel struck half-past nine, Margaret slowly raised her head, once more pressed her hands beside each cheek, once more kissed the bald head.

"Now don't sit up late, papa, for we're to have a long drive to-morrow. When you and Rodger get to talking, you never know when to stop." This assertion was not based upon a knowledge of facts, for Professor McVey and Rodger Latimer rarely gave more time to each other than conventional politeness required, but it was the illogical expression of a fear of a long talk that special night, for Margaret knew that Rodger had come to speak with her father regarding his professional location. As she rose from the back of her father's chair, Rodger Latimer also rose and stepped toward her with an extended hand.

"You will bid me good-night, Margery?" he said. In a flash, the expression of her face changed from an almost motherly tenderness, so womanly it was, to a girlish archness.

"Certainly sir, good-night," she replied, as she made him a profound courtesy. "I shall hope to see you in the morning," she added, throwing him a kiss from the tip of her fingers, as her head was turned over her shoulder toward him, as she tripped out of the room.

Rodger Latimer returned to his seat on the sofa, and looked into the fire, with a happy expression of contented proprietorship on his face. After a few moments he raised his eyes to encounter the steadily fixed gaze of Professor McVey. He hastened to speak:

"I fear that I am keeping you up, Professor, but I'll not detain you long."

"Oh no, you are not, I am very glad to see you, and will gladly hear all you have to say. Do not hasten, Rodger, but say all that you wish to."

"I *wish*," said the young man, "that I could have followed your advice in the choice of a profession. I have felt all through the past two years, that in studying law

I was placing myself in opposition to your wishes and judgment, and deeply regretted the necessity."

"And what was the necessity?" asked Professor McVey removing his searching eyes from Mr. Latimer's face to the fire.

"It lay in my own judgment and preference," replied Mr. Latimer; "you certainly will not deny that in the selection of a vocation a man should choose that for which his friends, and he himself, believes he is best fitted, especially if that choice is in harmony with his inclinations."

"You never should act in opposition to your judgment," said the professor, "the inclination perhaps is not worthy of as much consideration; but you must remember that it was your father, not I, that wished you to succeed to his place in the college. It was natural and right that I should do all I possibly could to accomplish his last wish, which seemed to me a very wise and proper one. To strive to fill as honorably as your father did, the chair of mathematics in a college of the rank of this, would have been a noble ambition for you, and in such a position your life might have been a decidedly happy and useful one. Edgewood is a desirable place of residence." A sneering smile for half a second flitted across the young man's face. "But what was it, Rodger, you particularly wished to speak of to-night?"

"I thought I would like to tell you that I have rented an office on Washington street, and shall commence practising in October."

"You think Clinton the best place in which to locate yourself?"

"I don't know that there is much difference in cities, either in the East or West; it's the man, not the place, that brings success or failure."

"To be sure," replied Professor McVey, "the main thing is to be doing something, to have some constant occupation, something for which a man is responsible, that requires him to go to work every morning, and holds him for the larger number of hours during the day; it don't matter so much what the work is," again an expression of dissent took possession of the young man's face, "provided it is obligatory and systematic." The professor suddenly wakened up; he was astride of his hobby. "There is no happiness without regular employment," he continued; "when will young men learn this, and set themselves to some stated methodical work? One of the evils of locating a college near a large city, is the great wealth possessed by some of its citizens; the large amount of money spent by some of the young men in Clinton is a curse to them, and their example is a snare to some of our students who are dependent upon their own exertions for a livelihood. It made me sad indeed, when I was in New York last month, to see how some of the sons of old friends of mine lived. It was lamentable; yachting, shooting, clubs, and the theater, seemed to fill out their lives. They had no interest in anything outside of themselves, no sympathy with any cause or organization whatever. They seemed to think their daily comfort the center of a revolving universe, in which their bath was a matter of the utmost importance, and as to their dinner, it was of such paramount consideration they gravitated toward it for hours, and seemed to think it worthy of their most mature thought. Those stalwart, well educated young men would sit round for hours in utter idleness, not knowing what to do with themselves, and would talk of killing time. What a wicked expression that is! They were being eaten up by sloth, their lives passed in utter idleness, cankering idleness, nor is it strange that such idleness leads to wickedness. I was told that some of those wealthy young men do not lead lives of absolute moral rectitude. I am very glad, Rodger, that you have decided to work at anything, anywhere."

"That was not a voluntary decision, sir, and while I believe that all you have said regarding a regular employment is true in the main, work with me is a necessity."

"What are your prospects, what are your plans?"

"My plans are, to begin the practice of law in Clinton this autumn. I hope to crowd my two feet down until I find standing room, and then I must fight for it, work for it, perhaps, would be better to say.'

"You are well equipped for the effort, Rodger," said Professor McVey; "let me see, how old are you?"

"I am twenty-eight."

"What a heritage is youth!" said the professor, with earnestness, rising to his feet and leaning his elbow on a corner of the mantelpiece, and resting his large head against his thin white hand. "Why, my young friend, what a life you have before you! Twenty-eight years old, with unimpaired health, and the mental discipline given by the literary and law course at Harvard. You certainly occupy vantage ground at the beginning of the contest."

"It's not a question of health or of will; but competition is sharp, and every inch that I gain I must struggle for. I have no doubt of the ultimate outcome, of that I am sure. I cannot, or at least I do not expect any pecuniary assistance from my uncle; I suppose he feels he has done his full duty toward me, in meeting the expenses of my college education, and sending me through the law-school. He handed me, last week, a receipted rent bill for my office this coming year, and he has given me quite a fair law library; he gave me a check for fifteen hundred dollars, with the receipted rent bill, saying as he placed it in my hand, 'Now Rodger, there is money enough to pay your first year's expenses, and by Gad! if you can't swim after that, you better sink.'" Mr. Latimer smiled good humoredly as he repeated the remark of the brusque business man, but gentle Professor McVey started as with a nervous shock, the words seemed to him brutally cruel. With a little, meaningless laugh Mr. Latimer continued, dashing right into the subject nearest his heart, and the one he especially came to speak of that night. "I did not wish to leave Edgewood, professor, without speaking to you regarding my engagement with your daughter. I beg that you will consent to our being married as soon as I have a home to offer her."

Professor McVey reseated himself, and gazed into the fire with a troubled expression. He had always been a bookworm, and from boyhood up, an enthusiastic philologist. For many years he had been a teacher of ancient languages, and had lived more in the past. than the present. He knew Grecians and Romans better than his own countrymen, the issues of the nineteenth century were trivial to him, compared with those of the first, and no poet or statesman of modern times, gave him the intellectual pleasure, or commanded his reverence, as did those of hundreds of years ago. The streets of Athens, her shaded walks, her Acropolis, were more real to him than the elms and buildings of his Yale Alma Mater. His library and classroom bounded his world, and the scientific and religious struggles of to-day, the vital questions of capital and labor, civil service reform and national finance, elicited from him but little attention, and no interest, so pre-occupied was his mind with ancient philosophy and poetry. It was said that only once was he ever seen by his students to shed tears, and that was one day when he was reading to an outgoing class Socrates' Apology. As he gave utterance to the lofty sentiments of the Greek sage, his enthusiasm kindled, a color flushed his pale face, his eye lighted up with unusual fire, and his voice trembled with emotion; higher and higher rose the tide of his feelings, till at last he burst into tears. But this teacher, who could become so possessed of the noblest passion as he read the words of Socrates, passed through our civil war, without any desire to understand the underlying causes of the contest, and with his sympathies hardly touched by the sufferings of either side. He lived in another time, his heart was fixed upon other things. But after all, this Greek teacher knew, when he stopped to think of it, that death comes to all; his own wife Millicent, whose portrait hung over the mantel right before him, and to which he now turned his troubled eyes from the fire, had been laid under the sod five years before. Every time he went to the city he saw the marble stone that marked her grave, gleaming white through the trees of Oakwood cemetery. His Millicent, that gentle New England girl, whom he first saw in the church, on "The Green," of a village on Long Island sound, that gentle wife who never said nay to her catechism, her husband, or society; that gentle wife was gone from his house, and he and Margaret were alone together. Some day, he must die—Margaret alone! utterly alone! The look of painful uncertainty suddenly left his face as he turned toward Mr. Latimer, and said, as impetuously as it was possible for him to speak: "Rodger, be married this autumn, and live here with us, and go into the city every day to your business. As I think of it, this is Margaret's house, left her by her mother, so it will be yours. Be married, and live here."

The blood flew into Mr. Latimer's face, flushing it deep

red, over the high forehead to the roots of the short hair.

"Live here as your guest? Impossible, sir!"

"And why not?" asked the professor.

"If I succeed as I hope to, I must live in Clinton. I must identify myself with the city, make acquaintances among the business men, and become a part of its society, as far as I can. I hope to make a home for Margaret in the city."

"And take her there to live?" asked the alarmed father.

"If I live there, I suppose she will live with me, that is, if I have the honor and happiness of making her my wife."

Professor McVey leaned wearily back in his chair; a shadow had fallen upon his path, and it seemed to him just then, that it would never pass off. For the first time, he had faced the possibility of a separation from his daughter. "Sixty-five is not so very old," he thought as he closed his eyes, "and she is only twenty; why may we not have many happy years here together, in our own dear home." Everything seemed vague and uncertain, he could not imagine a life without Margaret, and his mind was simply paralyzed, as he attempted to grasp such a thought. Mr. Latimer looked at the pallid face quivering with emotion, across the chasm that yawns between youth and age, but ignorant, and unconsciously selfish as he was, his heart was touched by the suffering aspect of the old man, which was that of one shrinking from an impending blow. He hastened to speak: "I could not possibly be married for a year or so, my financial condition would not permit it. I think Margaret and I love each other enough to wait patiently, until my income would reasonably warrant our marriage, but when that time comes, professor, it must not occasion a separation between you and Margaret. To rob you of your daughter would be a poor return for all of your love for my father, and your kindness to myself. I hope you will consent that we all live together somewhere, either here, or in Clinton."

"Any way, any way, Rodger, only do not take Margaret from me," said the professor as he slowly opened his eyes. The conversation was ended for the night, and very soon Mr. Latimer took his leave for the boarding house, where he had occupied rooms during the Harvard vacations, for the last four years, since the death of his father had broken up his own home in Edgewood. Professor McVey bade him good-night at the front door, which he closed after him, turned the key in the lock, and slowly mounted the stairs, carrying to his chamber a sadder heart than he had known, since the face of his gentle wife was covered from his sight in that very room.

CHAPTER II.

The next morning, Margaret saw that something was the matter with her father. He scarcely tasted his coffee, and she noticed that his bacon and muffin remained untouched on his plate. He did not sit at the table more than one-half of the time he usually spent over his breakfast, but went to his study and seated himself before the brightly burning wood fire. A fire was frequently needed in August, both morning and evening, in that lake region, to make a house comfortable. He placed his thin, cold hands near the crackling blaze for a few minutes, and then took up the morning paper; but Margaret saw that he was not reading, for his eyes were fixed immovably on one place. As the clock struck nine, he cast off his slippers, took his shoehorn from a corner of the mantel, and put on his shoes. While doing this, he said to Margaret who was sitting near, "I must go a little earlier than usual this morning, Margaret, as I have to take the proof of our library catalogue back to Morrison to-day; they wish to get it into press as soon as possible."

Margaret seated herself on the carpet at her father's feet, as had been her habit for years, and tied up his shoe strings, and buttoned his gaiters around his ankles. "I shall not be home to luncheon," the professor continued, in a sad voice, as he placed his hand lightly on the loose knot of soft hair that was close to his knee. It was an unusual caress from him, and the sad tone and gentle touch, filled Margaret's eyes with tears. She bent low over the dear feet, yes, even the shoe strings and gaiter buttons were dear to her. "I think," he continued, "that I will stop in and take lunch with Miss Sargent, and come home on the three-thirty train; that will give us two hours for either a ride or a drive, whichever you choose, my child."

Margaret opened the screen door for him, and stood on the upper step, as he passed down from the piazza; when he was two steps below her, she threw her arms around his neck, and held him tightly, as she rested her chin on his shoulder.

"Papa, what did Rodger say to you last night," she asked," that made you sad? you ought to tell all that you and he talked about."

"How do you know that he said anything that made me sad?"

"Oh, I know, I guess it; don't you know that we women can guess everything?" she asked, as she gave him a little impetuous hug. "Now you must tell me what it was, or I shall be real unhappy."

"He did not say much of anything, excepting that he wished to take you to Clinton to live with him." Both stood very still; Margaret's face turned rosy for a moment, and her eyes grew large and luminous, but only for a moment, for the anxiety of the daughter just then, dominated the sweetheart. Never before had they spoken together of Rodger, as holding any special relation to the family. Professor McVey knew that the diamond that had sparkled on Margaret's finger for the last year, had been placed there by Rodger; he knew that Rodger, all of his life, had come to the house as though it were his own home, and why shouldn't he, the only child of his own dearest friend, his classmate, and associate college professor for years, the friend who had died in his arms four years ago? He knew—but that was so dream like, in such a far away future—that Rodger and Margaret would be married some day; but it never seemed to him that this, his own little Margaret, who flitted around his **house,** and was always by to cut **his** magazines and foreign papers, and pour out his coffee **and light his** cigar, and button his gaiters, was the Margaret who **was to marry** Rodger; that was some **other Margaret, a girl in a book, or** one out in **the world somewhere.** And Margaret had always kept her blissful dreams **and reveries close within** her own heart, and why should she not **; there were no de-** cisions to be made, no questions to settle, only **the pres-** ent hour, crowded full of happiness, to be enjoyed. **She** could talk of Rodger, as Professor Latimer's son, **of** Rodger, the Harvard student, the law student, the friend who brought her books and rode with her in her father's absence, but Rodger the lover! ah, that was a very different matter. The future marriage was almost as indefinite an affair to her, as to her father; *that* was far off, impossible to realize, and little thought of. To be sure, she had dreamed of a home with Rodger, of opening the door for his coming, of the evenings together with books, **all** alone, they two, within the sacred four walls of home, of the long talks before the blazing fire, of the dainty table, with its delicate linen and china, a home where all was a sweet medley of color and warmth, and where, over all, an**d** through all, was tender, brooding love; yes, such a home there was somewhere, but whether in the clouds, or in the air, or on the earth, this dreaming maiden heart never stopped to think or ask, the present was too satisfying to be disturbed by anticipations or calculations. But Rodger's statement last evening that he was to live in Clinton, and that he wished **to** have Margaret live there with him, brought the **misty future of the** father's indefinite thought crashing **into** the present, with a sickening reality to Professor McVey; and the sad voice and dejected air of **the** loved father, smote the daughter's heart with a sharp pain, and awakened all of her sympathy.

"Take me to Clinton to live with him!" repeated Margaret after a moment's silence. "O he could not have said that, papa; you must have misunderstood him."

"No, no, Margaret, that was just what he said," replied Professor McVey in a broken voice.

"But not for a long time yet, papa?"

"I know, not now, I don't remember just when, but it was to be sometime."

"Now papa," said Margaret, "you and I have something to say about that, and I never, never, never, will leave you, and go and live in Clinton." She emphasized each repeated never, with a little pressure on her father's chest, right under his chin, with her clasped hands. "If Rodger wishes," she continued, "to come here and live with us, all right. Auntie will give him the nicest dinner, and he may ride with you and me, and sit on the sofa and read in the evenings and smoke his cigars, and we all will be real good to him, but if he wants to live in Clinton and be worth a million, and make a chief-justice of himself, he must do it alone. We won't have our nice times spoilt, because he is determined to be rich and great, will we, you dear old papa?" And then she gave a downright close hug to the neck she held, and pressed the side of her head against the old man's ear. For an instant it was a question of breath with Professor McVey, but even with the choking sensation in his throat, it was one of the happiest moments of his life. Away flew all fear; that hateful future went back to its mists; Clinton faded into indistinctness, Athens and Rome took their old solid places again, and the philosophers came out with togas free from dust, and crowded poor Rodger Latimer into dreamy obscurity.

"No, no, Margaret, we will not, if you say so."

"And I do say so," quickly interrupted Margaret. "And now papa, you must go, or you won't have time to get your proof and catch the 10:30 train. Don't get off the cars till they have stopped perfectly still, will you? Did you know that Mr. Dickinson stepped off at Stanhope station yesterday, before the cars stopped, and sprained his ankle? I'll have the carriage at the depot for you, and we will drive right on from there; perhaps we'd better not ride this evening, as it is growing warmer; what do you think?"

"Just as you like, Margaret, it is immaterial to me; but I think there is a prospect of a comfortably cool day."

Margaret was satisfied with the cheerful tone of her father's voice; he was at peace again. She watched him as he went briskly on under the elms and maples, that entirely shaded the sidewalk from the rays of the warm August sun that had scattered the fog of the night before, and as he turned the corner toward the college, she walked slowly into the house, down the length of the hall, and entered the room back of her father's study, by opening a door, and pushing aside one of the double portieres that hung within. This was Margaret's special room, library, sitting room, music room, all in one. Margaret's "Sans-Souci," her father called it. The only two windows in the room, which were west windows, looked into an old apple orchard, that was dearly loved by Margaret; some of the trees were so near the house, that one standing by the window could, in May, pluck handfuls of apple blossoms from the outstretching boughs, and in the autumn, gather the red and yellow apples in the same way. Frequently in the springtime, Margaret would have a "stretcher" placed under the trees, on which

she would lie, gazing up into the canopy of white and
pink blossoms and green leaves, that entirely shut out the
blue sky. Here she would yield herself to the dreamy
reveries of youth and love, the twilight dimness that surrounded her being broken only by the hum of insects and
sleepy twitter of birds. There were three doors in the
room, one from the hall, one entering her father's study,
and the third opening onto the south piazza. The
piazza was heavily covered with ivy, which Margaret had
cut and trimmed in low arches between the pillars, giving the piazza the appearance of a shaded arcade. All
of the furniture of Margaret's room was dainty and choice,
but there was one piece that deserves a moment's special
attention. This was an elaborately carved ebony lounge,
that possessed an unusual history. A Mrs. Lundom White,
an ambitious society woman of Clinton, and a prominent
member of the leading woman's literary club of that city,
found in Florence an old ebony chest of huge proportions,
which by an outlay of money sufficient to have purchased
and stocked a Western farm, she placed in the hands of a
Clinton cabinet-maker. Under her directions, this chest,
every inch of which was most beautifully carved, was
converted into two settees, the straight, square backs of
which, and the straight, square arms, and front piece that
reached to the floor, being entirely composed of the curious
carving. One of these settees Mrs. Lundom White placed
in the spacious hall of her own city residence, the other
she gave to her "dear friend Professor McVey, the dearest man in the world," as she declared, "and just the one
to appreciate that lovely old carving, such an antiquarian
as he is!" Professor McVey never thought, and certainly Mrs. Lundom White never once said, that the gift
of the settee was prompted by a sense of obligation that
she felt toward the professor, for the assistance which he

had rendered her in the preparation of the literary papers that she had read from time to time, before "The New Era" club. These essays, that were entitled "The Greeks and Their Literature," "Hypatia and Her Compeers," had been placed in his hands by her for revisal, and had received the most copious corrections and annotations. It was really a great pleasure for Professor McVey, to restore in Mrs. White's manuscript, his old Greek friends to their right minds, and correct the anachronisms therein. The reading of these essays gave her an enviable reputation in the club; one of its members, a lady of high social position, wrote to a friend of hers residing in London, to whom she had given Mrs. White a letter of introduction, "You will find that Mrs. White has an exhaustive knowledge of the Greeks, their art, customs and literature." It was a warm day early in December that Mrs. White took one of her papers to the professor, and sat in his study with an expression of pensive penitence on her face.

"You know dear Professor, that I am growing old," she said, "and I feel that I ought to give less time to society, and more to books and reflection. It is very kind in you to help me, you live in such an Eden out here under these trees, that you can't realize how difficult it is for me in that crowded city to be good, but I'm determined to try, and give more time to books. Please don't say anything to any one about my poor attempts at self improvement," she continued, as with a benign smile he took the manuscript from her faultlessly gloved hand. When the society woman had taken herself back to the city, she exclaimed to her sister, as she threw off her wraps in her luxuriously furnished bedroom: "I declare Marie, I feel as though I had just crawled out of my coffin. I wouldn't live in Edgewood for all of America. You've no idea of the place,

Professor McVey's house is as still as the grave, and he looks as though he had sat right there for a thousand years; but I must say that he was very polite to me, and he will get my paper in fine shape. The poor old goosie quite brightened up, when I talked of Conway, and of the people we used to know there. Now mind, don't you for your life ever let any one know that I went to Professor McVey's. We go to the theater with Mrs. Richmond to-night, don't we?" continued Mrs. White, suddenly changing the subject. "I'm glad Grey Whitridge is to be there, now go and take a nap, so you will look bright."

And so it came, that the Florentine ebony chest rested at last in the shape of a settee in Margaret's room, where her father had directed it to be placed, on its arrival from Clinton. As Margaret entered her room after bidding her father good-bye on the piazza, she closed the door behind her, dropped the portiere over it, and seated herself in a wicker chair beside the center table, and gazing unconsciously at the ebony settee, she was lost in thought, until recalled by a knock at the hall door.

CHAPTER III.

Only four persons ever asked for admittance to Margaret's Sans-Souci. They were her father, Miss Sargent of Clinton, her Aunt Deborah, and Rodger Latimer. She knew, by the peculiar rap, who it was that stood outside of the hall door waiting to enter, and as her eyes moved from the ebony settee to the double portiere, which opened at her bidding, her face flushed radiantly. Rodger Latimer stepped quickly to her side, dropped on one knee, and put his arm across the back of her chair, then by placing the other hand beneath her chin, he laid her head upon his arm so that he could look in the upturned face.

"A curt good-night you gave me last evening, Margery; are you not sorry this morning, that you treated me so badly?" he asked.

"I did not treat you badly, but very nicely. You came to see papa, and I was very courteous to his guest."

"To see papa!" repeated Mr. Latimer; "well, I came this morning to see you, so good-morning, love." Slowly and tenderly he kissed the smiling lips, and then held the sweet head close to his breast with his large white hand. The girl's heart was heavy with happiness, as she felt the gentle pressure of the strong arm around her shoulders, and the touch of the hand upon her head. The August sunlight came through the vine arches of the south piazza, and rested in its yellow brightness on the floor, just within the open door, the clock ticked on the mantel, and the katydids sang out in chorus from the old apple trees, while the crickets chirped from the twilight depths below. After a little, Mr. Latimer's fingers commenced playing with the curls on Margaret's forehead, then she turned her head back against his arm, and said: "Nobody is allowed to touch my front hair."

"Is that so?" he asked, as he continued to draw the soft hair through his fingers, and rearrange the curls over the brow, gazing as he did so on the happy girlish face, with an earnestness that caused the eyelids to droop with a tremulous motion. Again he kissed the full lips as tenderly as a mother might have kissed a half-sleeping child. "I wonder if you know how beautiful you are, Margery," he asked, "you are so fairy-like, and ethereal with your changing color, and great blue eyes, that are twice as large as usual to-day; no, don't shut them up, let me look at them, if you will not look at me. I came to have a good long talk with you, but there's a wonderful heavenly air about you this morning, that makes me feel as though I was in church, kneeling before a saint."

"Nonsense, Rodger," said Margaret, putting his hand aside, as she arose, and drew a large chair close to the end of the table, "here is your chair, let us have the good long talk now, which you may begin by telling me every word that you and papa said to each other, last night."

Mr. Latimer took the seat designated, and proceeded very deliberately to light a cigar, and then he smoked in silence, with his eyes fixed on the ceiling. Margaret waited for him to speak.

"Tell you all that your father and I said last evening," he repeated after a while. "I hardly remember all, Margery, but I can tell you all that we said about you, or you and me, which was very little. I told him that I expected to have an income two years from now, that would warrant our being married, and I hoped when that time came, he would give his consent to the marriage. He seemed startled, absolutely discomfited, routed, at the thought of your ever leaving him, but he was very kind, and I think would consent to anything that did **not take** you from him."

"Our marriage is so **far in the future**," said Margaret, "that it is hardly **worth while making** him unhappy about it."

"Oh, **I told him at last, that** everything **should be as** he wished. Perhaps," **continued** Mr Latimer, "**that I was** mistaken, but I thought that the idea **of being separated** from you distressed him, and as you say, **there is no** necessity of annoying him about an event a year or two distant. I was more than ever confirmed, while talking with him last evening, **in my** belief **of the great** influence surrounding circumstances have in **the** development of character. What a **man is, depends** after all on where he lives, and what **a** difference **there is in places.** Edgewood is a sleepy old town, **compared with** Cambridge, but your father seems to think **that a life here, on** three thousand dollars a year, is the **best there could be in** this world."

"He finds it a very pleasant life," **said** Margaret.

"Certainly," replied Rodger, "with **his** profession, and at his age, this is just the place for **him,** but a young man might as well live in the catacombs; there is no society here, and the difficulty of getting **to** the city and back, cuts off all amusements."

"I don't know," said Margaret, "our society people frequently go down to the opera and theaters."

"Frequently!" repeated Mr. Latimer with derision; "a dozen times during the winter, and then it's a break-neck race for them to come home to dinner, dress and rush back to the depot, and half of the time they have to leave in the middle of the closing act to catch the last train home. I'm sick of depots and suburban trains," he added, looking gloomily on the floor. After a moment he raised his eyes to meet Margaret's fixed on him with a very serious look in them. "Margery, you think me selfish and discontented, don't you?" he asked with a smile.

"Indeed I do not!" she replied with animation. "I only think you are ambitious, but you are no more ambitious for yourself than I am for you."

"Come now, what would you like to have me do?"

"Work hard in your profession," Margaret replied, "and make the leading lawyer in Clinton; to be always on the right side of every question, to have men and women who are in distress feel sure that they can count on your sympathy and assistance, and every leader of a reformation know that you, and your eloquence, and reputation and influence will be on his side to help him to success."

"Why, Margery, how am I to get all of this eloquence, and influence, and reputation, to help all of these distressed men and women, and reformers?" Mr. Latimer asked, as he leaned forward and possessed himself of the little hand that lay on the arm of the wicker chair. "All such anticipations have no firmer foundation than a girl's love."

"Yes they have," she replied, "you possess brains enough to make all such anticipations come true, and after awhile, Rodger, before you are an old man, you will be one of the great men of the country." The eyes of the enthusiastic girl filled with tears as she continued, "And then you will do all of those great and good things that we talked of when we were at Lausanne." Mr. Latimer took the third finger of the little hand he held and kissed the ring that encircled it, which he had placed there a year before, as he and Margaret were sitting on one of the terraced hillsides of Lausanne. The college vacations of the two previous summers had been passed in Europe by Margaret and Mr. Latimer, with Professor McVey and Miss Sargent, a lady who was an old friend of the McVeys.

"That summer seems like an idyl, Margery, as I look back on it," said Mr. Latimer; "what a different world this is from that we then dreamed, and how different our life must be from what we then planned, or rather thought it would be, for very few plans either of us laid, as we floated through those months of music and flowers, of mountains and lakes, of moonlight nights, and starry skies. And that day under the grape vines!" Mr. Latimer placed the hand he held against his cheek, as a vague expression of retrospection came over his face, and he looked out of the west window at the white clouds lazily resting above the apple trees. "What a lovely time it was. I wonder," he added, drawing Margaret's hand softly down his cheek, "if it will ever come again."

"Come again!" exclaimed Margaret, "it has always been with me, and I don't know Rodger, what you mean when you say this is such a different world; it is the same world to me, and I think life will be just what I then thought it was to be."

"I declare, Margery," said Mr. Latimer, "you and your father are a pair of artless children, living here in this nest among the trees, with heaven within hands' reach: you darling, you don't know anything more of life, than a dove in the twilight."

"Why, Rodger, I'm not such a child, nor have I lived in a box. I've seen something of the world."

"Yes," he replied, "quite a number of its square miles, but how much of life? You have had, say, six months in Europe, closely surrounded by Miss Sargent, your father and myself, then a dozen dinners, and as many operas and theaters in Clinton, always attended, either by Miss Sargent or me; most of your life has been passed here with the poets and philosophers, among these vines and trees. And as for your father, he knows ten times as much about the ancients as the moderns; when he speaks of the Greeks and Romans, he speaks of them as though they were living men, and of those old times as though they were of paramount living interest to-day, but the moment you commence to talk with him of the people, or the issues of the present, he is as vague and impracticable as a child. Why Margery, he knows no more of the ambitions and needs of the young men of the present·day than did old Diogenes himself." Mr. Latimer left his chair, and walked back and forth across the room, with an expression of moody discontent on his face; he stopped before one of the open windows, but saw neither the red and yellow apples hanging among the green leaves, nor felt the influence of the dusky silence below the trees.

Margaret observed him intently for a few moments, then asked, "On what points do you and papa differ so much?"

"On all practical ones; he thinks a life in Edgewood desirable, I think it insufferable, not worth having. One gets a very different view of life, from the Boston outlook, than from this monastic loophole."

"Which is the truer?" asked Margaret.

"Both are true, I suppose; but if you wish to ask, which is the most desirable, there is no comparison. Live in such a town as this, with these saints and ancients, on twenty-five hundred dollars a year!" Mr. Latimer's nostrils fairly distended with scorn. He went back to his chair and reseated himself. "You may think me unreasonable, Margery, but nothing short of fifteen thousand dollars a year, and a first class social and professional position in Clinton will satisfy me!"

"Will that satisfy you?"

"As near as anything can satisfy a mortal. I know, your philosophers **say that no one is** satisfied in this world, but this is all **the world I know anything** of, and **as** Emerson **says, one world at a time.**" He smiled good-naturedly, **as Margaret laughed aloud.**

"I doubt if Emerson **made** the **same application of that thought,** as you did just now," **she said.**

"**Well** Margery, Grey Whitridge seems **satisfied with the life** his ten thousand a year enables him **to** lead. I **dined** with him last summer at the Dorchester Club, the day before he sailed, and I didn't **see** any evidence of discontent, or **unhappiness in** him, **nor** in Walt Richmond, or young Barstow, **who dined with** us; they were about **as gay a set of fellows as one** would care **to** meet, not any more **satisfied though than** some of the Harvard men, with their **horses and yachts.** There **is** no use of denying it **Margery, this life is not worth** much without money."

"I've never met Mr. Barstow," **said Margaret, "and I** have seen but little of Mr. Richmond, but **I don't** think the Richmonds a happy family. Ethel is absolutely blasé at nineteen. I called to **see her** regarding the flower **mission one morning at eleven o'**clock, and she was not out **of bed.** I **don't see much** use of her ever getting up, she goes through everything in such a listless way, as though nothing paid, and Mrs. Richmond is always fretting about something, either the cook is in fault, or the coachman is drunk, or her last dress is a failure. I spent a day there last winter, and **I was** glad to get away from both, the half-dead daughter and the complaining mother. What's the use of all **their money,** if it don't bring **them** happiness? as to Grey Whitridge, I have seen him only twice, and both times **at** the Assembly. He certainly has a fine figure, but I can't understand why he is called so handsome. His finely shaped head, and clear-cut features, seem to me physical accidents, inherited lines, without any individual character back of them; he strikes me as a man who would have no higher thought than well fitting clothes, and well served dinners. But, Rodger, you are more of a man than Grey Whitridge, and I know that such a life as he leads would never satisfy you, for any length of time at least."

"I don't know about that," said Mr. Latimer. "I think his life ought to satisfy any one; there is not a more popular man in Clinton, he is considered the greatest matrimonial prize in the city. Everybody is delighted with an invitation to his theater parties, and I don't know a man anywhere who is a better judge of a dinner; he's a fine horseman, and a good shot they say, and with all, a downright good natured, affable fellow; I would like such a position in Clinton society as he has."

"And can't you have it?" asked Margaret.

"Have it!" repeated Mr. Latimer, "with my empty purse! He asked me last spring if I would not like to have him propose my name for membership in the Dorchester Club; he would be amazed should I tell him that every dollar I possessed, for a twelvemonths' board and clothes, was fifteen hundred. I might go in society as a sort of available young man, a convenient dancing partner, when one was needed, a good fellow enough among men, to be invited to dinner at the club, with the sons of society families, but not a man to be invited to the wealthy homes, and be presented to the daughters of the house." Mr. Latimer was walking the floor again. "No, Margery, a young man without money, or expectations, cannot have a desirable social position; I have seen that demonstrated over and over in Clinton, and in Boston, and a man of any self respect, will not accept one of those tolerated-for-convenience-sake positions, that some brainless fellows hold. I cannot bring myself to dance attendance on some rich matron, so I shall stay out of society entirely, until I can make an income sufficient to take me there, on the top of the wave. It is a dismal prospect, but I shall have to submit."

Margaret sat silent; she could not understand how life could open out before such a man as Rodger Latimer, in any other way than as a boundless arena of mental activity and delight. She was not old enough to correctly value the youth, health, superior natural ability and thorough educational discipline that Mr. Latimer possessed, so she did not place these advantages in one scale, and toss into the other the dinners, dogs and horses of which he had been speaking; and accurately weigh one against the other, but she had a vague idea that he was wrong in his comparative estimates. She regarded him closely as he walked back and forth, his clear gray eyes fixed upon the floor, his head bent slightly forward, and his hands crossed behind his back.

"It must be, Rodger," she said after a little, "that as you say, there is a difference in places, and the thoughts they suggest, and the tastes they cultivate. I can't for my life, see anything so very desirable in the society which you admire; perhaps I'm not adapted to it, and I'm sure that I do not like it. I've seen very little of it I know, but I've seen enough to know that it would never satisfy me. I do not enjoy the dinners of which you speak so highly; there are twenty different dishes served, and if I only taste of each I'm made physically uncomfortable, and then what a babel of talk on uninteresting subjects! I get nothing out of it but weariness. The theater and opera give me much more pleasure, when I can go quietly with you or Aunt Helen.   I don't like the theater parties which you seem to.   I was invited by Mrs. White, to hear Irving, and she had a party of six or eight, and what a jumble the evening was of Irving and Terry, Assembly dances and Hamlet, receptions and Ophelia; I did not enjoy it at all.   How much better to go and listen to an artist in a quiet way."

"Then you would think it better for me," said Mr. Latimer stopping in his walk near Margaret, "to sit alone this winter, if I go to the theater at all, in the parquet and study Hamlet?   I think it would be much pleasanter to sit in Mrs. White's box, with her sister, Miss Edwards, or with Ethel Richmond and Grey Whitridge, and after the play go to the Bellevue for a nice little supper."

"Then why don't you do it?"

"Simply because I have not the money; how could I give a theater party, at an expense of a hundred, or a hundred and fifty dollars?   None but society men, of an assured social position, are invited to such places."

"And that assured social position depends upon wealth?"

"Almost entirely," replied Mr. Latimer, "as he commenced to walk the floor again.   "You may call it unmanly if you choose, Margery, but I absolutely dread, with a smarting, shrinking dread, the next two years in Clinton.   I have seen enough to know how it will be.   At Harvard my position among the students was a pleasant one; Uncle Gill allowed me plenty of money, and I was known, by the Boston men at least, as the nephew of Gilbert Latimer, who is regarded as a very wealthy man in Boston; no one thought anything about my personal wealth or poverty; my cigars were always of the best, and I always had an abundance of money, so it was taken for granted, if thought of at all, that I could command what-

ever I chose.   But it is different in Clinton.   I have felt
the difference, even in the little that I have dropped into
Clinton society, in the last two years, and now I have to
squarely face the thing.   You may wonder why I do not
go to Boston, or New York, but Uncle Gill advised me to
stay out of Boston, and he gave me distinctly to understand that I was henceforth to depend upon myself, and
as to New York, it was the judgment of several friends
of mine—young lawyers—and also of Judge Sargent,
that on the whole, Clinton offered stronger inducements
to a young man, than any other city.   I had thought of
Omaha, but Judge Sargent advised against that.   I've
tried, Margery, to settle the question with careful consideration, and I hope that I've made no mistake.   I'm not
afraid of work; I think I shall enjoy it.   As a matter of
course, the first year or two of waiting for business, will
be trying, but every year it will grow better.   Judge
Sargent told me yesterday, that he could throw some business in my hands, and I feel sure that I shall succeed in
the end, both in making money and in gaining a professional position.   I wouldn't mind, if I could work under
desirable social conditions, but I don't like to think of
the close economy of living on fifteen hundred dollars a
year, when most of the young men whom I now meet in
Clinton, spend from four to ten thousand a year, and
some of them have neither brains nor culture.   If it were
not for their money, they would be dropped out of society
in twenty-four hours, and its doors would be barred
against them.   Think of the difference! they with their
clubs, opera boxes, horses for driving and riding, invited
everywhere, frequently two and three invitations for an
evening; and I in a second class boarding house, a penni-
less attorney!"

"Rodger, I don't believe a word of what you say," said

Margaret, as she crossed her arms on the corner of the table, and looked up in his face, as he halted in his walk beside her; "it cannot be otherwise, than that a man of your intellect, fine personal appearance, and conversational ability, will be popular, and have a splendid time in any city. It's natural that it should be so, it's according to law, as papa says, it's the effect of a cause."

"You're too ignorant of the laws of society," said Mr. Latimer, "and of its underlying causes, to know anything of the relative effects of money, or no money."

"Well Rodger, if what you say is true, I'm glad that I do live among the trees, with poets and philosophers, where worth holds its true position, and is not beaten down by advantages that are impersonal, and often accidental. I am glad that I haven't lost my faith in what is right."

"But Margery," interrupted Mr. Latimer, "all of this may be right, even as you use the word; money has its rights, society customs have their rights."

"There's something wrong somewhere," she replied, "when the advantages of society are withheld from such a man as you, simply because he has a small income, and are given to another man who is inferior in every way, excepting that he has money. If these things of which you speak are really advantageous additions to one's happiness and development, it's your right to have them, and somewhere there is a great wrong in their being withheld from you. I don't see the matter very clearly, but I have faith in the right, and in the end it will assert itself, and we shall see it, and acknowledge it. Wait a few years, you and Grey Whitridge are both young men, you say he lives a life of self-indulgent pleasure; if you live a life of intellectual activity, and are true to moral principle, and are not the happiest man in the end, what becomes of

Plato's and Montaigne's maxims and philosophy? and the Bible? and of God's justice, Rodger? You used to have faith in all of these; where has it gone?"

"Just where Plato's might have gone, perhaps, in his lifetime, hadn't he enjoyed all of the advantages of wealth. I tell you Margery, much of this religion and philosophy, learned at home and in Sunday Schools, goes like dew, when we get out in the hot world, and see what God does, or at least permits to be done. There is nothing like being knocked down by daily facts, to take this nonsense of religion and philosophy out of one."

The smile died out of Margaret's face. "You ought not to talk so Rodger," she said; "you don't believe what you say, you know you don't."

Before Mr. Latimer could reply, there was a light rap at the door, and Margaret's Aunt Deborah entered and handed her a telegram. Mr. Latimer noticed the sudden look of alarm with which she opened it.

"Is your father away, Margery?" he asked. She finished reading the dispatch before replying.

"Yes," she said, "he went to the city on the ten-thirty train, to take the library catalogue to Morrison's, and was to take luncheon with Aunt Helen, and return this afternoon; this is from Aunt Helen; she says that papa will remain there over night. Doctor Brandon, of Rutgers College, is to dine with her, and she wishes papa to meet him. Papa must have gone to see her before going to Morrison's, or this couldn't have reached us so soon."

Suddenly Margaret sprang up, and clapping her hands, commenced to dance around the room. "Now Rodger, let us have a day in the woods! Auntie will put us up a luncheon, wont you, Aunt Deb? And we wont come home until dinner," sang Margaret to the rollicking air, "We won't go home till morning," which she had frequently heard at night from the students, as they went through the town in their noisy bouts. She caught Mr. Latimer by the arm, and whirled him down the room in rapid circles, as she whistled a waltz from Nanon.   At last she stopped in front of quiet Aunt Deborah.

"Shall we go, Rodger?" she asked, catching her breath.

"Certainly we will.   A luncheon in the woods will be worth more than all of the philosophy of your old Plato. But Margery," he continued, leading her to the center table, "where did you get this beautiful copy of Montaigne?" and he laid his hand on an English edition soft as satin, and beautiful to look upon.

"I found it at Morrison's."

"Rather solid reading for a girl, but not as bad as this," he pursued, taking up a volume of Mill.

"Why do you say bad? you wouldn't if you knew how much good Mill has done me, how he has helped me to think for myself."

"Think for yourself! good Jove! what's coming next!"

"Yes," answered Margaret seriously, "and how that thinking has steadied me."

"Why Margery, this is metaphysics, and reading metaphysics will spoil you, will make you strong minded." He pronounced the last words with a wry face.   The volume of Mill that he held in his hand as he was talking, opened of itself, where Margaret had slipped between the leaves, a mother of pearl paper knife to keep her place; it was a beautiful paper cutter, with lovely chameleon hues of pearly white, azure and purple; dainty and feminine.   As his eyes rested on the paper knife, Margaret placed over the volume of Mill, Blackmore's Lorna Doone.

"This is not metaphysics, Rodger; have you read Lorna Doone?" she asked.

"No."

"Well, you must, it's a perfect love story, and the descriptions of scenery are so simple and natural, and yet so original, their quiet beauty is wonderful; we'll take it with us, I'll read you some of the descriptions. But you must read it yourself, every word of it, it's all so delightful, nothing commonplace in it."

The girl's hand was resting on Mr. Latimer's arm, he glanced from the beautiful volume of Montaigne to the delicate paper-knife, then his eyes rested on the enthusiastic face at his shoulder.

"What a strange compound you are, Margery, of child and woman," he said, taking her hand in his own, "dainty bindings, and dainty paper cutter, and enthusiasm over Lorna's love—read your metaphysics, if you like, or anything else, nothing could spoil you, you little impulsive woman, nothing in the universe. Now for the woods and luncheon," he cried, as he gave the hand a little squeeze, "only you will have to drive round by Howland's, so I can get some cigars."

CHAPTER IV.

As soon as Margaret's phaeton drove away from the house, Aunt Deborah closed the piazza door in Margaret's room, to keep out the bugs and flies, and lowered the window shades, to prevent the sun from fading the rugs. Faithful Deborah Bond! a woman who never thought of a mission, or a sphere, in connection with herself, but who, as a child, on the twenty-five acre farm that lay close to a New England village, was the one of all the children to be trusted with the baby, to whom, when a child, a half holiday meant more time to help around the house, and mend the baby's clothes; who as a young woman, never thought of lover or husband for herself, who never was even a bridesmaid; but whose pride and love centered in her pretty sister Millicent. This woman thought it a providential call when she received a letter one day, that the pretty sister, whose health had failed after years of wifehood, needed her in her Western home. She responded to the call, and took upon herself the duties of nurse and housekeeper, in Professor McVey's house in Edgewood. When the gentle Millicent died one evening, it was Aunt Deborah who folded the hands of the dead wife and mother, soothed the weeping daughter to sleep, staid up all night with the bereaved husband, sitting beside him in sympathetic silence, placing a cup of tea in his hand as the night waned, and at last persuading him to lie down on the lounge, where he soon dropped off in a sleep of exhaustion. Duty done to the dead and the living, she leaned her head against the straight, high back of the rocking chair she was sitting in, and in thirty seconds was sound asleep. No one seemed to think of it,

but ever after that evening, it was Deborah's hand that
oiled the machinery of Professor McVey's creakless household. Happy woman! with no yearnings, no question-
ings, no ambitions, no insomnia, no indigestion. In her
housekeeping, the dinners were never late, the buttons
never off, the coffee never muddy; the curtains were
always white, but no one knew when they were washed;
the house always clean, but no one ever saw a broom or a
duster; the larder always answered any emergency of
extra luncheon, or a double number for dinner; there were
no flies in the house, and rarely a mosquito on the piazza.
Yet Deborah Bond never seemed to have anything to do,
or looked as though she had anything on her mind. Her
creed she never thought of, the Westminster Assembly
settled that in 1645; her philosophy could be condensed
in the one sentence, " Take things as you find them, and
make the best of them." Out of this philosophy there
came to her a life as regular as the tides, and as satisfying as the seasons. Happy woman! who worked to sure
issues, and rejoiced in the work of her hands. Professor
McVey did not know how much of daily comfort he owed
to the quiet woman whom he instinctively treated with a
respectful reserve, but Margaret did know that " Aunt
Deb was the best woman in the world," and was always
just at hand if she wished for anything, and never annoyed
her with questions or advice. She loved her aunt in
exactly the way such a woman would choose to be loved,
with a calm, undemonstrative affection that never startled
or embarrassed her.

Mr. Latimer and Margaret were as happy as the day,
as they drove toward the woods. The weather vanes of
the town pointed to the north, but no breeze was felt, not
a leaf stirred, the grass was fresh and green from late
rains, and the air was clear and cool. The sky was blue

as June, and the white clouds, in long sweeps of thin, torn mist with irregular edges, rested motionless across the blue. Margaret drove toward a little spring that she knew well, in a wood, and there they unpacked their luncheon basket, chattering merrily all of the time. Margaret laughed at Mr. Latimer because he was so clumsy in breaking the ice into small pieces for the cold tea, and Mr. Latimer laughed at Margaret because there was no knife in the basket with which to cut the chicken and cake, and declared that he would have to do the housekeeping when they were married. "All Mill's fault," he said with a sly glance, as he produced a good sized pocket knife and proceeded to disjoint the roasted chicken. They wakened the birds that had been hushed into a noonday sleep by the profound stillness of the forest, and the twittering birds aroused the crickets, that commenced chirping in all directions. Luncheon over, Mr. Latimer said:

"Let the things be Margery; we'll pack them after awhile. I want to smoke now, and you read to me from that enchanting Lorna Doone of yours." After giving her the book, he threw the laprobe on the ground and placed a carriage cushion on it for a pillow, then he stretched himself out close by her side, as she sat on the grass leaning against a tree, turning his head so that he could see the fair face with the long lashes, and the sweet curves of the moving lips. He cared little for Lorna Doone, or the outlaws; Margaret's face filled his eye, and thought of her his mind, even as his ear was filled with the musical low tones of her voice, that were very restful and soothing. Margaret read on, absorbed in the book, until suddenly, startled by a heavy breathing, she looked round to see Mr. Latimer fast asleep, with hands clasped over his breast, and his head leaning a little one side toward her.

She scarcely breathed for fear she might awaken him; she had never seen him asleep before, **and** she gazed on him with shy curiosity.   He might **waken up any** minute and catch her looking at him **so earnestly, she** thought, but no, he slept soundly on: **how handsome he** looked, but how funny it was to hear **him** breathe **so heavily, then** she wondered **if** that was **what** they called snoring.   **Now** she could look at him as much as she chose, and he not know it.   How still he lay, and how white and large his hands were, and what beautiful pink nails, almost as pink as her own.   Then she looked at her nails and very slowly put out one hand; glancing up at his **face** to see that he was not waking up, **she** leaned **over,** stretched out one finger and placing **the nail as** close **to** one of his as she could without **touching** his finger, **she** compared the nails in solemn silence for a moment, then **folded** her hands in her lap and continued gazing at him.   **How** broad the chest was that supported the white hands.   **Aunt** Deb said her father had a narrow chest that indicated consumption, in some branch of the McVey family. The Latimers must have been strong for generations to have produced such a chest as that, and how tanned his throat and face were, all but his forehead, and what a pretty dimple that was in **his chin,** she would like to lay the tip of her little finger **in** it; such a little cleft in such a large chin; then how regularly his lips moved, and with every breath came that puff that made the sound of heavy breathing.   For an instant she thought that she would like to kiss him, then her face blushed rosy all over at the thought; no! she would not touch him for the world! But she never moved her eyes from his face, she looked at his dark moustache, and then to his hair, so soft and silky, and she raised her hand and drew one of the rings of hair over her forehead out between her fingers. "It looks soft as mine," she thought, and how straight the parting was, exactly in the middle, and not a single hair across it; the hair seemed to grow lower in the middle than on the sides, just as it did on Byron's head, and how the short hair clung to the soft white skin, and how much larger and heavier his head looked, lying there, than when he was sitting up. She wondered if a barber parted his hair, or if Rodger did it himself; whether he took care of his own nails, or had a manicure to do it. At this point of her observations and wonderings, a fly lit on Mr. Latimer's face and Margaret brushed it away with her handkerchief. At last she seemed satisfied with gazing, and noiselessly turned the leaves of her book as she read to herself; every few seconds looking up and waving her handkerchief over Mr. Latimer's head to keep the flies away. The birds became quiet, the crickets droned in a dreamy way, and stillness reigned in the forest. An hour passed, and then as Margaret glanced from her book to wave her handkerchief over Mr. Latimer's head, she met his wide open eyes fixed on her face, but as she looked, the lids slowly dropped over his eyes again, and she turned to her book, but when in a few minutes she raised her head to wave her handkerchief, the eyes were open, and with more expression in them. Soon Mr. Latimer turned over on his side and leaning on his elbow, rested his head upon his hand, then after a little he sat up and clasped his hands around his knees. Margaret did not speak, but continued her reading. Mr. Latimer looked at the dishes and the remains of the luncheon strewed on the grass, looked off through the woods, and then fixed his eyes upon Margaret.

" Well, Margery, have you had a good time?" he quietly asked.

"Yes, a lovely time," she smilingly replied.

"I must have been sound asleep, my cigar has gone

out," he said, as he reached for his cigar that he had laid on the grass when he felt himself growing sleepy; he brushed the ashes off it and tossed it away from him.

"Sound asleep! I should think you had. Why, Rodger, you slept over an hour."

"O no, that can't be," he replied, taking out his watch and looking at it. "Cæsar's ghost! it's half-past four! Now that was not treating you well, Margery. I don't see how I slept so long, or went to sleep at all for that matter, but you have a nap now," he continued with a smile, "and I'll keep the flies off you."

" No, thank you, I'm not sleepy. I never sleep in the daytime."

" Nor do I."

"Unless you're in the woods being read to."

"It was that stupid book of yours, Margery, that did it."

"The next time I'll bring Mill," rejoined Margaret, saucily. Mr. Latimer reached out his hand and gave her ear a little pinch. " But come, Rodger, you said you would have to do the housekeeping, so please pack the basket."

"No, I'm not to do the housekeeping yet. I went to sleep, and that was doing my share for the day. If you'll pack the basket, I'll cut all of the goldenrod that I can carry in my arms for you."

The basket was packed, and they wandered off in a ravine, and through lowland woods for flowers. At seven o'clock they reached home with a carriage load of goldenrod, blue gentian and cat-tails, ready for one of Aunt Deborah's beautiful dinners.

"Where shall we sit, Rodger?" asked Margaret, as they rose from the table, "in my room, or on the piazza?"

"On the front piazza in the moonlight, unless you care to be within doors," replied Mr. Latimer.

They went to the piazza, and Margaret located herself in the hammock, leaning her head and shoulders back against a cushion, and resting her feet on a large velvet mat that partially covered the floor. Mr. Latimer drew the sea-chair to her side and seated himself in it, and after striking a match on the railing near by, lit a cigar, then placed his feet on the railing, leaned his head back, and looked into the tree tops. Margaret was looking at him.

"What compensation, Rodger, do you suppose women have for not smoking?" she asked after awhile.

"Watching us as we smoke," was the reply.

"And that's compensation?"

"Ample," said Mr. Latimer; "you are the unselfish sex. You find more happiness in seeing other people happy than in any self-indulgence. Don't you see how perfectly Providence has arranged it? But what are you going to do all of this next winter, Margery?"

"Just what I did all of last winter, I suppose. I shall look after papa, read and sew a little, go in society some, run down to the city when there are good operas and theaters, and write a great many long letters to you. What are you going to do all winter?"

"Don't talk of my next winter, I hate to think of it. We've had such a perfect day, I don't wish it marred by having any unpleasant thoughts thrust on me." It was full ten minutes before either of them spoke again, then Mr. Latimer said: "How lovely it was under the trees by that spring! seems to me you know all of the pretty places in the woods, and just where the gold-enrod grows. How lovely it is out here to-night, see how bright the stars are." Margaret glanced from Mr. Latimer's face to the stars overhead but said nothing; after a little he continued, "For the first time in my life

Margery, I have to-night an idea of what you and your father find in this Edgewood life. How pure and calm it is, how unlike the crowd, and heat and noise of Clinton. It don't seem possible that we are only ten miles from that dirty city; just now I feel as though I would like to live here forever." One of his hands rested on the arm of the sea-chair, and as he ceased speaking, Margaret laid her hand softly upon it; instantly he turned his hand, and took hers in a close clasp.

"The stars are very bright for so clear a moonlight night," said Margaret after a long silence; "this is like some of our old Lausanne evenings; after all Rodger, last summer was not to be the happiest of our lives; we always speak of it as such a happy time, but why has not to-day been just as happy as any of those happy days?"

"It has love, it has," replied Mr. Latimer, "no one ought to ask for a happier day than this has been." He turned his head and looked at the girlish face leaning against the cushion, and into the large luminous eyes full of love, holding within them a beauty far surpassing that of moon or stars. Occasionally a footfall had been heard in the distance; it had come nearer and sounded louder, passed by, grown fainter, and died away into silence. The passers by grew fewer and fewer, and then they ceased entirely, and all was silent on the street of this country town, in the early evening. The last robin had twittered itself to sleep long ago, and the katydids stopped their song; the sacred silence of night rested upon the earth. The stars passed noiselessly on, Jupiter came from the east and marching toward the zenith threw his brightest rays on Rodger and Margaret as they sat side by side, the Pleiades all saw the happy pair, and clustering closer together, swept through the heavens singing their song of love. Vega and Mars peeped through the leaves, but a fleecy cloud on watch, floated between and hid the lovers from their gaze; the half moon in the south drew a veil of yellow mist across her face, and the wind with finger on her lips, crept away through the silent night.

CHAPTER V.

One cool morning in the first week of November, as Mr. Latimer was stepping from the sidewalk into the hall of the block in which his office was located, in the city of Clinton, he met Mr. Grey Whitridge.

"Have you just returned to the city, Mr. Latimer?" asked Grey Whitridge, after the young men had heartily greeted each other.

"O no, I have been here at work for six weeks or more."

"Is that possible! At work? May I ask at what?"

"At my profession, practicing law, although I can't say that I'm doing much practicing just now. I am going through the necessary transition stage of a beginner. Step up to my office and have a cigar, and tell me of your summer." The two men stepped into the elevator, and in a few moments were seated in Mr. Latimer's office.

"You have an unusually pleasant office, Mr Latimer, with all of these south windows," said Grey Whitridge, looking around the room, and as he lighted the cigar Mr. Latimer gave him, he added: "This is a very fine cigar, where do you get them? I've had a world of trouble about my cigars; seems to me there are no cigars as fine as we used to smoke ten years ago. I was out of all patience in London with the vile stuff I was compelled to use there."

"Did you have a pleasant time in London?" asked Mr. Latimer.

"No, we had dreadful weather, the worst this year that I ever saw there; it was a wet season. I had such a constant cold I could not enjoy society at all, so I went into the country to shoot, and had the poorest of luck."

"You seem to have had a combination of misfortunes," said Mr. Latimer.

"Yes, and then I went over to Paris; the rain crossed with me, and there was a misunderstanding between myself and some friends that were to meet me there, and I missed them, which was a great disappointment. It was beautiful weather the few days that I spent in Switzerland, on the mountains, but I care little for natural scenery, simply as such, so the fine weather there was of no special advantage to me."

"How much of one's pleasure in traveling depends upon the weather!" said Latimer, not knowing what else to say.

"Yes, I thought so on my return voyage."

"Did you have a rough passage?"

"The sailors did not call it so, but I thought it decidedly rough. We had heavy fogs and rain, and a rough sea nearly all the eight days that we were out; then one of the passengers died, and a lady went insane from sea sickness, or from the remedies she took to relieve her sea sickness. I've always considered myself a good sailor, but I'll confess the sea got the upper hand of me this trip. I've been over eight times, and all of the discomfort of fifteen of the passages put together would not equal what I suffered this return voyage. I don't believe I'll ever go to Europe again. I'll spend my summers in this country, but it's a serious question where one can pass the summer months most pleasantly. I never cared for shooting much, and I care less for it every year. I expected to find great enjoyment in salmon fishing, when I joined the Neytaya Club, but salmon fishing is too hard work, it's a tax physically and mentally; I never shall try it again. On the whole I'm glad the summer is past. I really believe one can get about as much out of life here in the city as anywhere. Clinton is to be very gay this winter, they say. Everything is hazy and uncertain yet, but definite programmes will begin to come out soon. I have just heard that the Blackwells are to be home next week, and that they will open their house. You know the Blackwells?"

"No, or at least I have simply met Mr. and Mrs. Blackwell at a formal dinner."

"They have two lovely daughters, who were educated abroad. They finished their studies last year, but Mrs. Blackwell wished to keep them out of society another year, and thought that would be impossible if they returned to their own home, so they passed last winter in Dresden; but they will have their house opened by the first of the month, and you will find them charming people. Mrs. Richmond told me yesterday, that the prospects were for an early and gay season."

Mr. Latimer had nothing to say in reply to Grey Whitridge's society gossip. What could he reply to it? He could neither deny nor affirm; what was the approaching season to him? Gay Mrs. Richmond, the Blackwells' beautiful home and lovely daughters, did not come within range of his practical knowledge. Visions of operas, dances, dinners, carriages and flowers, rose before him, as part and parcel of Grey Whitridge's coming winter, nor did the vision flit before him and pass away, but staid in his mind, each moment assuming a more beautiful and desirable aspect. He looked at Grey Whitridge, who belonged to the second generation of wealth, and who had never known an hour of either physical or mental striving; there he sat, so surfeited with the good things of earth, that his pleasure in London was destroyed by a cold he had taken, Paris ruined by rain, he found shooting on a lord's estate stupid, and Switzerland scenery flat, and now the very best of Clinton's society awaited him with its lovely women, beautiful homes, clubs, and gay men. Bitterness filled Mr. Latimer's soul, his proud, sensitive nature writhed in pain, but he only said in an unruffled voice, as he struck a match and handed it to Grey Whitridge, "You have let your cigar go out, Mr. Whitridge."

After Mr. Whitridge had his cigar well lighted he said: " You must have a large number of acquaintances in Clinton, Mr. Latimer, although your long absence at Harvard has prevented your ever enjoying one of our society seasons."

" No, I have not many acquaintances in the city. I have a few valued friends, but not any general acquaintances. You must remember that my last six winters have been passed in Cambridge."

"Well, I congratulate you on your prospects for this winter. I have been in society for eight or ten years" (Grey Whitridge was thirty-eight years old) "and I wish I could begin again with the zest of ten years ago. If I had made this world, I would have given all men unlimited wealth and youth."

" And all women ?" interrogated Mr. Latimer, with a smile.

" Equal youth and perfect beauty," replied Grey Whitridge, without an answering smile. "But, Mr. Latimer, we are not going to permit you to hide yourself in this office." Grey Whitridge turned one scrutinizing glance on Mr. Latimer, and estimated him from the top of his large, dark brown head, to the tip of his fashionably-made shoe; he passed upon his clear, intellectual eye, shapely hands, well fitting clothes, gentlemanly manner, well modulated voice, linen, necktie, and watchguard. The verdict was," He'll do; unusual man, handsome fellow, somebody new; yes, I'll bring him out." "I presume," he said, "that you have come out of college with great ambition, at least this office looks like it. Ah! Latimer, it don't pay, there's nothing pays less than work. If a poor devil is compelled to do it, I suppose there is no dodging it, but I pity him. Yes, you smile, I know. I've heard it all, and I can repeat it about as well as the parson himself, but it is all a lie from beginning to end, a fine-spun theory that no one believes. Now yesterday, for instance, at Trinity Church, Dr. Moore preached a sermon to young men; it was specially prepared for young men who have come here this autumn to find employment in business houses. It was the old cant on the dignity of human nature, nobleness of labor, and the satisfying results of honest toil. The old doctor ought to be shied out of his pulpit into the lake, if he don't know enough to know that there was nothing but rhetoric in his sermon, from beginning to end."

"Suppose he does know, what then?" asked Mr. Latimer.

"O, I suppose he would have had to preach it all the same, but don't you make a mistake, Latimer; I've seen many do it. As a matter of course, if you find pleasure in the study and practice of law, I would do it, for happiness is what we're all after. Some men may find pleasure in pursuing law year after year, but I doubt it. Judge Kent's position is a desirable one, so is Monroe's, and Judge Sargent's; they don't do much, and do it about as they please. I can easily imagine that a practice like theirs might make an agreeable life; but Mr. Prentice tells me that he worked very hard for twenty years after he was admitted to the bar, and he says no man can succeed in the profession, who is not willing to work early and late, and give up everything but his work. Now, why should a man do this when there is no pecuniary necessity? It's an ambition that I can't understand. Then Mr. Prentice says that few succeed with all of their hard work, that this city is full of lawyers, who hardly make a living, and that young men, especially, have a hard time of it; that with the most faithful work, they can't hope for more than a bare subsistence. What a doleful prospect looming up before young men who are compelled to earn their bread? I tell you work is a curse, to be borne if a man can't rid himself of it, but it doesn't pay. Now with you it is all so different. Pardon me, Mr. Latimer," he continued, as he turned to Mr. Latimer with a flattering air of respectful deference, "but I wish I had your advantages of youth and person. Why, Latimer, you have the world before you to choose from; before spring, half the women in society will be in love with you, and you will have to look out for jealous husbands, and bald-headed fathers, who will wonder what your intentions are."

Mr. Latimer felt his heart beat faster with gratified vanity as he listened to the words of Grey Whitridge, who was one of the acknowledged authorities of Clinton society. The opening of the door fortunately saved him from attempting some necessary reply, for really he had nothing at all to say to Grey Whitridge's long talk. As a strange man entered the room, Grey Whitridge took his leave. Mr. Latimer asked the long-waited for client, as he took the stranger to be, to excuse him for a moment, and he stepped outside of the door with Grey Whitridge, who said to him on parting:

"You must join the Dorchester Club, Mr. Latimer. Have you an engagement for this evening? I'll drive round for you after dinner, if you would like to go and see Mrs. Richmond. Where are your rooms?"

Mr. Latimer told him that he was engaged for the evening, but said nothing as to the location of his boarding house on Hillson street.

"Very well," replied Grey Whitridge, "I'll see you to-morrow."

The strange man proved to be, not a wealthy client, but a man in search of some one of whom Mr. Latimer knew nothing, and he immediately left. Mr. Latimer went to the window of his office, that overlooked one of the principal business streets of the city, and gazed down upon Grey Whitridge, who stood on the edge of the sidewalk, talking with Mr. Walt Richmond, who was seated in his tilbury. The young men spoke together for a few moments, then Grey Whitridge took a seat beside Mr. Richmond and they drove off. Mr. Latimer turned from the window and stood alone in his vacant office. His air was dejected, his face gloomy and angry. He walked slowly to a chair that was at the end of the large table in the center of the room, and sat down. As he raised his arm to rest it upon the table, he saw the end of Mr. Whitridge's cigar, that he had left there. He took it up, and threw it savagely across the room.

"D—n the man!" he growled between his teeth, then he sank into moody thought. "What a fool I was to stay in Clinton. I hope I shall never see Whitridge again—come to my boarding house!" In imagination he saw the raised eyebrows, and the ill-concealed disgust, and the polite leavetaking of the society man, from the small room, in the long block of a dozen houses, on Hillson street. He saw himself dodging into his office all winter, to avoid meeting Grey Whitridge, or some one of his friends, and in imagination he heard the inquiries that would be made for him, by the few young men he knew, for a week or so at the first of the season—why not at the opera, or theater, or at the club? Inquiries made of Grey Whitridge as to his whereabouts, and imagined his replies —practicing law, no money, dependent upon himself; and the answering comments—fine fellow, hard luck to have to drudge and grind. Six weeks, and not a client yet! Only some copying, and looking up some authorities for Judge Sargent. The years rose before him, slowly adding themselves together, years of hard, uncongenial toil; not of speechmaking on great elemental principles, or celebrated criminal cases, in a crowded courtroom, the day beginning with, " May it please your honor," and closing amid a crowd of friends, and members of the bar, congratulating him on his eloquence and unanswerable arguments, all of which would be reported in the next morning's city papers; but days of uninspiring work, bending his back over that table in endless writing.

Then after awhile he might get some collecting to do, and after another while, he might be retained in unimportant suits, and all for what? To be able to occupy that one room on Hillson street, and pay for his monotonous breakfasts, luncheons at the business men's counters of some restaurant, and equally monotonous dinners. After many years perhaps, he would be able to marry Margaret McVey and have her board with him in that same house, or possibly at one a grade better. The thought of Margaret McVey had no power to quell the tumult of his mind, or cast a cheering ray into his future. From his office windows, during the last month, he had looked down on the increasing crowds in the street, as the society people gradually returned from their summer's journeyings, and the beautiful women, and rapidly passing carriages, with their prancing horses and smart coachmen, gave a bright hue to life, in comparison with which Edgewood, and Margaret McVey's quiet home, rose before him as flat and stale. From the isolation of his office, he had looked on passing millionaires, merchants, railroad magnates, bankers, and celebrated lawyers, whose names were in every daily paper, and some of whom were men of national reputation; a few of these he had met in society; others he merely knew by sight, but they, and their wives, and sons and daughters, seemed to him the happy dwellers in Elysium. He saw the deference paid to men of large wealth by their fellows and he considered their position the most desirable one on earth. He was not aware that in drawing such an inference he was committing the blunder common to youth, that of over-estimating the power of wealth to confer happiness, and under-estimating the amount of happiness that comes from the simple gratification of the natural appetites and affections. Over the wall, that a moneyed caste had built as high as any barrier of Indian caste, he could in his imagination, hear the music, and dancing, and laughter and song, of well-bred and well-dressed men and women; with his feverish mind's eye he could see spacious rooms covered with soft carpets, flooded by a subdued light, the air sweet with the odor of flowers; could see Ethel Richmond waltzing down the Assembly Hall, on Grey Whitridge's arm, and Marie Edwards with Walt Richmond, and then came to him over this insurmountable barrier, the sound of merry voices at dinner tables, and the roll of carriages through the streets on their way to the parks and theaters. His mind had dwelt so much on the power and grandeur that wealth conferred, and saw so clearly the line of demarcation between, not wealth and poverty, but wealth and competence, that life without wealth, seemed to him a poor gift, but with it, of inexhaustible capabilities. Grey Whitridge's conversation with him that morning, had only confirmed him

in these views.   He roused himself from his bitter fore-
casting of the future with a start, turning sick and faint
as he leaned his elbow on the table, and rested his head
on his hand. Where should he go, how rid himself of this
unbearable prospect of poverty and mortification.   For
two hours he paced the floor of his office, in which time a
dozen projects were harbored and abandoned.   Among
these, were the ideas of speculating in stocks, going onto
a Western ranch, appealing to his uncle for sufficient
money to give him a social position until he could earn
one, and blowing his brains out with his pistol.   Turn
which way he would, his logical mind was thrown back
against the rock of steady work, and its legitimate results.
The lines deepened around his mouth, and his face took
on the desperate look of an animal at bay.   Always in
the past, he had possessed the advantages of wealth, as
much so, as though he had been born to a large estate,
and his soul revolted from the circumscribed, distasteful
life that lay before him.   After a while the stupor of nervous exhaustion came over him, dulling his pain; he sat
in a chair by the window, took up the morning paper, and
mechanically ran his eye down its columns.

CHAPTER VI.

That same morning Mrs. Lundom James White was sitting in her library before an anthracite coal fire, looking over the morning paper, which her husband had thrown down, when the maid announced to him that the horses were waiting. Suddenly she turned and cried, " Marie, come here !"

Marie Edwards rose from the sofa in the south bay-window, where she had been sitting in the sun, and crossed the room in her slow, stately way at her sister's bidding.

" Listen to this," said Mrs. White; then she read aloud the following item:

" A dispatch from Boston announces the death of Gilbert H. Latimer in that city last evening at six o'clock. His death, which was wholly unexpected, was caused by apoplexy. Mr. Latimer was born in Buffalo, N. Y., April 13, 1820. He was a member of the Commercial Exchange in Buffalo for many years. In 1870 he became interested in Western railroads, and removed from Buffalo to Boston, in which city he has since resided. He was a successful business man, and died possessed of several millions. Mr. Gilbert Latimer was a bachelor, but his courteous, genial temperament gained for him numerous friends. He was a man of great benevolence, and was actively interested in several charitable institutions of Boston. His only known relative is Mr. Rodger Latimer, a brilliant young attorney of this city, who is the only child of the late Professor Latimer of Edgewood College."

You remember Rodger Latimer, don't you, Marie?" asked Mrs. White, as she laid the paper across her lap, and looked up with an expression of alert interest.

"Yes, and he *is* a brilliant man." After several minutes of unbroken silence Marie continued, "He refused your invitation to join the Assembly, didn't he?"

"Yes he did, and I was disappointed, for he is an agreeable man, and a fine dancer. Don't you remember how beautifully he and Ethel Richmond danced together last winter?"

"I wonder why he refused."

"I don't know, there's something strange about it; he seems fond of society, and fond of dancing. I wonder—" Mrs. White leaned forward, crossed her hands on her knees, and gazed into the fire. Her sister waited full five minutes in silence, then impatiently asked, "You wonder at what?" It was another five minutes before reflective Mrs. White deigned a reply.

"It may be Marie, that Mr. Latimer's poor. The excuse he gave me was, that he couldn't spare time from his professional duties; he said he was very much interested in his profession, and if he made a success of it, he must devote himself to it. Perhaps he's dependent upon his practice; if that was his reason for refusing my invitation, this death of his uncle will remove it, for it must be that his uncle would leave him something handsome, even if he didn't give him all of his property." Both ladies gazed into the fire with serious, diplomatic faces.

"Newspaper reports can't be relied on," said Mrs. White after a little. "I wish I knew," then followed another silence that was broken by Marie.

"Suppose his uncle did leave him money; how do you know he cares for society? he may like his profession better than he likes dancing, and shut himself up to it."

"Fiddle-de-dee! how do I know anything? I know young men, and if he gets a million from his uncle, and don't go into Clinton society this winter, he will be a different young man from any I ever saw. The thing is to be sure of the fact; I don't want to make a blunder. The will may not be published." Again Mrs. White relapsed into another silence of ten minutes, after which she rose and went to the portieres that hung between the library and dining-room, parted them, and thrusting her head forward, looked around the dining-room; when she had convinced herself that no servant was within hearing, she returned to her seat.

"I've changed my mind about Grey Whitridge," she said in a low voice; "I really don't know what to think of him, but I don't believe he wants to get married; why hasn't he been here since his return? Mrs. Richmond told me last evening that Mr. Richmond overheard him say, when Mr. Barstow was rallying him about being engaged to Edith Morrison, that he was not engaged and had no idea of being; that he had much rather flirt with young married women than to get married."

"What a speech for a man to make!" exclaimed Marie. "Grey Whitridge ought to be ashamed of himself. I don't think Edith Morrison is much of a girl, but if that is the way he talks, she's too good for him."

"I don't believe he's very good; you know he was educated in Germany, and then he has so much money, and nothing to do," rejoined Mrs. White. "It's enough to spoil any man to be petted as he has been for the last four or five years. I should think he would be sick to death of being run after and complimented."

"He's a rather heavy man to entertain," said Marie.

'Yes, because he is entertained so much, he just leans back to be entertained; he's found out that we are willing to take him, and do all of the entertaining ourselves, but he can be charming if he chooses."

"He don't very often choose."

" No, but don t you remember how well he talked last spring, at our Lord Harrod's dinner? he seemed to know London, and English affairs as well as Lord Harrod himself." Again the two women sank into silence, Mrs. White gazing into the fire with contracted brows; after awhile she spoke: "Now, Marie, I'll find out in some way about Rodger Latimer's affairs; you leave it all to me."

" Leave it to you, Harriet!" exclaimed Marie in a petulant voice, "do you suppose I'm going to do anything? The Lord knows I would if I could, but what can a girl do nowadays?" Marie's usually handsome face was anything but handsome as she relapsed into silence, shadowed as it was with an expression of discontent and resentment. Mrs. White raisd her eyes from the fire to her sister's face, with a quick, impatient jerk of her head, but as her eyes remained fixed upon Marie, the expression of impatience changed to one of sympathy and earnest thought.

"I know," she said, "that all of our plans seem to fail, but there's no use in looking in that discouraged way; one would suppose we had come to the end of all things. You're only twenty-four; girls don't marry as young as they used to; we'll make this winter tell in some way. I've about made up my mind that Grey Whitridge will never marry. I don't believe he wants a home and wife of his own."

"I don't know why he should; he has a dozen homes or more in Clinton now, and heaven only knows how many in Washington and New York; as long as other men's wives pet and humor him as they do, what does he want of a wife of his own?"

"That's an ill-natured speech, Marie. What do you know of his position in New York or Washington society?"

"Nothing, only what I know of his position here, and

what I hear and read of New York and Washington society, and he is frequently in both places. If he is invited out as much there, and danced with, and flirted with there, as he is here by married women, the poor fellow hasn't time to think of getting married."

"I don't think he finds his time passes unpleasantly," said Mrs. White, growing a little ill-natured herself.

"No, I presume not. I dare say he likes it all, but really I do believe he is getting a little cloyed by all of the honey he has had poured down his throat, and is growing tired of all women, married and single."

"Well, he's not the only man in the world. Let him go; there's half a dozen right here worth as much as he in every respect, and then who knows what strangers we may have in town during the winter. I am determined that you shall visit Washington this season. When I was there I did not see as handsome a girl as you, in all of the crowds. I don't believe James will let me go again this winter, but I'll manage it. I thought it all out one night when I couldn't sleep. The McClures are going to spend January in Washington, and they know the best people there, the society people."

"I see; but Mrs. McClure may not wish to chaperone any one but Ada. You know, Harriet, that a mother don't care to have a girl that is handsomer than her own daughter constantly around. I never did think much of your Washington plan."

"No, you don't usually think much of any of my plans, but I think I've managed my own social matters very well." Marie hastened to appease her wealthy sister:

"Come, come, Harriet, you know I think you're the smartest woman in the world. I'm sure I've done just what you wished me to do for the last three years."

"Yes, and you'll not be sorry, only be patient, and

don't do anything in haste.   I'm so afraid you'll fall in love with some of these men who have just enough to drag along."

"You needn't be alarmed," interrupted Marie.   "I saw enough of the disadvantages of poverty before I came here, and have seen enough of the advantages of money since I have lived in Clinton, to keep me from making a fool of myself."

Mrs. White took the paper from her knee and read the obituary notice over again to herself.   "This uncle's property may be over-estimated," she said, laying the paper again on her lap.   "Fortunes usually are; but then he must have been a rich man, for he seems to have had some prominence.   'Several millions,' " it says, referring to the paper on her lap; "suppose he had only one million, and gave only half of that to his nephew, it would be a handsome fortune to begin with, and he could easily go on in Clinton with such a start and become a very rich man.   'A son of T. C. Latimer of Edgewood College;' that must be Professor McVey's friend, the Professor Latimer I've heard him frequently speak of."

Mrs. White leaned her head back against her chair and gazed at the ceiling for a few moments in earnest thought, then went to a writing table that stood in the room, and slowly, with great care, wrote a note, looking absently out of a window opposite for several consecutive minutes between the sentences.   When it was finished she sat with her eyes fixed on it for some little time; evidently it did not suit her, for she tore it up and threw the bits in the waste basket, and commenced another.   Marie meantime was looking into the fire at swiftly-moving panoramic scenes created by her memory.   The first picture was of her father's store in the New England village; in one corner of this store was the postoffice, at the counter her father sold calico, muslin, lamp chimneys and wicks and coal oil, sugar, tea, coffee, shovels, rakes and grass seed, together with cheap fish-hooks and lines to impecunious summer tourists, who did not aspire to the ownership of a hand-made, hexagonal, split bamboo rod. Then across the coals quickly followed a view of her sister's marriage to the Clinton iron merchant, when Marie was ten years old, Harriet twenty, and the iron merchant forty-five. The next picture was of the four years of school life that she passed as a pupil in a seminary, where her sister paid her bills, and then of the two years she had taught in another seminary as an assistant teacher. All through, as a sort of background to these pictures, ran a dull gray of economy, spring suits made over from her sister's last year's ones, the sewing being done after study hours had passed in the evenings—mended gloves, mitts manufactured from her sister's worn silk gloves by cutting off the fingers and hemming them round the hand, patched walking boots, and home-made bonnets and hats. Then followed a view of her arrival four years before in Clinton. She closed her eyes as she thought over the delirium of that first winter, with its novel splendor and gaiety, but opened them and gazed into the fire as the last three seemingly endless, years of her life passed before her, with their tangled plans and efforts and disappointments. These three years of effort on Marie Edwards' part to establish herself as the mistress of a wealthy home, had crystallized the artless girl into a managing society woman of great tact and complete self-control; a much deeper and shrewder woman than her less selfish and less intellectual sister, Harriet, gave her credit for being.

"Listen to this and see what you think of it," said Mrs. White, as she stood by her sister's side with her finished note in her hand.

Dear Mr. Latimer:

Can you dine with us informally, next Tuesday, at half-past six? I have not heard a word of my dear old friend Professor McVey for months, and probably you can give me some information regarding him. And then I wish for an opportunity to appeal to your kind heart, to reconsider your decision not to join our Assembly this winter. The committee had numbered you among my special friends, and I have some little pride in showing that they were not mistaken. Please come as an old friend; you will meet no one beside the family.

Very sincerely,
HARRIET F. WHITE.

1326 Madison Avenue.
  Nov. 6th, 188—

"This is the seventh, not the sixth," said Marie.

" I know it, you goosie," replied Mrs. White. " I dated it back; do you suppose I would write that invitation to-day, with this notice of his uncle's death coming out in this morning's paper?" Mrs. White touched the bell, and ordered the answering maid to call her coachman.

" Now Michael," she said, when the obsequious man stood before her, " I wish you to pay strict attention to what I say, as this is an important business matter, and you must be sure and make no mistake. I wish you to take this note to Mr. Rodger Latimer's office; he is a young lawyer, who has just opened an office down town. I don't know where his office is, you can find it some way; take this note to his office and leave it for him, and be sure and tell the man, or whoever you see, to say to Mr. Latimer when they give him the note, that you were sent with it yesterday and could not find his office, and that you are very sorry, and hope that it will make no difference with Mr. Latimer; you understand, Michael; this is some business that I ought to have attended to yesterday, and you be sure to say to the man, to tell Mr. Latimer that you were sent yesterday. Go over to Newman street and take the car if you can go quicker that way, but if not, take a horse. You are sure that you understand?" The quick-witted Irishman assured her that he understood, and left the room with his eyes fixed on the floor. Mrs. White went back to the fire and placed one hand on the mantel, as she rested her foot on the fender, and drew up her dress skirt, so that the heat could strike her ankle.

"Do you think that safe?" asked Marie.

"Yes," replied Mrs. White, "Michael knows too much, to ever say a word." She gazed abstractedly into the fire as she added: "No knowing what old Latimer did with his property; I wish I knew."

It was not many days before all of Rodger Latimer's friends knew, that his uncle's property had been equally divided; and that Rodger Latimer received one-half, the other half being given to several charitable institutions in Boston.

CHAPTER VII.

It would seem on first thought, that Rodger Latimer's
course in life was now a perfectly straight one. That
there was nothing for him to do, but marry Margaret
McVey and go happily through the years, enjoying all of
the blessings of the love and wealth Providence had so
bountifully bestowed upon him. But human nature is of
complex organization. Mr. Latimer at this time had no
other thought but that of marrying Margaret sometime in
the near future, and settling down in his own home, as an
orderly and useful citizen of Clinton. But when all of the
nightmare horrors of poverty and mortification that had
laid hold of him, were dispelled by the pleasant shock of
a shower of gold, his first thought was, that now he could
become a part of the brilliant dash he had seen flying past
him, and that all of the glittering paraphernalia of society
life was within his reach. The prospect was intoxicating;
he could not turn his back on the fleeting forms of beauty
that beckoned him to follow into the bewildering maze
before him, and settle down as the staid husband of a
simple village girl. The barriers had been thrown down,
and every path in the Elysian fields was open to his feet;
his heart beat high with joyous emotions, his judgment
was led by a disordered fancy, and he was eager to leave
the narrow circle of his personal life, and enter the boundless land of unsurpassing beauty, that for weeks he had
caught glimpses of, from the gloomy solitude of his office.
Life assumed a new phase; it was set to music, and all in
high notes. His first pleasant experience was the selecting of rooms at the Bellevue, the purchasing of pictures,
rugs and bric-a-brac, a saddle horse and a team. He

feared at times that it might all be a dream, and that he would waken to find the old life of toil and economy a bitter reality: but he lay down to sleep, arose to eat, and walk among men, and there remained the solid fact of wealth to his credit. He wondered at times that the earthquake that had elevated his personal life to such a pleasing altitude, had not caused the slightest tremor of the earth beyond the small portion covered by his own feet. For a few days he was congratulated by his friends on his inheritance of a fortune; then men met him as though the present order had held from the beginning. Soon he was afloat on the waves of society, invitations poured in upon him, and Grey Whitridge was always at his elbow to advise in selecting the most desirable. He would have liked to have accepted them all, and in his heart, he regretted his inability to be in half a dozen places at the same time.

A short time after his pleasant entrance into society a celebrated actor came to Clinton to fill an engagement. He had been long heralded, and much talked of, and Mr. Latimer received invitations to several of the parties that had been formed for the opening night, but unfortunately important business called him to a neighboring city, and he had no idea that he could finish his business and return in time for the first night of the theater. He regretfully refused all of the invitations, being careful to state the reason for his refusal. Much to his surprise, however, he dispatched his business with unexpected rapidity, and found that he could, by traveling part of one night, reach Clinton early in the evening before the play began. He telegraphed to his hotel for a ticket to be obtained for him, and started for home, where he found a ticket for a seat in the parquet awaiting him. He entered the opera house a few moments before the curtain rose, and had scarcely seated himself, before two ushers came to him, one with an invitation from Mrs. Richmond, and the other with a like invitation from Mrs. Lefarve to a seat in their respective boxes. Before he could rise to his feet, a third usher approached with an invitation from Mrs. Lundom White, to her box. He slightly bowed to Mrs. Richmond and Mrs. Lefarve, whose boxes were side by side, and then glanced up to Mrs. White, who was on the opposite side of the house, leaning forward as her arm rested on the front of her box, smiling down on him. There flashed into his mind a remembrance of that kind invitation of Mrs. White's, to her family table and fireside, sent him when he was a poor attorney, and her almost persistent urgency that he join the Assembly. He acknowledged her smiling recognition, and soon was seated in her box beside Mr. White, directly back of Marie Edwards, who immediately turned her chair so that as she faced the stage her side was toward Mr. Latimer. Miss Edwards welcomed him with a smile that was peculiar to herself, a smile that never seemed to stir the lips, but consisted of a brightening flash over the face, not of color, for color was never seen in Marie Edwards' face, but a flash of pleased recognition, and the holding of the man's eye for one slight moment, with an expression of intense delight that made him feel, that of all living mortals, he was the most welcome. It mattered not how frequently a man might receive this salutation, repetition could not dull the effect of that rapt, instantaneous gaze. There was the advantage in such an unspoken greeting, that only the receiver was aware of it. Each man to whom the young woman pleased to accord this welcome, thought himself the one specially favored, and prized a greeting that was no hackneyed form of speech, words cheapened until worthless, by being spoken impartially to all. No one

would have thought for a moment that Mr. Latimer was
flattered by the attention which he had received, but under
his dignity of manner there was a delightful flutter of
gratified vanity.   Clinton's best society was out that
night to welcome the great actor, and Mr. Latimer had
seen the opera-glasses turned on him as the three ushers
stood around him, with the flattering recognition which
they brought from three of Clinton's social leaders at the
same time.   As he walked up the aisle on his way to Mrs.
White's box, he was aware that hundreds of eyes were
gazing on him, and there came to his mind the remark
Grey Whitridge had made that miserable morning in his
office, the morning that he had first met him after his
return from Europe in the autumn, " Pardon me, Latimer,
but I wish I had your advantages of person."   Rodger
Latimer knew that he was a handsome man, and he knew
also that he was a well dressed man, knowledge that went
far in keeping him undisturbed under the scrutiny of
numberless eyes.   When the curtain dropped on the closing
of the second act, he went over to Mrs. Richmond's box
and stood beside her and her delicate looking daughter,
Ethel, for a few moments in animated conversation, and
then stepped into Mrs. Lefarve's box, to thank her also
for her courtesy.

"Why didn't you come and sit with me, you naughty
man," said sprightly Mrs. Lefarve, a woman of twenty-
seven, as she playfully beat Mr. Latimer's hand with
her fan. "We had just this one place, and I determined
to have the handsomest man in the house occupy it, and
when you wouldn't come, I wouldn't let any one have it."

Mr. Latimer spent a few moments in complimentary
raillery, and then returned to Marie Edwards' side, with a
Jacqueminot rose from Mrs. Lefarve's bouquet, in the
buttonhole of his coat.   She had given it to him with the

remark: "You must wear my color, if you do sit with Mrs. White."

When Marie Edwards noticed the rose, she took a Bon Silene from her own bouquet and handed him, holding out her other hand for Mrs. Lefarve's Jacqueminot, which Mr. Latimer covered with one hand, as he slightly shook his head, reaching at the same time for the proffered Bon Silene, with an expression of smiling entreaty. Miss Edwards answered his look with one of her peculiar flashes, as she laid her rose on her white wrap on her knee, and immediately turned her attention to the stage. Mr. Latimer was fond of the theater and usually gave his undivided attention to the play, but just then the girl at his side distracted his thought. His eyes wandered to the beautiful white throat, and rested on the curve where the cheek sloped to the neck, under the exquisitely formed ear. All was graceful undulation, from the low broad brow, down the nose, across the clear white cheeks, over the full lips and round chin, to the large white throat, where the perfect lines expanded into the velvety softness of the neck, plainly shown by the square cut corsage, and expanded still more into the full bust that rose and fell, with every breath, under the bodice of some soft white fabric. After a little, he resolutely turned his eyes to the stage, but it was only a few moments before he was looking at the well formed hand under which lay the coveted rose, and from the hand his eyes slowly traveled up over the arm, and bust, and neck, and cheek, and rested upon the drooping lids that seemed charged by the lightning that lay beneath. When the play closed, he was much more under the influence of Marie Edwards than of the great tragedian. As they left the box Miss Edwards placed the rose that she had detached from her bouquet, between the first and second finger of the hand that held her flowers, thus keeping it separate from the others. Mr. Latimer noticed this, and as they stood close together in the crowded passage way, he touched it with one finger, and said:

"Am I not to be honored with the keeping of that rose, Miss Edwards?"

"You do not understand women, Mr. Latimer," Miss Edwards replied in a soft voice, with the lids low down over the brown eyes. In the crowd her face was near his as she continued: "No gentleman can wear the colors of two ladies at the same time."

As she said this, she suddenly raised her eyes to his a moment, and then veiled them again. Quickly his hand went beneath his coat lapel, the pin was drawn out, and the Jacqueminot lay on the top of Miss Edwards' bouquet, as with a whispered, "Permit me," he took the Bon Silene and placed it where Mrs. Lefarve's flowers rested a moment before.

"Come and take a cup of tea with us to-morrow," said Mrs. White to Mr. Latimer, as he was closing their carriage door, after he bade them good-night; "then we will all go together to Mrs. McClure's. I know you are to be at her dinner and theater party, and it will be lovely for us all to go together—tea at five, remember."

The first thing Marie Edwards did after closing her bedroom door on her return home, was to take a tiny vase from the mantel, step to her bathroom and fill it with water, and after placing Mrs. Lefarve's Jacqueminot in it, set it on a corner of her bureau. Then she seated herself in her usual stately way in a chair in front of the bureau, and fixed her eyes upon the solitary rose, with what would have seemed to a spectator of the pantomime, a most ridiculous gravity. But never did a general fix his eyes upon the map, outlining his first move in a campaign, with greater interest, than Marie gazed at the half-crushed Jacqueminot. It was the result of her arrows tried on new game. The opening of the door aroused her.

"Why Marie, what have you been doing? haven't you got your things off yet?" asked Mrs. White, who came forward wrapped in a long flannel gown placed over her nightgown, her feet thrust into a pair of bedroom slippers. "I'm not a bit sleepy; it's that coffee at dinner. I won't drink any more of it. James is fast asleep; I declare it don't take a man but half a minute to undress, and the other half to go to sleep."

Mrs. White curled up in a large chair, and laid her cheek against the back. Her years of society life had not destroyed her desire to talk over every dinner, funeral, or theater that she attended. Mr. White, who was a good sleeper, and was not particularly fond of society, said to his talkative wife one night as he was settling himself to sleep, after returning from a dinner: "This talking parties over, is as bad as having to go to them twice; if you can't stop talking things over after we get home, and go to bed and go to sleep, we better give up going out." Poor Mrs. White never offended again in that way, and she declared that one of the comforts of having her sister in the house, was that she could talk things over with her. Cautious Marie never complained, no matter how late Mrs. White staid in her room at night, or how many times she was compelled to lay down her book during the day.

"Wasn't that a splendid play?" asked Mrs. White as she cuddled herself up in her chair, "and what a full house 'twas; it was just lovely. Say, Marie, did you notice Mrs. Lefarve looking at you?"

"No."

"She just watched you all of the time after Mr. Latimer came in our box. When he came back from speaking to ner, I looked right at her, and she saw I noticed the way she stared at you, and she stopped it. I don't believe she looked at you again."

"I don't know why she should stare at me," said Marie.

"I suppose it was because Mr. Latimer chose to come and sit with us, when both she and Mrs. Richmond had invited him to their boxes. When I saw those other ushers, I was dreadfully afraid he wouldn't come." Marie said nothing, and after a moment's silence Mrs. White continued, "What a lovely dress that was of Mrs. Von Stein's; did you notice it?"

"No."

"It was lovely. I suppose it is one she brought back with her, she has splendid taste in dress. I suppose her dinner next week will be an elaborate affair. How pale Ethel Richmond looked to-night, I should think her mother would feel anxious about her. I should, if she was my daughter. Did you notice how well Mr. Bassett looked?"

"No."

"You know he saw the midnight sun, and was in Spain and Algiers. He told me he had a delightful trip, perfect weather everywhere, and not a single accident or unpleasant occurrence." Mrs. White sat in silence a short time looking at her sister, who was seated before the mirror, brushing her back hair. After a little she said: "Marie, you'll take cold without anything over your shoulders."

"No, I think not."

"What's the matter of you to-night? didn't you have a pleasant time? Seems to me you're not very happy," said Mrs. White, giving her gown a tuck around her feet.

"Why yes, I had a delightful time," replied Marie, rousing herself from her abstraction, "and I'm sure that

I'm happy. I think we had a charming evening. I was delighted with everything."

"Was Mr. Latimer as agreeable as usual? I was mortally afraid that James would go to talking to him about his old iron. Mr. Latimer don't know a thing about iron, and then I wished you to have a chance of talking with him. Isn't he a handsome man?"

"Yes, he is handsome," replied Marie, "and he is very unlike these other men who have been in society so long. It's a positive pleasure to meet a man of his enthusiasm. Mr. Whitridge and Mr. Bassett, and all of them are so mechanical, they say everything in a mechanical way, just as though they had been saying that same thing, in that same way, for fifty years. If they express any enthusiasm, it is so evidently assumed, it only increases the artificial impression."

"I think you're a pretty severe critic Marie; all of those are agreeable men. You must remember that Mr. Latimer's much younger than they are. I don't believe there's as young a man in society as he."

"I don't know," said Marie, "as it is possible to be born in society, and live in it, without losing the last spark of spontaneity one has. The souls of some of these people we meet, have been in society for generations. Some physiologist says that a person can inherit mental discipline. I wonder if they can't also inherit *ennui*, and be born blasé."

"I don't know what you mean, Marie," said Mrs. White, looking at her sister as though she questioned whether she was in her right mind or not.

"I mean," explained Marie, "that Mr. Latimer is, what half a dozen of the unmarried men who visit here, wish they were, and pretend they are. He really enjoys life, from his cup of coffee in the morning, to that good-night at the carriage door, at midnight When he talks to you, he don't have to throw his soul in his eyes, as Mr. Whitridge does, for it's already there; and what a difference it does make."

"But you ought to remember that this is all new to Mr. Latimer," said Mrs. White; "neither his father nor grandfather had money."

"I should suppose he was well born."

"Oh, the Latimers are a good family, a splendid family. Professor McVey told me all about them one day, when I was in Edgewood. He and Rodger's father were great friends, but you see this wealth and society is new to Mr. Latimer "

"He has traveled," said Marie, "and is really the best, the most thoroughly educated man I have met in Clinton."

"I don't mean that," replied Mrs. White; "it's this society that's new to him. He's studied all of his life, and seen no society outside of Edgewood, and you've no idea what a washed out set they are, only they never had any color to wash out." Marie made no reply as she brushed her dark chestnut hair, looking into the mirror with a preoccupied air. Every few minutes she would give the mass of hair a few twists, then shake it out, and continue the brushing.

"I presume this is a new life to Mr. Latimer," pursued Mrs. White; "you never could know Marie, how delightful this city life was to me, for two years after I was married. It did seem as though this world was too beautiful. I couldn't get used to it. I saw other people didn't feel as I did about it, and I tried not to show it, for I knew they had had it always. I used to shut myself in my room, and back away from the mirror, and walk up to it, looking at my dresses. It did seem so good to wear a dress that I hadn't made myself, and such lovely dresses, that cost so much. And then to drive down the avenue in my own carriage, and have people bow to me from the sidewalk!" Mrs. White burst into a laugh. "It seems too ridiculous, don't it?"

"I don't see anything ridiculous about it," answered Marie, "it was natural—if you only had sense enough to keep the new experience to yourself."

"Oh, I did that. Sometimes I would talk a little to James, and he would laugh just as though it pleased him, especially when I would tell him that we must not spend so much money, that we were living too fast, and he would be ruined if we weren't more economical. But it did seem to me that first year as though no one could stand such a constant outlay of money, it took my breath away. After a while I got used to it, and then how natural and matter-of-course it all was."

Marie brushed away at her hair in silence. Presently Mrs. White exclaimed: "What a handsome girl you are, Marie! I declare a girl who has such shoulders and arms as you have, ought to have the credit of them. It's too bad that James makes such a fuss about low necks."

"I don't care to wear low necks or short sleeves," said Marie, as she passed her left hand down her bare right arm, from shoulders to wrist. "Miss Johnson fits me well."

"I should think she did! I was looking at you to-night, that white dress fits you beautifully, not a wrinkle in it. You looked beautiful to-night; what will you wear to-morrow?"

"I don't know."

"I want you to look your best. Alice McClure has a fine figure, but it's nothing to yours! Say Marie, I've just thought of something. Mr. Latimer must take a part in our play; he would make a perfect Rubo, to your Ardano.

Won't that be delightful?" exclaimed Mrs. White enthusiastically starting up, and untangling her feet from the long woolen gown; "it is strange I never thought of it before."

"I don't know about that," replied Marie. "I don't know as I wish to act in a play with him."

"But you will have to take the part of Ardano, you said you would, and Mrs. Von Stein and Mrs. Richmond would never forgive you if gave it up."

"I don't intend to give it up," said Marie, "but I don't know about Mr. Latimer taking the character of Rubo. I should have to think about that."

"You know they all said you might make your choice of a Rubo."

"Yes," replied Marie, "but you know as well as I do, that it would never answer for me to express the least preference in the affair. I'm the only girl in the play, and I think some of those married women look upon me as a sort of intruder any way. When Mr. Lefarve cast the play, I think several of the ladies were dissatisfied; you see Ardano is a prominent character. I think several wished for it."

"You're mistaken, Marie; Mrs. Von Stein and Mrs. Lefarve are intimate friends, and Mr. Lefarve very likely had gone over every character with Mrs. Von Stein, before he gave them out. But you will have nothing to do with it; I will manage it."

"Don't let it be decided for a week at least," said Marie, "then I'll tell you."

"Bless me," said Mrs. White getting out of her nest in the big chair, "how late we are talking, and we shall have to be up late to-morrow night." She leaned over her sister and kissed her, and then went noiselessly to her room.

CHAPTER VIII.

Rodger Latimer was a man who lived in the present.

Present gratification appealed much more strongly to his nature—which was a poetical, sensuous one—than did future consequences. He was logical and well balanced, yet the esthetical luxuriousness of wealthy society, possessed a subtle charm for him, which it would have been impossible for him to have accounted for, even to himself. As Mrs. White said, society life was a new experience to him. In Harvard he had known young men, at least the best of them, in Edgewood he had known mature scholars. As to women, he did not remember his mother, he had a more than conventional acquaintance with Miss Sargent— a woman forty-five years old, the sister of Judge Sargent, a bachelor, with whom she lived in the quiet elegance inherited wealth made possible—and he had a slight acquaintance with half a dozen Clinton ladies. The only woman he really knew, was Margaret McVey, and he had never cared to go beneath the fascinations of her personal attractions, to the creative forces of her life, and gain a knowledge of the constituent elements of her character, those potentialities of all suffering and action in each individual personality. He was utterly ignorant of the machinery of society and of housekeeping. He was an intuitive, rather than a critical, judge of the furnishings of a room, of a dinner table, or the completeness of a woman's dress. He felt rather than saw harmonious combinations and beautiful effects, and the artistic costumes worn by Miss Edwards, that he ardently admired, were to him a part of the woman, that in some mysterious way must have been evolved from her inner consciousness.

It was to him as though she simply stood and **was** clothed
about, with soft fabrics that clung to her regal form **in**
obedience to the law of natural selection. As the unconscious lily in the perfection **of its bloom** under the moonlight, so she stood in **the mornings, in the soft** light that
came through **the** buff-colored **shades of Mrs.** White's
library windows, draped **in clinging, creamy white:** or as
a rose in its glory under a **July sun, she** stood **in the flood**
of gas light, wrapped about in crimson, that, creeping up
from the trailing folds that lay in glowing circles around
her feet, passionately encircled her waist and bust, and
threw an ardent glow over the clear white cheek, and
touched the chestnut hair with an added warmth.

After his return from the theater that opening night,
Mr. Latimer sat long in his room before his grate fire.
When he first sat down in gown and slippers, he held a
lighted cigar between his lips, but it soon went **out,** and
he seemed unconscious of the fact, as he lay back in his
chair, gazing at times into the fire, then looking fixedly
at the ceiling, but most of the time sitting motionless
with closed eyes. Every sense had been gratified that
evening; every nerve had thrilled with pleasurable sen-
sations. After a little he laid his cigar on the table by
his side and took up Miss Edwards' rose that was lying
there, and as he leaned back again in the chair he placed the
rose to his lips and gave himself up to a delightful reverie.
In imagination he saw Marie Edwards as plainly as when
he sat by her side an hour before; he was gazing on her
face and watched her quivering eyelids slowly rise, and
his pulse kept time to their motion, faster and faster, as
the eyelids rose higher; then the one challenging, yield-
ing, thrilling flash, and he opened his lips to breathe, as
the eyelashes instantly lay upon the white cheek again.
The rounded throat, the soft line under the ear, the reg-

ular rise and fall of the Juno bust, were all before him, and the sight drove the blood tumultuously through his veins. "There never was such a woman before," he thought. "How unlike all other women, how different from Margaret McVey." With the thought of Margaret McVey, he suddenly opened his eyes, and sat bolt upright.

"I declare I must write to that girl," he said aloud; "it's a week or more since I have written." It had been over three weeks since his last letter. He laid the rose on the table at his side, crossed his legs, and leaned forward, resting one arm on his knee as he gazed into the fire. "Confound it, I wish I wasn't engaged," he thought; "a man has no business to engage himself before he knows all sorts of women. What a figure Marie Edwards has! I wonder if Margaret knows of this money that Uncle Gill left me; yes, I wrote her about it—no, I don't know as I did; I wonder if I did? I declare I don't believe I have written her as often as I ought to, but she always told me never to make a duty of writing, if I didn't write from one six months to another. She don't care for money, she don't like theaters, or dinners, or society. How beautiful Miss Edwards looked at Mrs. Bassett's! I'm going to the McClures with her; how much she adds to a dinner; tea at five; I hope there'll be no one there; how delightful Clinton society is! I wonder if there is any better in the United States. I don't believe there is in Boston or New York. I wonder if Paris or London are better? Whitridge didn't like London last summer. I don't know much of Europe; never have been there unless Margaret McVey was with me. What an idiot I was! Margaret wouldn't like Paris or London: what a queen in society Miss Edwards is? What eyes!" Rodger Latimer faintly smiled, and closed his own eyes; he was again lost in an enchanted world; he retained no connected thought, no distinct memory, but was wrapped in the witchery of a spell that obliterated the past with any obligation it might contain, and that did not evoke from the future any embarrassing complications of situations, that might demand an explanation or decision from himself. He was aware of nothing besides a satisfying present. At the expiration of half an hour, he quietly rose and prepared for bed. His last thought as he dropped off to sleep was of Marie Edwards, of the tea with her the next day, and the long evening to be passed in her presence afterward.

CHAPTER IX

True to her word, Mrs. White managed the affair with such adroitness, that Mrs. Von Stein thought the idea of Mr. Latimer's eminent fitness for the part of Rubo, in her forthcoming play, originated in her own mind. She sent him a note, asking him to come and see her.

"You know, Mr. Latimer," she said, when seated in her drawing-room with him, "we wish a man of quickness, and of adaptation, and withal, one of leisure."

When Mr. Latimer assured her that it would give him great pleasure to serve the ladies in any possible way, but that he doubted his ability, and suggested his friend Mr. Whitridge, as a man who had experience in amateur theatricals, she would not hear to it.

"No, no," she said, "we wish you to take the part of Rubo. Then Mr. Whitridge is the lover, you know, your sister Ardano's lover, and you are the watchful brother. I'ts so funny where you drag Mr. Lefarve off of Mr. Whitridge. You'd just die to see Mr. Lefarve; he flies at Mr. Whitridge as though he would kill him, and Mr. Lefarve is such a peculiar looking man, thoroughly French looking, he would really make a better Italian than Mr. Whitridge. I declare we ought to have those parts changed. I fear Mr. Lefarve made a mistake there in his casting, don't you think so ? You have the most conspicuous part in the play. "

"What is the play? I haven't seen it yet."

"Then you have your lines to commit," said Mrs. Von Stein, taking a copy of the play from the pile that lay on the sofa beside her, and handing it to Mr. Latimer. "It's a lovely play, full of hits. Mr. Lefarve translated and adapted it specially for us." It was a French society play, one of those intensely intellectual productions, that are considered capable of repaying days of study and numberless rehearsals. There was in it, an indiscreet young wife and jealous husband, a handsome Italian tenor, who fell in love with the wife, and then followed a succession of tragi-comic situations, where fortuitous circumstances brought the wife and Italian into association, wholly unpremeditated and unlooked for, on the part of the wife, that aroused the most irrational jealousy in the young husband, who was personated by Mr. Lefarve. In one scene he nearly choked the Italian to death, but explanations from the wife, and a promise from the handsome tenor to exile himself from the country of the married pair, saved his life. The hysterical wife fell into the arms of the appeased husband, and the curtain dropped, after general harmony had been created by a full understanding of the innocence of all parties, except that of the inflammable, susceptible singer, who consented to an eternal exile from American shores. Rodger Latimer, in the character of Rubo, the brother of the indiscreet wife, was always hovering over his sister's path as a guardian angel, full of advice and assistance. He was ubiquitous on the stage, appearing always at the right moment, even standing between his sister and any misconstruction that society might put on her conduct. He flew from the infuriated husband to the infatuated lover, intent upon explaining questionable appearances, and convincing the husband of the guilelessness of his wife's nature. And through all of his sister's thoughtless conduct, and the unfortunate circumstances that surrounded her, he succeeded in protecting her from gossip, without wounding her by severe criticism, or curtailing her social pleasures by any over-cautious restraint.

Mr. Latimer set himself to learn his part in the play, in the odd moments that he could catch between his social engagements. He frequently met Miss Edwards, scarcely a day passing without his seeing her for a few moments, at least. Sometimes it would be for only a few moments in a bookstore, or he would ride beside her carriage as she was out for a drive. Owing to Mrs. White's great kindness, he found himself a frequently-invited guest to her house. The winter was not far advanced before in some way, he could hardly tell how it came about, his Sunday dinners were taken at her house. He feared at times that he might be trespassing upon her hospitality, and one day when he intimated as much, Mrs. White, in a dear motherly way, said to him:

"What in the world should you go back to your lonely room for? Professor McVey will never forgive me if I don't look after you; we'll have some music after dinner if you'll stay; Marie and Polly will sing for us."

The name of McVey was fast losing its power to disturb him. How far off Edgewood seemed! McVey? yes, and his father who had been dead for years, used to live in Edgewood. Hazy as an incoherent memory, was that old life, as he glanced at the queenly girl sitting in the bay-window, with a halo of yellow glory around her, thrown from the southern sun through the buff shades. One flash from those grand eyes destroyed his past, and left him no desire for a future; the present held for him the fullness of life, and it was a measureless, unfathomable fullness. Mrs. White had cordial allies in her efforts to keep Mr. Latimer for Sunday afternoons, in her husband and two little daughters, Polly and Dora, girls of six and eight years of age. Mr. White was not much of a talker, he was too heavily weighted to be loquacious, his soul having chained to it an iron furnace, and a wholesale hardware store. But he frequently would rouse himself from his corner on the sofa, and **supplement** Mrs. White's invitation.

" Better stay, Latimer," he would say, "if you care for the lives of these two women. They don't know what to do with themselves after coming from church."

The two little girls were put to bed at eight o'clock, and saw very little of any guests who might be in the house to dinner on week days, when the family dined at night. But two o'clock was the Sunday hour for dinner, and Mr. White insisted on having his children with him, the only day of the week that he was at home, so Sunday afternoon was a sort of family gala day, directed and ruled over by the two little girls. Mr. Latimer, and Polly and Dora, were the best of friends, and when he was there on Sunday, they claimed from him one story at least, which he usually related to them, as they sat on his knees, with their arms around his neck. The little girls were not the only ones entertained at such times. Mrs. White would sit near by, delighted with the delight of the children, and even Lundom James White—whom business men called the closest old screw in the State; so sharp, there was nothing to be made by doing business with him, as he knew just when he got a man screwed down to the last sixteenth of a cent profit—this hard business man would listen to every word of the story, with a tender smile on his prematurely wrinkled face, watching his little girls as they sat so still, with their eyes fixed intently upon Mr. Latimer, who observed with pleasure that Marie Edwards' attention was also fixed upon him, and his two absorbed listeners, for whom he recollected or improvised a story. He little thought, however, that Miss Edwards was equally indifferent to the children's pleasure, and to the fate of the fairy who visited the sun to gather a basket full of beautiful gifts for good little girls. Marie Edwards was building a palace of her own, and on more solid foundations than fairy gifts. She was always glad when the children had been taken up stairs to bed, releasing her prince from the thraldom of their arms, to devote himself to her. It was Mr. Latimer, who was very fond of children, that took the little girls up stairs on Sunday nights, perched on his strong shoulders, their four arms clinging to his head, the children filling the house with screams of laughter, as he pinched their dangling legs on the way. Had it ever occurred to Mr. Latimer to inquire why they were never interrupted by visitors, Sunday evening, in a house that was rarely without visitors, the butler could have told him, that Mrs. White had given orders that the family should be excused to all who came, on Sunday evenings whenever Mr. Latimer was there, unless some special friend of Mr. White's called, and then he was to be taken to Mr. White's private room. It frequently happened that such a friend did call, an old-time, or business friend, and then Mr. White would leave the library for his own room. It also frequently happened, that soon after Mr. White had gone from the library on such Sunday evenings, a maid would enter with a message from the nurse, that the children wished to see their mother in the nursery. These happenings would frequently leave Mr. Latimer alone with Miss Edwards, in the large quiet library, where he would sometimes read aloud to her, and sometimes she would read to him. He never sat near her, but was content to rest in the atmosphere of her presence, gazing upon the face and form of the peerless creature in white, and to wait patiently for the uplifting of those grand eyelids to disclose the light they hid. He never thought of how little she talked when they were alone together; the hours seemed to him wanting in nothing. The inspiration of her listening face awakened the best there was in him, and he talked a great deal of books, and of art, and of life. At times his mental excitement carried him into waters far beyond her depth, and he enlarged upon the relation of nation to nation, the development which the race was working out for itself, and the probable beautiful outcome of all tangled human affairs. She listened to all that he said with eager attention, as though she feared to lose one word that fell from his lips. How beautiful she looked to him, with the constant play of rising and falling eyelids, her whole being seemingly absorbed in the thought to which he gave utterance. Had Rodger Latimer been told that he was living in an imaginary world, fashioned and impressed by his own excited mind, that his infatuation was a sensuous one, and that Marie Edwards was playing a part, he would have accused the speaker of blasphemy, and smitten him in a white heat. He said to himself, again and again, that he loved Marie Edwards, and that he never had loved Margaret McVey. This was the first delirium of his life, and he called it the first love. It would have been useless for any one to have told him, that he vastly overrated Miss Edwards' beauty of person, and warmth of nature; he could no more correctly estimate her qualities of person or mind, than could the man with senses dulled, and faculties stimulated into supernatural intensity by a dose of hasheesh, estimate correctly the length of the passing minute, or the relative size of objects within his view. He did attempt to reason regarding his relation to Margaret, but made a sad jumble of it. He said to himself, not only that he did not love her, but also that he could not marry her; he declared to himself that he did love Marie Edwards, but there he stopped. That he loved her was enough. All of his life centered in the present hour in her presence, and he was never from under her influence, for his ardent imagination took with him as he went forth from her bodily presence, each line of form, and sweep of eyelid, each quiver of lip, and electric flash of brown eyes. He felt that Margaret was an intruder, that not even a thought of her ought to come within the magic circle, where he and Marie Edwards stood alone. Sometimes he would sit down to his table, to seriously think of his irksome relation to Margaret, usually on the receipt of a letter from her, in answer to one of his own, for he continued to write to her at long intervals. His letters were short, and contained nothing regarding his own personal life, neither of his inner world of thought and feeling, or of his relation to society, but such length as he gave them, was spun out by comments on sermons, theaters, and books, or descriptions of pictures. They were such letters as might have passed between two people for ten years, and given no more knowledge of the individual writers to each other, than would the same number of lines cut from a daily paper, and sent in an envelope. When he did set himself to look over matters, he usually ended about where he began; with thinking that he must say something to her of his state of mind sometime, but not now; that there was time enough in the future to straighten the affair out. At this stage of his thinking, he was apt to slip her letters into his table drawer, relegate her personality to oblivion, for another period of blissful weeks. It was but natural that as his feeling grew more ardent toward Marie Edwards, Margaret should fade out of his life until she almost ceased to be to him a living being. Only when he wrote her a few lines, or received a reply, did she assume the reality of a flesh and blood girl, to whom he was engaged to be married; and then he often became irritated and resentful in his feelings, as though his recognition of their engagement, was asserting a claim to a relationship to which she had no natural right. He argued to himself, that if she could only be made to see the eternal fitness of things, she probably would regard herself as some unfortunately misplaced body, and would gladly take herself out of the way, anywhere, only that she cause no disturbance in the beautiful harmony of those spiritual laws, that control the movements of human hearts in the heaven of love. Had he been called upon to analyze this feeling of resentment, which he certainly felt toward her, he probably would have declared it to be a revolt of his being, from unharmonious environment, instead of acknowledging it as an old-fashioned stirring of conscience. But neither thought of her, or feelings toward her, came with any frequency to him, so engrossed was he by the beautiful life that surrounded him. His health had never been injured by dissipation, or injudicious study, his tastes were cultivated and an ardent temperament whetted his appetite for every pleasure, and to these pleasures he yielded himself without reservation. A month's absence from Marie Edwards would have restored the equilibrium of his nature, and a few weeks of solitary reflection, necessitated either by sickness, or an absence from society, would have given him a just estimate of the men and women about him, and of his relation to them. But he saw Marie Edwards every day, and spent most of his waking hours amid the soft illusions of social amusements and entertainments.

CHAPTER X.

One Saturday evening, the members of the Amateur Club met at Mrs. Von Stein's for a rehearsal in her mansard theater. It was the first rehearsal that Mr. Latimer had been able to attend, so pressing were his social engagements. None of the actors had committed their lines perfectly, and the books, which all had declared at the previous rehearsal, should be laid aside this evening, had to be called into requisition, much to the disappointment of the managers. They all did the best they could, but there was no attempt to carry out the details of the play, and the rehearsal was, after all, but little more than a careful reading of the individual parts, under the manager's critical direction. There was some attempt at grouping, and some little acting, in the simplest scenes, but nothing was thorough or finished. Mr. Latimer, with book in hand, followed out to the last detail, the part of each man and woman as they successively passed through the manager's hands. He closely observed, not only what each did and said on that night of partial rehearsal, but what they would do and say, when the characters as they had been cast, were acted in all particulars as designated in the copy of " Parlor Theatricals," which he held in his hand. He carefully scanned each situation Miss Edwards would be placed in, when she acted the part of Mr. Lefarve's giddy wife, who by her beauty and vivacity, inspired the Italian tenor—Mr. Whitridge—with a tragic passion for her. No one beside Miss Edwards, who never lost an expression or action of Mr. Latimer's when they were together, noticed his critical observance, or the expression of displeasure that at times rested upon his countenance.

"I shall hope to see you to-morrow, Miss Edwards," he said as he bade her good-night. "Mrs. White has again kindly invited me to spend the day with her."

The next evening as they were sitting alone together, Mr. Latimer turned the conversation on the forthcoming play, of which he and Miss Edwards had never befoie spoken to each other.

"These amateur theatricals are new to me," he said.

"And to me also," replied Miss Edwards.

"Have you never taken part in one before?" he asked.

"No," she replied, but she said nothing farther, for she felt that there was something back of Mr. Latimer's serious tone, which she did not understand, and she was afraid to do more than follow his lead, until she could get hold of his underlying thought or purpose.

"Mrs. Von Stein seemed disappointed that we did not know our parts," said Mr. Latimer.

"Yes, I fear she was," replied cautious Miss Edwards. "Mrs. Von Stein has been very kind, and has given a great deal of time to this play; really she and Mr. Le-farve were the originators of the whole thing."

Mr. Latimer sat in silence looking at the chestnut head, and drooping eyelids. After a little he said:

"It strikes me that this is rather a peculiar play, but perhaps my ignorance of French parlor plays may account for the unpleasant impression that this one has made on me."

Miss Edwards made no reply; she was fearful she might not say the right thing if she spoke; and concluded that it was safest for her to say nothing. After a few moments Mr. Latimer continued: "Yet, this play is not one-half as objectionable as some that we all go to see at the theater; many of which, I am perfectly willing to say, I exceedingly dislike. I can understand why Marie Laurent refuses to play any maternal part, that is not sweet and noble. She will not personate a cruel or a tyrannical, or a selfish mother, and she is right. When the word mother has become a synonym for tenderness and forbearance and unselfishness, why should the few abnormal instances of selfishness and wickedness, be typified upon the stage, to outrage our sense of justice? And it is the same with the other relations of life, especially so that of wife; if there are a few monstrosities holding that relation, who have no sense of the sacredness of their duties, why should these moral distortions be forced upon us, any more than painful physical distortions? The moral sense is as much outraged and pained by the one, as the sympathies are taxed, and the esthetical nature pained by the other." Mr. Latimer evinced more feeling as he spoke than he was aware of.

"I agree with you perfectly," said Miss Edwards, "and I am glad to hear you speak as you do."

Mr. Latimer's face flushed with pleasure: "I hope I am not narrow regarding the drama," he continued, "I have no sympathy with the tirade indulged in by the clergy against theaters; I think we go to the theater for pleasure, not instruction, but it certainly ought to be a pure pleasure, not a demoralizing one. I respect, as well as admire Modjeska, she is a lovely woman, but I wish she would select different plays from some we have seen her in."

"You like her Rosalind?" asked Miss Edwards.

"Yes, and her Mary Stuart, which is as perfect a piece of acting as I ever saw. But to think that the woman who can come upon the stage, with the majestic grandeur of her Mary Stuart, should debase herself to the playing of Odette. Her Mary Stuart is wonderful. I never fail to see it, when I am where she is playing it."

"Do you consider that the best acting you ever saw?" asked Miss Edwards.

"No—I can hardly say that; nothing can surpass Salvini's Othello."

"And yet Othello is a cruel husband, who kills his wife," said Miss Edwards.

"I think Salvini's Othello," replied Mr. Latimer, "leaves an impression, not of a cruel personality, but rather of a cruel passion, stalking before us, in all of its naked hideousness; the last shred of concealing drapery torn off. It is just a thing to be hated and condemned. Its blind fury and roaring rage may have an element of chilling horror in them, but the horror we feel, is akin to that with which we beheld a violent thunder storm, when the lightning twists itself through the black clouds and then dashes in broad, blazing sheets over half of the heavens. Salvini's genius lifts the passion out of personality, and the man is nothing, the passion everything."

Miss Edwards was listening intently, with her brown eyes fully opened, fixed upon Mr. Latimer's face. She was a flattering audience, and as Mr. Latimer looked at her he forgot Salvini, and for the time, the end he had in view, when he turned the conversation upon theaters and actors. Presently he resumed: "But all of this is very different," he said, "from some of Modjeska's plays; even she has not, no one can have, genius enough to rid themselves of the abhorrent personality which they sometimes represent. The fact is, the personality is about all there is in some of these objectionable plays, for they are written with no genius. And right here is the difficulty with these silly parlor theatricals; they are adroitly written perhaps, but with no talent, and they cannot be acted with any power. They may be cleverly given at times, but at best, it is an approximation to the correct representation of a person's externality, so none but harmless externalities, or realities, should be given, nothing that we could object to in real life, either in sentiment or manner."

"That is very true," said Miss Edwards.

Mr. Latimer looked at her a moment in silence, then he rose from his chair and commenced to walk back and forth across the room. Miss Edwards did not, at all, understand the drift of his talk; she felt convinced that he had something on his mind, but she could not even guess at its nature. She did not wish to turn the conversation away from the present subject, for fear of impressing him as lacking sympathy with his mood and turn of thought, but she dared say no more than give her assent to his opinions, lest she pitch herself in some quagmire, by an irrelevant utterance. So she remained silent as he walked the floor, with head slightly bowed and hands behind his back. At last he stood still beside the table near which she sat.

"Miss Edwards?" he said, then ceased speaking in evident embarrassment. She uttered only one word in a soft, persuasive tone.

"Yes?" she interrogated.

"I don't know but that you will think me very presuming; indeed, I seem so to myself," he continued, with increasing embarrassment, "but I have a great favor to ask of you. I have no right to ask it, I know," he hurriedly added.

She turned her face full upon him as she said: "There is nothing, Mr. Latimer, that you can ask of me that I would not gladly grant. I wish there was something that I could do for you, in return for your many kindnesses to me."

"Kindnesses!" he exclaimed. "I don't know of what you speak."

"Perhaps you may not regard it as much, but I was

thinking this morning that for months I had been surrounded **by** the most beautiful flowers and the best of
books, for which I was indebted to your thoughtful kindness." Miss Edwards with **seeming** unconsciousness, raised
her hand and toyed with **three roses worn on the** bosom of
her dress that she had taken **from a bowl on** the table that
held several dozen of the same **kind, which Mr.** Latimer
had sent her the day before.

"I beg of you not to speak of such slight things," said
Mr. Latimer, in a voice full of feeling; "it has given me
the greatest pleasure to see that you cared enough for
either the flowers or books to let them remain near you."

"I'll not question that," she replied with a beautiful
smile, "remembering that the good Book says, 'It's more
blessed **to** give than to receive,' if you will only believe
that it will give me pleasure to render you any slight
service that is in my power, and will be good enough to
ask it without the least hesitation. Really," she added,
seeing that he still hesitated, "I shall feel complimented
to know that it is possible for me to **render** you a
service."

Nothing could be more charmingly winning than her
voice and manner. It was with a great effort that Mr.
Latimer refrained from throwing himself at her feet, but
he quietly turned and walked the floor again, and Miss
Edwards saw that his face was pale with emotion. After
a little time, in which nothing had been said by either of
them, he stopped behind her chair and looked down on
her as she sat with her elbow resting on the arm of the
chair, and her head leaning on her hand in a way that
gave him a full view of the side of her face. He gazed
down on the warm chestnut hair, the drooping eyelids,
rounded cheek, and red lips just now quivering with
emotion, and on the superb neck and bust.

"Miss Edwards, do you care especially to take the part of Ardano in the play?" he asked hesitatingly.

"Not in the least," she replied in a cheerful, decided tone. "On the contrary, I should be glad to be excused from the whole thing."

"I am delighted to hear you say so!" he exclaimed.

"I only consented to take the part," said Miss Edwards, unhesitatingly, feeling that now she stood on firm ground, "to please my sister. She was very anxious that I should, and she and Mrs. Von Stein and Mrs. Lefarve pressed it on me, so at last I consented."

"You may think it strange that I should speak of the matter to you," said Mr. Latimer, "and it is strange. Perhaps you cannot understand it, when I say that it pains me to think of you in many of the situations that you would be compelled to occupy as the Ardano of that play."   .

Miss Edwards was silent; she could not understand his motive in asking of her what he did, but she instantly decided to give up the play if he wished it. Why did he wish it? she asked herself with a flutter of heart, and she dared not hope all that might possibly be inferred from his words and manner. He was gazing intently upon her face.

"It's a great deal for me to ask," he pursued. "I have no right to ask it, and yet I cannot refrain from doing so. It's right that you should know the reason for such a request; let me try and tell you." He was silent a moment or two, then continued: "Mrs. Von Stein has given me the part of Ardano's brother; pardon me, Miss Edwards, but permit me to speak as a brother might. You must not think it strange that during this winter, in the happy hours of my association with you, I have come to regard you with all of the interest a brother might feel;

and it distressed me last evening to see you, even in jest, holding the relations that you were compelled to, to Mr. Lefarve and Mr. Whitridge. And think for a moment how much more objectionable, in the inference at least, it will be when the play is fully carried out."

Mr. Latimer ceased speaking, and waited as though expecting some reply. When none came he hastily added in a tone of apprehension: "You think me unreasonable? You cannot agree with me?"

"I fully agree with you," replied Miss Edwards, "and I don't think you at all unreasonable. Let me speak to you frankly." Her head drooped slightly, and her voice sank so low Mr. Latimer was compelled to lean down from his height, a little over her, to catch her words. "I never liked the play. I always disliked my part; I felt sometimes that I could not take it, but what was I to do? I didn't like to displease my sister, and I had no one to help me out of it."

"Then you will not take it?" Mr. Latimer eagerly asked.

"No, certainly not, if you wish me not to." The slight, but yet evident emphasis on the word you, possessed the power to bring a deep flush of delight into Mr. Latimer's face.

"Thank you! thank you, Marie," he exclaimed; he had never called her Marie before. "How can I ever repay you! what a relief it is to know that I shall not see you again in any of the situations of last evening; I felt that I could not bear to have those men touch your hand; how hateful the whole thing was to me! How can I repay you?" In his excitement he had leaned over the chair, and had rested one of his hands lightly on Miss Edwards' right shoulder. As he asked, "How can I repay you?" she raised her left hand and laid it very softly upon his hand, as she replied:

"By always being my good, true friend."

That electric touch pulled apart the last strand of his self control. In a moment the impulsive man was on his knees by the side of the chair, and had taken the beautiful head in his arms, and was kissing the hair and brow, and closed eyes, and pouring out such words of burning love as Marie Edwards had never heard before.

Two hours afterward, Miss Edwards let Mr. Latimer out of the front door, turning the key and fastening the chain behind him with her own hands. Then she went back through the dimly lighted hall to the library, where she sat down in the chair beside the table which she had occupied most of the evening. She was alone in the large room; she leaned her head against the back of the chair and closed her eyes, to live it all over again, as any loving girl would have done. An hour after, she turned out the side gas lights, extinguished the coal oil lamps, and noiselessly went up stairs, turning the gas off in the hall as she passed through. The hour had not been one of dreamy, love-making remembrances, but one filled with the forecastings of a calculating woman of the world. Though she had been delightfully startled by Mr. Latimer's impetuosity, and very sweet to her had been his words of love and adoration, the after-thoughts were of the life of assured position and social influence which the man of wealth could bestow upon her, rather than of his protestations of affection.

As Miss Edwards turned the light up in her own room, she saw her sister lying on the edge of the bed, in her nightgown, wrapped in a blanket, looking straight at her with wide open eyes.

"Harriet! why are you not in bed, and fast asleep?" she asked.

"I wanted you to tell me all about it before I went to bed," said Mrs. White.

"About what?" asked Miss Edwards with a smile.

"O you know! about what Mr. Latimer said to you; come, tell me all about it."

"How do you know he said anything?" asked Miss Edwards, as she stood in front of her bureau unbuttoning her dress and looking at herself in the glass.

"Now don't be so provoking, Marie. I'm dying to know; do tell me all about it."

"Well, he don't like my being in that play of yours, and wishes me to give up the part of Ardano."

"Marie Edwards! you don't say that was all he has been talking about for these three hours?" asked Mrs. White, sitting on the edge of the bed, as she tightly held the blanket around her shoulders.

"I think it's considerable," replied Miss Edwards, "and you will have to manage it for me, and get me off. He has a great deal of feeling about it. It will never do. I must give it up."

"Give it up!" exclaimed Mrs. White; "what will Mrs. Von Stein say? Why don't he like it, what's the matter? I declare, I'm out of all patience." Mrs. White threw off her blanket and stood up in her lamb's wool slippers, as straight as a section of lightning rod. "I don't know," she continued energetically, "what right he had to ask you to leave the play. If that is all he has to say, it's none of his concern; how long he staid! I sent Vilas to bed and told him I would lock up and put the lights out myself, and I coaxed James up stairs as soon as old Perry left, for fear he would go in the library, for I really thought Mr. Latimer had something special to say to you. I was sure he was in love with you. If he isn't I'll give up that I know anything about men. He's acted for six weeks as though he was perfectly dazed. Want you to leave the play!" Mrs. White shook out her blanket, and threw it over her shoulders as she said: "I'm going to bed, it's nearly one, there's time enough to talk that play matter over to-morrow."

Miss Edwards took her by the arm, as she was going toward the door. "Stay, Harriet," she said, "I have something to tell you. But you will take cold; cuddle up in that chair."

Mrs. White curled up in the large chair designated, and Marie, sitting in front of the bureau, commenced to brush her hair, which she usually brushed for half an hour every night, to keep it bright and soft. She seemed in no haste to speak, and Mrs. White waited in impatient silence a few moments, then said:

"Well, what have you to tell me, Marie? Do speak."

"What a hurry you are in, Harriet," said Marie, smilingly, as she drew the brush the length of her hair; "but Mr. Latimer did tell me that he loved me."

"And asked you to marry him?"

"No, there wasn't a word said about marriage, but with a man of Mr. Latimer's type, words of love are based on marriage."

"I don't know," said Mrs. White; "young men nowadays are slippery as eels, but Mr. Latimer don't seem like most other young men."

"He's very different, I always told you he was."

"But did he really tell you that he loved you?" asked Mrs. White; "in a way that he wished to marry you?"

"Yes, he did really tell me that he loved me," replied Marie laughingly, as she imitated Mrs. White's intonations. Then she added very seriously, "I wonder if it's possible for a man to love a woman as he says he loves me? There's something beautiful in it, and something dreadful, too." Marie lapsed into thought. Poor Mrs. White was eager for the whole story, and when was there ever a woman not eager to hear the last detail in a girl's love affair.

"What did he say?" asked Mrs. White; "how do you know that he loves you so much?"

"Know!" exclaimed Marie; "by the way he looks, and moves, and speaks; why, every look of his eye, and tone of his voice, and touch of his hands, are declarations of love. I don't suppose I ought to tell what he said."

"Yes, you should, every word of it," insisted Mrs. White.

"But he calls me his queen, his darling, his angel, and his life, and hope, and soul, all in one breath. He seems to think me the most beautiful woman that ever lived, or can live."

"Any one could see," said Mrs. White, "that he thought you were very handsome, from the way he looks at you. I declare I've sometimes been afraid that other people would notice it, and laugh about it. It's not any seem with him, he really thinks so. You certainly think he's honest in all he says?"

"Honest as heaven! I've seen something of men and have been made love to somewhat, but I never met a man like Rodger." Mrs. White's face broke out all over in a satisfied, triumphant smile, as Marie said "Rodger."

"That settles it," she thought; "they'll be married."

Marie continued: "It's strange what confidence I feel in him; I would as soon expect the moon to fall out of the sky as for him to utter a dishonest word, or do anything that was not exactly right. How differently I feel about his going away to-night without saying a word of marriage, from what I would if it had been any other man I know, or ever have known, for matter of that."

"But didn't he say anything about your marrying him?" asked Mrs. White.

"No; he called me his wife, his darling wife, in some of his rhapsodies, and said that his whole life was to be spent in making me happy, but he didn't come down to serious talk about our being married. It makes no difference with him; I feel as sure of him as though I had had a public betrothal, or were married. He feels every word he says, through and through. I wouldn't have let any other man kiss me as he did, and hold my hands, before he had asked me in plain English to be his wife, and asked permission to speak to you or James."

As Marie finished speaking the brush lay idly on her knee, and for a few moments she seemed lost in thought, with her eyes fixed on vacancy. The expression of her face was sad and hard; wasn't it the memory of a bitter lesson learned that made it so?

"But he will talk about it the next time he sees you, won't he?" said Mrs. White, "or do you suppose he will go on with just his love making?"

"I shouldn't be surprised if he were here in the morning," replied Marie, "pressing for a speedy marriage, and talking the whole matter over with you."

Happy Mrs. White! She folded her hands over the blanket and straightened her head up against the back of the chair, and assumed the air of the affectionate elder sister and general adviser. The comparative merits of brocade with pearls, and velvet with diamonds, for her dress, as she stood at the altar near the bride, passed through her mind; and Mrs. Von Stein and Mrs. Richmond there to see! She gave a tug to the blanket, folding it closer about her breast, and clasped her hands again over the folds, envying no reigning queen under her royal purple. She gazed at her sister with the old affection, but with it there was mingled a new expression of rapidly increasing deference.

"I declare, Marie, you're a happy girl," she said after a little. "We'll have a splendid evening church wedding, won't we? just as handsome as it can be made, the very best of everything. I know James will be delighted to do it; he was always proud of you, and you know Mr. Latimer's a great favorite of his. You *are* a happy girl Marie, Mr. Latimer's a great match, the best in Clinton; and then he's so kind-hearted, just see how much Polly and Dora think of him. You'll have everything, just think of it! Such luck don't come to many girls. He has money, and is fine looking, and is intellectual, loves you, and then he's good, which is something after all."

Marie had come out of her sad retrospection, whatever it had been, and was quietly brushing her hair, with an expression of perfect contentment on her face. She scarcely heard her sister's enumeration of the desirable qualities possessed by her lover, which she had counted over herself many times during the past weeks, both the inherent, and adventitious ones, although she had not ranked them exactly as Mrs. White had just done.

"You always were a dear good girl," continued Mrs. White, "and I hope you'll be very happy. Wont James be delighted! Say, Marie, when will you be married? I'm so glad you're to live in Clinton."

"I shall be married next May or June," replied Marie. "I know Rodger will wish for an early marriage, and I dislike long engagements."

"Let me see—" said Mrs. White, "this is the middle of February, March—April—May. Why Marie! that will give you only three or three and a half months to get ready in."

"That's time enough."

"Where will you spend the summer?"

"I don't care where, anywhere Rodger chooses."

"Will you keep house next winter?"

"Certainly I shall," replied Marie with decision.

"Yes, I suppose Mr. Latimer will wish for his own home, he seems very domestic," said Mrs. White.

"I shall wish for mine, whether he wishes for his or not," responded Marie.

"How strange it sounds," said Mrs. White tenderly, "to hear you talk of keeping house, and being married."

"It don't seem so very strange to me," said Marie, "it seems natural, just as it should be."

"Yes, it certainly is just as it should be," replied Mrs. White. "Wont Mrs. Richmond and Mrs. Von Stein be surprised, and then the Blackwells! Mrs. Blackwell has been particularly attentive to Mr. Latimer; she told me she regarded him as being a most exemplary young man. I wonder if she wouldn't have been glad to have had him marry her Marion."

"I'm sure," said Marie, "that I don't know anything about that; but Harriet, we must go to bed. Here it is two o'clock," continued Marie, taking her watch from the bureau and looking at it. "I shall be up late to-morrow night, and must go to bed. I suppose Rodger will spend every evening here now, unless we are out somewhere. Suppose you tell Susan when she comes in your room in the morning, not to come in here till I ring. If my curtains are not raised, and no one opens the door, perhaps I may sleep an hour or two later."

CHAPTER XI

Rodger Latimer did not go to Mrs. White's the next morning, as Miss Edwards fancied he might, but he sat himself down to write a letter to Margaret McVey, and found that it was not quite as easy a task as he had anticipated. At first he dashed off several pages full of his love for Marie Edwards, which on reading over struck him as not being in very good taste under the circumstances. Then he indited another, from a lofty moral standpoint of duty to one's self, and the supremacy of the law of love and the obligation of obedience to that law. This suited him some better, but he was far from being satisfied with it. After a few turns across the room, he opened his table drawer, into which he was in the habit of throwing miscellaneous letters, and sorted the contents, selecting out Margaret's letters and placing them on the table by themselves; then he arranged them in chronological order beginning with the previous August. He opened several of those written in August and September, glanced at the beginning, read a few lines and laid them aside with an expression of annoyance on his face; he turned from them, as from something distasteful. After looking at half a dozen written later in the winter he arose and went to the fireplace and rested his arm on a corner of the mantel, and gazed into the fire. After a little he raised his eyes to an engraving of Titian's Sleeping Venus that was in an exquisite frame on a small easel on the mantel. A thought seemed to strike him; he took the Venus from the frame and placed therein a cabinet photograph of Marie Edwards, that she gave him the night before. It was a side view; the head drooped a little, and the eyes were cast down; the dress was as décolleté as any of the ladies in Mr. Lundom White's family dared wear, the light played upon the soft curves, and undulating lines, in a way that brought out their voluptuous sweetness. How enchanting was the glow that crept from beneath the more than half-closed lids, and lay caught below the delicate lashes! How lovely the meeting of cheek and neck, the well-rounded shoulders and swelling bust covered with a mist of illusion lace! Mr. Latimer's face was transformed as he gazed upon the picture before him, his eyes glowed with excitement, and his lips parted with intense emotion. After a little he turned to the table to finish his task, taking Marie's picture, which he placed on the table directly in front of him. He commenced to read Margaret's letters again, several of which he put aside after giving them a hasty glance, then he read one clear through, and another, and another, from the beginning to the end. There were not many of them all together, and very few written after the first of November. It was these last ones that he read carefully through. As he finished the last one, dated something like a month back, he rested his elbow on the table, and his head on his hand. He drew before him a sheet of paper, and dipped his pen in the ink, and placing his hand in a writing position, held the pen above the paper. But his eye caught Marie Edwards' face, and all thoughts of the unwritten letter fled from his mind, while he lived over the blissful hours passed with her the evening before. It might have been ten minutes or an hour, that he was lost in thought, he did not know; but presently he came to himself, and then he threw down his pen, leaned back in his chair and gazed into the fire, from which he turned in half an hour to take in his hand several of Margaret's letters which he carefully re-read.

As he finished them he took up his pen, and again held it over the paper. " Evidently we both were mistaken," he said aloud, and he re-read **again one of the latest letters.** " Those letters certainly **indicate a change," he thought,** " a gradual change. She **was very young when we became** engaged, a mere child; she was inexperienced, **knew** nothing of men. That letter of last month **is not at all** like those of September; how do I know what **men she** has met this winter. She was probably mistaken in **her** feelings toward me, as I certainly was, regarding mine toward her; it is better that we found it out **at** this early day; she may not love another, she may have just found out that she does **not** love me. Her **father** is about all **she wants;** I never knew **any one so** easily satisfied. That miserable Edgewood! **I shall never** go there again, but I must **write her** something. I'm glad she don't love me, it will **make** the whole thing easier. **It** is right, she would say so herself. I should say so to her, if she had discovered that she was mistaken." He **put** the pen **to** the paper and wrote rapidly. It was not a long letter; he addressed and stamped it, touched his bell, and gave **the** letter to the man who appeared, with an order to **send** it to the postoffice immediately. He turned back **from** the door, cheerfully humming a strain of a popular opera, kissed Marie's picture, ordered his carriage, and went to take luncheon with Mrs. White and Marie Edwards.

CHAPTER XII.

When Rodger Latimer bade Margaret good-bye, the day he left Edgewood to go to New York, which was the day following the one he spent in the woods with her, the evening of which they passed on the piazza together, that beautiful August evening!—he promised to return and spend a few of the autumn days with her.

"My vacation is over, Margery," he said, "and I must get to work, but I'll run up, for at least one day, the last of September, and we'll have a great many evenings together this winter. But because I'm to be so near, you must not stop writing to me. You don't know how much your letters are to me."

Margaret realized that her lover was no exception to the average man, in his dislike of letter writing, and she had accepted this fact in the early years of their correspondence, with a common sense amiability, after she was once thoroughly convinced that he really did set a positive value on her letters. During the years of this correspondence, she might not have written him a larger number of letters than he her, but the pages of hers frequently outnumbered the lines of his. Short as his letters often were, they had been frequent enough, and long enough, to give her a knowledge of his daily life, and were so unreservedly confidential in their character, they prevented any strangeness from growing up between them during his long college absences. After he left her in August to go to New York, his letters came with their usual regularity and frequency, but soon after his return to Clinton, they came very irregularly, and she felt a lack of something in them, which she could not define, and for many weeks

III

did not attempt to define. The facts of his daily life were given; she knew something of his boarding house on Hillson street, of his pleasant office, and of his hours of copying, and wearisome waiting for clients; and she was not surprised at his evident restlessness, and chafing under the dragging monotony of his daily task; but was surprised, and a little hurt by his seeming loss of interest in her life, and in her father, and all that pertained to Edgewood, and indeed to all of their past life together. He delayed his promised visit to her from week to week, till at last October came, and the leaves had fallen from the trees, and the autumn beauty of the country town had gone. Gradually Margaret grew thoughtful and silent, but no positive fear possessed her regarding either Rodger's affection for her, or their future happiness together, until one November day, when she opened a letter from him, and her eyes rested on the unusual address with which it began. He had always called her Margery when they were small children, and all through their happy after years, and had never called her anything else, and no one beside him, had ever called her that.

The members of her household and her familiar friends would about as soon have taken Mr. Latimer's purse from his pocket, as to have taken the name of Margery from his lips, and used it themselves. Instead of the dear familiar Margery, this letter she held in her hand began with the conventional address of " My dear Margaret." As she read it, her head whirled, and she was in an instant the victim of a strange hallucination. She lost her personal identity for a moment, and dropped her eyes down the page—only a dozen lines or so—to see who wrote the letter. Yes, it was from Rodger, there was his name in full, but who was it written to? She looked again at the address, " My dear Margaret," and she thought, " Margery must be dead, and Rodger has written to tell me so." All of this passed in a moment, and she was herself again, but permeated with a presentiment of some impending calamity. She read the letter carefully; there was nothing unusual in it, in nothing was it different from those she had received from him for many weeks past. She re-read it, lingering on each word, vainly trying to extract from it a quality it did not possess. For the first time in her acquaintance with Rodger, she felt that something was wrong between them. She felt that this letter which she held in her hand, that stared at her in such a hard, cruel way, was indicative of a wrong somewhere. She turned to her desk, and took from its drawer, a number of his late letters, that had impressed her as lacking some old and well-known element, and after reading these, she selected some of those written the previous winter and spring, and read them through. Oh! what a difference! so fond! so warm! Not long nor effusive, but breathing in every line, the calm, tender love, that had so brooded her life with its sheltering warmth. For an hour she sat in painful, incoherent thought, with accelerated pulse, and a buzzing in her ears, then she went to her bedroom, and putting on her hat and jacket, started for the woods back of the college. The exercise and fresh air, restored the circulation of her blood to its normal rate, which cleared her brain. And as she seated herself at the root of a tree to grapple with facts, she resolutely set herself to eliminate all that might be imaginary, all that might be the outgrowth of a morbid state of mind, and steadily look at the simple facts of the case. It was a difficult task; half of the time she was in tears, and frequently she was so mastered by her apprehensions of coming evil, that she sat motionless, shivering and shrinking as it were, from some approaching ill. But

8 Rodger Latimer's Mistake.

with all of her will power, she turned from the present to the past, and brought before herself all of the years of her acquaintance with Rodger, and her knowledge of his character, in order, if possible, to account to herself, for the evident change in his feelings toward her. She could not remember the time when she had not known Rodger; there was no experience of her life that he had not shared, no transition period through which they had not walked side by side. He had participated in all of her childhood's plays and in the studies of her girlhood, he had been her companion in society, and she had never taken a trip at home or abroad, unaccompanied by him. They had prepared for confirmation together, and knelt side by side at the altar, when the good Bishop laid his hands on their heads. As she thought of that Sabbath morning, she said to herself: " The man who knelt beside me there, cannot be false, he cannot do a wicked thing." Then she thought of the many years, when his absences in Harvard were shortened, and brightened by his regular letters, and of the delightful holidays, and summer vacations, when he was a daily inmate of their home, and their lives went on as smoothly as the even sweep of a great river through a level country. It all came back to her, it was a tangle of thought, a confused mixture of retrospection and reasoning, but out of it, at the end of an hour or more, two conclusions stood clear and distinct in her mind. One that she must not be childishly suspicious, or hasty in her judgments of Rodger; the other, that come what might, her father must not suffer on her account. Whatever she might be compelled to suffer in any way, she must so bear it, and so manage it, that her father would not know that she suffered at all.

As Margaret, on her return from the woods, went to her room to dress for dinner, she was appalled by the appearance of her face, as reflected from the mirror; her eyes were red and swollen, her hair was in confusion across her forehead, and her cheeks were covered with purple spots. As she was wondering what she should do to hide the effects of her weeping, her Aunt Deborah came into the room.

"Why, Margaret McVey! What in the world's the matter of you?" she exclaimed, as she caught sight of the face in the mirror.

Margaret turned toward her and laughed in a rueful way. "There's no denying it auntie," she said, "I've been out in the woods, having a good cry, and see what a fright I've made of myself."

"Crying! about what?" asked Miss Bond in a tone of alarm.

"It would be difficult to tell," Margaret replied, "I guess I'm not quite well to-day. "I'm nervous perhaps; but I felt like crying, and I just cried, I had no idea it would make me look like this, it's dreadful! I wouldn't care if it was not for papa, he will be distressed to think that I've been crying and he can't be made to believe that I cried for nothing, only just because I was nervous and felt like crying. What shall I do with my face?"

"Crying for nothing seems silly employment," said Miss Bond, "but it's much better than having something to cry for. Really, Margaret, I thought you had more sense. Your father would be distressed to see that face of yours; you'd better wash it in cold water, and lie down and have a nap. Your father came home at three, and when I told him you were out, he said he would take the phaeton and drive around for Professor Hitchcock, who was anxious to see some lots he talks of buying, and asked your father to drive him down to them. He said you could follow on your horse, if you chose to ride in this wind; they went the north road; they can't be back before half-past five, so you'll have two hours for a nap. Lie down, and I'll call you at five."

As Miss Bond closed the door behind her, after comfortably covering Margaret on the bed, and drawing down the window shades, her heart ached for the suffering girl. She had not been deceived by Margaret's evasions, but believed there must be some serious cause for such tears, and she feared that Rodger Latimer was in some way responsible for them. She had been speculating for weeks, over Mr. Latimer's long continued absence.

"Only ten miles away," she had said to herself, "and not been here since August!" But kind, cautious woman that she was, she did not appear to notice his neglect, nor would she have Margaret suspect that she even detected in her face or manner, more than Margaret chose to tell her in plain speech. Two hours afterward when Margaret was ready to go down to dinner, she was not at all satisfied with the appearance of her pale face, with its swollen eyelids. She put on a red woolen dress, so as to look as bright as possible and as she entered the dining-room, her aunt was surprised that she looked as well as she did. Margaret tarried a moment beside her father's chair, on her way to her own place, to kiss him, and as she chatted in her usual merry way, and her voice gave no evidence of a sad heart, he observed nothing unusual in her. The evening passed in the customary way in the professor's study, Aunt Deborah busy with her sewing, and Margaret with her book. Professor McVey occupied his own large chair in front of the bright wood fire; at his side was a small table, on which stood a double student lamp, and around the lamp lay his foreign papers and reviews, and home magazines, to which he always gave his evening hours. As the hands of the clock on the mantel were nearing ten, Professor McVey threw the end of his cigar into the fire, and leaned back, with his eye upon the dial, as though watching for bedtime to come.   Aunt Deborah had gone to her room half an hour before.

"You look tired, papa," said Margaret gently, as she leaned over the back of his chair and placed her hands tenderly on either side of his face.   "I hope you did not drive too far with Professor Hitchcock; you better go to bed."

"No, I don't know that I drove too far, but I shall go to bed soon.   Did you wish to drive this afternoon, my child?   I feared perhaps you might be disappointed when you returned, and found that I had the carriage, but Professor Hitchcock requested me to go with him to look at some lots he thinks of purchasing, and I hardly knew how to refuse him."

"Oh, you ought to have gone with him," replied Margaret; "I didn't care to drive, it was a little chilly.   I'm afraid we shan't have many more of our nice drives this fall, papa, the roads are getting muddy."   Margaret leaned down and rested her pale cheek on her father's bald head.   How soft and warm it felt to him! he closed his eyes in peaceful contentment.   But after a little, he suddenly opened them and without stirring his head, he said:

"You have not told me Margaret, of your, or rather Rodger Latimer's good fortune."   Margaret's heart gave a bound; she raised her head, but gently, so as not to startle her father, and took her already trembling hands from his face.   "Has he not yet written to you of it?"

"I've heard of nothing, what is it?" she asked.

"Professor Hitchcock told me this afternoon, that Gilbert Latimer died in Boston last week, and left Rodger a million or more, and you haven't heard of it?"

"No," replied Margaret, calling up all her power of will to steady her voice; "Rodger knows I don't care for money, and so would not hasten to tell me that. But who told Professor Hitchcock?"

"He saw it in the 'Clinton Press,' and also in a Boston paper that he takes." Both were silent. Professor Mc-Vey's thought was, "Will the possession of that amount of money hasten Margaret's marriage?" and Margaret was trying to answer to herself the question, "How will that money influence Rodger's life?" All of Rodger's bitter talk regarding his social positon in Clinton, came quickly to her mind; she felt that she must be alone. The apprehension of coming ill, that had possessed her with such appalling power that afternoon in the woods, again seized her. Her limbs trembled beneath her weight, she leaned heavily aginst the back of her father's chair. She recalled the conversation between her father and herself one morning in August, regarding her leaving him, when she married Rodger, and she vividly remembered his distressed face, and broken voice. Much as she wished to be alone in her room, she felt that she must first remove any possible fear from the dear father's heart, and send him to bed in peace.

"Well papa," she said in a steady voice, as she again placed her hands on either side of his face, and leaned her cheek on his head, "I don't know as I'm glad Rodger has that money, I don't believe it will make him any happier, or a better man; he'll have to keep it, and spend it. Suppose some one had left us a million, and we should have to move into the city and spend it, how unhappy it would make us; we never could be as happy anywhere else as we have been here. How happy we have been here!" She gave him a little hug with her hands, as she kissed the top of his head. "You dear papa," she continued, "we never could be happier than we have been here, could we? and we're not rich."

"Then my child," said the professor, "I need not fear that you will marry Rodger soon, and live in Clinton, if you are so happy here?"

"No indeed, you need not," Margaret cried, as she kissed him again and again. "But let us go to bed now, and be thankful that no one has left us a million. I'll fix the fire and put the lights out."

Margaret picked the fallen brands up, and piled them together, and placed the wire screen before the fire, chatting all of the time in a cheerful way to her father, who, instead of going up to bed, sat still in his chair looking at her. After she had arranged the screen, and turned down the lamp that was on the table by his side, she commenced to turn off the light of the large lamp that stood on the center table. "Now papa, here goes," she cried, "the last light; I do believe you're too tired to go up stairs."

"No I'm not, but seems to me you are in unusual haste to put the lights out to-night."

"You know," replied Margaret, "that you would never go to bed if you hadn't me to drive you off; you would sit up all night and get sick." She placed her hand on her father's arm and led him across the room, which was only lighted now, by the hall lamp casting its rays through the open door. "And I heard auntie tell Mary," she pursued, "to have some of that nice corn bread for breakfast, and we must be up ready for it." She led him across the hall to the bottom of the stairs, and stepped aside for him to pass up before her. When half way up the stairs, she reached over the banlster to turn off the hall light, and looking up at her father who stood in the hall above, looking down on her, she said:

"Go on papa, I wont put the light out until I hear you shut your door."

He waited a moment, gazing **on the loved face** turned upward toward him; at **the soft rings of fluffy** hair, the affectionate blue eyes, **and delicate, full lips,** parted with a smile; then turned **and went** to his **room,** feeling that indefinite years of peaceful happiness stretched **out** before him.

Poor Margaret's powers of self-control had been sorely taxed; as the sound of her father's closing door reached her she dropped her mask, and the face, that the leaping flame of the expiring hall light shone on, was one of appalling wretchedness. She went qui**ckly** to her room, closed and locked her door, and threw herself on her knees beside the bed. Bitter waters overflowed her, utter darkness enveloped her, she crouched to **the** floor, covered her face with her hands, and cried in her agony: "Father, help me!" Margaret's faith in the existence of a personal God was an implicit one; that this personal God was her Heavenly Father she truly believed; a belief in answers to prayer, and a faith in special providences, had been the faith of all her life. The first impulse of her heart in this dire necessity, was to fly to the Omnipotent for help. Morning and night as long as she could remember, she had knelt in prayer. Her petitions for herself were of a general nature, but in her sweet believing, she had asked for all possible good to come to her father and Rodger. She had been assured every Sunday from the pulpit, that the condition to the answer of any petition was faith on the part of the suppliant, and the facts of her daily life seemed to attest a believing petitioner, and a good Giver. But that irrepressible cry of anguish to her God that night, was a different petition from any that had ever before passed her lips. Her generalizations had been of lightning rapidity, in the few moments that she leaned over her father's chair, after he told her the news of Rodger's inheritance. From the facts of Rodger's dread of poverty, his desire for social position, his infrequent letters, their lack of expressed affection, and that ominously conventional letter being written a week after his inheritance of wealth had been published in several newspapers; she drew the fearful conclusion that Rodger did not love her as he used to, and if he had not positively taken himself away from her, there was imminent danger of his doing so. Where could she go for help? Not to Aunt Deborah, she could do nothing; not to her father, he must not even know of her needs; not to Rodger, oh! hitherto, unfailing source of help and counsel! No human being could help her, God must. As she knelt in her desolate agony, she said to herself: "God can; He holds all men's hearts in His hand, He loves me. He'll bring Rodger back. Oh! Father, Father!" And again there went from the thick darkness of earth a despairing cry into the unknown. Hours of wrestling and of anguish passed. Margaret had not abandoned hope, but the terrible fear, the dreadful apprehension that Rodger was lost to her, brought an agony that was beyond words. At times she would lie motionless on the edge of the bed, her wide open eyes staring into the darkness, then she would sit just as motionless on the side of the bed, with her head bent low on her breast. Hour after hour, alone in the night the contest raged between her being and her destiny. There seemed closing around her iron bars, that her girlish hands were powerless to break; there seemed pressing down upon her a load, that she could neither avert nor bear. Rodger was drifting away, taking all of life with him. Only ten miles from her! and it was as though seas and mountains, and deserts swept between them. How she had loved him, how trusted him! and was this to be the end? The words spoken by the Bishop as his hands rested on her head, when she knelt in confirmation, came to her mind: "Defend, O Lord, this thy child." Yes, the Infinite Father was her only hope, from Him alone could succor come; and He would bring her out of this woful agony. Morning came at last. Margaret did not know whether she had slept or not. The sound of the rising-bell rung in the hall below, for the half hour before breakfast, brought to her mind the thought of her father. She took off her clothes, none of which she had laid aside the night before, and proceeded to take a cold bath, and dress herself in her usual morning wrapper. She was faint and sick, and shivered as she walked about her room. But she went down stairs, saw that the fire was burning brightly in her father's study, and met him as was her custom, at the foot of the stairs as he came down to breakfast. She seated herself at the table with her back to the light, and neither during breakfast time, nor in the hour which she and her father passed together in the study after breakfast, did unobserving Professor McVey notice her pale face. As Margaret sat at his feet tying his shoes, and buttoning his gaiters, it was with the greatest difficulty that she could keep back her tears. She felt so lonely and stricken, she would have been glad just then, to fold her arms around her father's knees, and lay her head upon them, and die.

"Is anything the matter with the buttons, my child?" asked the professor. Margaret was not aware that her hands were lying idly across his feet.

"No, papa," Margaret replied in a voice that would have arrested the attention of almost any other man, "the buttons are all right, and now the shoes are on," she said, as she fastened the last button, and gave the feet a little caressing pressure. She held his overcoat for him, and opened the front door, giving him the usual good-bye kiss, as he passed out, carefully keeping herself in the shadow of the open door.

The weeks following this first awakening of Margaret's fears, were weeks of alternating hope and fear. She had always looked over, at least one daily paper, and kept herself well informed regarding home and foreign affairs, from a natural desire that she possessed for all kinds of information, and also that she might be able to talk with her father upon any subject that might interest him; but during these weeks of anxiety, she read the dailies with more than usual attention. She examined the papers to find which one had the best society reports, and subscribed for it, and there was hardly a day that she did not scan two or three Clinton dailies, for their society notes. She frequently saw the name of Mr. Rodger Latimer, a notice of him, as being present at an opera, or theater. Sometimes he was spoken of as occupying a seat in Mrs. Lundom White's box, sometimes as a guest of Mrs. Richmond, or of Mrs. Blackwell. Several times "A brilliant theater party" was reported, as given by Mr. Rodger Latimer, and she saw in the paper at one time, that he had replied to a toast at a Harvard dinner, and again that he was a guest at some sort of a banquet. There was hardly an account of any important social event, or of any gathering of Clinton's best society people, in which his name did not appear. There were days during these weeks of painful uncertainty, in which her feverish restlessness drove her from one employment to another, from one room to another, from book to book; and often from the house, across the country for miles, from which long walks she would return totally exhausted. Other days she would hardly leave her "Sans-Souci," but would lie

on her Florentine lounge for hours, with her **face turned**
to the wall. Several times she revolved **in her mind the**
feasibility of going to Clinton, **and** spending **a few days**
with **Miss Sargent, and from Judge** Sargent's house,
sending a note to Rodger, **informing him that she** was
there, and that she **wished to see him. Then as** she
asked herself, what could **she** say **to him, should** he
come in compliance with her request, she abandoned that
scheme, as she had on second thought abandoned all
schemes of approaching him, that she had harbored from
time to time. Look at the matter in any way she might,
she could discover no method of bettering her condition;
there was absolutely nothing that she could do, but wait
in suffering and silence. Rodger knew that she loved
him, knew that she was there—only ten miles, less than
an hour's ride from his office! **If he chose** to come to
her, he could and would **come; but if he did not** choose?
God was her only refuge, morning **and** evening, midnight and noon; lying on her bed in the darkness, sitting
in the silence of her "Sans-Souci," and **walking far** out
on the country roads; her prayers were unceasing, that
she might be guided, and that Rodger might be influenced
by some supernatural power to return to her.

Miss Bond, unlike Professor McVey, noticed every
change of Margaret's face, with the natural solicitude of
a kind woman accustomed all her life long, to think of
and care for others. It distressed her severely, to see
the color leaving the girl's cheeks, the large eyes growing larger, and the lips losing their beautiful curves.
Deborah was not a woman of intense feeling, but she
possessed quick sympathies, and was sorely grieved by
Margaret's sufferings. Although Margaret had never
talked with her regarding her engagement to Rodger
Latimer, she perfectly understood the relation that the

young people held to each other; and she as perfectly understood that Rodger's unfaithfulness was the cause of all of Margaret's sorrow. She knew, as well as Margaret herself, that nothing that she could do, or say, would avail to heal her wound, or have the least influence over Rodger. As soon as her father was out of the house, all of Margaret's assumed cheerfulness of voice and manner was laid aside, and she looked as wretched as she felt. She knew that she could not conceal from her aunt, week after week, the fact that she was suffering, and she did not make the attempt. So these two women lived under the same roof, and ate at the same table, during all of these weeks; one slowly drifting farther and farther into darkness; the other standing by, in utter helplessness, unable to give either aid or comfort.

In December, Margaret received another letter from Rodger. When her eyes fell upon the familiar writing, as it was handed her by the clerk in the postoffice, the blood surged up into her head, and for a moment she feared falling to the floor. She held it tightly in her hand, and hastened home. Who could tell what that letter might contain? Possibly words of explanation, and pleadings for forgiveness, and all of the old utterances of love so long dear to her! Perhaps she had been hasty in her judgments; men are so different from women! Dear Rodger! If he did really love her, and came back to her, how happy she would be, and how gladly she would let the past go, and never speak of it. She locked herself in her own room, and sat down with hat and cloak on, and tore open the envelope—only one small sheet, and no writing on the last page, which was clear and white. The thought that it was nothing more than one of the short letters he had been in the habit of writing for months, seized her; with sickening fear and trembling fingers she unfolded the sheet of paper—one page, and part of another, written the day before. The address was, " Dear Margaret," not even *my* dear Margaret. She let the letter slip to the floor, and leaned her head on the table by her side, in blind, unthinking misery. She did not weep, she did not think, she uttered no reproach or prayer. The keen disappointment showed how far from dead was hope in her heart. An hour afterward she read the conventionally friendly letter, and mechanically placed it in a drawer, where she kept the letters Rodger had written her for the few months past, apart from those of the years before.

CHAPTER XIII

The next door neighbor on one side of Professor Mc-Vey, was a family by the name of Herman. Mr. Herman was a member of a small manufacturing establishment of some kind, in Clinton. He was punctual in business, paid his debts, lived up to his agreements, was an indulgent husband and a kind father. Every Sunday morning found him in his church pew, and every pleasant Sunday afternoon found him out driving with his family. His greatest dissipations were a mild cigar and a glass of claret. Perhaps it was in obedience to some law of nature, looking to the balancing of the race from generation to generation, that this equable, practical man, had married an eccentric woman. Whatever the cause, the fact was, that Mr. Herman when about twenty-six years of age, had married Isabel Wasmansdorf, who was the daughter of a New England mother, and a German father. Mrs. Wasmansdorf was first cousin to Mrs. Lundom White's mother. In 1870 Mr. Herman located himself in business in Clinton, and purchased a pleasant house in Edgewood, next to Professor McVey, for a home for his wife and infant daughter. Mrs. Herman was a woman of theories and moods, and while she was not of unkind heart, she was an irresponsible talker. Her emotions were turbulent, and when excited, she would rattle on about people and facts, in an illogical and inconsequential way, that sealed the lips of every cautious person in her presence, for fear that the simplest words they might utter, would be misrepresented sometime in the future. She indulged in ill-natured gossip about very few people, but when she was speaking of her somewhat removed cousin, Mrs. Lundom White,—between whom and herself there was no love lost—her temper, rather than her judgment, was responsible for her utterances. Mrs. White declared that Belle Herman was a ridiculous woman, who made a perfect fright of herself in dress, and was not to be depended upon; a woman with whom she would hold none but the most conventional relations.

"I really am afraid to have her in my house," she said to her sister, Miss Edwards. "You never know what she will say about you as soon as she is out of your sight, and how she twists things! I don't know as she means to tell downright lies, but it amounts to the same thing in the end, for she never gives a truthful account of anything, or anybody; and then how she does talk! and on what ridiculous subjects. Say what you like, she isn't well balanced."

Mrs. Herman quite prided herself on her relationship to the wealthy Mrs. Lundom White of Clinton. The two ladies left their New England homes for the West, about the same time, but under different circumstances. Mrs. White, as the wife of an opulent iron man, moved into an elegantly appointed home, and before many years had passed, occupied a leading place in society. Mrs. Herman, as the wife of a young man just beginning business for himself, entered a pretty, but inexpensive home in a suburban town. Her father in New England was a man of larger wealth than the father of Mrs. White, and in her childhood she had lived in a much more comfortable way than had her cousin. As soon as each woman was adjusted to her personal surroundings, and had had time to measure advantages with her immediate neighbors and acquaintances, Mrs. White was filled with exultation over her good luck; and while Mrs. Herman was contented with her relative position, among her Edgewood acquaintances, her soul was filled with envy, as soon as she encompassed Mrs. White's grandeur. In her heart, she berated the fortune that had been so lavish of favors to her poorer cousin. She felt that Mrs. White's brougham, and victoria, and saddle horse, were personal affronts to herself, as long as she could afford only a comfortable family carriage. And the sight of Mrs. White's rugs, cut-glass and pictures, soured her temper to that degree, that when surrounded by them, it was with the greatest difficulty she could speak pleasantly to the lady of the house, or to any guests that might happen to be present, when she was visiting Mrs. White. But with all of her envy and anger, she determined not to lose sight of any practical advantage that might accrue to herself, from her cousin's wealthy marriage, and her active imagination foresaw many ways in which she might make Mrs. White's money and position, subserve her own pleasure and profit. But when within the first year of her residence in Edgewood, Mrs. White had made her feel that there was not to be the least intimacy between the families, her wrath knew no bounds. What little practical sense she had, combined with her pride, kept her silent upon the subject, when talking with any one besides her husband, through all of the succeeding years, in which Mrs. White never deviated from the course which she had first lain down. But poor Mr. Herman had the full benefit of his wife's wrath.

"To think what airs Hat Edwards takes on herself, and toward me, too," said Mrs. Herman to her husband, at the breakfast table, one morning late in December, when she had, the day before, paid a visit to Mrs. White, for the purpose of seeing some new dresses which she had heard that lady had received from Europe, through a friend who had just returned. Mr. Herman was absent

9 Rodger Latimer's Mistake.

when his wife reached home, so she had had no opportunity of relating to him the result of her visit to her cousin, until she met him at the breakfast table. When Mrs. Herman spoke of Mrs. White in society, it was as her "dear Cousin Hattie;" when talking to her husband, the dear cousin was designated as "Hat Edwards," or simply "Hat," if her anger waxed particularly hot. "I wanted to see that new street dress of hers," she continued, "that Mrs. Higgins brought her from Paris, and she knew it as well as I did, but to do my very best I couldn't even get her up to her bedroom. There she sat all of the time in that library, and was *so* polite, so *dreadfully* kind, but I could no more get near her, than I could near Queen Victoria. I was so mad, I could have bitten her head off; so sweet, and smiling, and polite—and then Mrs. Campbell came in to luncheon—I know she was invited, for Hat had a regular five-story-and-a-mansard luncheon. She was exactly as formal to me as she was to Mrs. Campbell; no one would ever have dreamed that I was a relative. I declare I don't believe that I'll go there again; here I have spent the whole day, tired myself to death, and I don't know a thing more about her than I did before I went. I didn't see any of her dresses, and how on earth shall I make that new dress of mine? And I don't know anything about her reception that they say she is going to have, and I wanted to hear all about that dinner at General Austin's, that last evening's paper said she attended. Dear me, it is too bad!"

An hour after this outburst, Mrs. Herman rang Professor McVey's door bell. Margaret was lying on her Florentine settee, with closed eyes, going over in her mind, the same old routine of thought. A hundred times she had asked herself the same question, raised the same answering hypothesis; rejected it, grasped it again, thrown it aside, and reached out for some more probable explanation of Rodger's conduct. A hundred times she cried out that she could not bear it, that the dreadful suspense would kill her, and yet she lived on, growing a little thinner and paler every day, but never relaxing for a moment in her gentle care of her father, or uttering a cry in the hearing of her aunt. She was aroused from her painful reflections by the entrance of her aunt, who said to her:

"Mrs. Herman's in the parlor, and wishes to see you."

"Must I see that woman, auntie?" asked Margaret. "Is it anything special, or do you suppose she has just come in for a call? I wonder if she wants that Kensington pattern for her table scarf; she spoke of making one for Christmas."

"I don't know," replied Miss Bond; "I stopped and talked with her for ten minutes to see if I could find out what she came for and save you the trouble of seeing her, but she asked so positively for you I had to come."

"I suppose I must see her," said Margaret, as she smoothed her hair down with her hands. When she entered the parlor, which was across the hall from Professor McVey's study, Mrs. Herman, who was a slight woman, skipped across the room to meet her, uttering at the same time unintelligible monosyllables in a sort of cooing sound. She placed her hands on Margaret's shoulders and kissed her repeatedly, after which she placed one arm round her, and gave her a close hug.

"You darling pet," she cried; "it's an age since I saw you." Then she kissed her again. "How pale you look, but how pretty you are! You have this horrid cold, haven't you? It's just dreadful, but everybody has it this awful weather. I didn't sleep at all last night, I coughed so, and Mr. Herman is sick too, and both the children, and I declare Matilda is coming down, and she is such a good nurse; what could I do without her? Novalis, the dear little pet, has had a dreadful time for a week, and it's too bad, for our weather is so good I wanted him to be out of doors; it's so much healthier to be out of doors, don't you think so? Mr. Herman and I do; we've been out so much this last week, and Mr. Herman says he never felt better in his life than he does now; isn't it delightful?"

Mrs. Herman had been running on without stopping for breath, her arm around Margaret, who patiently waited for the pause which she knew would come after Mrs. Herman had run herself down in her contradictory garrulousness.

"Pray be seated, Mrs. Herman," said Margaret. "I'm glad to know that Mr. Herman is well; I hope the children will soon be over their colds."

"Dear me," said Mrs. Herman, "the children are just as well as any little tots can be; they're all well but me, but then I'm never well. Mr. Herman says it's all because I do so much; that I do more than any two ladies in the city would think of doing. He says I read myself to death, but I can't be lazy; I never could. Now, last night— were you out last night? Wasn't it lovely? Such a moon!" Mrs. Herman, who never stopped for a reply to any of her questions, but jumped abruptly from one subject to another, leaned over and placed one hand on Margaret's knee, as she continued: "What a lovely wrapper that is! Was it made in the city? You're just a poem sitting there in that wrapper. I *must* have a new dress, and I don't know what to get. You can wear anything, you're so pretty. I'm going to ask Mr. Herman to get me such a wrapper as this, but I'm not so pretty as you are; it wouldn't look as well on me. Isn't it too bad that we have to grow old and ugly?   But Mr. Herman says that I am just as pretty as I ever was."   Mrs. Herman covered her face with both of her hands for an instant, her fingers outspread over her eyes, and with a simpering laugh went on: "Ridiculous, isn't it, to call a woman like me pretty? But then it's well enough for every husband to think his wife is good looking, don't you think so?   I don't believe married people ought to get prosy, and not love each other, do you?   Mr. Herman is just as much of a beau as he was before we were married, and I think it's nice.   I got so tired in the city yesterday that I've been cross ever since.   I don't think a woman ought to be cross, do you? But Mr. Herman says I'm never cross, but you see I'm so worried about this dress; it's my best street dress, and I went in to see Cousin Hattie about it, she has such exquisite taste; the dress she had on was just a dream. You know I promised Cousin Hattie that I would come and see how your father was.   What a dear man he is! He knows so much.   Dear pet!   How pretty you *are!*" exclaimed Mrs. Herman rapturously, placing both of her hands on Margaret's lap, as she was sitting on the sofa beside her; "but your dear father is well, isn't he?   I told Cousin Hattie I thought he was, or I should have heard of it.   She said she hadn't seen your father for ever so long.   You remember Cousin Hattie, don't you?   She's coming out to spend a week with me next summer.   I haven't asked her yet, but I'm going to next June or May perhaps, when the apple trees are in blossom; they're so sweet, don't you think so?"

Margaret declared that she did, which declaration Mrs. Herman never heard, for she was miles away from the apple blossoms before Margarat could give her assent.

"I didn't see any of Cousin Hattie's street dresses," she rattled on, "for she had on a tea-gown, but that was just too lovely for anything.   Cousin Marie came in from a drive while I was there, and she had on a tailor-made dress, and it was lovely too, but I couldn't wear such a dress as that, I'm so slight.   I don't think I'm thin, do you?   Mr. Herman says I'm just plump.   I wouldn't be thin.   I don't blame men for not liking skinny women, do you?   But Marie is so much larger than I am; she's tall and large.   Do you know her?"

"No," replied Margaret, "I never saw her."

"Marie wears white so much," said Mrs. Herman dashing on, "but I couldn't wear a light colored street dress; just imagine a light dress, back and forth on the cars." Mrs. Herman clasped her hands together, and filled the room with her thin, tinkling laughter.   "It'll do for Marie," she continued, "for she has cousin Hattie's carriage.   Do you know Miss McVey, what I heard? They say cousin Marie is to be married soon—that Mr. Latimer, you remember him, don't you?—is very devoted to her, and that they are to be married soon.   I never knew him, but I knew his father a little; he was such a sweet man! don't you think so? I saw Mrs. Holland in Smith & Green's and she told me all about it.   I hadn't seen her for six months. Mrs. Holland don't know cousin Hattie very well, but she often meets her on the board of the Old Ladies' Home, and she has seen cousin Marie at the opera. Cousin Hattie always has a box.   I don't think those boxes are as good to see from, as the parquet chairs, do you? O, about Marie; Mrs. Holland says Mr. Latimer is with Marie at the opera every night; I mean when there is one, and Mrs. Holland is there; Mr. Latimer is very wealthy, you know. Some cousin of his died in India last summer, and left him two hundred millions, or two hundred thousand, I don't know which, but he's awfully rich any way, and he's going to marry Marie

Edwards soon. She don't like me I know; she's a smart girl, she always was, but she hasn't a cent in the world. Cousin Hattie gives her all of her clothes; she is handsome, but not as handsome as she thinks she is. I knew the Edwards girls before they ever heard of Clinton." The rancorous feeling against the opulent Mrs. Lundom White was rising in Mrs. Herman's heart, and with the thought that Cousin Marie might marry as wealthy a man as Cousin Hattie had, came feelings of intense dislike toward Marie also, but her natural caution enabled her to curb her resentment. Fortunately she was too much engrossed by her feelings toward the "Edwards girls" to notice Margaret's increased pallor, or the fact that she had placed her hands under her crossed arms, so that it would have been impossible for Mrs. Herman to have touched one of the cold fingers, had she been disposed. Poor, tortured Margaret, found that the efforts she had been making for weeks to control and suppress herself, in the presence of her father, had developed a power that enabled her to simulate calmness and unconcern under this ordeal.

"Will your cousin, Mrs. White, be pleased to have her sister marry Mr. Latimer?" asked Margaret in a pause of Mrs. Herman's talk.

"As a matter of course she'll be delighted; why shouldn't she? Marie has no home, and I don't believe that Hattie cares to have her live with her, though it will be very nice for Cousin Hattie to have her live in Clinton, in an elegant home, with her own carriage and all that. It's not every day that two sisters have such luck."

"What kind of a girl is your Cousin Marie?" asked Margaret.

"She is called beautiful; you never saw her? She don't look at all like Cousin Hattie. She's large and fat; I don't

think she is so very handsome, although her eyes are
lovely, and she has lovely hair. She isn't my first cousin,
you know, so it isn't so bad if I don't like her. I
don't think it is right for people to talk about their own
blood, but she is only my third cousin, and that isn't very
near, do you think it is? Mrs. Holland says everybody
thinks Marie is beautiful; the most beautiful girl in Clinton—I guess she said, but I don't think so, she's too
big." Mrs. Herman arranged her wrap around her own
slight shoulders, as she pursued her subject: "She is sort
of slow and heavy, she doesn't say much; I never heard her
talk at all, but then I never saw much of her. Cousin
Hattie is always urging me to go and see them, but they
live so far up, and I always have so much to do in the
city that I never have time; it's real tiresome to spend a
day in the city shopping, don't you think so? Last
Thanksgiving, no, the year before—I declare! how time
flies; Mr. Herman and I dined with Cousin Hattie, and
Marie was there, that's the most I ever saw of her. She
was there only to dinner; just at the table, I don't know
where she went after dinner up stairs, or off for a drive,
perhaps, but I don't think it was treating Mr. Herman
and me with much attention, to go off in that way, do
you? It didn't make any difference about the good time
we had, for she was just as stupid as she could be when
she was there; I don't like stupid people, do you? but I
must go home; I promised to take darling Novalis down
street. I wish I knew what to do about my dress. How
nice it is to have no more trouble about one's dresses than
Cousin Hattie has, and if Marie marries Mr. Latimer, she
can have everything she wants without any trouble to herself. I used to see Mr. Latimer around here, but I
haven't seen him in Edgewood for a long time. Don't he
ever come here any more? didn't he go to Europe once

with you and your father, or was that some other young man? I don't believe Marie Edwards would marry him, if he wasn't rich, and I declare I don't blame her for liking money; it's nice to have all the servants and carriages one wishes, and not have to bother one's head about clothes; don't you think so?"

"Did Mrs. White tell you of her sister's engagement?" asked Margaret.

"No, I didn't see her after Mrs. Holland told me what she knew."

"Then she knew," said Margaret, in a voice she could hardly control, "that your cousin, Miss Edwards, was engaged to Mr. Latimer?" and involuntarily her left thumb folded into the palm of the hand, and moved back and forth across the diamond ring on her third finger.

"Well now, it's all mixed up in my mind. I don't think she did say Marie was really positively engaged, and that she knew it, for if she'd said that, I would have been angry that Hattie hadn't told me all about it when I was there; don't you think she ought to have told me? But she said every one was talking about it, and that Mr. Latimer was dead in love with Marie, and she had been told they were to be married soon. She knows them both by sight, that's all; she noticed them so often in Hattie's box. She inquired who they were, and a gentleman friend of hers told her the lady was Miss Edwards, a sister to Mrs. White, and the gentleman was a Mr. Latimer, who was soon to marry Miss Edwards. I think that was all she knew, but that looks as though Marie was going to marry him, don't you think so? But I *must* go home," declared Mrs. Herman, as she rose from the sofa. "Do come and see me," she said, as she kissed Margaret, "and tell me what to do with that dreadful dress of mine; you never come over any more." She placed her hands on the tips of Margaret's shoulders, and slowly moved them up to her neck, resting them against the lace ruffle in the neck of her dress. "What a sweet little neck you have," she said. "How pretty you are! This is a new dress, isn't it? I wish my dress was done; here it is the last of December, and my best winter dress not done! Don't you think it is too bad? but we've had such a dreadful time this fall, company all of the time, and Novalis sick, and Edith was not well all last month. I have had just a dreadful time, and dear me, there is that Browning Club to-night! I don't see how I can go, but I must!"

Would the woman never go? thought Margaret, never take her hands off of her shoulders and her eyes off of her face, and leave her alone to herself?

CHAPTER XIV.

When evening came, Margaret and her father were sitting in the study with their books and papers. She was holding an open book in her hand, on which her eyes were fixed, but she was neither reading nor thinking of the book in the least. Between her eyes and its pages was a girl robed in white, with lovely eyes, of no particular hue, and beautiful hair. Margaret had fallen into the habit of idly holding an open book while her thoughts were upon Rodger, when she and her father were sitting together in the evenings, so that there would be no apparent change in the habitual occupation of their evenings. The long continued silence of the room, unbroken by the rustling of her father's paper, or any movement on his part, suddenly arrested her attention, and she raised her eyes to meet those of her father fixed intently on her face, with an anxious expression. It was such a questioning look as she had never before seen him fix upon her. Her face flushed, she hesitated a moment, then went to him, taking the paper from his knee as she seated herself on his lap, and leaned her head upon his shoulder.

"What is it, papa?" she asked, as she placed one of her hands against the side of his face.

"My child, you do not look well," replied the professor, as he put both of his arms around her. His voice was full of tenderness and solicitude; for the first time he had that evening noticed the change in his daughter, and was startled by the sight of her pale face.

"I am not quite well, papa," said Margaret; "in fact, I am almost sick. Mrs. Herman was in this morning for an hour or more, and she spoke of my dreadful cold."

"Is it only a cold, my darling?"

"What else can it be? I took cold three weeks ago, and I haven't been well since."

"Yes, I knew you took a slight cold that evening at the college, but I did not apprehend anything serious would come from so slight an exposure. You look seriously ill."

"Well, I'm not seriously ill, papa, you may be sure of that, but colds hang on so long this winter. Mrs. Herman said that all of her family were sick with them, Mr. Herman and all, and that Novalis is really quite sick. Why, Mrs. Herman looked miserable; I wonder if I look as bad as she does."

"You look very sick, my child."

"How can I look very sick when I'm not sick at all?" Margaret hastened to say. "It's only a mean, miserable cold; if I thought I looked as thin and pale as Mrs. Herman does with her cold, I would take malt or quinine."

"Take some of both, my child," said the professor; "have we any in the house? You better send George down to Howland's for some to-night, if we have not."

Margaret saw that her father was thoroughly alarmed about her and set herself at work to allay his fears. "No, we wont send George out to-night," she said, "but if auntie hasn't malt and quinine on her closet shelf, I'll send him in the morning. But I know she has both; you have no idea papa, what a wonderful closet that is of auntie's. It has everything in it; I know there are a hundred bottles of medicines on the shelf, all sorts of cough mixtures and twenty little homœopathic bottles— I really believe auntie is an eclectic—and there's no end of boxes and little rolls of things. You just cut your finger once, and see how many kinds of salve she will bring out for you to choose from, and all of them are sure cures, the best in the world. I know she has quinine and malt too, for I heard her say the other day, that Americans were coming to be a nation of nervous invalids, that they overworked, and brought on nervous exhaustion, and needed tonics, and concentrated nourishment; and that is exactly what malt and quinine are, and she would be sure to have on her shelf what the great American people universally needed. But I don't believe I need either; it can't be that I look as Mrs. Herman does with her cold. Do I look so dreadfully, papa?"

Margaret sat up straight on her father's knees, and placed her hands on his shoulders, and looked him full in the face as she continued, "Now take a good look at me papa, and tell me the truth."

The professor did look earnestly into the vivacious, laughing face. "Really, my child," he said. "You do look better than when you were sitting on the sofa by the table. I feared you were seriously ill: your face was not indicative of health."

"Over there, papa!" exclaimed Margaret, pointing to the table by which she had been sitting, "there, in the light of that green lamp shade! I should think I might have looked like a ghost. But here, in this light, I don't look so dreadfully, do I?" Adroit Margaret was sitting with her back to her father's lamp. "I would not look like Mrs. Herman for the world; colds are uncomfortable things to have, but it is too dreadful when they make one look like a scarecrow; do you think I look so very bad, papa?"

"No, I do not, my child," said the professor taking one of Margaret's hands in his, "but you say you have a cold, and are not well. You ought to take the greatest care of yourself; perhaps you better have a physician, my darling."

"That would be ridiculous," replied Margaret, "he would only laugh at me. One has to have a little patience with these provoking colds; you can't do much with them but leave them to take their own course. I don't need anything; I haven't much faith that anything will do me any good, but to make you feel more comfortable, papa, about me, I'll commence taking both malt and quinine to-morrow."

"Do, darling, it will make me feel more comfortable, and if they do not benefit you, you must take something besides, or have a physician. We can have any one come from the city you would like to see. What would you think of consulting Miss Sargent regarding a physician, if you have not confidence in Doctor Kean? She must know who is considered the best."

"I don't need any physician, dear papa; what makes you think I'm sick? You say I don't look sick."

"You do not now, my darling, but you looked very sick when you were sitting on the sofa."

"Yes, and if I should sit there now, you would see that it was all that green shade."

"Perhaps something was due to the light. Do not ever sit in that light again my child, and do not be careless of your health, and neglect your cold."

"I will not, papa," said Margaret, as she passed her hands caressingly down each side of his face, "and you will be careful and not take cold yourself, wont you? Mrs. Herman said Mr. Herman was quite sick, just with a cold, and had been for some time. It don't make much difference if we women have colds, but you men ought never to get sick; we have nothing to do, and can snug down by the fire, if we take cold and do nothing all day, but if you got sick, what would become of your classes? And then you would be miserable for so long a time.

Mrs. Herman says, that it is a peculiarity of colds this winter, they hold on so long. Now I don't expect to be well for weeks yet: just think of weeks of feeling miserable and taking quinine!"

Professor McVey leaned his head against the back of his chair, and looked into Margaret's face, that was flushed with the excitement of her determination to remove all apprehension regarding her from her father's heart.

"But must you feel miserable?" he asked, "cannot something be done to enable you to feel as well as usual, even if you cannot immediately throw off this cold?"

"I do feel well enough," said Margaret, "I haven't the least pain, or any uncomfortable feeling. I ought to have said look miserable, instead of feel miserable; one don't like to look like a fright, even if they feel well. But then the being well is of more importance than the looks, and you wont care, will you papa, if I am well, and feel well, how I look? or not so much so, I mean."

"As a matter of course, your health is of the first importance, but it would be difficult for me to convince myself that you were absolutely well, if you looked ill."

"I'm not ill in the least, but tonics may help throw off this cold, or rather brace up the system to bear it for weeks, as I suppose I shall have to, from what Mrs. Herman said, so I'll take quinine, and some of auntie's malt to-morrow; but papa, if I do look pale, you must not be concerned, for I may not be able to get entirely rid of this cold before warm weather comes in the spring. Professor Hitchcock told me, that he took cold one November, and never got rid of it before the next June." Margaret looked very sympathetic as she continued: "And he coughed dreadfully, and lost half of his flesh. Don't you remember what a miserable winter he had? it was two years ago this winter; I'm thankful I have no cough. One can afford to grow pale a little with a cold, if it don't settle on the lungs, and keep one coughing all of the time; I really think I ought to be thankful I'm escaping so much easier than most people. I am only losing a little of my color and flesh, which can be quickly gained when spring comes. I wish the spring would come, so we could ride again; there is nothing in all this world that I like as much as riding; and how fortunate it is that you like it too. Suppose you were like some stupid old papas, that don't like riding, what a time I would have," said Margaret, as she tied and untied her father's cravat and retied it in a sailor knot; then changed it into long bows, and then short ones.

"Papa, you will have to give me a salary as your valet," she continued. "I do believe I tie a prettier knot than you can. I wish there was a glass down here so you could see this one," and Margaret covered the bow which she had finished with her hand, and pressed it down against her father's neck to make it keep its shape. Professor McVey's soul was filled with peace; he was under the hands of his beloved child, whom he now believed was well and happy; and all that earth could give him, was her presence, and the knowledge of her happiness.

The next morning at the breakfast table, Margaret had a bottle of malt, and a box of quinine capsules by her plate, and she was very merry, passing each in turn to her father and aunt, insisting that they needed them as much as she; and with a playful pout, accusing them of selfishness, in managing to have her take the medicine for the family. Professor McVey had suffered from dyspepsia for years, and when he could not take solid food without distressing him, it was his habit to rely principally upon beef tea for nourishment. There was always a cup of this popular article of diet for invalids, beside his plate on the table, that he could take or not as he chose. Frequently when he was not inclined to take it, he would do so at the urgent suggestion of Margaret. Miss Bond thought that sometimes he refrained from drinking it, for the sole purpose of being coaxed to it by Margaret's affectionate playfulness. That morning after she had swallowed her dose of malt with a very wry face, she turned to her father and said:

"Now papa, let's trade; you take my quinine, and I'll take your beef tea."

"No, no my child," said the professor, "you need your quinine, and I do not."

"I do not need it at all," said Margaret, "and I think you and auntie are tyrannical conspirators, and I am your poor victim, but I'm in your power, so I submit," and she put in her mouth a three grain capsule. Her father finished his breakfast, leaving the beef tea untouched, which omission Margaret quickly noticed. She left her chair, and standing beside him, placed one arm around his neck, and taking the cup of beef tea in the other hand, peeped into it with mock gravity, and then shaking her head solemnly, she pressed her hand against the back of her father's head, saying, "Naughty papa." Then she held the cup close to his lips as she continued, "If I take malt and quinine, you must take beef tea."

"But I do not need it, my child."

"Yes you do, more than I need malt. Doctor Kean said you had nervous dyspepsia, and nobody ever said anything was the matter of me. I have to swallow both malt and quinine because I happened to sit by a lamp that had a green shade; no papa, you can't get away," she said, pressing her hand still harder on his head, "you've got to drink the last drop of it," and she held the cup close to his lips.

10 Rodger Latimer's Mistake.

"Suppose I will not take it, what then?" playfully asked the professor, as he looked into the merry eyes, so close to his own.

"Why then I'll hold you here all day, and your boys will have a good time," replied Margaret, as she gave him a little hug and a kiss; whereupon her father drank the beef tea, sipping it slowly, frequently stopping to protest, declaring that he was badly used; Margaret as frequently with the little hugs, insisting that he take the last drop.

The lamps in the study were changed that day, so that the one with a pink shade sat on the table by which Margaret usually read, and it cast over her face and neck a warm flush, as she occuped her usual corner of the sofa, and in this flush she looked bright and rosy. But the brightness was fast dying out of her life. The solitary figure of Rodger Latimer had haunted her night and day since the first doubt regarding him had entered her mind, but after that morning visit of Mrs. Herman's, the spectral figure was no longer solitary; it was always accompanied by a large girl dressed in white, with lovely eyes, and beautiful hair. The two heads, in close proximity bent over her as she lay on her lounge, the two figures stood side by side in the darkness, and gazed at her with fixed, expressionless faces, through the sleepless hours of her nights; in the wood, very close together, her lover and that unknown woman, glided noiselessly over the dead leaves by her side, as she took her daily exercise. Had Margaret been under the care of a physician at this time, he would have peremptorily insisted on a change of scene, and society, as the only hope of saving her from serious results, that might follow the mental strain she was evidently bearing, whatever the cause of the strain might be.

CHAPTER XV.

Christmas came and went, followed by New Year's, and while the holidays were not what could be called merry, in the McVey home, they passed in quietness and peace. Professor McVey was in the house more than usual, and Margaret never flagged in her affectionate attention and cheerful conversation. After the holidays, when Professor McVey went into his classes again he did not seem quite as strong as usual; but he had always been so thin and pale, neither Margaret nor her aunt noticed any change in his appearance. His hands and face and ears, could hardly look whiter than they had for years, but he certainly had less appetite, and he wearied easily. Early in February he commenced to lie on the lounge in his study, part of the evening, instead of sitting in his chair and reading all of the time. He slept well, felt no pain, and declared there was nothing the matter of him, but his being willing to lie down half an hour after dinner, and not eating as much as usual, was sufficient to alarm Margaret. She saw that any reference to his lack of strength annoyed him, so she never referred to his condition in his presence, but she made his beef tea herself, to know that it was strong, and perfectly prepared, and she added to the quantity usually put in his cup, and in her playful way insisted that he should take it with every meal. After a consultation with her aunt, she dropped a line to Dr. Kean, their family physician who resided in Clinton, who was a dear personal friend, as well as medical adviser, and asked him to come and see her father, and tell them whether or not anything really ailed him. In response to this request, about the middle of February

Doctor Kean went out to **Edgewood, on one of the late** afternoon trains, ostensibly **to dine with his old friend,** whom he had not seen for **months. After dinner Margaret** left them alone together in **the study, for an hour or two.** When she returned her father **was sitting on the sofa in** his shirt sleeves, his coat and waistcoat **were lying by his** side. To her questioning look of smiling **surprise, he** said:

"Doctor Kean has been giving me what **he calls a** physical examination, my child. He fancied I was not looking quite as well as usual, **and** persuaded me to be looked over, as he calls it."

"And I had **my** trouble **for my pains," said Doctor** Kean; "I thought at dinner, **your father did not look in** his **usual** vigor, but I find nothing **the matter with him.** Every organ is in a healthy condition, **and doing its work** well, not with much energy to be sure, but **then he is per-** fectly sound."

"I assured Margaret that there was **no** cause for **any** anxiety regarding my health," said the professor, **"that I** was perfectly well, but I do not think she was quite satisfied, and I am very glad that your judgment justifies the opinion that I held."

"Papa thought he did not need to take any beef tea, doctor," said Margaret, "but his appetite was not good, and it seemed to me, that he needed more nourishment than he possibly could get from the small quantity of food that he took."

"And you were quite right, little woman," replied the doctor. "There is no doubt but that you need the beef tea, McVey; you and I must not forget that we are grow- ing old, and can't do as we once did. What we need is nourishment and tonics, and less work. Margaret is right, beefsteak would be better, but if you cannot take that with a positive relish, take the tea, and plenty of it, and it would not be amiss if you add some sort of emulsion; a pancreatic emulsion would be good, and then, Margaret, give from six to ten grains of quinine a day. Try it for a few weeks, professor, and see the effect; say through this month, and next. This is the most trying season for invalids, and for such old fellows as you and I; and this climate is especially trying through March and April. It would be a good plan for you, and little Margaret here, to run down to Florida for six weeks this spring. I find that men over fifty need a great deal of rest and recreation. Couldn't you bring that around, Margaret?"

"Certainly we could," Margaret replied; "there's nothing to prevent our going. Papa has frequently taken part of the classes of the other professors, when it was necessary for them to be absent during term time, and I am sure that his classes could be provided for, as long as you thought best for him to be away from Edgewood."

"I beg of you, my dear sir," cried Professor McVey, "not to put any such notion into Margaret's head. I presume that I could arrange to leave my classes, as Margaret suggests, but it is not at all necessary, and I could not think of leaving unless it was a matter of absolute necessity."

"I understand all of that, my old friend," said the doctor, "and I don't advise you to leave now, but you may be sure that I don't wait until an absolute necessity stares me in the face, before I send a patient off in search of health. You know you always used to say I was an obstinate fellow, and I think it grows on me. If it is best, as a preventive, that you and Margaret go to Florida for four or five weeks, I hope you will be controlled by my judgment, and that Margaret will pack the trunks without a word of remonstrance, and both of you be off." · Doctor Kean, as he ceased speaking, laid his hand on Professor McVey's knee, and gave it a pinch of good comradeship.

"We shall both of us do as you say, dear doctor, there is no doubt about that," said the professor, "only do not send us off on a pleasure trip."

"I don't know about that, you ought to go just for pleasure, both of you, if there were not the least necessity; you have money enough, McVey, and why, at your time of life, shouldn't you do just as you please?"

"I am doing it in teaching Latin and Greek, and staying at home with Margaret," replied the professor.

"How hard it is for a man who has been busy all of his life, to learn to take things easy," said Doctor Kean, as he rose to his feet. "But I must be going to the depot, or I'll lose my train. Now Margaret, see that your father has plenty of nourishment, and tonics for the next few weeks; all sorts of good things to eat, remember, and plenty of sleep. If you are in the city during the next few weeks, professor, step in and let me see how you are doing. If you don't feel like coming down, I'll run out and smoke another cigar with you soon. Good-night, no, you sit still, Margaret'll let me out," continued the doctor as he placed his hand on Professor McVey's shoulder to prevent him from rising.

In the hall, as Margaret was holding the doctor's overcoat for him she said: "Now doctor, tell me the exact truth; you know me well enough to know that it will do."

"To be sure I do," replied the doctor, "and I would tell you the truth, no matter how serious it might be, but nothing ails your father, there's not a particle of disease about him; his circulation is not very strong, but he always was delicate. I presume there may be a little lack of assimilation, but at his age, with his indoor life, that is not strange.   He needs nothing but nourishment, and toning up a little.   Beef and quinine are the best things he can have.   I really think that it will be well for him to go South in order to get away from these spring winds, so I thought I would open the way to-night, and let him be thinking of it; not that he really needs it, but it will be a safe precaution.   Good-night, Margaret.   I am very glad that you sent for me; if you get at all anxious, and wish me to come at any time, telegraph, and I'll come immediately.   But don't allow yourself to be anxious, child," added the kind doctor, " for nothing really ails your father."

The next day—which was Thursday—Margaret received a note from Miss Sargent informing her that she had seen Doctor Kean the evening before, after his return from Edgewood, and had learned from him that Professor McVey was not quite well; after expressing her sympathy, she closed her note by saying, that if perfectly agreeable to Margaret and her father, she would spend Saturday with them at Edgewood.   Margaret replied immediately, urging her to come on Saturday and spend the Sabbath, and to bring her brother with her for the visit.   She sent George to the postoffice with her letter as soon as it was written, so that it might reach Miss Sargent early on Friday.   When the man returned he brought Margaret a number of letters.   The address on one of them was in Rodger Latimer's well known hand.   It had been weeks since she had heard from him.   The letter contained three well filled pages; only three pages in which to tell her that he loved another woman; that this woman loved him, and that they were to be married.   The sentences that seemed to him just, kind, and full of common sense when he wrote them; seemed to Margaret, cold, cruel and dishonorable, as she read them—daggers, with jagged edges, driven by a giant's strength into the heart of a dying woman. She had thought that she was prepared for anything; she had said to herself a hundred times, that Rodger loved her no longer, and that he did love the large girl in white, with lovely eyes and beautiful hair; and a hundred times, as she had looked at them as they stood side by side, gazing at her out of the darkness of the night, she said to herself—"Yes, that is his wife; if they only would go away and leave me alone!" She thought that she had accepted the truth of his love for this beautiful girl and his allegiance to her; and she had never dreamed that his plain statement of such a fact would be so different from the imagined fact. Margaret read the letter over several times in a calm, mechanical way, then leaned her head back against her chair, and closed her eyes; the lids were heavy, and the eyeballs hot. After a little she raised her head and looked around the room, and remembered that there was something she had to do. Not to answer Rodger's letter! that, she never could do. She had not one word to say to him, but she must return the letters that a man had written her who soon would be the husband of another woman. She looked at her hand, at the ring on her finger; looked at it in silence for several minutes, then drew it slowly off, as she might have closed the eyes of a dear one just dead. She did not shed a tear, and in half an hour or so, she slowly and noiselessly went through the silent house to the attic, and from a heap of pasteboard boxes, that her thrifty aunt had gathered there from time to time, she selected a large strong one, and carried it down to her sitting-room. In this she placed all of Rodger's letters, taking them from the drawer where she kept them, in packages of each six months' letters tied up by themselves with a pretty ribbon.

She slipped the ribbon off and packed the letters closely together. How many there were! Among them were all the telegrams that she had ever received from him; these she placed with the letters. Above them she laid half a dozen engravings that Rodger had sent her, and two tiny water-colors in their frames; and last of all, she put in four photographs of Rodger, which she folded in white tissue paper without looking at them. She placed the cover on, wrapped the box in strong brown paper, and fastened it securely. Then she took from the book shelves and the table, and the small stand at the head of her Florentine lounge, a dozen or more of books, Rodger's gifts, and made them into a safe package. After writing Rodger's address upon these two packages, she went out and ordered her carriage, and told the man that she wished him to drive her down street. Then she went to her room and put on her cloak and hat, winding a long veil around her head. Before going down stairs, she took from one of her bureau drawers a ring box, which she carried down with her, and in which she placed her diamond engagement ring, wrapping the box in several layers of paper to make a large package. The man, under her directions, placed the packages in the carriage, and drove to the express office, where she ordered them sent to Mr. Latimer. The package that contained the ring, she had the express agent seal, and she took a receipt for it which she placed in an envelope and had the agent himself direct to Rodger Latimer. This done, she returned home. As she dropped the portiere behind her as she entered her Sans-Souci, she stood and looked around. How still it was! what a sense of vacancy surrounded her! There were the empty open drawers of her writing table, the empty coils of ribbon on the floor; the vacant places, at intervals, on the bookshelves, and the absence of books on the tables. It was a dark February day, the sky was heavily clouded, but there was no wind; stillness reigned without and within the house; the only sound that struck her ear was the ticking of the clock on the mantel. It was twilight, but not the dreamy twilight following a bright sunset; it was a stealthily approaching of heavy gloom. She seemed alone in the universe, as she slowly crossed the room and seated herself in her little wicker chair beside the center table. She felt an inward tremor, and her breath came heavily; she pressed one hand upon her breast as her eyes rested upon the open drawer where Rodger's letters used to lie. She remembered the coming home after her mother's funeral, and how strange the house seemed as she sat in her father's lap in his study, where several kind friends were sitting with her father and aunt. That was nothing to the horror of this hour; alone in this silence. She leaned the side of her head upon some books, with her wide open, tearless eyes fixed upon the empty drawers of her writing table. The darkness of the winter day slowly descended, shutting from her sight every object in the room. She knew nothing of the passing of time, but her father's voice from the stairs, as he was on the way to his room, aroused her. She could not see him, for the first time in her life her power of will failed her. As she rose to her feet, a sharp pain shot through her head and she was obliged to lay hold of the back of the chair for a moment, to steady herself on her feet. After a little she very slowly walked into the dining-room, where she knew her aunt would be at that hour, superintending the laying of dinner. Miss Bond sprang forward as she caught sight of Margaret's face, but before she could speak, Margaret, holding onto the door knob, said:

"Auntie, will you tell papa that I have a headache and

have gone to bed? Just a headache, and that I will be well by morning. I want to sleep, that's all." Miss Bond was quickly by her side and caught hold of her left hand, that was hanging by her side. She felt the ring was gone, and knew all.

"Can I do anything for you, Margaret? Are you very sick?" she asked.

"No," said Margaret as she leaned against the door, "I'm very wretched, auntie, all you can do for me is to take care of papa and make him comfortable and happy. Tell him the pain is not much in my head, but I wish to sleep." Then she went to her bedroom, closed the door, and threw herself on the bed. About ten o'clock her aunt came into the dark room.

"What is it?" asked Margaret, in a low voice.

"It's only me, Margaret," replied her aunt, as she lighted the gas.

"What time is it? has papa gone to bed?" asked Margaret.

"It's ten o'clock; your father went to his room about fifteen minutes ago," said Miss Bond. "I've brought you a cup of tea and a bit of toast," she continued, as she went to the bedside with a small tray in her hand. Margaret thanked her gently, but said she could take nothing, yet to please her aunt, who begged of her to try and eat a mouthful; she sat up and took a bit of toast in her mouth. She chewed it and shifted it from side to side, but could not swallow. As she placed the morsel back on the tray, she said:

"I cannot, auntie, all I want is to be alone. I will be better in the morning."

Miss Bond was sorely grieved that she could do nothing, but she had sense enough to desist in her efforts, and in perfect silence to assist Margaret to undress and get into bed. At Margaret's request she turned the gas all off and left the room.

How often in this sorrowful world has impotent love cried in anguish: "What can I do for you?" and been answered in hardly a greater anguish: "Nothing, leave me alone!"

The next morning Margaret did not appear at the breakfast table, but her father quietly accepted Miss Bond's statement, that she thought it best not to awaken her, but to let her sleep her headache off. Professor McVey ate very little, and did not talk at all. Miss Bond was anxious that he should take his beef tea, which he set aside, but she dared only to make a suggestion to that effect, which he did not seem to notice. He would look from time to time at Margaret's vacant chair, as though he were trying to correct some inaccuracy of vision. Not to see Margaret at the table, was as un-natural as it would have been not to see the college, or his own house, as he approached the place where he had always seen them. He did not stop for his morning cigar, or newspaper, but went directly from the breakfast table to the hat-rack in the hall, where he courteously de-clined Miss Bond's proffered assistance in putting on his overcoat.

"You are sure, Deborah," he said, as he held the front door open, "that Margaret is not sick? that nothing more serious than a headache is the matter with her?"

"Yes, I'm very sure," Miss Bond replied; "she will be as well as usual when you come home at noon."

Professor McVey passed out quickly, but the cold air striking his ankles, disclosed to him the fact that he was on his way to the college in his slippers. He returned for his shoes and gaiters, but left the house as soon as possible, after he had put them on, which was a new and difficult task for him, and was only accomplished after he had buttoned the gaiters wrong three times. When Miss Bond went to Margaret's room, immediately after the professor left, she found her lying in bed, wide awake, with sunken eyes and white face. Her first words were. "Did papa take his beef tea and quinine, auntie?"

"No, I think not; I tried to persuade him to take them, but I don't believe he did, but he looks well this morning, Margaret, so don't worry about him. How do you feel?"

"Did you give papa his shoes and gaiters?" persisted Margaret.

"N-o," hesitatingly answered her aunt, for the first time thinking of the professor's shoes, and wondering if he would return for them, or wear his slippers all of the morning, and take his death of cold. As she was cogitating over the matter, she heard the front door open, and went into the hall and looking over the banisters, saw the professor come out of the study with his shoes on. She returned to Margaret's room and told her that her father was all right, that he had on both shoes and gaiters.

"I ought to have gotten up; it's selfish for me to lie in bed, and let dear papa go off in this way," said Margaret faintly as she gazed at the ceiling.

"Indeed I don't think it is, Margaret. Your father did well enough, he's looking better than usual this morning; I think you are the one to be taken care of; what can I get you? You must eat something, you better have a cup of coffee, and then turn over and go to sleep."

"I would like a cup of coffee," said Margaret, "very strong. I want to be up and looking well when papa comes to luncheon. But before I drink the coffee, I would like a little something to eat. Where is my quinine? I'll take some of that. But auntie! the very first thing—

can't you write a note to Aunt Helen; she's coming here to-morrow to spend the day, you know."

"I didn't know you expected her," said Miss Bond.

"She, and perhaps the judge. Write a note immediately please, and have George take it to the office for the noon mail; then she may get it to-night; she certainly will early in the morning, they have a delivery about their breakfast time. Say that I'm not well; not sick, you know, but have a cold and headache; and if convenient for them, we would like to see them next week Saturday, instead of to-morrow. Auntie, I cannot see anybody! By next Saturday I shall be strong again; give her my love, and write cordially, and say how disappointed I am, and say it will be a severe disappointment to us all, if they don't visit us next week. Dear Aunt Helen! how kind she was to me in Europe," said Margaret laying one arm across her eyes, as her aunt left the room to write the note. The first numbing shock and intense agony that followed it, were past, and Margaret lay in helpless exhaustion. The tears flowed from her eyes behind her arm, down the temples, upon the pillow. She wept in childish weakness at the thought of the dear European days, of which Miss Sargent was an inalienable part.

Professor McVey hurried home at noon to find the door opened for him as soon as his foot touched the piazza, and little hands ready to take off his overcoat and lead him to his chair in front of a crackling fire in his study. And when Margaret was in his lap, her arm around his neck, and her soft cheek against his pale, cold face, the old sense of happy contentment settled upon him.

CHAPTER XVI

Saturday morning, as Miss Sargent seated herself at her breakfast table in Clinton she found, with other mail matter by her plate, Miss Bond's letter of the day before. After reading it, she laid it aside from her other letters.

When she and her brother had finished their breakfast, they turned their chairs around from the table so as to face the blazing wood fire that always burned in the dining room. Judge Sargent used to say, that his only extravagance was a wood fire, and that he must have good wood and plenty of it, if he had to sell his horses to get it. While the butler was clearing the table, Judge Sargent read the morning paper, and Miss Sargent re-read Miss Bond's letter. As she sat there in the glow of the fire, she was a woman that any thoughtful person would turn to look at the second time. She was between forty-five and fifty years of age, and her stout matronly figure was clothed in a black and white foulard silk breakfast gown. Her head was large, and especially broad across the top from ear to ear, and was covered with an abundance of hair white as snow. This hair was twisted in one long, loose coil, that was thrown, in some deft way, up and down the back of the head, and across the top—a pile of silvery whiteness. Her brow was low and broad, and the front hair lay across the sides of her head in a plain, wavy surface. The skin of her face was nearly as white as her hair; not at all sallow, nor had it the least tinge of color, but was of a delicate fresh white. There were lines at the corners of the eyes that indicated years, but the lines of the mouth indicated sorrow. They were not simply deep marks, cut by the years into the tissues,

natural and expressionless, but they were lines full of
history, and of hope—to one who had eyes to read—a
record of struggles, and of victories; of strong passions,
met by a strong conscience and a strong will.   An artist,
who had painted her portrait once, said: " I always ex-
perienced pain, whenever I attempted to paint Miss Sargent's mouth.   It was a delight to transfer to canvas,
the majestic head, with its beautiful white hair, and her
grand pathetic eyes, but whenever I attempted to paint
her mouth, I broke down, the suffering so touched my
heart."   There was about her a peculiar air of depend-
ability.   One felt that she was strong, and wise, and good
and could be trusted; and that she was ready to give the
best of herself, whenever it could be of use to any one.

As the butler closed his pantry door after him, when
his work in the dining-room was finished, Miss Sargent
said to her brother:

" Would you like to go to Edgewood next week, and
spend Saturday with Professor McVey ?"

" I don't care particularly about it," replied the
judge.   He was ten years his sister's senior, and for
many years had not cared particularly about anything,
outside of his own home, and not much for anything
inside, excepting his wood fire, newspapers and books.

" Margaret sends us an invitation for next Saturday,"
said Miss Sargent, " and desires that we pass the Sabbath
with them.   I should think you might find it pleasant to
go, for a day at least."

" No I don't know as I care to; I don't like going away
from home, but I thought you said the other day that you
were going this week Saturday ?"

" I had intended going to-day, but Miss Bond writes
me that Margaret is not well, and so invites us for next
week."

"Margaret not well? I thought it was Professor McVey who was sick," said the judge, "didn't Doctor Kean say that?"

"Yes," replied his sister. "Professor McVey has been out of health for weeks, but Margaret is sick abed, with a headache, brought on, Miss Bond writes, by some trouble that she has had with Rodger Latimer. She thinks their engagement broken."

"You don't say so!" exclaimed the judge, turning toward his sister with an animation he rarely exhibited. "Why I thought they were to be married soon; what's the matter, who is to blame?"

"Mr. Latimer entirely," replied Miss Sargent.

"I have always thought well of Mr. Latimer," said the judge, "I cannot conceive of his doing anything dishonorable; what do you know of the affair?"

"Not very much. I have seen nothing of Margaret since last October. I hardly know how it is that I have been to Edgewood so little this last year; and neither Margaret or her father, have been here as much as usual. I hope I've not been remiss and neglected Margaret."

"Does Miss Bond say to you that the engagement is broken?"

"She says that she fears that it is," replied Miss Sargent, "and that Margaret has not been well for months, that she regards her as being in a worse condition than her father. I ought to have gone out there before this. You don't know Margaret as well as I do; she's a most lovely girl; as faultless as any human being can be."

"Well, why don't you go to-day, if you feel anxious about her?" asked the judge.

"I can't very well," replied his sister, with a smile, "when they write me not to. How could Rodger Latimer do such a thing!"

11 Rodger Latimer's Mistake.

"Are you sure they were engaged?" asked the judge, evincing the legal habit of his mind, by wishing first of all things to be sure of the fact.

"There can be no question about that," replied Miss Sargent.

"You liked Latimer, didn't you?" the judge asked.

"Yes, he seemed to possess an unusual depth of affection, and a peculiar delicacy of nature, and he certainly is a man of mind."

"I always regarded him as an able man," rejoined the judge. "Mr. Prentice was saying to me the other day, that he almost regretted Latimer's inheritance of his uncle's property, because it removed the necessity of his practicing law, and that he had mind enough to become in time a leading lawyer."

"How he has plunged into society!" said Miss Sargent. "What of his office, did he give it up?"

"He gave up all personal work in it; there was a sort of partnership formed between him and two men—the Mead Brothers, they are sometimes called—two brothers, they are older than Latimer, and both are capable men; but they have little property, and are having a hard time to get their share of business. It was a good thing for them. Latimer'll have no money out of it, but he don't need any, and it will be a place for him to begin again, if he ever should wish to resume practice. I think he is acting very foolishly, but after a little experience he may set himself to work again."

"He's an impetuous nature," said Miss Sargent, "and for a man who has been as much in the world, possesses a remarkable simplicity of character. But I know that he is all in fault, if there is any trouble between him and Margaret." The conversation dropped at this point, and Miss Sargent gazed into the fire, as her brother turned to reading his paper. In a few minutes he exclaimed:

"Hello! Helen! listen to this: 'Notable marriage to occur.' 'The number of matrimonial alliances between Boston and Clinton families, is to be increased by still one more. Miss Marie Edwards of this city,—a sister of Mrs. Lundom J. White—is to be married to Mr. Rodger Latimer of Boston. The date has not been determined on.'"

Miss Sargent sat speechless, gazing at her brother in blank astonishment. After a little she said:

"What paper is that? give it to me. That cannot be true; it's too dreadful!" She read the notice over and over, and then again fixed her eyes on her brother in dismay.

"Who is this girl? What's her name?" asked the judge.

"Poor Margaret! poor Margaret!" exclaimed Miss Sargent. "Marie Edwards? She's that large girl we dined with at Blackwell's last week; don't you remember her?"

"No."

"The only girl there; she's a great friend of Alice Blackwell's."

"I don't remember her," said the judge, "what sort of a girl is she?"

"I know very little of her," replied his sister. "She has the reputation of being a great society girl, and that's all I know of her. Dear little Margaret! I wish I could go to her. But you see she don't wish for me. It's just as I should have expected; she wishes to be alone, she must fight it out alone first. How could Rodger Latimer have done such a thing! I can hardly believe it; Latimer is not of Boston."

"His uncle, Gilbert Latimer, died there," said the judge, "so newspaper men connect the name of Latimer with Boston, I presume."

Miss Sargent re-read Miss Bond's letter. " It would not do for me to go before next Saturday," she said, "a week from to-day—how long it seems."

CHAPTER XVII

Margaret was so completely exhausted by the violence of her feelings Thursday night, and for want of sleep, that she went to sleep early Friday night, and slept until awakened by the rising bell Saturday morning. Nine hours of sound sleep restored the tone of her system. She awakened with every faculty of her mind possessed of its usual vigor. Since she read Rodger's letter Thursday afternoon, she had only felt keenly, deeply, suffering in every fiber of her being; but after the first overwhelming tide of anguish, that came with the wakening of memory Saturday morning, had subsided, she quieted into questioning thought. All day Saturday and Sunday, she was asking herself over and over, that question, that in some form or other, has perhaps been more frequently asked than any other since the world was made, "Why is this, why must it be?" She did not weep, neither did she pray. When doubts of Rodger first laid hold of her, she had prayed almost continually. She then went to God with a childish faith; believing that He could, and therefore would, right the great wrong; that He would insure the fulfilment of his laws, and see that truth and constancy received their natural reward. She reasoned that the God of nature would permit no unnatural thing to happen. But believe what she might, she felt that the facts were tightening around her, and what she termed an unnatural thing, seemed rapidly hastening to consummation, and no remonstrance was offered from any other source, than that which arose from her own woman's heart. Gradually she prayed less and less. She knew that she had prayed a great deal, she knew that she had believed in the answer to prayer; she also knew that her prayers had not been answered. Now that the crisis had come, that the one thing of all else in the universe, which she wished to retain, had been torn from her; now that the greatest sorrow which she could imagine, had overwhelmed her; she could only cry: "Why is it? must it be?"

Monday morning while revolving this subject of prayer in her mind, in a desultory sort of way, she went into the kitchen to speak to Christine, a pious Swede girl of a low order of intellect, regarding the proper washing of her father's flannels. She found the girl looking out of the window at the gathering clouds:

"Do you think it is going to rain, Christine, and wet your clothes?" kindly asked Margaret.

"No Miss, it ain't going to rain," replied the girl, leaving the window, and looking at Margaret with an inane grin on her face; "I have just went up stairs, and asked God not to let it rain."

"But, Christine, does God stop the rain because you ask him?"

"Yes, Miss, He knows I'm not strong. God loves me, and He won't let my clothes get rained on."

"Is that the reason He stops the rain from wetting your clothes, because He loves you?" asked Margaret.

"Yes, I talk to God, and He loves me. I'm saved. God talks to me. Oh, no, He won't let Christine's clothes get rained on, for I prayed to God."

"But, Christine," said Margaret, "it may be best that it should rain. God knows better than you."

"No, Miss, I talked to God last night. "I don't sleep, so I talk to God. He made it rain last week for me; the rainwater was gone, that other water makes the clothes bad; it hurted my hands; I asked God to make it rain, God loves me, He filled my tubs. God knows I'm not strong. He wants me to go to prayer-meeting to-night, so He won't let the rain wet my clothes." The little old Swede girl seesawed back and forth, from one foot to the other; her roving light gray eyes twinkling with excitement, as she continued: "You are saved, Miss; you know God loves me."

"Yes, Christine, I presume that He loves you, He loves us all. Suppose one of the poor men living down by the creek, had a sick wife and some little children, and he had to buy bread for them all, and all that he had to depend on was his garden; and his potatoes and corn, that he wished to sell for medicine for his wife, and bread for his children, were all drying up, and he was a good man, and God loved him, and he prayed God to send rain on his garden, the same day as you prayed God not to let it rain on your clothes, which of you would God hear?"

"I don't care for that man," answered Christine, after a moment's hesitation, in which she closed her teeth tightly, as she grinned from ear to ear. "I'm saved, and God loves me. He will be good to that poor man, but He won't let the rain come on Christine's clothes; when I pray to Him, He will stop the rain. Our minister says, if we believe, God will talk to us, and do just what we say. I believe God, and He will do what I say."

"You ought not to talk in that way, Christine, we ought to do what God says. He knows best."

"Yes, Miss," interrupted the girl, with a determined air, "God knows I love Him, and I talk to Him, and He will do what I say. He will not let it rain if I pray to Him. God knows I'm not strong."

Margaret gave her directions and returned to her room. She turned in disgust from the ignorant fanaticism of the Swede girl, who considered herself the first care of the Infinite, who, she believed, would direct natural laws with reference to her comfort; who believed that her faith possessed power to call the rain down into her wash-tubs, and to prevent its natural descent upon her clothes on the line. As she sat by her west window, that looked out upon the old apple orchard, where the trees stood gnarled and bare in the cold February rain, that was slowly falling in spite of Christine's prayers, she asked herself if there were not many who occupied an intellectual altitude as far above her, as she, above the ignorant Swede woman; who might from their nearer position to truth, regard her religious faith as narrow and fanatical and selfish, as she, from her superior position, considered Christine's senseless and unreasonable. She knew the pious servant was wrong, that she was the victim of an honest illusion. Happy in her credulity she might be, but mistaken, she most surely was. Under what errors was she herself living? And if wrong, how far wrong was she? What of the faith of her childhood? What did her father really believe? And Aunt Deb? Did her minister believe what he preached from Sabbath to Sabbath? or was his faith merely a hereditary one, and his pulpit utterances the habitual expressions of church formulas? She had tried to obey God, she was very sure she had done the best she had known; she had prayed, she had read the Bible, and tried to fashion her life after its principles, and heed all of its instructions. It was true this had not been a task, for its requirements were so reasonable and just, she naturally chose to do what they commanded; but what had it all amounted to? Rodger was gone, and her life was ruined. Why was it all permitted? Was she to blame? What wrong had she done that this retribution should come upon her? Or what mistake had she made, that this calamity should desolate her life? If she and Rodger were not to have been married, why their long acquaintance, their love for each other? Was all of this in conformity to natural law? Was this end the natural result of a cause? If so, what was the cause? Could any human intellect feel its way back from the effect to the cause? It all seemed very strange to her, she could not understand it. It seemed so natural to her that she and Rodger should love each other; they were specially fitted for each other in education, similarity of taste and temperament. It had seemed as though God had designed their marriage, and that only good and happiness could come to them, and all related to them, by their marrying. What was this wicked influence that had worked the defeat of so beautiful and natural a result? All of her ideas of a Supreme Being, and His government, seemed called in question. It was all a tangle and a jargon.

It did not look as though a wise Supreme Being had meted out her life in loving supervision, and it did seem as though every natural and moral law had been broken through to place her in the distressing position that she occupied. She left her seat by the window; not that the gloomy February outlook affected her in the least, she was too much engrossed by the sorrow of her heart to care for either sunshine or clouds, but she was intellectually weary of the inner strife. She picked up a book from the table, and seated herself to read. It was Motley's Dutch Republic, and she opened it where the bloody Alva was in the height of his career of devastation, and followed him page after page in his slaughter of the innocent, and oppression of the noble. Then she turned over a handful of leaves at random, to get away from that scene of carnage, and alighted upon the Calvinists and Armenians where they carved and toasted and fried each other as they got the chance. She had read the book

before, but the fatality that attended the cause of the
Silent Prince during so many years, and the horrible per-
secutions of the different Protestant sects of each other,
had never impressed her as strongly as at this time.   As
she read she was pursuing an undertow of thought on
cause and effect, natural and moral law, the injustice of
much of that suffering of which she was reading, and all
of the time she was struggling for an intellectual recognition of a benevolent, supernatural agency.   Her sense
of justice was outraged, her heart faint with sympathy,
and she turned sick at the terrible workings of such
savage hate and cruel bigotry against personal conscience
and individual judgment, and all done in the name of
Christ, for the glory of God, and in obedience to Him!
She threw the book from her with an expression of bitter
sorrow on her face, so bitter it verged upon anger and
revolt against some one, or some thing, whoever, or whatever, was responsible for the dreadful sufferings of those
noble men and women.   All of that tyranny and carnage
—she thought, that torturing and murdering might have
been the natural result of religious fanaticism, political
ambition, narrow education, and unconscious selfishness;
but what comfort would such a statement of the supremacy
of natural law have been to those innocent victims of the
rack, dungeon and flames?   She shuddered.   Was she a
creation in the order of law?—a creature of natural cause?
and a victim of law?   It was terrible to think of, but her
life looked like it; and was there no spiritual power above
natural law to rescue her?   She rose to her feet and
clasped her hands in front of her, then fell upon her
knees; not to pray, but from habit.   Prayer was useless:
this inexorable nature was blind and deaf, possessed of
neither love nor sympathy; cries and tears were in vain
before it.   She felt that she was on the track of a jugger-

naut car, ponderous, slow-coming, but not to be escaped: right on the track of this law that had been silently marching down the ages, never deviating, whether in its way lay the bud on the bush, to be brought out in the full bloom of June loveliness, the seed in the ground to be developed into bread; or a human brain it was manipulating into insanity, or a human heart out of which it was crushing the last red drop of life blood: never turning aside through all of the generations that in their turn had become the victims of its power. When the car reached her, in solemn majesty it would pass on, and that she was left ground to powder would be but the necessary fulfillment of its unconscious behest. "Just one more," she said to herself, as she thought of the thousands in the Netherlands suffering and dying for their country and church. What could she expect for herself? a girl with only a personal sorrow. Oh! the bitterness of it all! its hopelessness! "Why was it? Why must it be?" she cried. She did not think of her future, she did not know that she had any future. When Rodger went out of her life her individual life seemed ended. She buried her face in her hands, and shivered with fear. She was afraid of life, of the terrible influences at work, afraid of some impersonal power, unnamed, not in the least understood; that seemed to her to be devoid of knowledge, and reason, and love; and possessed of only force, absolute, eternal force. Before this power she crouched in bitter reproach and utter helplessness.

CHAPTER XVIII.

This expression of bitterness on Margaret's face struck Miss Sargent painfully, the following Saturday, as Margaret opened the front door to welcome her on her arrival at Professor McVey's. It was an expression she never had seen Margaret wear before, during their long acquaintance.

"I've been watching for you," said Margaret, as she raised both of her arms to Miss Sargent's neck, who kissed her again and again.

"I'm so glad to see you dear—how glad I am!" said Miss Sargent, looking down on Margaret as she retained her close in her arms. "You have not treated me well in not coming to see me oftener; but I know dear, it was your care for your father that kept you so closely at home, you dear, darling daughter, you! Yes, I'll take my cloak off in a minute, I just want to hug you a little," and Miss Sargent broke out into a cheerier laughter than the house had heard for months, as she gave Margaret another squeeze. All in the house felt her coming a blessing. None, even in thought recognized that she supplied a doleful need, but all felt an influence like the coming of spring, quickly upon a dreary winter, like a diffused warmth through a cold room, like the breaking of soft music upon a weird silence. The gloom of the house penetrated Miss Sargent through every fibre of her sensitive nature. She smiled at Margaret's playful prattle over her father, and tears filled her eyes as she smiled, to see how ignorant this sixty-five year old man was of the thorn in the breast of the nightingale that made the music of his life. There was, to her, something

vastly sadder in Margaret's light laugh and speech full
of loving raillery, than there would have been in her tears
and silence. She comprehended the effort the girl was
making, and it struck her as a dance on a grave, or a
laugh over a corpse. No one would have imagined
that she was analyzing the state and the relation to each
other of the three inmates of the house, with a penetration
that in a few hours enabled her to understand Professor
McVey's physical danger, and enough of Margaret's mental
anguish to cause her own soul to cry out within her, in
sympathy and prayer for her, and something of Miss
Bond's lack of appreciation of Margaret's condition.
While she was making these investigations, she was chatting at the dinner-table and round the study fire through
the evening, about the outside world in a hearty, breezy
way that awakened laughter, and also a curiosity that
she was delighted to gratify. Professsor McVey found
himself really interested in bits of gossip regarding his
city acquaintances, and enjoyed being opposed by Miss
Sargent in some of his views regarding the importance
of the study of Latin and Greek, and his deprecation of
the scientific tendencies of the age. A load seemed lifted
off of Aunt Deborah's shoulders by the mere presence of
this self-reliant, capable woman. But however great
Miss Sargent's power to entertain Professor McVey and
Miss Bond, she felt that nothing she said possessed the
least interest for Margaret, who sat in the friendly light
of the pink lamp shade, with her thin white hand over
her eyes. Miss Sargent saw that all of Margaret's apparent interest in the family group was assumed, and
that the sounds crossing and re-crossing from one speaker
to another that might fall upon her ear, carried no meaning to her pre-occupied mind. After they had parted for
the night, and the house was still, Miss Bond was startled

by a knock on her door. She opened it to find Miss Sargent standing without in the dark hall, wrapped in a large shawl.

"Pardon me for disturbing you, Miss Bond," said Miss Sargent, "but I wish to talk with you a little about Margaret and her father, and feared we might not have an opportunity to-morrow, as it is Sunday, and Professor McVey will probably be home all day, and I must return on an early train Monday morning."

"I shall be very glad to talk with you," said Miss Bond, as she seated her guest in a large chair, and placed a hassock for her feet.

. "Neither Margaret nor her father seem quite well," began Miss Sargent.

"No, they are not well," replied Miss Bond, "and I hardly know which is the worst, and I really do not know what is the matter of either of them. I think Margaret is as sick as her father, but I don't see as she has any real ailment."

"You spoke in your letter of the breaking of her engagement with Rodger Latimer, does she talk with you about it?" asked Miss Sargent.

"No," replied Miss Bond as she seated herself in a little rocking chair, opposite to Miss Sargent. "She has never said a word to me about it."

"Then from what do you draw your conclusions?"

"From what I have seen. I think Margaret knows that I know the engagement is broken, and is willing that I should know it. She don't wish her father to know anything of it, for fear it would worry him."

"When was Mr. Latimer here last?" asked Miss Sargent.

"It must have been sometime in August, about the middle of August, I guess."

"Was everything pleasant between them then?"

"It appeared to be," replied Miss Bond, "he was with her in her room for two hours or more—yes, I remember now, Professor McVey was at your house, and he telegraphed Margaret that he would not be at home until the next day, so she and Rodger took the phaeton and drove to the woods. I put them up a lunch, and they didn't get back until six, and then after dinner, they spent the evening on the piazza. They seemed very happy all day, as far as I could see."

"And he has not visited her since that day?" asked Miss Sargent.

"No."

"Do you know anything of the frequency of his letters, and when the correspondence ceased?"

"I used to frequently bring her letters from the office," replied Miss Bond. "Whoever goes down street, brings the mail. Last year, I know, she heard from him very frequently, but as far as I know, she hasn't had a letter from him for months. I don't believe I've brought her any for three months: it may have just happened so; she may have gotten them herself, or George may have brought them."

"You know that Mr. Latimer is to be married to a girl in Clinton, I suppose," said Miss Sargent.

"No, I didn't!" exclaimed Miss Bond, as she leaned forward and clasped her hands on her knees. "He must have treated Margaret shamefully! I don't believe they ever had the least quarrel; he has just left her: who is this girl?"

"Her name is Marie Edwards, she is a sister of Mrs. Lundom White. I first learned the fact from a notice in a newspaper, and thinking that possibly there might be some mistake about it, I paid Mrs. White a visit a few days after the engagement was announced in the paper. She is a talkative woman, and I felt sure that she would speak of it, if it were so, and I hadn't been in the house five minutes, before she told me of the engagement, and of a dinner that she gave to Mr. Latimer and some of his friends. She said they were to be married next May, or June, probably in May."

"You were not invited to the dinner, as one of Rodger's friends?" interrogated Miss Bond.

"No, Mr. Latimer is a man of too much sense, to wish me to be a guest at a dinner that was a sort of announcement to his friends of his engagement to Miss Edwards, after the two summers I spent in Europe with him and Margaret. But Margaret seems to me to be in a very bad condition, physically and mentally."

"I don't think she is well," replied Miss Bond.

"Well!" repeated Miss Sargent, "her condition is pitiful: how she has changed! I was shocked when I saw her, it was with the greatest effort that I controlled myself. I never saw a sadder face; there is something almost unearthly in her appearance. Have you noticed her hands? they are absolutely shrunken with pain. She seems so utterly bereft, utterly hopeless, and how she has isolated herself from all human sympathy. I cannot approach her as I used to; it seems as though an almost infinite space separated between us. Something must be done for her, but God only knows what." Miss Sargent wiped the tears from her eyes.

"Why, Miss Sargent, you frighten me," said Miss Bond, "I didn't know that Margaret was as sick as you say."

"You have seen the change come on gradually," replied Miss Sargent, "and so have not noticed it I suppose, and then Margaret has such a power of will; her self-repression is something terrible. But we must do what we can to get her away from Edgewood for awhile. Doctor Kean says that he feels anxious about Professor McVey."

"I thought the doctor said there was nothing the matter of him," said Miss Bond.

"He told me," replied Miss Sargent, "that there was no organic disease, only a gradual weakening, a sort of letting go his hold on life. But he said that when men of Professor McVey's age get into that condition, they seldom come out of it. Now it seems to me that Margaret and her father, better start immediately for Florida, and go prepared to stay two or three months. They both need the change."

"I don't believe either of them will go," said Miss Bond.

"Doctor Kean said Professor McVey might be compelled to go, in order to live through the spring," said Miss Sargent. "I'm sure if I repeat to Margaret what Doctor Kean said to me, she will hurry her father off."

"But you can't convince Professor McVey that he is sick; he won't go," said Miss Bond.

"I don't wish to convince him that he is sick," replied Miss Sargent; "that would have a depressing effect on him. I can influence him, if in no other way, through his affection for Margaret. It would never do to tell him what I think of Margaret's condition, but he is so alive to everything that bears on her happiness, he will go anywhere that is for her good."

"You cannot make him see it," persisted Miss Bond.

"Oh yes, I can, in ten minutes, and without alarming him either," cheerfully replied Miss Sargent.

And she did use her influence so effectively, that before sundown Sunday evening, it was decided that Margaret and her father would start for Florida the next Wednesday, to remain as long as seemed desirable to either of them, or as Doctor Kean might advise. This point

12 Rodger Latimer's Mistake.

gained, Miss Sargent turned her entire thought to Margaret's present condition. She was anxious to be of some little comfort, or assistance to Margaret, before her return home. But the woman, nearly half a century old, stood in awe before the girl of twenty. There was about Margaret the dignity of silence, and the majestic sacredness of sorrow. How to approach her, Miss Sargent did not know, and at times she questioned if it were best to try. But she could not bear the thought of going home, and leaving that delicate, suffering girl to go off to Florida with her sick father, without at least assuring her, in a warm, tender way, of her great love for her, and establishing to some degree, the old confidence between them, that had existed for years, but which now seemed entirely destroyed. But how was this to be done? While Margaret was a thoughtful hostess, observant of every courteous and affectionate attention, she gave Miss Sargent no opportunity to see her alone.

They all sat up late Sunday night, quietly talking around the study fire. As the clock struck eleven, Margaret in her usual gentle way, insisted that her father should go to bed.

"You know, papa," she said as she leaned over the back of his chair, and placed her hands on each side of his face, "that none of us can get away while you are talking, and we will all be down sick to-morrow, then Uncle John will never again let Aunt Helen come to see us. And you have a great deal to do before Wednesday. Just think, papa! roses in February, and sitting under orange trees!"

Miss Sargent rose to her feet, to supplement Margaret's efforts, as did Miss Bond also. Professor McVey reluctantly left his easy chair, and bright fire, although his daughter led him by one of his hands clasped in both of hers. She kissed him at the foot of the stairs, and turned from him to Miss Sargent, whom she also kissed good-night, and who passed up the stairs after Professor McVey. Margaret, instead of following them, returned to the study, which Miss Sargent observed from the hall above. She hesitated a moment, determined to make her own opportunity, descended the stairs, and entered the study, where she found Margaret sitting on the rug before the fire, with her hands clasped around her knees. Miss Sargent seated herself on a hassock by Margaret's side. For a while neither of them spoke, or in any way recognized the presence of the other. Margaret hadn't a word to say to any living mortal, and Miss Sargent didn't know what to say. She feared to give utterance to any commonplace remark, upon indifferent subjects; or even to speak of the approaching trip to Florida, or Professor McVey's health. Those subjects had been talked over between them during the day, and to touch upon an ordinary topic now, might cut off her last chance of getting nearer to Margaret, near enough to be of some comfort to her. So they sat in silence, both gazing into the fire. After a lapse of fifteen minutes, Miss Sargent turned her head toward Margaret, and looked at her intently. Margaret was conscious of her gaze, and in a few minutes she unclasped her hands from her knees, and laid one of them, the left one, on Miss Sargent's lap. Miss Sargent quietly clasped it in one of her own, and held it in a firm, gentle grasp for a few minutes, then she opened her hand that held it, and commenced to stroke it tenderly with her other hand. She was so afraid of hurting Margaret she dared not speak. After a little she ceased the motion of her hand, and fastened her eyes upon the ringless finger. When Margaret noticed that Miss Sargent was looking at her hand, she said in a measured, emotionless way:

"Aunt Helen, as a matter of course you know the fact, in knowing that, you know all there is to be known. If there was anything to tell, anything to say, I should wish to say it to you, but there is not." As she ceased speaking she drew her hand from Miss Sargent, and again clasped her knees, and continued her gazing into the fire.

Never in her life had Miss Sargent been at such an utter loss; every form of speech that rose before her mind, seemed a mocking platitude to utter in the presence of such suffering. Nothing but a denial of the fact could comfort Margaret now, and such denial Miss Sargent, alas, was powerless to give. She felt as she looked at the thin white face beside her, that Margaret had, in her searchings for some way out of this terrible sorrow, gone far deeper, and far beyond, any consolation that her human reason could give. But she must say something to the child she loved so much. Remembering Margaret's religious faith, as she had seen it manifested for many years, she thought to appeal to that. She placed one arm around Margaret and drew her head to her shoulder, and as she held her closely, she leaned her head upon the girl's forehead.

"All of this seems very hard, dear, cruel and hard," she said, "it seems so to me, I cannot understand it at all; it is a great trial of my faith, and I know, darling, it is a hundred times harder for you to bear, than I can even think. But some way it is right, blasphemous as that may sound to you." Margaret said nothing as her head rested upon Miss Sargent's shoulder. After a few moments' silence, Miss Sargent continued, "Now, yes, many years ago, I could look back on a great sorrow that came to me in my youth, that at the time seemed cruel, and more than I could bear; and now I see, not only that it was right, but I see just why it was right. When I was suffering, I could not believe that it ever could be for the best, but I came to feel that God does all things well; God saw through so many more years than I could. If I had seen all things as God saw them, at the time He permitted such a sorrow to come upon me—and as I saw them afterward, I should have done, regarding myself, had I possessed the power, just as God did. Oh if we could only believe in His wisdom and love, and trust Him, and wait for the outcome of our lives in patient faith." She softly kissed the head that leaned against her; Margaret breathed in a regular, quiet way, but said nothing. "We don't know," pursued Miss Sargent, "much about the future dear, even of our own lives here upon earth, much less of the great hereafter. Your Heavenly Father loves you tenderly, my darling; you cannot tell what He is even now planning for you, what He is doing for your future."

"Mixing a cup of wormwood and gall, probably," said Margaret, in a hard voice, as she raised her head, clasped her hands again around her knees, and gazed into the smoldering fire. Miss Sargent sat perfectly still; the tears rolled down her cheeks, and dropped on her hands that lay in her lap. In a few minutes Margaret turned toward her.

"Aunt Helen, I know how good you are, and I know that you love me," she said, as she threw both of her arms across Miss Sargent's lap; "don't think me ungrateful. You know that I love you dearly, and in all of this world, you are the only human being that I can go to for counsel, and I know that you will never fail me, for you never fail any one. If there was anything you could do for me I would ask it of you freely; neither you nor I can change or modify events, so there is no use in talking about them.

I know all about God's love, and quiescent waiting, and everything of that kind—all about it—there is nothing to be done."

"Nothing that I can do, my poor darling," said Miss Sargent, as she looked into the desolate face that was turned toward her; her tears were flowing from her eyes. It seemed to her as though she should weep her heart out over the forsaken girl.

"Nothing," replied Margaret. "Yes, there is something, Aunt Helen, that will be a help, and a comfort to me. Sometime, before long, I shall speak to papa regarding this affair—I shall tell him—that—that," Margaret stopped for a moment, but without any change in the expression of her face; the hesitation was for a moment only, then she resumed, speaking slowly and distinctly, with a business-like, mechanical accuracy: "I shall tell him that I shall never marry, and in order to make him feel perfectly comfortable regarding me, I shall talk of the pleasure of living with you, and having Uncle John look after me. As a matter of course, papa and Aunt Deb, and you, and Uncle John, will die before I do, that is according to nature. You understand, Aunt Helen, for myself I haven't a care. The future will bring its own events, and it is immaterial what they are, but papa must not have an anxious thought about me. So if you could say to him, in a way that will not startle him, and set him to thinking, that you are to care for me—you know just how to say it—he must not be disturbed, he must think I am perfectly happy, and that I will always be so, no matter what may happen."

"Yes, I understand you dear. I will make him feel that love and security will be yours under all circumstances, no matter what may happen, and will not designate the happenings. If you should outlive your father, Margaret, remember then you are to be my own child. Aunt Deborah is well enough, but I am to be first. I shall admit no claim before mine. You—"

"I was perfectly honest, Aunt Helen," interrupted Margaret, in whose face not an expression of interest or relief had been roused by Miss Sargent's affectionate declarations, "when I said that for myself I hadn't a thought." Nor had she. Life had done its worst to her. After the deathblow given, possible pin-pricks were not worth guarding against. "You are very kind," she continued, "but it was only of papa's quiet and happiness I was thinking, so please do this for me." Margaret drew her arms off Miss Sargent's lap, and clasped her hands again around her knees.

"Yes, dear, I can easily do that, but Margaret, you must let me speak to you of yourself for a moment," said Miss Sargent, as she placed both of her arms around Margaret and drew her close to her. "You are very mature for your age, my darling, so I shall speak plainly without fear of distressing you, and you know me well enough to know, that I mean every word that I say, to the fullest possible meaning of that word. No one can tell what the result is to be of your dear father's present condition. You have practical sense, and although you know nothing of business, you know that as long as people live, they have daily needs, and must have food and shelter. You must know too that your father has considerable property, and that brother John has the care of it. We will make your father feel perfectly happy regarding your present condition, and your future. Then, my darling, although you see nothing in life and no possible future before you, but the simple routine of existence— and I see very plainly that on this point you must be left to yourself and God, for think what you may, dear, there is a personal God who is caring for you—but this routine of your existence, darling, is to be spent in my arms, close to my heart. Don't say no, don't say what I suppose is true, that you don't care where it is spent; only let me say that I am getting to be an old woman, and you are my only child. Dear Margaret! how I have loved you all of these years!" exclaimed Miss Sargent, as she passionately pressed Margaret closer to her and kissed her hair and forehead. "I would like to take you home with me now, and never be separated from you another hour, only that I know your father needs you. But child, you are to belong to me, so remember darling, wont you, to write to me and send for me, the first moment I can be of use to you or your dear father?"

Oh! the wonderful power of human love! Margaret's sad eyes were filled with healing tears, as she raised them to Miss Sargent, and her lips lost their rigid tension, and quivered with emotion. She raised her hand and laid it softly on the side of Miss Sargent's face, the gentle caress which she so often gave her father!

"Yes, Aunt Helen, I'll write to you, and I'll live with you always." It was all she said, but it was enough.

"Bless you!" cried Miss Sargent, as she placed her hand lightly on Margaret's head, and held it close to her breast. The two women sat in silence, with clasped hands. The clock on the mantel above them ticked its monotonous to and fro, and the fire fell so low, that there were but a few coals in the ashes. Half an hour had passed, when Miss Sargent felt the clasp of Margaret's hand loosen, and her head press more heavily on her breast, and she knew that the sorrow-worn girl was asleep. She had kept many vigils during her life, beside the sick beds, and deathbeds, of her own household; in hospitals, sitting sometimes, the night hours through, as some unfortunate woman who had seen better days, was breathing out the life she was weary of; and saddest of all, in the city prison, beside erring, desperate women, whom she was striving to hold with the strong grasp of a woman's sympathy, and a Christian's faith. But she felt that never had she held a holier watch, than through this silent midnight hour, as she clasped to her heart in peaceful slumber this young girl, in whose soul the bitter waters of anguish had quenched all hope in life, and all faith in God.

CHAPTER XIX.

Professor McVey did not gain strength as Doctor Kean hoped he would, by a prolonged stay in a mild climate. He very much enjoyed the change from the snow and piercing winds of the North, to the balmy air and almost constant sunshine of the extreme south of Florida. He had never been in any of the Southern States before, nor had he ever passed the cold season in any mild climate. This was his first relief from the raw springs of the North, and it was as though he had passed into a new state of existence. His days seemed filled with a delicious languor, and everything pleased him. Even the sand flies and mosquitoes, that Margaret found annoying, did not seem to disturb him; but he gained no strength. Every day he took a little less exercise, and there was a gradual, although scarcely perceptible, decrease in the amount of food that he ate. When Margaret would press him to eat more freely, he would reply that he had all that his system demanded. One day he said to her, as she rather persistently recommended some delicacy that she had prepared for him:

"My child, I eat all that my appetite calls for. I would take more if I could, for everything tastes so good down here; this is a perfect climate, it makes physical existence a delight."

"But you eat so little, papa," said Margaret.

"A man needs but little food, living in this air," replied her father. "He gets much nutrition from these sea breezes. And remember, my child, that I am doing nothing, neither mentally nor physically."

Margaret was satisfied, and tranquilly watched beside

her father's lounge, which she had placed near the open door of their parlor, from which, across the sand, he had a distant view of the ocean. He would doze off half a dozen times a day, into a quiet and perfectly natural sleep, and when he wakened, always found Margaret by his side, with the book open at the place where she had left off reading, when she saw he was fast asleep. Then he would ask her to proceed with her reading, which she would do, but gradually her voice would mingle with the twitter of the birds in the rose bushes just outside the door, and he would be hushed to sleep again. As the heat increased with the advance of the season, by the advice of their resident physician, they moved Northward to St. Augustine, and then in a week or so afterward, again moved North, to Jacksonville; and by the middle of April, they were pleasantly located in Aiken, South Carolina. If it were possible, Professor McVey was more pleased with Aiken than ·with any of the places they had visited in Florida, and Margaret was delighted to find that her father seemed to gain strength, from the tonic air of the high altitude. He frequently would walk on the hotel piazza, and go out and gather for himself, bunches of the wonderful Aiken roses, that never ceased to delight him. Every day he would have Margaret drive him out to one of the pine groves that surrounded the place, when he would lean back against the soft cushions that Margaret arranged for him in the high-backed seat of their carriage, and listen to the wind in the pines. He never seemed to tire of the woods, and often insisted on staying out so late, that it required adroit management on Margaret's part to get him in, out of the night air, or before darkness was down on them. Those were peaceful, happy days for both father and daughter. Professor McVey had no care, suffered no pain. and was constantly attended by Margaret, who herself rendered him every service she possibly could, and was loth to have a servant touch him. Her tender ministrations, and the beautiful surroundings, combined to make those few spring months one of the happiest periods of Professor McVey's life. And Margaret wondered at her own serenity; she seemed to have passed from a world of snow and harsh winds, and horrible dreams, to one of balmy air, of flowers, and of beautiful realities. The preceding six months were as a terrible nightmare, from which she had awakened. When she thought of Rodger at all, it was of the Rodger of a year ago, of the dear Lausanne Rodger, who was in harmony with her present life, amid the roses and pines, and soft air full of the hum of bees, and song of birds. But she thought of Rodger very little, her mind was too fully occupied with her father, of whom she thought every waking moment, and often dreamed of at night.

Doctor Mackintosh, their Aiken physician, passed half an hour each day with his patient, pleasantly chatting, passing lightly from one subject to another, in a way that would amuse, rather than tire a sick man, and doing most of the talking himself. It never occurred to Margaret to study the physician's face for a report of her father's condition, nor would she have gained any information had she done so. The only time there was any peculiar expression on the face of the doctor, was when Margaret was busily attending to her father's needs, and his eye rested upon her. He evinced no anxiety when he was observing Professor McVey, but his face was full of solicitude, as he furtively regarded Margaret. One day he said to her:

"Do you expect any of your friends to join you this spring, Miss McVey, or are they too loyal to the North, to come down here and share this beautiful weather with us Southerners?"

"I don't think their loyalty to the North would keep any of our friends away from here," replied Margaret, "although their ignorance of your lovely country might. But we have no friends in our own town who have leisure to travel at this season. In a college town we all stay at home until the last of June, and then take a three months' vacation."

"I didn't know but that some of your Clinton friends might be coming to meet you," said the doctor. "Clinton usually sends a large delegation here during the spring months. This is, perhaps, rather late for any new comers, but May is a beautiful month on this tableland."

"No, not unless papa or I need some one to look after us, and we are both doing so well, that I feel almost ashamed to say that we are here for our health." As Margaret said this, she left her chair, and seated herself on the floor in front of the sofa, where her father was reclining, and as she took one of his hands and kissed it, she continued: "I suspect, papa, Doctor Mackintosh wonders why I insist upon his coming to see you every day, now that you feel so well; you tell him he must come, if only to say how much nourishment you better take—"

"No, no," interrupted the doctor, "I do not wonder at all, nor do I intend to be robbed of my daily visits to you; we doctors are hard to get rid of, when once called in, but I must be honest with you, for the sake of my professional reputation, otherwise I might be inclined to keep you and your father here, until the heat became injurious to you both. That was my reason for asking you if you expected any friends to join you here. If you do, they will have to come soon, for it is growing too warm for your father. This heat may be agreeable to Northerners, but it frequently is debilitating, and it would not be well for your father to remain in it much longer.   I am sorry to have to say this, for in advising you to take him back to the more invigorating air of your lake region, I am depriving myself of the pleasantest hour of my day."

Margaret was surprised; her father appeared very comfortable, and happy: he was quiet and satisfied with everything, he did not seem to care whether he staid in Aiken, or returned to Edgewood.   Of late he had seemed to grow indifferent, he never expressed a wish for anything; not even to stay in the pine woods, when Margaret said it was time for them to return to the hotel.

Doctor Mackintosh carried his point, and in a few days the trunks were repacked, and they were ready to begin their journey.   Margaret did not observe it at the time, but she afterward thought of how everything was at hand to expedite their departure.   Servants and horses, and all needed things supplied in some magical way, everything that could add to her father's comfort on his homeward trip.   And she knew, when she looked back to it, that it was kind Doctor Mackintosh that had saved her all thought and care in the preparations; and that it was his foresight that provided an ample supply of different tonics and nourishments for her father's use on the way.

"I see that you have not much knowledge of sickness, Miss McVey," said the doctor, to Margaret, on the morning of their departure, "although you are a perfect nurse, the very best I ever saw.   Your father is very comfortable this morning, and he will, without doubt, have a comfortable journey.   He probably will not leave his berth, in fact, he'd better lie quietly in it all of the way.   The journey will tire him less in that way, and at the best, these railroad trips are exhausting.   Let him sleep, but be sure and give him his medicine and nourishment regularly. Insist upon his taking them, even if he is a little averse to doing so. He seems very well this morning, but—I don't know—it is best to do a dozen unneeded things, rather than run the slightest chance that you may need something that we have neglected to provide; and possibly, your father may need a change of tonic when he reaches Clinton; so you better give me your Clinton physician's address, and I will telegraph him my opinion. Doctor Kean, did you say the name was? You will have a pleasant trip home I'm sure," pursued the doctor, "this fair weather is going to last a week, and these late rains will have laid all the dust. I am sure both of you will have a comfortable journey."

CHAPTER XX.

Margaret was both surprised and delighted, when she reached Clinton, early one evening, after her long railroad trip, to find Doctor Kean and Miss Sargent, at the Clinton depot waiting to greet her and her father. Both insisted on accompanying her and Professor McVey out to Edgewood, where the door of the old home was opened for them by Aunt Deborah. Doctor Kean assisted Professor McVey to his bedroom.

"No, no, we're going right up stairs," he said, when Miss Bond informed him that the professor's chair was ready for him, drawn up before the fire in the study. "I know how it is when a man comes home at night, from a long railroad journey. He wants to get his clothes off, and be rubbed down, and get into his own bed."

Professor McVey, who was slowly mounting the stairs, leaning on Doctor Kean's shoulder, looked up with an almost boyish roguery in his face, as he said:

"Oh, Jack, you take me for old Denmark, don't you?"

Doctor Kean broke into a merry laugh, as he replied: "You remember that, do you, old boy? What a horse that Denmark was! how you used to laugh at me, because I would rub his legs down myself, after I had trotted him; but I tell you, Mac, I loved that horse."

As they entered the professor's bedroom closely followed by Margaret and Miss Sargent, Doctor Kean said: "Now we'll just turn these women out, and I'll put you to bed myself. Do you remember how you used to sit up with me, professor, when I had that long pull of malarial fever? and you wouldn't let me have all the ice water I wanted to drink? What boys we were then!"

Miss Sargent and Margaret went down stairs, and left the two old friends together. Doctor Kean continued his cheerful talk, as he busied himself about the sick man, who paid little attention to anything around him. "We *were* boys in those days," pursued the doctor, "but that Black was a miserable old doctor. My instincts were all right; I knew he was mismanaging me most outrageously, all through the fever. Here, old fellow, your nightshirt is good and warm," said the doctor, as he brought the nightshirt he had been holding over the register, to Professor McVey, who was sitting on the side of the bed. "Put your arm in here; I declare, Prof. we won't have to give you much anti-fat for the next few months," said the doctor, as he took hold of his friend's bony arm to guide it into the sleeve. "Now let's have these shoes off. Yes, I know, Margaret always does it," replied Doctor Kean, to the professor's feeble inquiry for Margaret, when he stooped to untie the shoes. "But I can do it as well as she; I am not quite as slim as she is, or as I used to be, but I can stoop yet, I'm thankful to say. Now you begin to look right comfortable, McVey; here, just drink this warm milk, and lie down and I'll cover you up."

Professor McVey smiled as he laid his head upon his pillow, a vague, childish smile, and immediately dropped to sleep. Doctor Kean stood in watchful silence over him for a few moments; his face grew very sad, the tears slowly gathered in his eyes, and rolled down his cheeks. Then he stooped down and took the gaiters in his hand, and, glancing around the room, he crossed over and opened a closet door, and set the shoes down, and laid the gaiters across them; but, as he looked down on them, he thought of Margaret—they looked too life-like for her to find there in a few days—he took up the gaiters and cast his eyes around in search of a hiding place for them.

13 Rodger Latimer's Mistake.

After a moment's scanning of the capacity of the closet, he thrust them into the pocket of a coat that hung near by. He wiped the tears from his eyes, closed the closet door, and recrossing the room, leaned over his sick friend, who was in a deep sleep. Fearing that he was sleeping too heavily, he attempted to arouse him, which was a difficult task; but he persisted in his efforts until the professor was wide awake, and looked him full in the face.

"Are you awake, McVey?" asked the doctor.

"Why, certainly I'm awake, Jack." Doctor Kean remembered with a pang, that Professor McVey hadn't called him Jack, until this evening, for forty years. "What do you want? there's no use in your advising me against it; I shall go at all hazards." He turned his head on his pillow, slowly closed his eyes, and was going off to sleep again. Doctor Kean gently shook his shoulder, which again partially roused him. "Yes, yes," he muttered; "we'll go by the Wabash, Millicent, to Florida without change."

The doctor stood some time by the bedside in deep reflection, then he placed his fingers on Professor McVey's wrist for a moment, turned, and left the room, and descended the stairs to the study where the three women were sitting around the fire. Margaret immediately went to him.

"How is papa, doctor?" she asked in a cheerful voice.

"Right comfortable; but I want some supper, have you all been to supper?"

"No, we were waiting for you," said Margaret. "Aunt Deb says the steak is nearly ruined, so you take your supper now and I'll sit with papa."

"Yes, you go up and sit with him, little woman, but don't speak to him; he is sound asleep, and better not be disturbed."

As Margaret closed the door behind her, Doctor Kean stopped Miss Bond who was leaving the room to order the supper on the table. "Sit down, if you please, Miss Bond," he said; "I wish to say a word to you and Miss Sargent. Professor McVey is much worse than I expected to find him; he must have failed very rapidly in the last twenty-four hours. Doctor Mackintosh would never have permitted Margaret to have started on that long journey alone with her father, had he been in his present condition when he left Aiken. But in such cases there is frequently a rapid change in a short time; it is difficult to tell twelve hours ahead, sometimes, what a person's condition may be." The doctor blew his nose vigorously and wiped his eyes. "McVey may live a week or ten days, and then the dear fellow may pass away to-morrow. His mind wanders now; he talks of going to Florida by the Wabash, and fancies he is talking to his wife."

Miss Bond was filled with dismay, but the cheerful serenity of Miss Sargent's face only deepened into an expression of great seriousness.

"You must tell Margaret, Miss Sargent. I can't do it," said the doctor.

"How long do you think he may live?" asked Miss Sargent.

"I cannot tell, he may sink away in the next twenty-four hours, and he may live a week; but probably he will stay three or four days."

"You say his mind is wandering; isn't there danger that he may not be rational again?"

"Yes, great danger; he will suffer none, but will sleep most of the time, and drop off quietly—just stop breathing in his sleep. Perhaps it is as well so. Margaret will be spared some pangs."

Silence fell upon the three; they looked at each other

with a sense of some mysterious presence in the house. After a little, Miss Sargent said in a low tone:

"What do you think, doctor, of my not telling Margaret of her father's danger immediately? We are never ready to part with a friend, no matter how long a time of preparation we may have had. The end is always sudden, even if we have been expecting it for months; and there is little difference in the suffering, whether the parting comes without warning, or after long watching. Seems to me Margaret might be saved days of sorrow by not knowing that the end is near, until within a few hours of it, especially as her father will not be able to talk to her. If I tell her now, she will have days of agony; I know how it will be, she will not leave him for food, or sleep; but will hang over him, watching every breath, fearing it may be the last."

"You are quite right," said the doctor. "I'm glad you thought of it. Have Margaret take her food regularly, and go to bed and sleep regularly every night."

"When must you return to Clinton?" asked Miss Sargent.

"I must go back on the eleven o'clock train. Let me see, this is Saturday. I have an engagement at ten to-morrow, a consultation, but I can come up on the noon train and stay the rest of the day, until the midnight train. I'll be up every day and remain as long as I can. It might be well to have Doctor Hopkins come in to-morrow and see the professor, so that if anything should happen you could have a physician here in a few moments. But nothing will happen; he will continue just as he is now, quietly sleeping, to the end. All there is to do is to arouse him sufficiently to take the milk, and that liquid preparation. I hope, for Margaret's sake, that he will not come to himself enough to talk in a wandering way.

You and Miss Bond are all that are needed here, and then George is a reliable man."

Miss Sargent did not succeed quite as well as she expected in keeping Margaret's mind free from anxiety regarding her father. In the hour that she sat by his bedside, Saturday evening, when Doctor Kean was talking with her Aunt Deborah, and Miss Sargent was in the study below, Margaret had observed her father very closely. His deep sleep did not seem natural to her; it was true that he had slept and dozed a great deal for the three months past, but some way there was a look upon his face that evening she had never seen there before; it was not like the face of a natural sleeper, it was not as he had looked for the past week. The face was peaceful, even more than peaceful; there was on it an expression of deep restfulness, of permanent content. And yet it was a strange face to her: not in its physical lineaments, those were the same dear features of material molding; but it was as though there were two beings in the one lying on the bed before her. The material form, with its mechanical breathing, was familiar: but there was a spiritual presence looking through that attenuated, familiar face of flesh, that was strange; in it, back of it, but still a distinct individuality. It was her father, and yet not her father. She arose from the bedside, where she had been sitting with her eyes immovably fixed upon her father's face, and removed the shield from the side of the shade that Doctor Kean had placed there to intercept the light, and watching closely to see if the increased light disturbed him, gradually turned the gas up, throwing the light full upon her father's face, which continued in its perfect repose. Then she returned to the bedside and stood with hands clasped in front of her, with a face as white, but far from being as peaceful as the dear one she gazed upon. There Miss

Sargent found her, when she came to take her place by the bedside, so Margaret could go to her supper. Margaret went, as Miss Sargent desired her to, without a demur or question, but when they were making arrangements for the night, and both Miss Sargent and Miss Bond begged Margaret to go to bed and have a good night's sleep after her long journey, she quietly but positively refused. After changing her traveling dress for a warm wrapper she had a lounge brought into her father's room, and taking both of Miss Sargent's hands in hers, said to her:

"Aunt Helen, you must let me stay here all of the time. I cannot leave papa, I could not sleep a wink out of this room. You know I have been his nurse too long to be able to sleep away from him. I can sleep on this lounge, and if you think it best, if you think he is too sick for me to be left alone with him, suppose you stay here one part of the night, and Auntie Deb the other."

And so it was arranged. "We had better let her have her own way," said Miss Sargent to Miss Bond, as they were talking about it in the hall. Most of the night Margaret sat by her father's bedside, simply watching his quiet slumber; at times she would lean down low over him to catch the meaning of the muttered words that died away as she listened. Either Miss Sargent or Miss Bond sat on the other side of the bed throughout the night. Margaret wheeled the lounge into a position that enabled her, as she rested on it, to look directly upon her father's face. Here she would catch what sleep she could from time to time, when the room was perfectly quiet, but the slightest motion of the watcher sitting in the large arm-chair, or the least turning of her father's head upon his pillow, or a whispered mutter from his lips, brought her to her feet wide awake, and she would lean over him with a clear brain and steady hand. Miss Sargent feared she would be worn out, and suggested a trained nurse, but Margaret would not hear of it. So the hours passed as they pass in every chamber where one of the great transitions of existence is taking place. The days and nights came and went, Doctor Kean passed to and fro between Clinton and Professor McVey's house; in the sick room up stairs nothing was said but what was necessary to say regarding the dying man's needs. Miss Sargent wondered what Margaret was thinking of through all of those hours of alert attending; she could form no idea whether Margaret, who asked no questions, was aware of her father's immediate danger or not. Sometimes she thought she ought to speak plainly to her; and then she wished Margaret would interrogate her, as that would make the communication so much easier for her. But Margaret showed no disposition to ask for any information until late Tuesday afternoon. That afternoon she was crossing the lower hall with a glass of milk in her hand that she was taking to her father, just as the maid admitted Mrs. Herman, who immediately rushed to Margaret, and clasped her in her arms, regardless of the danger of spilling the milk over them both.

"You little darling, how glad I am to see you back again!" she cried. "Edgewood has been just desolate without you; but no wonder, you're such a belle! I declare I've missed you every hour." This assertion of Margaret's belleship was grotesque enough, as Margaret had rarely been in Edgewood society, and Mrs. Herman's protestation of hourly feeling her loss was based on the inadequate fact that she and Margaret for years had had the most casual acquaintance. But Margaret was too much occupied in her efforts to preserve her glass of milk, which she held at arms' length, to appreciate the ridiculousness of this affectionate onslaught upon her by her neighbor.

"What a nice time you must have had among the roses and oranges," continued Mrs. Herman. "I told Mr. Herman he ought to take me down there, for my lungs are not strong. But how pretty you look, you pet you; you are real pretty any way, and everybody says so. I am so glad you are back. We've missed you dreadfully; we'll have nice times together this summer, won't we? Where are you going after commencement? Let us go to the same place." Here she gave Margaret another hug. The milk swayed in the glass, and Margaret's eyes were fixed on it in dread of its splashing over. She placed her disengaged hand on Mrs. Herman's shoulders in an attempt to relieve herself, as she said:

"I am glad to see you looking well, Mrs. Herman, and glad to be at home again, but papa is quite ill, and I must go to him. I was just taking him this milk."

"O I'm so sorry," said Mrs. Herman, still holding Margaret by one arm, "but he'll be well soon, won't he? I know he will, you don't want to go to him just now. Your aunt is with him, isn't she? set down your glass of milk and come in the parlor. I want to tell you something, and show you something—but perhaps you're going to Marie's wedding. Are you invited?"

"No," replied Margaret, after a moment's hesitation. The past of four and five months ago, came rushing with a crash over the last eight and ten weeks, and a wave of feeling surged over her, making her head whirl, and her ears ring. During that moment of hesitation, Mrs. Herman took the glass from her hand, and set it on a table near by, and placing one arm around Margaret, drew her into the parlor, the door of which stood open, close to where they were standing.

"Just think of a large church wedding," said Mrs. Herman, "and to-morrow evening, the first of June, a real

Jnne wedding.   I don't know what to wear—you didn't
know anything about it? But then you were away so long!
I declare I never will let you go away again.   Yes, the
invitations were out more than two weeks ago, don't you
think they are pretty?   Cousin Hattie couldn't help
inviting me to the reception, how people would talk if
Marie didn't have her own family there."   Mrs. Herman
drew from her jacket pocket the invitation, which she
unfolded and handed to Margaret, who extended her
hand for it, as though she were in a dream.   As her eye
rested on it, she saw only the words—" Rodger Latimer"
—" Marie Edwards"—" Marriage"—"June first."   Had
June come? to-morrow, June first?   Mrs. Herman rattled
on.
  " It's to be a splendid affair, everybody's invited, both
to the church and reception.   I mean everybody who is
anybody.   I wanted a new dress, I told Mr. Herman;
I ought to have one, don't you think I ought? but my
white silk is just as good as new, and Mr. Herman said it
was good enough.   It's a lovely dress, don't you think
so? and then Marie hasn't been any too attentive to me,
and I won't go to the expense of a new dress for her wedding, would you?   You ought to see the present I got for
her, it's just the loveliest pie-knife—solid—with an ox-
idized handle, it's too lovely for anything.   I wanted to
keep it for myself, but I couldn't do that. As a matter of
course I had to give her something, but what will a pie-
knife be to her, with all of Mr. Latimer's money?   I expect she'll look beautiful, and so will Hattie.   What a
grand chance this will be for Hat to spread herself, I
shouldn't wonder if she made herself look like a peacock,
and what airs she will put on!   It will be almost as good
for her as being married again herself; a great deal better! for she didn't have any wedding at all, not near as

nice as mine. I had a real pretty wedding, but why don't you sit down, Miss McVey, how tired you look, pet; here sit down on the sofa by me and rest."

Mrs. Herman rose from the sofa, where she had seated herself when she entered the room, and placed her arm around Margaret, who had been standing all of the time, with her eyes fixed in a vacant stare on the invitation which she held in her hand. She had not heard one word of Mrs. Herman's rattling talk.

"No, no, Mrs. Herman," said Margaret, thoroughly aroused to her situation, "I cannot stay a moment longer; papa is really very ill and needs me. You must excuse me, my dear Mrs. Herman, but I must go immediately. I will ask my aunt to come to you, if you wish to see her."

Margaret placed Mrs. Herman's invitation back in her hand, and quickly left the room. She took the glass of milk from the table in the hall and passed rapidly up the stairs. In going to her father's room, she had to pass the chamber Miss Sargent always occupied when she visited them, and which had come to be spoken of in the house, as "Aunt Helen's room." As Margaret passed it now, the door was open, and she saw Miss Sargent sitting in a chair, facing the door, on the opposite side of a center table, on which one of her arms was resting, as she was looking straight before her, with an expression of the deepest sadness on her face. Something in the expression arrested Margaret's steps, pre-occupied as her mind was with thoughts of Rodger Latimer; she was alarmed by the look of anxious apprehension. She entered the room, placed the glass of milk on the table, and stood close by Miss Sargent, gazing intently into the eyes that were raised to hers. The tears gathered in Miss Sargent's eyes, until they flowed down her cheeks. Margaret's heart sank within her. Kneeling down by the weeping woman, she asked:

"What is it, Aunt Helen? Do you think papa is worse?"

"My poor, dear darling! how can you bear it?" said Miss Sargent, as she placed her arms around Margaret, who raised her head, put both of her hands against Miss Sargent's breast and leaned back so that she could look Miss Sargent in the face.

"Aunt Helen!" she cried, in a low, unnatural voice, full of anguish.

Miss Sargent said nothing, but placed both of her hands over Margaret's that were on her breast, with a loving pressure. After a moment's silence, Margaret exclaimed in the same low-pitched, unnatural voice:

"Tell me, it cannot be! Aunt Helen, it cannot be! is papa in danger?"

Miss Sargent made no reply, but gave a closer pressure of the hands as a fresh flow of tears fell from her eyes.

"Tell me, Aunt Helen!" cried Margaret, as her eyes suddenly grew large, and a look of terror came into her face. Miss Sargent again placed her arms around the girl, and drew her to her bosom, as she said:

"Oh! my darling! we shall have to let him go—he is passing from us."

"Not now! you don't mean now!" cried Margaret, springing to her feet.

"He may stay with us a day or two longer, or he may leave us in the morning," said Miss Sargent.

Margaret turned and quickly entered her father's silent chamber. The window shades were down to keep out the afternoon sun; Miss Bond sat by the bed where the dying man lay so still and white, that Margaret's heart ceased to beat for an instant, as she leaned over him. As her eyes become accustomed to the dim light of the room, and she gazed intently on his face, she could not see that it had changed since the last Saturday evening, when she, for the first time, noticed what she called an unnatural look on it. There was, perhaps, a look of little deeper restfulness, a more marked absence of her father's individual expression, and a more marked presence of a strange solemnity that struck her with awe, but that was all. Neither during the night nor through all of the next day could Margaret be persuaded to leave her father's bedside. She would catch a few moments of sleep as she leaned her head upon her hand, and she would drink the cup of beef tea that Miss Sargent gave her, but she only shook her head when either her Aunt Deborah or Miss Sargent begged her to lie on the lounge which they had rolled close to the bedside for her. She sat for hours holding her father's hand in hers, which never returned the loving pressure, but lay motionless in any position in which she placed it. Doctor Kean came on the noon train, but Margaret did not notice his entrance; she was oblivious of everything but the dear father lying so still before her. She asked no questions, she made no comments, but sat in silence holding the cold hand, with her eyes fixed upon the white face. As soon as the sun went down, Miss Bond raised the shades of the west windows. The sky was cloudless. At the horizon lay a broad band of soft olive hue, that melted into a purplish tint above, that threw a warm glow over the earth and sky, touching a few small clouds that floated in the air, midway toward the zenith, with a bright, delicate rose color. A soft twilight filled the chamber where in perfect silence, the four friends stood in the presence of mortality.

"Speak to him, Margaret," said Doctor Kean, in a

whisper. Margaret leaned her head close to her father, and in a low tone called:

"Papa! dear papa!" but there was no recognition of the voice that never before had been, by him, unheeded.

"Speak louder," said the doctor, as he stood by Margaret's side.

Margaret elevated her voice a little. "Dear papa! Papa?" Suddenly the old look flashed back in Professor McVey's face, the look of answering affection so dear to Margaret, and although the half open eyelids were not raised, a smile of perfect recognition parted the lips. Margaret was intensely excited, she grasped both of her father's hands in her own; it was but for an instant, a gray shadow fell upon the face, both the smile and expression of answering love passed, the breath stopped, and in holy majesty, like sculptured marble, lay the head of the good man on his pillow.

Margaret burst into a paroxysm of tears. Miss Sargent gently led her into her own room, where she placed her on her bed, lying down herself beside her. She tenderly took the suffering girl in her arms, and held her close. Margaret wept in silence. Miss Sargent also wept, but as she wept, her thoughts wandered off to the city church, down whose aisle at that hour, a bride was passing, on the arm of Rodger Latimer.

CHAPTER XXI

The last of July found Miss Sargent and Margaret located in a hotel on Mackinaw Island. Miss Sargent had suggested to Margaret, immediately after her father's funeral, that she and Miss Bond, and Margaret, go to Europe for a year, but she found that Margaret was not inclined to go so far from the old home. Then she persuaded her to spend a few weeks at Mackinaw. "It will build you up, and give you an appetite," she said to Margaret, "and you will sleep so well, you cannot help sleeping up there in that bracing atmosphere."

Miss Bond declined to accompany them, as she wished to renovate the house, and then she declared that she ought to go to New England and visit some cousins that she had not seen for years. Mackinaw proved to be all that Miss Sargent had predicted; the change of scene and the pure air, did Margaret good, and although she gained neither flesh nor color, the nervous tension of her system relaxed, and she slept naturally. She could not be called cheerful, but either the healthy surroundings or the influence of Miss Sargent's abiding serenity, induced a natural quietness of spirit, that was in pleasing contrast to the painful self-repression of the preceding winter.

After they had been there a week or more, Miss Sargent saw with pleasure, that Margaret was becoming interested in a group of young women, who had taken rooms at the hotel where they were stopping; there were six of them, and they evidently were teachers from Clinton. They all were merry, healthy girls, intent upon getting the greatest possible enjoyment out of a summer's vacation; there was neither a gloomy one, or discontented one among them.   Every morning brought them together on the piazza, in consultation regarding the plans for the day, and every evening brought them in from some excursion on the lake, or over the island, with arms full of ferns and grasses, or hands full of stones, picked up on the shore.   One morning Margaret was standing alone, leaning against one of the pillars of the piazza, and the young women were huddled around a pile of small luncheon baskets, discussing the best way of reaching a certain point they were desirous of visiting.   One of them glanced from time to time, at the pale girl, dressed in deep mourning, who was standing in lonely isolation, not far from the merry group ; then after a little, the heads of the six were drawn close together in a whispered consultation, which resulted in the young woman who had first observed Margaret, approaching her.

"We are going to walk part way around the island to-day, and take our luncheon on the rocks," she said, "and we all would be delighted to have you go with us, if you have no pleasanter plan for your day."   .

Margaret's face flushed with surprise, to be thus addressed by a stranger, but her native good sense, and kindness of heart, rightly interpreted the attention, and she immediately replied that she would be glad to go.   It took but a few moments for her to run up stairs for her hat, and to gain Miss Sargent's consent to the excursion, before she joined the girls, who were sitting on the steps of the piazza waiting for her.   The one who had first addressed Margaret, rose to meet her, and introduced herself as Jennie Hobert, a Kindergarten teacher in Clinton.   Margaret responded by giving her name, then Miss Hobert introduced her to each of her friends.   They started across the lawn, most of the girls proceeding in a half dancing way, keeping time to the strains of a popular opera, that was sang in a spirited style by several of the girls.

It was late in the afternoon when the party returned, wearied by the long walk they had taken, and Margaret went immediately to her room to lie down, only stopping a moment in Miss Sargent's room, which she had to cross to reach her own, to give her a kiss. After tea, as they were sitting alone in their room, on a small sofa they had rolled to the window, from which she could see the waves of the lake touched into brightness by the full moon, Miss Sargent asked:

"Have you had a pleasant day, dear?"

"Yes, a very pleasant one," Margaret replied, "those girls were a revelation to me."

"In what way?"

"You would not suppose, Aunt Helen, that every one of them is dependent upon herself, and that they all have earned, by their own teaching, all the money they have. They buy their own clothes, and they pay for this trip, which they are taking, out of money they have earned this last year: Miss Hobert told me so."

"I am not surprised; I have met such people before," replied Miss Sargent.

"But they are real ladies, they are well bred; did you notice how well dressed they are? Miss Hobert is positively beautiful, and she is well read, but I think she is of a good family."

"She looks like a gentlewoman," said Miss Sargent; "I saw her on the piazza, a few evenings ago, and inquired who she was. They are all fine looking girls; I'm not surprised by what you say of them."

"But I did not know," said Margaret, "that teachers in public schools were ever such accomplished ladies."

"O yes, they sometimes are," replied Miss Sargent;

"there are different types and different classes of teachers; probably these young women have been drawn together by a similarity of taste, and are all of refined natures."

"How happy they seem!" said Margaret. "It didn't seem to me to-day, as I listened to their laughter and gay talk, that any of them had ever had a sorrow or a sad hour."

"They are out for a good time," said Miss Sargent; "and if they have sorrows, they probably have the good sense to leave them at home."

"It cannot be a very serious sorrow that can be left behind," said Margaret, in a sad voice.

"My darling," said Miss Sargent, taking one of Margaret's hands in her own; "I do not wonder that the careless glee of those girls impressed you strongly; you look upon life out of a world of which they probably know nothing, at least I hope they do not." Miss Sargent was anxious that Margaret should talk with her about herself and her father. While she respected the sorrow of the young girl, she knew that her reticence tempted to a morbid state of mind. She was too well acquainted with the depths of the human heart to be surprised at Margaret's silence regarding Rodger Latimer, but she had hoped each day, since Professor McVey's burial, that Margaret would speak of the one so dear to them both, and that by the exchange of tender memories between them, her heart might find some relief. Only once had she approached the subject, and then Margaret had turned from it. But as they sat together that evening, when Margaret raised the hand that had clasped hers, and held it to her face; Miss Sargent thought that she would try again to break through the reserve that she feared might tend to a self-repression and introspection that would create an unhealthy mental condition.

"You say that all of those girls are teachers," resumed Miss Sargent; "may it not be that their occupation accounts somewhat for their happiness? I heard your dear father once say, that he considered constant employment one of the necessary conditions of happiness. How wise and just he always was! As I have been looking over these beautiful waves since we have been sitting here, my thoughts have been of him. This holy evening, with the clear sky, and few stars, and bright moon, and that far reaching lake, all seem in harmony with his beautiful life and with the beautiful world which I love to think of his now inhabiting." Margaret said nothing, and Miss Sargent continued: "The memory of such a life as you lived with your father is a rich heritage, my darling, how thankful I am that you have it; and then to know that we all shall be together again, think of it, Margaret!"

"Do you really believe that we shall all be together again?" asked Margaret.

"Certainly I do. How could any one believe in the justice of God, and not believe it? Existence would be a poor thing if this life were all; it would be a cause without an effect; a miserable defeat and failure."

"Oh, Aunt Helen! how I wish I could have your faith," cried Margaret; "but I cannot, I cannot; it's all a horrible tangle to me. I see no justice or love anywhere."

"How can you say so, Margaret, when you think of your father's beautiful life and beautiful death?"

"And you call his death beautiful!" exclaimed Margaret. "I think it was dreadful! It was dreadful to watch the separation of body and spirit. I tried to understand it as I looked at him—three days dying! The spirit trying to leave the body, to get away from matter,

As I sat there that last night, I thought of what Aunt Deb once told me of the birth of Mrs. Hitchcock's babe —perhaps she ought not to have talked to me of such things—it was horrible! A rent mother and a screaming child; that was the combination of spirit and matter, and there was my own dear father going through the separation of spirit and matter. He didn't know, couldn't speak to me, couldn't hear my voice, and *that* you call a beautiful death! It's all dreadful to me; the earth seemed determined not to let him go, and yet he was not here. What a—being dragged out of one world into another! And we have nothing to do with it all; neither birth nor death. Your God joins spirit and matter at a wailing birth, and separates them at a groaning death."

"Margaret! such talk is horrible!" cried Miss Sargent, taking both of Margaret's hands in hers, "how can you arraign Providence in this way? why will you refuse to look at facts in a reasonable, Christian way? My poor darling, sorrow has blinded your eyes."

"No, I think tears have washed my eyes clear at last, so that now I am able to see facts, and tell them from superstitions," replied Margaret bitterly. "What fancies I used to have!" she continued, leaning back on the sofa, as she drew her hands from Miss Sargent, and dropped them into her own lap, and gazed out of the window into the lovely night, without seeing one of its glories. "My life was full of beautiful fancies, and I peopled my future with them; but it's better to know the facts, whatever they may be, than to be cheated by fancies. I don't pretend to understand why any one thing is, as it is, nor do I see that any one knows much more about the affairs of this world than I do. Your George Macdonald, of whom you think so much, goes a great way round, and a great many ways across, but I can't see that he reaches any point, excepting that we don't know, and we must trust God. You ask how can any one believe in a just God, and not believe in a beautiful immortality? I don't like your logic. At last, I have come to look at facts steadily, no matter how hideous they may be, but as I said, I don't pretend to understand them. I don't see why that wind storm last night, didn't take some of the ugly trees down there, but it didn't, all of them stand just as firm as they did yesterday; but that perfect maple that we were admiring so much, was torn up by the roots, and even the branches rent off, as though done in a fury. As I looked at it this morning, it seemed like a dying creature, it lay there so broken and helpless, there was a sort of dying pathos in its twisted branches. And why is it, that one woman stands in her glory, regally crowned by love, and happiness, and every good thing this world can give, while another is cast down into utter darkness and desolation? Is it according to law, as scientists say? an inevitable consequence—consequence of what? superior beauty, grace, and intellect? or is it a reward of right doing? obedience, kindnesses done to others? The 'well done' of your just God, spoken positively, and loudly, so that all the world may hear and rejoice with the blest creature? This is all for development, perhaps you will say; develop one by sunshine and joy, and another by tears and suffering? I only speak of facts, I haven't any more theories, facts have destroyed all that I ever had."

Margaret ceased speaking, and Miss Sargent made no reply; both gazed silently into the night. Miss Sargent knew too well, that this was not the cry of a bereaved heart, for a dear departed one; but the outcry of a deceived and outraged heart, for a living love, that was more to it than all of the universe beside. She knew how great the anguish must be, that gave rise to such bitter words as Margaret had spoken, and she was startled by the subtle reach of the girl's thought, whose mind seemed to have been brought to a swift maturity by suffering, and she felt that it would be equally vain to offer argument or consolation, to such an one, so she sat speechless, as the moon passed up the clear sky, and the moving waters tossed the glancing beams from one wave to another. After half an hour had passed in this silence, Miss Sargent, who possessed an unusually sweet contralto voice, commenced to sing in a soft tone the beautiful lines of Lyle, beginning:

> "Abide with me! Fast falls the eventide
> The darkness deepens—Lord, with me abide!
> When other helpers fail, and comforts flee,
> Help of the helpless, O abide with me."

The silent night bent over the two women, as the words of prayerful entreaty, in a woman's voice, went up to the heavens. As Miss Sargent began the third stanza, she noticed tears glistening on Margaret's eyelashes, then she placed both of her arms around her, and drew her head to her bosom, and while she held her close, she continued singing the hymn, in a voice tremulous with tenderness. As she finished the last line—"In life, in death, O Lord abide with me;" Margaret was quietly weeping, holding Miss Sargent's hand again, against her cheek.

The next morning, Margaret was in a gentle mood. "Aunt Helen," she said with a sweet smile, and a wistful look in her blue eye, "I wish to talk with you about something, and I fear you will not agree with me."

"I cannot imagine that we would disagree on any subject of practical importance, my dear; what is it?"

"What am I to do next winter?" abruptly asked Margaret.

Miss Sargent was taken by surprise, but replied instantly: "You are to live with me and brother John, go in as much society as you choose, read, practice your music, perhaps assist me a little in my work for the Home of the Friendless, and the Orphan Asylum, if you will; and then in January, we'll go to Cuba for a while."

They were walking on the lake shore, and Margaret pressed the arm on which her hand rested. "All of that is just like you, Aunt Helen," she said, "but it will not do, I cannot live in Clinton. I can never go in society there, or anywhere else, and I cannot live an idle life, I may not have been of much use to any one in my past life but I have always had some little responsibility, and have always been busy. Now, all duties and employments seem taken out of my hands; I have nothing to do, and am utterly useless in every way. No, no, let me go on," entreated Margaret, as Miss Sargent, with a deprecating exclamation, placed her hand on Margaret's, that rested on her arm. "I must do something, I cannot live unless I do. You would have been surprised, to have heard those girls talk yesterday about their different schools, and matters relating to them. I got a glimpse into a strange and busy life, it seemed full of interest to them, and indeed, they seem to be doing a great deal of good. Miss Hobert is really a beautiful girl; she tells me she has a sister living in Edgewood, a widow, with one little girl, her name is Bray—the sister's name,—her husband was a dentist, and died two years ago; Miss Hobert is teaching a kindergarten, and Mrs. Bray is going to teach, as soon as she can get a situation. She has just finished her course of study, and has taught in a charity kindergarten, for a year. Now I talked the matter all over with Miss Hobert yesterday, and I would like to fit myself for a kindergarten teacher. I shall have to go to Glendale twice a week for instruction, and teach every morning in one of the charity kindergartens, to obtain a practical knowledge of the system. I always liked children; my mornings would be taken up with teaching, and my afternoons in going to Glendale, and my evenings in study, and in preparing the work for the next day. Miss Hobert told me all about it; she says there's a large class this year, and two lovely girls in it, girls of refinement and good breeding—they are from St. Louis, and have an uncle in Clinton, with whom they are staying. I could go back and forth between Clinton and Glendale with them. Now what do you think of my plan?"

"I can hardly give an opinion now, my dear, I know too little about kindergartens, nothing beside the theory. I never was in one in my life. The system is a good one. I have incidentally heard some talk between Mrs. Black and Mrs. Whiting regarding their kindergarten association, but I didn't pay much attention to it. I know Mrs. Black thinks the charity kindergartens are the most efficacious means of purifying and elevating the depraved masses, and she's a woman of good judgment, and wide experience. But, Margaret, do you really think that you ought to teach? What will your Uncle John say to such a scheme? I fear he never will consent to it."

"There is no ought about it," said Margaret. "I do not pretend that I am conscientiously moved to this, it's not a charitable scheme, it's a matter of judgment, purely selfish; I feel an absolute necessity of having some constant employment; what shall it be? I cannot go in society, I have no heart for it, what shall I do?"

"Well, I see no insuperable objection to your wishes," said Miss Sargent; "we will investigate the matter when we return."

"The class school opens at Glendale, the first of October," said Margaret, "but Aunt Helen, the charity kindergartens open somewhere from the first to the middle of September."

"We can go home whenever you choose," explained Miss Sargent. "I will see Mrs Black, she is the president of a kindergarten association, and can give me any information that we may need."

As Miss Sargent finished speaking, they overtook Miss Hobert, who was walking alone on the beach; Margaret presented her to Miss Sargent, who invited her to join them in their walk, and she soon left the two girls to continue their ramble together, while she returned to the hotel to write some letters. On her table in her room, among other letters, she found one from Rodger Latimer, dated the previous week at Cape May. It was addressed to her Clinton residence, and had been forwarded.

In it he said:

"* * * I have just heard of the death of Professor McVey, and I was shocked that my dear old friend could have been dead two months, and I have known nothing of it. I can only account for my ignorance, by the fact, that at the time of his death I was traveling, and frequently missed seeing the daily paper. I cannot grasp the fact that Professor McVey is gone, that the peaceful home in Edgewood is broken up. It always seemed some way. as though that house and its inmates were outside of the common everyday world; it was a hallowed spot, apart from the strife and heat of ordinary life. It seems this morning, as though half of a lifetime had passed since I was there, and it is really only one year. I knew few men whose personality stands out before me as vividly as does that of Professor McVey. With all of his childish simplicity of character, he possessed well defined opinions upon all matters, and where any moral principle was involved, expressed those opinions in such unequivocal language, that the halo of a saint seemed to surround him. I shall always regard it as one of the privileges of my life, that I had the friendship of such a man, and for years felt his benign influence on my character. I am grieved beyond the power of words to express, to think that I shall never see him again; I wish that I could have been near him, that I might have ministered to him in some way. I know that he was surrounded by devoted friends who left nothing undone, that there was no place vacant for me, by the side of the man who held my honored father in his arms, as he was dying. I know that I had forfeited my right to a place beside him, and it adds to the poignancy of my grief this morning, to feel that was so.   To you he has been dead more than two months, to me he died this morning, and I feel that I cannot have it so, and I did not even know that he was sick! How could it have been, that for weeks and months, he was surely descending into the grave, and I know nothing of it!   I seem to be wakening from a delirium, to find, that when I was not myself, something of great value passed out of my life, and was gone forever.   Pardon me, my dear Miss Sargent, for what may seem to you an unmanly expression of grief, but you cannot know the shock it was to me, to be suddenly told, in the midst of all this gaiety, that my friend had been dead for more than two months.   You and your brother were with him to the last, I know; how they all loved you! and I know the comfort you were to them.   I wish there was something that I might do for Miss Bond and Margaret, but I perfectly understand that there is nothing.   I know that all that man and woman can do, you and your brother will do.   May I ask you to write me something of our dear friend's illness and death? and of the welfare of Margaret and her aunt?   All that I could learn was, that he gradually failed in health, through the three months preceding the end."

The letter closed by saying:

"I suppose we shall return to Clinton, sometime in September, or October."

There was no other reference than this indirect one to his wife.   For a long time, after she finished reading the letter, Miss Sargent was lost in thought; she seemed to have forgotten the other letters, that lay on the table before her.   After awhile, she said aloud, as she placed the letter back in its envelope: "Poor fellow, he always had a warm heart, Margaret must not see this."   And she slipped the letter underneath the letters and paper, in her traveling writing desk.

CHAPTER XXII

After Miss Sargent and Margaret returned home from Mackinaw, Miss Sargent made the inquiries regarding kindergartens that she promised she would and was ready to receive Margaret as she came into her room, early one morning, on one of the last days of September.

"Are you not well, dear?" she asked as she kissed her, "you do not look very merry in anticipation of your new life."

"I don't feel at all merry, this is a necessity to me, Aunt Helen, not a pleasure. Did you see Mrs. Black?"

"Yes, and she says you will have to spend two afternoons in each week, with the class in Glendale, under the care of the principal of the training class. I went to the Union Depot, and got a time table of that division and your train does not reach the city, from Glendale, until five o'clock. You must pass the night here, when you go out to Glendale, it will be too late for you to go home, at least when the days are shorter."

"Oh no, it will not," replied Margaret, "George will meet me at the depot, and I shall not be alone at the Union Depot, for quite a number of girls will have to return to the city on that train."

"You don't suppose for a moment, do you, Margaret, that I would hear of your going alone, from one depot to another, at that time in the evening?"

"Why certainly I do, why not?"

"You don't know much about this city, child, that depot is located in one of the worst parts of the city; it isn't safe for women to be there alone, unless in broad daylight. Either John or I will meet you every evening."

"Now, Aunt Helen, if I go into this kindergarten, I propose doing it as other girls do. If you think it is an unwise thing for me to attempt, and are going to feel uncomfortable about it, and feel that you must guard me, and be with me, I will abandon the whole project. I could not permit Uncle John to feel that he was compelled to meet me at the depot; just think of you, and Uncle John, feeling that you must come with your carriage for me twice a week! I cannot have that, I'll give the whole thing up."

"No, not yet. I'll be frank with you Margaret, I have a growing conviction that you ought not to undertake it, but it is not a conviction founded on knowledge. Let us go and look into it somewhat, neither you nor I know anything of kindergartens. Mrs. Black talks eloquently of taking the little waifs out of the street, and snatching them from destruction—and every word she says is true —but on the other hand, Doctor Kean says that kinder-garten teaching requires more nervous force than any other kind of teaching, and frequently brings on nervous exhaustion. He says—and there is a great deal of sense in it—that only girls of firm health should undertake it, that it is no place for a young girl of delicate nervous organization. But let us go on, and see something for ourselves. Lee is at the door waiting for us."

Margaret rose to her feet in consternation. "You are not going to that charity school in your carriage, are you?" she asked.

"Why not?" inquired Miss Sargent.

"Pardon me, it is selfish," replied Margaret, "but as I shall always go on the street cars, I thought we would go that way this morning."

"Margaret! go up to 900 Leek street, on the cars, and walk a block in that region!"

"Why, I shall do it every morning." said Margaret.

"Indeed, you'll not! you'll go every morning in the carriage, Lee'll drive you."

"But Aunt Helen—" began Margaret in a broken voice.

Miss Sargent suddenly changed her manner.

"Well, on the whole, Margaret," she said, in a quiet, acquiescing tone, "we better go, as you say, on the street cars; I have never been on them, on that street, but can find our way."

The carriage was ordered back to the stable, and Miss Sargent and Margaret walked four blocks, and took the car on Leek street. Before the conductor notified them that they had reached their destination, Margaret began to wonder how many miles they had traveled. The car stopped a short distance from the crossing. "Can't get any nearer," said the conductor, "we're blocked here, that school's just around that corner, four doors to the right."

Miss Sargent and Margaret alighted from the car, into the muddy street, and picked their way to the sidewalk. They were near the corner of Leek and Forty-fifth street, which street they had to cross, but there was at the crossing of the two streets, one of those tangles of wagons and omnibuses, that frequently occur on crowded streets, and a policeman was endeavoring to clear the way. Miss Sargent and Margaret were compelled to wait until a passage could be opened, surrounded as they were, by a jostling crowd of rough and dirty men. Forty-fifth street was the direct route between two depots, in different parts of the city, and about thirty German emigrants who were passing through the city, had reached the Leek street crossing, just as the stoppage occurred. They did not understand what the difficulty was, and they seemed to fear that they were in some kind of danger. There arose profanity, and threats, and loud confused cries on every side. A giant of a man, not many steps away, was particularly excited. He swung his arms, and poured out volleys of oaths in his native tongue. A lad in his teens stood near him, loaded down with long bags, full of some sort of stuff. The boy was pale and thin, and his long, damp hair clung to the sides of his face, in a way that gave him a wild, half-crazy look. The giant seemed to have some authority over the lad. Miss Sargent, who understood German well, told Margaret that he was the boy's father—and he evidently was displeased with something the boy had done, or had not done, and was vociferating fiercely over him. The boy was frightened, and replied in pleading tones, but the wrath of the man rapidly rose, . and soon got beyond his control. He raised his great foot, with its heavy shoe, and kicked the boy in the stomach. The brutal blow caused the sickly looking lad to bend over nearly double, as groans of pain broke from his lips. Miss Sargent had fast hold of Margaret's hand, who, as she witnessed the cruelty of the beastly man, turned deathly white, as her eyes opened wide in horror.

"Oh! Aunt Helen!" she cried, as she clutched Miss Sargent's hand, "don't let him! do something for him, do help that boy!"

"Be quiet, Margaret," replied Miss Sargent, "we can do nothing, but get ourselves safely out of this, if we can."

"Speak to the policeman, Aunt Helen—see! he is going to strike him again. Oh! don't let him!"

The angry man had crowded the boy against a flight of rickety old steps that led into the second story of one of the high brick buildings that was near, against which he pushed him violently, as he railed at him in a coarse, loud voice. The frightened, half-starved looking boy, had dropped his bags, and put up his hands to shield his head from anticipated blows. Margaret turned away, white to the tips of her lips, Miss Sargent looked around her, scanning the buildings, to see if she could discover any place into which they might slip, and hide themselves, until the policeman had succeeded in opening the way. But it was a vain search. Every third building was a saloon; and gambling dens, and dance houses were on every side. Right in front of her was a place called: "Bob's Exchange," over the next door was a sign that read: "New Old Clothes," on the other hand was, "Cleveland Pool Rooms." She looked across the way, and her eye met, "De Steffano's Italian Liquors." As she abandoned all thought of seeking a refuge in one of the buildings, from the crowding, pushing, swearing mass about them, a tap on a window close by, attracted her attention. She and Margaret turned simultaneously; as they looked toward the window, Miss Sargent threw her arm about Margaret's shoulders, and quickly turned her around, so as to prevent her, if possible, from seeing the repulsive object that stood in a window, that reached almost to the floor. He was a middle aged man, broad and fat, with bleared eyes, and red, swollen nose and lips. His red flannel shirt was open, disclosing a purple throat and hairy chest. His trousers came only half way up over his obese abdomen, around which they were fastened by an old striped suspender, that was used as a girth. He paid no attention to Miss Sargent, but his eyes were fixed on Margaret, and as she turned, when he tapped on the glass, he leered at her in a frightful way. Miss Sargent's first thought was, to shield Margaret from the knowledge of the existence of such an animal; but as she looked in her face, as she wheeled her about, she saw that it was an unnecessary precaution on her part. Girlish purity was its own shield; the obscene creature was to Margaret, a dirty, ill-dressed man, and nothing more. She recognized no danger, she felt no fear. At that moment, the mass commenced to move across the street that had been cleared by the policeman, who stood on the crossing swinging his club, to keep the horses back, until the pedestrians could pass. As Miss Sargent, tightly holding Margaret's arm, hastened over, there came into her mind some lines that she had read somewhere: " A man with a foul mind, might go through heaven and think it vile, while a saint would walk unharmed, save for pity, through the nether world." But as she looked on Margaret's delicate face, she shuddered to think of the danger such a girl would unconsciously encounter, were she compelled to pass alone daily, through such a locality. A few steps from the corner, the words: "Charity Kindergarten," painted in black letters on a pine board, that leaned against the house, beside a closed door, that opened from a narrow platform raised a few inches above the sidewalk, indicated that they had reached the place of their search.

The upper half of the door was of glass, through which as Miss Sargent knocked for admittance, they were seen by a young woman in the room, who immediately opened the door for them. The room was about sixty feet long, and eighteen or twenty wide. The ceiling was high, and it, as well as the walls, was dark with dirt and smoke. On the walls, hung at intervals, were wreaths woven of evergreen, and red and white paper flowers; between the wreaths were placed mottoes in gilt, and different colored paper letters, pasted on pasteboard. Some of the mottoes were taken from the Scriptures, and read: " Love one another," " Bear one another's burdens." The word " Love," which was Froebel's universal motto,

was pasted on the wall in several places, surrounded by
chains made of red and white paper links, that had been
woven together by the children. Down the length of
the room were placed seven low tables surrounded by
children's chairs, small wooden chairs with low backs.
There were ten chairs around each table. About one-
half of the chairs were occupied by children, and a group
of twenty-five or thirty girls and boys,. from three to
eight years of age, were standing together at the lower
end of the room. They evidently had just come in from
the street. A few of them wore clean clothes, and had
clean hands and faces, but most of them were dirty and
ill clad. Two of the teachers, girls of twenty or more,
were moving among the children of the group, and taking
first one and then another, to a sink in a corner of the
room, where there was a water faucet, and a large tin
wash dish, a piece of soap, and several crash towels. The
hands and face of each dirty child were thoroughly
washed, the hair combed and brushed, and long clean
aprons, made of checked white and blue gingham, were put
on the little girls, and on some of the boys, who seemed
pleased with the fresh garment. But others of the boys
obstinately refused "to be made girls of," as they said,
and were permitted to take their places at the tables, in
the ragged, dirty clothes they wore from home. The
director of the school was a Miss West, a girl of twenty-
five, robust and healthy looking. She had broad shoulders,
a large waist, coarse black hair, a round, pleasant face and
great composure of manner. There were five young
looking girls, and a pale, large-eyed woman, of thirty
perhaps, who seemed to rank as teachers. Margaret to
her delight, saw Miss Hobert midway in the room, and
immediately went to her. Miss Hobert introduced the
pale woman to Margaret, as her sister, Mrs. Bray, who
lived in Edgewood.

"Do you teach here?" asked Margaret of Miss Hobert.

"No, I'm engaged in a private kindergarten, but I taught here two years ago, and I'm visiting this school to-day, as we teachers say. I have come to spend the day with sister; my school don't open until next month." As one of the teachers seated herself at an old looking piano, and commenced to strike the chords in a slow manner, Miss Hobert added: "They're going to begin now; let me get you some chairs, I'll come back after a little."

As soon as the music commenced, the children seated themselves around the tables, each table being filled by those near the same age. One, called the "baby table," was surrounded by little ones not more than three years old. At each table was a teacher. Miss West seemed to be responsible for two tables, at which were the older children. A teacher seated herself in one of the small chairs, at each table, and they all, teachers and pupils, bowed their heads upon their hands, that were clasped, and rested on the table before them. The girl at the piano continued striking the chords, until all of the little ones were in their places, then she left the piano, seated herself at her table, and dropped her head upon her hands. When the room was perfectly quiet, Miss West, with bowed head, commenced to repeat in a low devotional tone, in which she was joined by all in the room, these words:

> "Now before we work to-day,
> We must not forget to pray
> To God, who kept us through the night,
> And woke us with the morning light.
>
> "Help us, Lord, to love Thee more,
> Than we ever loved before,
> In our work, and in our play,
> Be Thou with us, through the day. Amen."

During the repeating of this prayer, the efforts of the teachers seemed to be directed to the keeping of each

15 Rodger Latimer's Mistake.

little head bowed in a devout attitude: and it was a hard task. Some of the stupidest looking children leaned their foreheads immovably upon their clasped hands, but most of them raised their heads every few seconds, to have them pushed down again, by the hand of the teacher placed upon the top of the head. Her hand flew around the table in its soft, but determined pressure upon the uprising heads, she and the children all of the time repeating their morning prayer. The baby table, naturally enough, was least under control. In spite of the teacher's ability, the baby heads could not be kept down. Some of them pushed her hand away from their heads, when she attempted to hold them still, and one struck her in the face. Through this half amusing, and half pathetic scene, Margaret had kept herself in becoming composure, until one of the babies slipped out of its chair, and shot under the table, and a boy seated at an adjoining table, who was looking at her, cried out: " Miss West, look at that kid under the shelf." This compelled her to cover her mouth with her handkerchief to conceal her laughter.

After these opening devotions, the children, at the several tables, were given either sets of blocks, colored worsted balls, packages of splints, or long narrow strips of glazed, colored paper; out of which materials they were directed to build houses, make fences, and braid, or weave mats. They were questioned as to the color, form and number of articles with which they played, but to convey to the children's mind the information which the teachers were required to impart in this way, did not seem one-half as difficult as keeping order among them. Miss West would come, from time to time, and stand beside Miss Sargent for a few moments, and give explanations of their system, and dilate upon its benevolent aspects. She did not know that Margaret anticipated joining the class of that year, but supposed that the ladies were only curious visitors. Miss Sargent had said to Margaret, as they entered the room: "We better not say anything about your wishing to teach; let us find out what there is to be done, before we speak of that." Miss Sargent, when talking with Miss West, dwelt only upon the generalities of Frœbel's theory, but when Miss Hobert sat by her, she asked all manner of questions. All conversation had to be carried on in a loud voice, as the children at the various tables created a great deal of noise. Some were laughing loudly, and some talking to their mates, and some calling, "Teacher, teacher," at the top of their voice, and there was scarcely five consecutive minutes, in which some child did not scream out, either in pain, fright, or anger, because it was struck, or its hair was pulled by some other child. The teachers were constantly busy walking around their tables, bending over first one child, then another, as they sat in their little chairs, soothing, reproving, and instructing, as the case might require, and not seeming to expect any very near approximation to either order, or silence.

"Did you teach in this room, Miss Hobert?" asked Miss Sargent.

"Yes, a year," replied Miss Hobert.

"Did you find it pleasant?"

"No, I did not, but I learned a great deal."

"What did you find unpleasant about it?" asked Miss Sargent.

Miss Hobert hesitated a moment, then replied: "The personal contact with these children is not pleasant; I did not like to wash them, or touch their heads."

"But were you compelled to do that?" interrogated Margaret.

"Certainly I was; didn't you see the teachers washing them, when you first came in?"

"Y-e-s," said Margaret, "but I did not suppose that was one of their duties."

"It has to be done; Margaret, and who is to do it if not the teachers?" asked Miss Sargent.

"Certainly," said Margaret; "but they are dirty, their heads must be dirty," she continued, turning to Miss Hobert.

"Dirty! they are absolutely filthy, and some of them diseased. Look at that boy's head, close to sister; you cannot know how hard this has been for her." Miss Hobert looked very sad as her eyes rested upon the pale, tired face of her widowed sister, who was stooping beside a boy at her table in order to show him how to weave the mat he was working on. His head was a mass of half-healed sores, his eyelids were inflamed, and the corners of his mouth were full of pimples. Margaret began to notice the children individually; hitherto she had glanced over them collectively.

"What an unhappy looking lot of children," she said.

"Yes, and worse than that," added Miss Sargent. "Such an intellectually and morally mutilated lot."

'Where do they come from? where do they live? whose children are they?" asked Margaret. "I did not know that there were any such children in this world."

"They come out of the rooms, above and back of the saloons around here," answered Miss Hobert.

"And they are the children of such men and women as surrounded us out there on the sidewalk an hour ago," added Miss Sargent.

"But how do these colored children get in here?" asked Margaret.

"They have the same right as white ones," replied Miss Hobert, "and really they are our brightest and cleanest children.   See that one at the second table; he's the most promising child at that table."

" He's an average negro child for any place," said Miss Sargent, "but those white children are far from an average. He looks healthy, and is not deformed, his eyes are bright and natural, but excepting his eyes there's hardly a healthy eye at that table."

"These poor children all seem to have something the matter of their eyes," said Miss Hobert. " They are cross-eyed or have inflamed eyes, are blind in one eye, or half blind in both."

A loud yell from the colored boy interrupted her. Miss Sargent started, and Margaret sprang forward, but seeing that neither Miss Hobert nor any one beside herself was disturbed in the least, she resumed her seat.

"Why don't you punish that boy?" she asked of Miss Hobert. "I saw it all, and the colored child did nothing to him, but that young brute fixed his mean looking eyes on him, then he slowly shook his fist, as though weighing it, and deliberately struck him on his back with all of his strength.   Why don't you go and see about it?"

"We never interfere with each other's tables, Miss McVey; the teachers don't like it.   Miss West is the only one who ever makes a suggestion to any teacher regarding one of her pupils. Each teacher is responsible for her own table.   That is a dreadful boy, his name's John Navigator; he's a brutal fellow, as you say, and he don't seem to improve."

" He looks like an embryo butcher," said Miss Sargent, as her eye rested upon the boy who had given the unprovoked blow.   He had a large frame, square shoulders, bony hands and a pyramidal-shaped head, with a heavy jaw for base.   His eyes were small and deep set under his receding forehead.   "He don't seem to have any compunctions of conscience for what he has done," added Miss Sargent.

"Conscience!" exclaimed Miss Hobert. "I suppose he has one and that it is our business to find it and cultivate it, but he has been here over a year and has evinced thus far nothing but a stolid brute nature."

"Do you notice much improvement in the children?" asked Miss Sargent.

"Yes, a great deal," replied Miss Hobert. 'Do you see that boy at the third table, he is standing up now, with those trousers made of light brown at the back, and white in front? His name is Isaiah Younger; isn't it a queer name? He was a perfect imp a year ago. He would lie, swear and fight, we could do nothing with him for months, and now he is gentle and obedient, and rarely speaks a wrong word."

"He looks badly born," said Miss Sargent. "What a missile that John Navigator will make in the hands of some anarchist in a few years," she pursued, looking at John, whose dull red eyes, as they were fixed on the colored boy he had struck, were full of a sort of savage gratification in the boy's suffering, that was shown by his restrained sobs.

"What is the matter with that little girl sitting off there all alone?" asked Margaret, indicating by her gaze, a scrofulous looking child, with thin bow legs, and a bloated body. A teacher had placed the little girl in a chair set against the wall, away from all of the tables, and she was screaming with wide open mouth, as the tears ran down her face.

"She has been naughty," said Miss Hobert, "perhaps she has quarreled with the other children. If the children are not good we punish them by making them sit by themselves; in that way they learn to be kind and unselfish with their mates."

"Why don't you make her stop crying so loud?"

" Oh, let her cry it out, she will stop herself, when she finds it does no good." Turning to Miss Sargent, Miss Hobert continued: "You see our system is one of natural retribution. Froebel says: 'The conquest of self-seeking egoism, is the aim of education.' I suppose he means to teach the Bible principle, of love one another. When children learn that selfishness does not pay, they are willing to do what love and justice require."

" It will be a long time before the world at large can be made to believe that selfishness don't pay," said Miss Sargent.

" Yes, I suppose so," replied Miss Hobert, "and it must be a long time before the class to which these children belong, are actuated by unselfish motives, and are ruled, or rather, rule themselves, by principles of justice, acknowledging the rights of others."

"There you have it, Miss Hobert; if this kindergarten system can instil correct ideas of individual rights into the children of this class, and prove to them that happiness can only come to them by respecting these rights; and train them into an observance of other's rights, you will more than one-half settle questions that vex our statesmen and philanthropists."

"That is Froebel's idea—self-culture—not restriction and punishment, as much as self-control, and the natural setting back upon the offender, of the result of his actions."

"May I go close to those tables, Miss Hobert?" asked Margaret.

" Yes, let us go." The two girls walked slowly round each table, and Margaret frequently stopped and spoke to some child that turned in its chair to stare at her. A little girl with very watery blue eyes, and an almost imbecile expression of face, laid hold of her dress skirt. Margaret reached out her hand to pat the child's hand, but when she saw the half-healed ulcers on the little hand, a qualm passed over her, and she gently released her dress and passed on.   One child with large black eyes, but a sadly pinched mouth Miss Hobert addressed as May Rubenstine, and the little girl that sat next, as Becky Rosenthal.

" Are they Jews?" asked Margaret.

"Yes, and sharp ones," replied Miss Hobert.   They made a circuit of all the tables, and Margaret returned to her seat with such a languid step, and face so full of sympathetic pain, that Miss Sargent was alarmed.   Margaret's usually pale face had been of an almost ghastly hue since she beheld the distressing scene between the German boy and his father, but as she sat down in her chair, when she returned from her walk around the children's tables, she looked sick and faint.   Miss Sargent rose, and looked at her watch.

"I think it is time to leave," she said.

"I wish you could stay until the children go on the circle," said Miss Hobert; "if you have never seen them, it might interest you."

"Let us stay, Aunt Helen," said Margaret.

"Very well," replied Miss Sargent, who had made up her mind that it would be well for Margaret to stay until she was satisfied with her investigation, "but is it impossible to have a little fresh air in this room? this atmosphere is positively foul."

"We find great difficulty in having pure air, with so many of these ill-kept children in a room.   I will see if the back windows are open."

As Miss Hobert went down the room, her sister, Mrs. Bray, passed Miss Sargent, leading a crying child by the hand.   It was a nice looking little girl, and she was sobbing as though her heart would break.

"What is the matter?" asked Miss Sargent.

"She's crying for her mother," replied Mrs. Bray. "She's a new scholar, and feels a little strange. I'm going to take her home. She doesn't belong to my table, but I know where she lives, it is back of a saloon of the lowest kind. Her father keeps the saloon, and there is no reaching her mother's room, without going through the saloon. It's a fearful place for any woman to enter, but it is better that I go, than the young girl at whose table the child belongs." Mrs. Bray passed out of the door with the child. In five minutes she returned, and stopped beside Miss Sargent's chair to say:

"It was well Miss Nichols did not take Molly Bloss home. When I was coming back through the saloon, a half drunken man placed himself right in my way, and asked me to drink with him."

"Was it Miss Nichols' duty to take the child home?" asked Miss Sargent.

"Yes." Miss Sargent and Margaret looked into each other's eyes. "They usually remain until we close at noon," continued Mrs. Bray, "but occasionally we have to take one home." She passed on to her table, holding her hand to her head as though it pained her. The colored boy spoke to her, and she dropped into a chair by his side, to give him the assistance that he needed in some paper braiding that he was trying to do. But she was interrupted in this, and the employment of all of the children stopped, by one of the teachers, a Miss Lane, going to the piano, and playing a lively march. All of the children in the room rose, and marched in single file onto a painted circle that was marked out on the floor in the back part of the room. It was nearly the diameter of the width of the room, and there was an inner circle of less diameter. Both circles were crossed, at right angles, by broad painted bands, that cut them into quarters. The children arranged themselves on the outer circle, and to the music of the piano went through evolutions of marching and simple calisthenic exercises, that brought into play both hands and feet. They all joined hands at one time, forming two circles, and by graceful, rapid movements, formed what they called a basket figure. At another time, twenty of them stooped to the floor, and hopped about as birds, and were fed with imaginary seed, scattered from the aprons of the teachers, who moved among them, keeping step to the music, with their aprons gathered up in one hand, while with the other, they went through the motion of scattering seed broadcast. This amusement seemed to be highly enjoyed by the children, who clapped their hands—mostly out of time, and capered around contrary to all rules. The teachers would place them back on the circle, when they danced off, and instruct them to keep all their movements in time with the music. The lively music must have been heard in the street, for as the door was shaken violently, Miss Sargent looked around, to see eight or ten heads close together at the glass in the door, some belonging to boys just tall enough to look through the lower panes, and others to boys who must have been twelve and sixteen years old. They were having their own fun outside of the door, and danced upon the doorstep and knocked their toes against the door, while they tapped upon the glass with their fingers, keeping time with the piano with both feet and hands. Miss West glanced toward them, but paid no other attention to their presence, or their shaking the door for admittance. Margaret concluded in her own mind, that this outside participation must be of daily occurrence, as it attracted so little attention, and she wondered why the boys were not admitted to play with the children on the circle. One little fellow, who wore very short trousers, and very heavy shoes, but had on no stockings, went off and danced by himself in a corner. His little legs flew in a double shuffle, with such rapid accuracy, that one could but think that in his own home he had seen dancing of that kind well done. Every few minutes she would stop, and rub first the back of one of his little legs, then the other, with the upper part of his heavy shoes, with a gratified expression of face, as though congratulating himself on his own proficiency. After fifteen or twenty minutes of these varied exercises, the music changed from its lively strains, to a popular religious air usually called, " Jesus loves me," and the children, under the leadership of their teachers, commenced to march around the circle singing:

> "Jesus loves me! this I know,
> For the Bible tells me so.
> Little ones to Him belong,
> They are weak, but He is strong.
> Yes, Jesus loves me,
> Yes, Jesus loves me,
> Yes, Jesus loves me,
> The Bible tells me so."

This appeared to be the closing of the circle exercises, preparatory to marching the children to their seats. While engaged in the lively exercises of calisthenics and games, each little one's attention was engrossed by its own bodily exercises, but when they came to the monotonous marching, they seemed to have thought and energy to devote to each other, and all around the ring, as they were keeping step in their marching to the religious song they were singing, two-thirds of the children began to tease the child in front of it. One boy took hold of the braids of hair hanging from the head of a girl in front of him and

twitching them, drove her as he would a horse.   A little
girl caught the skirt of the dress of a still smaller girl in
front of her and drawing it so tightly that the child could
not step, tripped her up on her nose.   Wo to the boy
who had a button in sight on the back of his clothes!   It
was seized by the one behind him, and twisted and
twitched until the thread gave way and it came off of
the garment, or the wearer was pulled by the force
applied, out of his place on the circle.   Apron strings and
suspenders were laid hold of wherever seen, but the
loose hair hanging around the necks of the girls was the
most convenient source of fun and torture, and not many
heads escaped.   Big boys pulled the hair of big girls,
and girls of the same size laid hold of each other's flying
locks with a playful and half diabolical fury.

"Seems to me these children pull hair to the tune of
'Jesus loves me,'" said Margaret to Miss Sargent, as cries
arose from some of the smaller children.   Very few
uttered any complaints if they were hurt; they kept it to
themselves and struggled to retaliate.   At last the sixty
children were seated again around their little tables and
Margaret expressed the wish to go home.   Miss West
urged her to remain until noon.

"These children have a luncheon in about half an
hour," she said; "perhaps it might interest you to see
that."

"Thank you," replied Miss Sargent, as she glanced at
Margaret's pale face.   "I think we must return.   May I
ask you, Miss West, if all pupils studying kindergarten
are obliged to teach in schools similar to this?   Are they
compelled to do it, I mean, in order to fit themselves as
teachers?"

"Yes, they must teach for one year in some one of the
schools under the direction of the Froebel Association.

We regard this as one of our best and pleasantest schools. It is in a demoralized locality, but after all the children compare favorably with those in any of the charity schools."

"And there are no schools in which girls can gain what you call practical knowledge, excepting these?"

"No, not any that I know of. Some girls teach during the morning for one year, and some for two years, but they usually finish the course in one year, and then after that they are paid a salary if they take a position. Now, there are more teachers than positions, although I teach in two schools."

" Is that possible!" exclaimed Miss Sargent. " You must have perfect health."

"I have splendid health," replied Miss West. "I did double duty the year I studied, and now I teach in two kindergartens. I stay here until half-past twelve, and then at two I have a school three miles from here."

"I am surprised that you have a nerve left in your body. I should think that you would be insane," said Miss Sargent.

"That is just what enables me to do it; I never had a nerve in my body; I don't know what nerves are," said Miss West, with a pleasant smile. "I never lose an hour's sleep; I never have a pain of any kind; nor do I ever feel tired."

"There is certainly then, a beautiful fitness between you and your profession," said Miss Sargent, with an answering smile, as she extended her hand in farewell. "This is a much needed mission, and I am thankful that it has so capable a leader."

Miss Sargent placed Margaret in the corner of the Leek street car, when they entered it, and seated herself between her and a rough looking man who was holding a tub of paint in his lap. As they alighted, forty minutes afterward, at the cross street that led near to Miss Sargent's residence, Margaret said:

"I'll go on to the depot, Aunt Helen, I shall be in time for the 12:30 train." Her voice plainly indicated her nervous exhaustion and mental depression.

Miss Sargent took firm hold of her hand. "Don't talk now, Margaret," she said; "you must come home with me, so please don't say a word, dear."

Margaret walked on, too tired and miserable to have a preference, or make a decision. Miss Sargent led her to her own chamber, as soon as they entered the house, and took off her bonnet, and jacket, and dress, with her own hands; and after enveloping her in one of her own—much too large—bedroom gowns, she placed her on the bed to rest. She leaned down and kissed the pale, spiritless face on the pillow, as she said:

"You are tired out, Margaret, that's all; it has been a hard day for you. Go to sleep, dear; a nap and a cup of tea will bring you out all right."

"I don't feel as though I should ever sleep again, those poor, miserable children will haunt me as long as I live," said Margaret, as she closed her eyes, and a shiver ran over her frame. "What a dreadful world this is; I never dreamed there was such misery in it."

"I ought not to have permitted you to go there, Margaret, I see it now; you're not strong enough for such a sudden outlook on the sufferings of that class. I have seen a great deal of them, but the sight of those unfortunate children affected me very much."

"What has God made this world for? It is dreadful!" said Margaret, opening her eyes that looked like those of a pursued animal. "How can He let such things be!"

"Remember, Margaret, 'What I do thou knowest not now; but thou shalt know hereafter.'"

"If He knows Himself, He knows more than we can even guess at," said Margaret.

"It is to be hoped He does. No doubt, Margaret, if we knew all that God knows, we should do just as He does. But, darling, we will talk it all over after you have had a nap and something to eat; you must have the nap first to quiet your nerves." While Miss Sargent was talking she had drawn down the window shades and had wet the end of a towel and laid it on Margaret's forehead and eyes. "Now I will lie on the lounge here," she said, "where I always take my noon nap, and let us both go to sleep for an hour."

Margaret felt very sure that she could not go to sleep, but in less than fifteen minutes the hot eyes were closed in slumber, and the excited pulse was falling to its normal pace.

An hour and a half afterward, Margaret was sitting in a large chair, still wrapped in Miss Sargent's gown, that crossed over her breast from shoulder to shoulder, and had the sleeves turned up half way to the elbow. The chair was drawn close to a table on which Miss Sargent had ordered luncheon served.

"It sounds selfish, Aunt Helen," said Margaret, "but if Uncle John was at home we couldn't have this cosy luncheon up stairs here in your room."

"He's having a good time somewhere," replied Miss Sargent.

"Don't this seem like heaven?" said Margaret, looking around the room, as she held the leg of a broiled bird between her thumb and finger. "How pretty your curtains are! and your pictures never looked so beautiful. What a horrid old room that was! Just smell this tea! Aunt Helen," exclaimed Margaret, as she held her face over the steaming cup, "this is my second cup, and I shall want another, I know."

"Well, it is here, darling," replied Miss Sargent, as she took the lid off of the little teapot that was over a spirit-lamp in front of her, and stirred the leaves with a teaspoon. She was delighted to see Margaret looking even one-half cheerful again. She could hardly keep her eyes off of the wan face opposite to her, or the tears from her eyes as she gazed on it.

"I must go home on the four o'clock train," said Margaret. "Auntie Deb will wonder what has become of me."

"I telegraphed her that you were here, and would like to have George meet you at the 5:30 train; was that right, dear?"

"Perfectly; how thoughtful you are of everybody, Aunt Helen; if I wasn't tangled up so, in this big gown of yours, I'd go round there and hug you," said Margaret, with a smile on her thin face, that Miss Sargent thought made her look even more pitiful than tears.

"No matter, dear, I'll take the hug on faith, until you have finished your tea." And she smiled, with such a world of love in her benign face, that Margaret exclaimed:

"I declare, Aunt Helen, you *are* a handsome woman! I wish you would go to the glass and look at yourself."

Miss Sargent laughed aloud. "It almost paid us," she said, "to go to that Leek street kindergarten, we enjoy so much more the pretty things in our own home, after seeing that unlovely room; you must have had Miss Lane in your mind's eye just now, as you were looking at me." It was an unfortunate speech, Miss Sargent instantly saw; a shadow fell upon Margaret's face, which she could not drive off, turn the conversation any way she would, Margaret was evidently pre-occupied with sad thoughts.

"There's no use dodging the point, Aunt Helen," she said after a little, "I cannot teach in that kindergarten."

"As a matter of course you can't; it would be madness to think of it, it would kill you."

"I am so sorry for those teachers," said Margaret.

"I don't know why you should say that," rejoined Miss Sargent. "Mrs. Bray is certainly an unhappy looking woman, those other teachers looked well and happy."

"Miss West did, I'm sure," said Margaret.

"She must be a very strong girl," added Miss Sargent, "but you and she resemble each other, about as much as brother John resembles a pugilist. I wish this world had more like her. Such physically strong people, of tough mental fiber, are specially adapted to do such work. Their surroundings don't seem to make them uncomfortable. Give such people plenty to eat, warmth, and time to sleep, and they will have an even sort of happiness, put them wherever you will."

"What a pity," said Margaret, "that every girl who lives isn't of that organization."

"I don't think so," replied Miss Sargent. "When I look into the heart of an ascension lily, and my soul follows its leading, out beyond bread, and shelter, and fuel, into a world as real as this material one, but where there are no material needs, I feel that the lily has as true a practical use, as has a peck of corn. I have a great respect for these strong, practical people, made of serviceable clay; but in this practical age, and time of great need for such people, don't let us forget that it was God himself that made other types, and that He has use for them. That charity kindergarten work is a peculiarly trying work, and it will probably be done by two classes of workers. One is a class of saints, that in hoars of solitary prayer and reflection, learn lessons of self-renunciation and fortitude, that enable them to devote themselves to the service of others, regardless of circumstances or surroundings—and there is a larger number of these saints, both men and women, than is generally known—but the most of this kindergarten work will be done by young women who are dependent upon themselves, and who choose it as a means of earning their bread. The majority of these will find it pleasant enough employment, because their early surroundings were not such as to cultivate delicate tastes; but many of these will make it only a stepping stone to something that pays better, or something they like better. Mrs. Black tells me that many of their kindergarten teachers are leaving them, and going into the public schools as teachers." Miss Sargent was silent for a moment, but as Margaret said nothing, she continued: "I must say that I share Mrs. Black's enthusiasm regarding kindergartens; there ought to be one in connection with each of our public schools. Any one who has seen as much as I have of adult criminals, in prisons and Magdalen asylums, can have but little faith in the reformation of depraved men and women, those who have fixed habits of crime. We are soon brought to see that our only hope is in getting hold of the children, and training them into a better life. But Margaret, you can do nothing in kindergarten teaching, you haven't the health, you could not endure the going to Glendale for instruction, and teaching in the city school, one week. And your teaching in such a place as we were in this morning, is not to be thought of."

"I know it," said Margaret, looking gloomily out of the window. "I wonder what I am to do for the next ten years."

"Do not try and settle your life ten years ahead, darling, you never have had an idle day yet; something will come to you, demanding your attention, that will be in harmony with both your judgment and taste, and will not injure your health; have patience, dear."

CHAPTER XXIII

On entering the car of the suburban train, a little after five o'clock, Margaret's eye fell upon Mrs. Bray, who was sitting with her head leaning against the car window, with her eyes closed as though in weariness. Margaret took a seat across the aisle, a little back of her. When half way to Edgewood, she observed that Mrs. Bray drew her black veil over her face, and she could see that behind it she was wiping the tears from her eyes. Immediately her sympathies went out toward the sorrowing woman. As they alighted from the car, she went to Mrs. Bray, and invited her to take a seat in her carriage.

"Let me take you home, please," she said, "I have two seats, you must be tired, after standing on your feet in that school all of the morning."

Mrs. Bray was touched by the kind attention. "Thank you, I am tired," she replied, and gladly accepted a seat beside Margaret, on the back seat of the phaeton. Margaret found that Mrs. Bray lived only four blocks from her own home. She felt that Mrs. Bray was in trouble, and while she kept up a running talk on commonplace subjects, she was wondering what the matter could be, and was resolving in her own mind ways of finding out, so that she might be of use to her. When they reached the house where Mrs. Bray said she had rooms, Margaret alighted, and insisted on carrying a parcel that Mrs. Bray had brought from the city, to the door for her, in order to prolong her stay with her, hoping each moment that something would happen that would disclose to her a way of serving the distressed woman. Mrs. Bray politely opened the gate for Margaret to pass through, without saying a word. Margaret thought she seemed afraid to trust her voice to speak. They had taken but a few steps on the board walk that led to the house, when the front door opened, and a little girl came bounding down the walk, and threw her arms around Mrs. Bray's neck, who stooped to take the child in her arms. She was a pretty, delicate looking girl, apparently about six years old, with soft brown eyes and a heavy, straight bang of brown hair. She was tastily dressed, and wore fine stockings and shoes. The mother and child embraced and kissed each other in the most affectionate manner.

"This is my little Eloise, Miss- McVey," said Mrs. Bray, as she rose to her feet.

Margaret stooped to the ground, and placed her arm around the child, whom she kissed repeatedly. Little Eloise immediately made friends with her, and rested her arm on Margaret's shoulder, as she retained her stooping posture.

" Is that your horse?" she asked, pointing to Margaret's horse. "Yes, dear; would you like to take a drive?" said Margaret.

"Yes! yes!" exclaimed Eloise; she ran to her mother crying, "May I mamma? Oh! please let me! the lady asked me, and I didn't say a word to her about it first; please let me!"

"Do let her go, Mrs. Bray; the horse is gentle, and my man is perfectly reliable, we have had him five years. Would you feel safe to let her go alone with George, so that you could give me half an hour of your time? I know that I'm asking a great deal, especially as you are so tired, but I need some information very much that I think you can give me, and we could have a talk while this little maiden is having an airing."

Mrs. Bray could not deny the eager child the rare

pleasure of a drive, and she invited Margaret to her room, which was a lower front one, opening from the hall. Eloise was soon arrayed in hat and jacket, and both Margaret and Mrs. Bray walked down to the carriage to see her off.

"Here, George, is a little girl you are to take good care of, and give a nice drive," said Margaret; "you must go where she says, and watch her closely, that she don't fall out."

Margaret placed Eloise on the front seat beside George, who moved along so that she could sit very near the middle of the seat. He smiled good-naturedly as he placed the lap-robe across her, tucking it in tightly underneath her; then he offered her the ends of the long lines that were buckled together, as he said: "Would the little lady like to drive?" Eloise took the lines in both hands, and turned with a delighted face to her mother, as she exclaimed:

"Oh! mamma, mamma! I'm going to drive the horse!"

Margaret stepped close to the carriage, and said in a low voice to George: "Go to Sanders' and bring me, when you come back, a basket of his best grapes—two baskets, one of Concords, and one of Catawbas. Be out about half or three-quarters of an hour."

As Margaret re-entered Mrs. Bray's room she was painfully struck by its air of poverty, which was out of keeping with both Mrs. Bray's and her daughter's appearance and manner. A creton curtain partitioned off one corner of the room, behind which was a bed. A small coal oil stove stood on a box that had a newspaper pinned around it. A small table covered with a flowered red and white cotton cloth, three wooden chairs and a small rocking-chair, completed the furnishing of the room. Mrs. Bray offered the rocking-chair to Margaret, and she seated herself at the end of the table on which she rested her elbow as she supported her head upon her hand. She was pale and looked physically exhausted, but the look of physical weariness was overshadowed by an expression of mental pain, a look of anxious fear that was in her face. Margaret's heart was full of sympathy, but Mrs. Bray's manner of gentle dignity forbade any familiar approach to personal matters. With delicate tact, Margaret immediately opened the conversation by speaking of herself.

"You are very kind, Mrs. Bray," she said, "in permitting me to take your time, but I feel that you are possessed of knowledge that may be of great value in assisting me in making an important decision, but perhaps you are too weary to-night,—shall I defer my questions until some other time?—shall I call and see you to-morrow?"

"O no, I'm not too tired to talk with you,—I shall be very glad to give you any information I may possess, but I can't imagine what it is I know that can be of any value to you."

"It's about this kindergarten teaching," said Margaret.

"Kindergarten teaching!" exclaimed Mrs. Bray.

"Yes; that was the reason of my being at your school this morning," said Margaret. "I wished to see what there was in it; I wish to teach. My aunt had seen Mrs. Black about my going to Glendale to join the class there."

Mrs. Bray raised her head with an expression of great surprise on her face. "Do I understand you, Miss McVey," she said, "that you wish to teach in a kindergarten? you, yourself?"

"Yes, that was my thought when I went to your kindergarten this morning," answered Margaret.

"But—pardon me, I thought—I understood my sister to say—you wish to teach? Excuse me, but why do you think of it?"

"Why?" repeated Margaret in a sad tone, as she looked at Mrs. Bray, with eyes fast filling with tears. Mrs. Bray's pale face flushed as she hastened to say:

"I beg your pardon, Miss McVey, but I could not imagine any such necessity."

Margaret was as tired as Mrs. Bray. She was trembling from nervous exhaustion. "Necessity!" she exclaimed, repeating Mrs. Bray's words. The dire necessity of something in her life so smote upon her that the gathering tears were forced from her eyes by the pain that crowded her heart. Mrs. Bray was shocked by what she thought was the result of her rude question.

"My dear Miss McVey," she said, leaning toward Margaret, "forgive me. I must have misunderstood; I have pained you,—how can I be of use to you? If you think of studying kindergarten, let me beg of you not to do it. It won't pay you; it is very hard, very trying work, and—" Mrs. Bray stopped abruptly, shut her lips tightly together, and clasped her hands rigidly in her lap.

"And what? Mrs. Bray, please tell me all about it."

"All about it!" repeated Mrs. Bray, covering her face with both hands, which she rested on the table before her. The tired woman broke entirely down and sobbed like a child. It was as though a long continued self-control had at last given way, and she was powerless to repress either her tears or sobs. For a few minutes Margaret sat perfectly still; she offered no consolation, she spoke no word of sympathy. Then as the first convulsive outburst of grief subsided, she drew her chair close to the side of the table, and reaching out her hand, laid it gently on Mrs. Bray's shoulders, as she said:

"These necessities of life are **terrible things, my dear** Mrs. Bray; perhaps you and I might **be of some help and** comfort to each other, if **we only knew it." As her sweet** voice fell upon Mrs. **Bray's ear, it was like healing balm** to her heart. She did not **analyze the tone, she could not** have done so, had she been aware that **there was any** peculiar compound to analyze. She only felt the **influence** of a spirit that was full **of** a gentle sympathy **born of a** sorrow of its own, and a cheerful helpfulness inherent **in** a character much stronger, and more self-reliant than her own. Margaret said no more, but quietly waited **for the** confidence that she felt sure would come; waited with **her** hand resting upon the shoulder **of** the weeping **woman.** After a little Mrs. Bray's sobs **ceased, and then she raised** her face from **her** hands, **and pushed her disordered hair** back from her forehead; **she looked straight at Margaret** with her red eyes and swollen lids, **but said** nothing.

"If you could, dear Mrs. Bray, tell **me** all about your kindergarten experience," said Margaret, "it might be of great use to me, and perhaps—perhaps we might be **of** help to each other."

"I don't know why I should not **tell** you all about it," said Mrs. Bray, as she began to cry again, the tears rolling down her cheeks as fast as she wiped them off. "You must excuse this weakness," she continued, "I am not always so childish, "but to-day I'm thoroughly worn out, and thoroughly discouraged. Whatever else you attempt don't go into kindergarten teaching, I beg of you, Miss McVey. To think how hard I have worked for the last year—I have gone through everything—and this is the result. But you don't know what I mean. In telling you about my kindergarten teaching, I must tell you something of myself. I never expected to teach at all— oh! Miss McVey, I had such a pretty home when my husband was alive.   He was a dentist, and growing into a good practice, but two years ago he died, he was sick only a few weeks, not dangerously sick for more than three days."   Mrs. Bray placed one hand across her eyes for a moment, then continued, "When the business was settled, I had nothing but the household furniture.   We had paid something on our home, but I lost it, the title was not good, you can't understand about business. I don't know much about it, but there were some debts, and I sold the good will of the office, and when all was settled, there was no money left.   Mr. Bray had his life insured as soon as Eloise was born, but he forgot to pay, and that ran out six months before he died, so I lost that.   I had not a single friend or relative that could assist me, and I was left with Eloise and our household furniture, and not twenty dollars in the world.   I had to do something for our support, and was advised by my sister and several friends, to fit myself for a kindergarten teacher. So I had an auction, and sold the furniture—it was dreadful to see at what prices the articles went—I kept enough to furnish two rooms for Eloise and myself, but most of that had to go, piece by piece, to pay my grocery bill, and we came here to live in this one room."   Mrs. Bray had ceased weeping, and talked as though it was a relief to give utterance to her sorrow.   "I was as careful as I could be," she continued, "but my fare into the city, and out to Glendale, and then a few books that I had to have and some material, all counted up, and I was frightened to see how fast the money went.   I worked very hard all last year, and endured all kinds of exposure; last winter I waded through the snow to the depot, to catch the early train, just plunging through drifts, and had wet feet and damp clothes all day, and several days I taught in that schoolroom with our thermometer at forty.   I kept my cloak and overshoes on all of the morning, but I took dreadful colds, really I was hardly free from a cold all last winter. The days that I went to Glendale I had to ride, in the four trips, two from here to the city, and then out to Glendale and back; forty-eight miles on the cars, and walk about four miles, leaving home at seven in the morning, and getting back at six in the evening, and frequently, during the spring, wet to my skin by the rain; I had overshoes, and rubber leggins, and a waterproof, but you can't walk a mile in a driving rain without getting wet. But I didn't mind all of that exposure as much as the personal contact with those filthy, diseased children. Some of the teachers don't seem to feel that at all, but it was something sickening to me, and I did not seem to get used to it."

Mrs. Bray stopped a moment, and Margaret asked: "Where did Eloise stay, when you were absent from her all day?"

"The woman I rent this room of is a kind, respectable woman, and is very fond of Eloise, so she looked after her. But it was very hard for me to leave that little girl all day, she seemed to feel my being away so much. Often I have cried all of the way into the city, because it was so hard for me to take her little arms from my neck, when it was time for me to go to the depot. I had an idea of taking a room in the city, so that I would not have to be away from her for so long a time, but I found that it would cost me double what it did to live out here. Oh! how tired and discouraged I used to feel, but there was nothing to do, but keep right on, and now, Miss McVey, after I have been through all of this, and got my certificate, I cannot get a situation." Again Mrs. Bray began to weep. "My last dollar is spent, and God only knows what I am to do."

"Do you mean that you cannot get a place to teach?" asked Margaret.

"Not a place that will pay my expenses. The best I can do is twenty-two dollars a month, and take out six dollars and thirty-six cents, for my monthly railroad ticket, that would leave me only fifteen seventy-five, for rent, fuel, clothes, and provisions for myself and Eloise. But my sister clothes Eloise."

"Can't you open a kindergarten here? wouldn't that pay you better than going into the city?" asked Margaret.

"I have thought that all over," replied Mrs. Bray, "but there is one here, a small one, taught by a Miss Allen. She is living with her mother, they have some little income, but she told me that her kindergarten wouldn't more than half pay her expenses."

"But are there not enough children in this town to support two kindergartens?" asked Margaret.

"There ought to be," said Mrs. Bray, "but if Miss Allen can't make hers pay, it would be folly for me to attempt to open a second one. You may think me very weak, but I am utterly discouraged, Miss McVey; there seems to be no place for Eloise and me in this world, I feel as though I would like to take her in my arms, and lie down in my grave. How little the dear child knows of the life that is before her." Mrs. Bray laid her head on her hands, and cried without trying to control herself.

"Instead of thinking you are weak," said Margaret, "I think you have been very brave and strong, but it does seem to me that something might be done, here at home, in the way of a kindergarten."

"But think of the expense," said Mrs. Bray. "I would have to have one large schoolroom, or two small ones, we must have a circle, a kindergarten without a circle wouldn't be a kindergarten, and then the furnishing and rent for the rooms.   Miss Allen has ten scholars, that is ten dollars a week; I couldn't get that number, and I would have to run in debt for rent and furnishing. Kindergarten furnishing is expensive, our tables and chairs, and all the materials are expensive.   And then I would have to rent a piano, I have none."

"Is the usual charge a dollar a week for tuition?" asked Margaret.

"Yes, in a private kindergarten," replied Mrs. Bray, as Eloise came bounding into the room, with hair flying, and cheeks aglow.   She rushed into her mother's arms, exclaiming:

"Oh! mamma! I've had such a good time! George got me some grapes, just see them!   I ate two bunches, big ones, you eat some, they're so good!"   The child ran to one of the baskets of grapes that George had brought in and placed on the floor, and taking a bunch, flew back to her mother, and commenced picking the grapes from the stem, and stuffing them into her mother's mouth.   Mrs. Bray placed her arm around the excited child, and took the grapes from her hand.

Margaret rose to take her departure, Mrs. Bray begged her to take at least one basket of grapes home with her, but Eloise flew back to the baskets, and leaning over them, spread out her little arms, as she exclaimed:

"They are mine! George gave them to me, didn't you, George?"   Mrs. Bray's face flushed, but Margaret stooping, placed her arm around the spontaneous child, and said:

"Yes, they are yours, George did get them for you, I don't wish for them, my house is full of grapes.   But Eloise, you must come and see me," Margaret continued, as she put her hand beneath the child's chin, and turned the sweet, fresh face toward her; "I haven't any mother, but I live with my auntie, and she loves little girls dearly, almost as much as I do.   Will you come and see us?"

The child threw both arms around Margaret's neck as she exclaimed:

"Yes! I will! now? shall I go home with you? I love you!" and the little arms tightened around Margaret's neck.

"Not to-day," said Margaret, "your mother wouldn't let you go to-night, but very soon, you and your mother must come."   At the outside door, where Margaret held Mrs. Bray's hand in parting, she said:

"You will not go to the city to-morrow?"

"No, there is nothing for me to do there, I was there to-day only to supply the place of a teacher who was not well.   I am almost sick.   I shall rest to-morrow, then I must start out and look for some place.   I must do something, if I can find nothing better, I shall take one of those situations at twenty-two dollars a month."

"Please don't go to the city until I see you again," said Margaret, "I'm about sick myself, but I'll try and see you by day after to-morrow.   I have a scheme that I am very desirous of carrying out, and I cannot do so, without assistance from you."

With that understanding Margaret went home.   Aunt Deborah had tea on the table five minutes after she entered the house.

"You don't seem hungry, Margaret, are you sick?" asked Miss Bond, as she observed that Margaret had pushed her plate one side, and was only sipping her tea.

"No, I'm not sick, but I'm very tired.   I lunched late with Aunt Helen.   The truth is I'm heart sick, I've seen suffering enough to-day to kill one."

"Where have you been?" inquired Miss Bond.

"I'll tell you all about it after tea," answered Margaret.

They soon adjourned to the study, which they made their sitting-room, occupying it just as they had done in Professor McVey's lifetime, Margaret laid down on the lounge, and then proceeded to give Miss Bond an account of what she had seen during the day, closing with a touching description of Mrs. Bray's condition, that awakened all of Miss Bond's sympathy.

"I have a plan," said Margaret, when she had finished her recital, "that I think is a good one, if it meets your approval. You know that I thought of teaching in a city kindergarten; I see now that I cannot do that, but I would like to have a kindergarten here in the house for Mrs. Bray. She understands the system thoroughly; I can play the piano for her, and render her some assistance with the children if I choose. It will give her a pleasant place to work, and enable her to earn enough to support herself and Eloise. Her little girl is a lovely child, as natural as a bird, and full of childish enthusiasm, you couldn't help loving her if you saw her."

"Where did you think of having this kindergarten?" asked Miss Bond.

"In the parlor," replied Margaret.

"In the parlor!" exclaimed Miss Bond, "you don't mean in *our* parlor! our large parlor?"

"Yes I do; that is, if you have no objections. This is your home as much as mine, Auntie Deb, and I wouldn't think, for a moment of doing anything that would interfere with your comfort or happiness. But neither you or I care for society, how little use we make of that parlor." Margaret hurried on so as to get in all of her points, before Deborah had taken a position. "It has not been opened for six months, it does no one any good. Mrs. Bray is a suffering woman, alone, and without means, with that little girl dependent on her. It would melt your heart to look at her, and hear her talk, she's not a strong woman, either physically or mentally, but is a gentle, shrinking creature, that needs some one to take care of her. Now if I can get the scholars—it all hinges on that—I'll try to-morrow, I'll go to all of my acquaintances who have small children, and if I can get the scholars, and you should think best, we could take out that furniture and pack it away up stairs somewhere, and I would get the little tables and chairs, and move my piano into the room, and in less than a week we might have a lovely kindergarten in there, and Mrs. Bray would be as happy as a queen. She is a real lady, auntie, and the little children who would come to the house, would all be nice, dear little creatures, just as sweet and pretty as they could be. You and I have nothing to do, and we ought to come in contact with the outside world somewhat, and you might find Mrs. Bray a pleasant person to talk with sometimes."

"I have plenty to do, Margaret," said Miss Bond, but Margaret thought of the many hours she had devoted to her aunt, reading books to her that she did not care at all for herself, and going to places where she did not care to go, in order to keep the kind-hearted woman from becoming lonely in the house, out of which had been taken the object of her greatest care. Miss Bond added: "But I see no objection to your plan, only what will you do for a carpet? and the hall carpet, too, the children will ruin that."

"I don't care for the parlor carpet, let it wear out, I never did like it, and as for the hall, we'll have the front of it covered with oilcloth, or heavy linen."

"But who is to pay for the tables and chairs of which you speak?" asked Miss Bond.

"I am," replied Margaret, "I ought to do some good

with the money I have, and how could I put some of it to a better use, than assisting that fatherless child and needy woman?"

"I declare, Margaret, you ought to have been a preacher; you could convince anybody of anything." Margaret smiled over her easy conquest.

"Now, what do you think of my plan?" asked Margaret. "You see, Mrs. Bray will have clear, all of the tuition of the children, she will have no rent to pay, or expense for warming her room. I don't know what we can do for a circle."

"A circle, what's that?" asked Miss Bond. As soon as Margaret explained the meaning, and the necessity of a kindergarten circle, Miss Bond said:

"Oh, I could make one in the center of the parlor that would answer perfectly, and it would be the diameter of the width of the room; that would be large enough."

"What would you make it of?" asked Margaret.

"Some broad bias bands of strong white cloth, or bright colored cloth, if you think best. White linen duck would be good, sewed right onto the carpet, or nailed down with flat headed brass nails."

As soon as Miss Bond became interested in Margaret's project, she applied herself energetically to push it forward, and hastened Margaret off the next day on her tour of solicitation for scholars, which proved a more successful one than either had anticipated. Twenty children were pledged, without Margaret approaching any of the families that patronized Miss Allen's class. "Suppose we say eighteen, Aunt Deb," said Margaret, as they sat at the tea-table, when she was giving an account of her experience during the day. "Somebody always fails to come to time, that will be eighteen dollars a week. You see kindergarten tuition is a dollar a week, let me see—

four times eight are thirty-two; yes, that will be—seventy-two dollars a month. Am I right? yes, it will be seventy-two dollars, just think of it! Perhaps we'd better give a wider margin; say we are sure of fifteen pupils, that will give sixty dollars a month. We shall get that positively, and no car fare, or schoolroom rent, for Mrs. Bray to pay. How much better that will be than going into the city, for twenty-two a month, and now she can have Eloise with her all of the time. I will run over and see her now, and you send George for me at half-past eight."

"Why do you go to-night, Margaret? you look very tired, you will make yourself sick."

"I am tired," replied Margaret, leaning her head on her hand, "but Mrs. Bray told me yesterday that she hadn't a dollar, and I presume that she would like to get to work as soon as possible. I told everybody that the school would open next week. I must see Mrs. Bray to get a list of the furniture, and what she calls materials, and order them to-morrow. I'll go down to the city in the morning. I declare!" she exclaimed, raising her head from her hand, and opening her eyes wide, " I ought not to have gone into this without consulting Aunt Helen, I utterly forgot it, I'll see her the first thing in the morning, but I don't believe she'll object."

Margaret found Mrs. Bray down with a neuralgic headache, but she insisted that Margaret should sit beside her bed, and tell her, to the last detail, of all her plans. When Margaret had laid the whole affair before her, she said: "But you calculate on the basis of fifteen pupils; two-thirds of the tuition must go to you. You supply the room, and fuel and piano. I cannot consent to take more than twenty dollars a month, and that will be very much better than going into the city at twenty-two.

You are very kind, but this is a matter of business justice; there are necessities in your life, **as well as in** mine."

Margaret made no reply for several **minutes, then** laying her hand on Mrs. **Bray's, that rested on the** edge of the bed, she said **in a sad voice: "The** necessities in my life, my dear Mrs. Bray, **are not pecuniary ones.** As you intimated yesterday, that **you** inferred **from** something your sister had said to you, I have a comfortable income, more than sufficient for **my** personal needs. My mother died years ago, and my dear father left me last spring; I live alone in the old home with **a** maiden aunt, we two in the house alone. It is very quiet and **lonely. We go** in no society, we don't choose to. I **thought I would** like **to** study kindergarten, **you know all about it, my** parlor is no use to me, and **the house has to be heated any** way. If you **will open a kindergarten there, I can** render a little assistance in playing the **piano, and you** can teach me, give me the practical knowledge — the theoretical I do not care **to** have—**I once thought I would** like it, but now I do not care at all about **it. It will be** a delight to both my aunt and myself, to have those sweet children in the house; my aunt is very fond of children, and their presence, and the kindergarten music will break the gloom and silence of the house." Margaret was feeling her way, was trying to delicately accomplish her object. "That will more than compensate me for any outlay that I may make, to say nothing of the information that I shall obtain from you, and how much pleasanter to get it in that way, than to have to go through all of the exertion and exposure that you suffered last year. **As** to the sixty dollars a month, you will fairly earn it, **and I** have no need of it, I shall receive more than an equivalent for what I pay out, in the arrangement. I have set my heart on the plan, and have more than money enough to carry it out, and shall be seriously disappointed if you do not feel that you can assist me. And then, auntie and I will have your little darling part of the time. She is a lovely child, Mrs. Bray, and it will be a positive pleasure to have her with us all of the time if you would only give her to us!" Margaret laughed merrily as she said this, and pressed Mrs. Bray's hand. "Sixty dollars a month is not a large income for you and Eloise," Margaret continued, "especially as it will be for only eight months of the year. Didn't you tell me that kindergartens had only eight months of school a year?" Mrs. Bray was lying perfectly still, with one arm thrown across her face. As she made no reply to Margaret's question, Margaret continued, "That will be only four hundred and eighty dollars a year, if we have fifteen pupils, and only six hundred and forty, if all come who have promised, I don't see how you can live on that, but it is better than twenty-two a month, and then, perhaps your school will grow. I will keep the accounts and collect the money, for awhile at any rate, for you will be very busy at first. I felt so sure, Mrs. Bray, that your judgment would coincide with mine, and that you would not refuse to assist me in carrying out my wishes, that I brought with me the first month's collection, which I will advance. You must have had heavy expenses in gaining your kindergarten knowledge." Margaret opened her purse, and placed within Mrs. Bray's hand that she held, eight ten dollar bills. Mrs. Bray's fingers clasped the bills, and she threw her arm around Margaret's neck and drew her head down to her own, as she burst into sobs, and for a few minutes sobbed hysterically; Margaret strove to quiet her, and at last succeeded.

"You don't know what it is," said Mrs. Bray, when sufficiently composed to speak distinctly, "to be in debt, and not have a dollar to pay with. I heve a two months' grocery bill that is not paid, and I have fairly dreaded going down street. They hesitate when I give an order in that grocery, and I dare not go to another without money. Loan me this eighty dollars, Miss McVey, if you can, and let me pay my debts. Can it be possible that I shall have eighty dollars a month! what an angel you are! what suffering you are saving me from."

Margaret continued to insist that the obligation, in the end would be on her side, and her cheerful, practical way of looking at matters, very soon completely restored Mrs. Bray's composure; she got off of the bed, declaring that her head was well.

"I seem to have crept from under a mountain, how light I feel!" she said, as she was looking over a catalogue that lay on the table, in order to make out a list of her furniture, and kindergarten material for Margaret.

Miss Sargent approved of Margaret's plans, and Miss Bond completed her ingenious circle, the furniture came, the little tables and chairs were arranged in the parlor, and on the appointed day, Margaret was seated at the piano, as Mrs. Bray, looking ten years younger, was superintending the twenty children—every one came—who fluttered around her like so many birds, with their bright faces, well kept hair, and pretty dresses. Miss Bond was as much pleased as the youngest child present, with the novelty of the scene. She was seated a little one side, holding Eloise, for whom she had conceived a great fondness, on her lap. The fondness seemed fully returned, for the child had one arm around Miss Bond's neck and from time to time, she would draw her head down, so that she could whisper in her ear, something about "our kindergarten." Margaret not only supplied whatever music was necessary, but both she and Miss Bond, under Mrs. Bray's direction, prepared colored papers, counted out splints, and divided the blocks among the children, and made themselves useful in various ways. Miss Bond was surprised when the clock struck twelve, and wondered where the time had gone. She insisted that Mrs. Bray and Eloise should stay to luncheon with Margaret and herself, and much to Margaret's amusement, the usually quiet woman talked incessantly about the morning's exercises, the children's laughable mistakes, and their enthusiastic interest. Poor Margaret's sad heart was sorely taxed, but no one would have suspected it, as she went through the morning routine. Nor did she hasten Mrs. Bray's departure after luncheon, and she listened with patient gentleness to Eloise's prattle, and kissed her again and again, at the front door, sending both mother and child to their humble home with hearts full of happiness. But as soon as the door was closed on them, she went into the study and dropped into her father's large chair. "What a mechanical thing it all is," she thought, as she leaned back and closed her eyes. "How little these happy children know what is before them; and those wretched children in the mission, what miserable little sufferers! how far the bitter waters spread; what suffering Mrs. Bray had last year, husband dead, money gone, in debt." Then her mind ran over the last year of her own life, sorrow within and without, and it seemed that hers was no special experience, every one of the men, women and children, on Leek street had hearts that suffered, and eyes that wept; they did not suffer in the way she did, but in their own hard way, and were they to blame for their miserable situation? what could it mean, where did it all tend? Here consecutive thought ceased, and her thoughts wandered off into vague, broken, uselessly-repeated questions.

A few days after, as Margaret was sitting in Miss Sargent's room, Miss Sargent said to her: "Do you get any happiness out of your kindergarten, Margaret, beyond the consciousness of the relief that you have given Mrs. Bray?"

"It breaks the day," Margaret replied, "and I find that it is well to have a duty to look forward to. You may think it strange, Aunt Helen, but the simple fact that I am to be in that room, down to the piano at nine o'clock, is a good thing for me; I know that I am of use there, that something depends on me."

"But will you be compelled to hold yourself to that all winter?"

"Oh, no," replied Margaret. "I shall begin next week to teach Eloise the tunes that are of daily use to her mother; she has a remarkable ear for music, she hangs around the piano constantly. She can easily learn the chords, and the simple tunes that I play for the children. I believe after awhile I will give her regular instructions, and if her improvement warrants it, I'll underake her musical education, and when she is old enough, I'll place her with competent teachers. Aunt Deb thinks she will make another Vogner. It's wonderful, the delight Aunt Deb finds in those children, I never saw her as happy."

"I'm surprised at that," said Miss Sargent. "I would have supposed the confusion of having so many children in the house would have annoyed her, she is such a particular housekeeper."

"No, it does not seem to," replied Margaret. "She seems delighted with the whole thing, and so do the servants. You would have laughed to have seen them yesterday, when the children were on the circle. Mary and Christine came in and stood at the lower end of the room, watching the exercises with a sort of surprised delight, and there was George, standing outside, with his arms leaning on the window-sill—we had all of the windows open—and he looked as pleased as a boy at a circus.   It really will be a good thing for the household, having that kindergarten there."   Margaret looked out of a window near by, as she ceased speaking, with eyes full of dumb, grinding pain.

Miss Sargent gazed for a few moments upon the pale face, and then she broke the silence.

'Don't go home to-day, Margaret," she said, "they can get on some way without you to-morrow morning, dear; stay in and pass the night with me."

"Not to-night, Aunt Helen, I'll come down next week; I shall have to come in Tuesday, to order some books for Mrs. Bray."

"And then you'll pass the night?"

"Yes, and I shall be down Thursday too, and perhaps I'll stay then."

The next Thursday afternoon, Margaret concluded the purchase of some books which she had examined the Tuesday before, on her way to Miss Sargent's.   The bookstore was located on Western avenue, which ran parallel with Union avenue, where Miss Sargent resided.   The next parallel street was Leek street.   As is frequently the case in large cities, there was but one block between opulence and poverty, happiness and misery, respectability and crime.   Union avenue was one of the most beautiful streets in America.   It was the main thoroughfare to the fashionable driving park, and during the driving hours of the day was a gay scene, made up of prancing horses, elegant carriages, and well dressed men and women. Margaret crossed from Western avenue to Union avenue, which she reached about the hour that society people were on their way to the park, and there was such a stream of swiftly moving carriages, **three and four abreast, that she** was compelled to **wait a moment on the corner for a chance** to cross to **the other side, on which Miss Sargent's** residence was located. It was a warm October day, and a bright yellow sunlight **was reflected from the mountings** of the harnesses, and **the swinging chains that bedecked** the horses, and from **the polished surface of the carriages.** Margaret glanced up and **down the street; there seemed** no end or beginning of the **gay procession; all was** swift motion and flashing brightness, **as the hundreds of** equipages rolled by her with their pleasure-seeking occupants. **As** Margaret stepped forward to attempt **the** passage of the crossing, her eye was arrested by **a** victoria passing **directly** in front of her, **Leaning back in it,** in luxurious **ease, sat Rodger Latimer, and beside him was** a beautiful woman, **richly dressed.** His head **was** turned **toward** the lady, who sat on the side next to Margaret, **and thus** she saw him full in the **face.** He looked in strong **health, and** full of happiness. There was a smile **on his lips and in his** eyes as he gazed upon the woman's **face, and listened to** something that she was saying. **The victoria** passed swiftly and neither of its occupants saw the slight figure draped in black, or the white face, from which a pair of large, sunken eyes looked out upon them. Margaret quickly crossed the street, heedless of any danger that might menace her from the rapidly passing horses. Instead of going up Union avenue to Judge Sargent's residence that was a few blocks above where she was, she kept straight on and crossed to Leek street. The second of time in which her eye had rested upon Rodger's face, completed the desolation of her heart, that hitherto seemed to lack **no** element of complete woe. She had been like an exhausted creature lying alone in the night on the bare earth, beaten upon by a storm; but the cold and rain,

the isolation and darkness, were not enough; out of the
heavens came a broad blaze of blinding brightness, and
from the glorious splendor that covered the dome in
swiftly sweeping light, descended the scathing lightning,
that with a dart smote every nerve with an instantaneous
agony that seemed to kill as it struck. Her intense nature rocked and shivered in anguish as the vision of
Rodger's happy face leaning toward that beautiful woman
passed by her; then the October brightness turned to
night, and a numbness crept over her. She did not think,
but rather felt, that she must get away from the happiness
of that avenue, it was no place for her. She moved like
one walking in sleep, and her thoughts were disconnected,
and dragged along as though her brain was paralyzed by
an opiate. Instinctively she turned in her inarticulate
misery to the dwelling places of the miserable. Just as
she reached Leek street, a car was passing, going down;
it stopped to let off passengers, and she stepped on. She
had a long nun's veiling veil on her arm which she wound
around her head and face. The conductor had to speak
to her twice, and even touch her on the shoulder, before
she responded to his call for her fare. The car took her
within a few blocks of the Edgewood depot, and when it
stopped and all of the passengers left, she mechanically
stepped to the sidewalk. Then she looked around, col-
lected herself a little, hesitated a moment, walked on to
the depot, and seated herself in the first outgoing Edgewood train. When she reached the depot in Edgewood,
she went into a telegraph office and sent a few words to
Miss Sargent, and then walked rapidly homeward, choos-
ing the least frequented way. George was raking the
leaves off the lawn, the front door was open, and the
quiet hush of the after-sunset hour rested on the place.
Margaret met no one in the hall as she passed through it

to her own "Sans Souci." The west windows were open, and the red and yellow of the evening sky cast a tender glow into the silent room, but she did not feel its beauty, nor did she think of this as her home for the coming winter, made comfortable by the superintendency of her Aunt Deborah, a home that would hold some slight daily occupation for herself, in connection with the little children she had gathered there, and the bereft woman whose life she had changed from one of fearful apprehension to a sweet contentment. She thought of nothing as she sank exhaustedly into a chair, and she saw nothing, but Rodger beside the beautiful woman in the victoria, the view of which had burned itself into her brain.

CHAPTER XXIV

Mrs. Rodger Latimer's summer had been a successful pleasure seeking. A few weeks before the wedding, her lover had expressed the opinion that a summer abroad, they two alone, amid the lakes of England or mountains of Switzerland, would be, of all things, the most charming; and Marie had immediately declared that nothing would delight her more. But some way, Mr. Latimer hardly knew how, their arrangements culminated in an itinerary of American watering places. He and Mrs. White planned the tour. He could not remember that Marie ever expressed a wish or uttered one word regarding the various places under discussion, and yet he felt sure that she was pleased with the plans made by Mrs. White and himself. So instead of quiet drives in the English lake region, alone with his bride, he had drives on the Newport and Long Branch beaches. In place of the seclusion of English country inns, there was the noise and crowd of fashionable hotels. He soon became conscious that they attracted attention wherever they located themselves, for a longer or shorter time; and he thought it natural enough that Marie's personal beauty should do this, and he reproached himself for not feeling greater gratification on account of the sensation she produced, as he saw her, morning after morning, and evening after evening, dressed in beautiful costumes, and wearing the rare jewels that he had been delighted to bestow upon her; surrounded by men who vied with each other in offering her attention and adulation. He often turned away with the wish that the summer was past, and he and his wife were located in their own home. He was tired of dances and dinners, of Newport polo and Saratoga coaching, of yachting, and of crowds and noise; and longed for quiet evenings alone with his beautiful wife. He expressed none of this weariness, however, or his desire for an early return home, to Marie, for he saw that she was very happy in the gaiety of these fashionable places.

"You don't seem to care much for any of these beautiful women, Rodger," said Marie to him one day in Saratoga; "I thought you were fond of ladies' society."

"No, my love, I don't believe I am; if I ever was I'm so no longer. You're the only woman in the world I care to look at," he replied, as he drew her to him with lover like fondness. "Come, let us go up into the pine grove for a walk, away from all of these people."

"O I can't, Rodger," Marie replied. "It would be delightful, but I have an engagement. Don't you know that I'm to drive with Colonel Moran? He has his coach here, and has invited a party to go to the lake. I'm so sorry you're not going."

Mr. Latimer stood on the hotel piazza and saw his wife drive off, seated beside Colonel Moran. He watched them out of sight, and then went to his room in search of a book, wishing that October would come. When it did come, he was among the earliest travelers that returned from seashore and mountain, from Europe and California, to take possession of the homes that had been unswathed from summer packings, and made ready for winter occupancy. Marie was willing to return early, in order to see that everything was to her mind in her house before the season opened. Mr. Latimer had rented, for the year, a beautiful residence on one of the fashionable avenues; that was furnished as completely as wealth and cultured taste could furnish a house. The place belonged to an acquaintance of his, one of Clinton's wealthiest citizens, whose wife was in ill health, and decided to take a year's rest in Europe.

"Only for one year, you say," replied Marie, when her husband consulted her regarding the feasibility of their taking a furnished house. "Yes, it may answer for one year, then we will have our own home."

"I shall be very sorry, my love, if our not living in our own house will make any difference with your happiness," said Mr. Latimer; "but you know we make the home for each other, wherever we are; and we shall be alone by our own fireside, and then it is really a pleasant house and beautifully furnished."

"Yes, the house is well enough," said Marie, "but there's an air about living anywhere, out of one's own house, that is not agreeable. It's a little different for a woman to be mistress of her own house."

At last every arrangement was complete in house and stable, and Mr. Latimer was full of blissful anticipations. Now, his beautiful wife would belong to him, now, they would have long evenings together for reading, beside the open fire, with shades drawn down, to shut out even the momentary gaze of passers-by. His house was to be his castle. Now he could become acquainted with Marie, whom he felt he knew less of, since his marriage, than before; and how delicious would be the revelations of love that awaited him! Full of such dreams of home life, Mr. Latimer, one evening after dinner, when they had been settled in this house several weeks, took Marie's hand as they entered the library, and said:

"Now what shall I read to you love, or what will you read to me?" He moved a large chair for her in front of the fire, and seating himself beside a small table, on which stood a lamp of wondrous beauty, commenced cutting the leaves of a magazine. He had scarcely ran his paper-knife twice through the leaves, when the butler put aside the portieres, and announced, " Mr. and Mrs. Therbert." An expression of delight instantly lit up Mrs. Latimer's face. She met her guests with rapturous exclamations.

" This is lovely in you, to come and see us so soon, in this informal way, I'm delighted to see you!"

The ladies kissed each other in an affectionate manner, and sat down side by side on the sofa. Mr. Latimer laid his book on the table with well-concealed vexation. There were but few people he would have welcomed to his anticipated paradise that evening, and neither Mr. or Mrs. Therbert were of the number. Mrs. Therbert he had always disliked; he considered her a vain, heartless woman, in whom love of approbation had eaten out the core of all womanly affection, and he felt a slight indignation as he saw her kiss his wife so fondly. The conversation flowed glibly without much effort on his part as host, to keep it up. The ladies chatted of the past summer, of the places they had respectively visited, and the people they had met. Mr. Therbert immediately plunged into speculations regarding the business prospects of the approaching winter. Mr. Latimer furtively looked at the clock on the mantel. Nine o'clock, they would leave soon, and he and Marie would have at least two hours to themselves. As he was consoling himself with this thought, the butler announced, " Mrs. Lundom White." As this lady came down the room, Mrs. Therbert clapped her hands, and exclaimed:

" I waited for you, I haven't said a word to Mrs. Latimer about it."

" So you knew Harriet was coming," said Marie, as she kissed her sister, and placed her in an easy chair, "but what conspiracy are you two in now?"

"It's no conspiracy at all, Marie," said Mrs. White, "and I supposed you and Mrs. Therbert would have the whole thing settled by this time. I could not come any sooner," turning to Mrs. Therbert, "Mr. and Mrs. Edmunds came in, and have just left."

"Well, what is it, Harriet, I'm dying of curiosity," said Mrs. Latimer.

"It's about the dancing class; you see Marie, that I can't give so much time to it, and Mrs. Therbert and Mrs. Edmunds wish you to take my place."

"Why, Harriet, I wouldn't do it for the world. I don't think it would be in good taste."

"I would like to know why?" asked Mrs. Therbert.

"So should I," rejoined Mrs. White.

. "Simply because I've been married so short a time," replied Mrs. Latimer.

"What of that?" said Mrs. Therbert, who had been prominent in Clinton society for nearly ten years, "that doesn't make the least difference, you're not like a stranger, you know Clinton society as well as any of us. You have had four full seasons, and you will be compelled now to take a leading position."

"As a matter of course," added Mrs. White, "you will entertain a great deal, and there's no earthly reason why you shouldn't relieve me. Now, be good, Marie, and do as we all wish you to."

"Why, Harriet, don't speak in that way, I would be delighted to do it, if I thought it best. But I'll do it," quickly added Mrs. Latimer, as she saw a look of displeasure settling on her sister's face. "I'll give up my own judgment to you, and Mrs. Therbert."

"We'll have a lovely time this winter," said Mrs. Therbert, reaching out her hand to give Mrs. Latimer's hand an affectionate pressure. "You come to my house to-morrow, and we'll revise the invitation list.   Or I'll come here if you prefer.   Yes, I'll stop here on my way down town.   Don't you think Mrs. White, that we better get the invitations out soon, so we can make a choice of evenings, before they are taken?"

"I don't know as there is any hurry," replied Mrs. White, "it is early in November yet."

"But it's going to be very gay this winter," said Mrs. Therbert, "and do our best, we can't have them ready before the twentieth."

"Well, do as you like, you and Marie are to make all of the arrangements, we all agreed that we would be satisfied with whatever you did," said Mrs. White.

"We expect you to lead the German for us," said Mrs. Therbert, turning to Mr. Latimer, "sometime during the winter; now don't say you wont, Mr. Latimer," she exclaimed, as that gentleman shook his head with a faint smile.   We can't let you off.   You led that one so beautifully last winter, and now that dear Marie and I are responsible for all the parties this season, we want to have them all as beautiful as possible."

"You must not depend on me, Mrs. Therbert, it will not be possible for me to serve you in that way," said Mr. Latimer.   The three ladies broke out in a chorus of remonstrance, that was swelled by Mr. Therbert's bass voice.

"Of course he will do it," said Marie, "he could not be so ungracious, I'll answer for him."

As the ladies continued their talk, Mrs. Latimer might have doubted her ability to make her assurance good, had she noticed, and been able to interpret, the slight drooping of the corners of her husband's mouth, and a latent flash in his eye.   At half-past ten, Mrs. White rose to leave.

"You will go in our carriage, wont you, Mrs. White?" asked Mrs. Therbert, rising also.

" Yes, I sent mine back," replied Mrs. White.

Mr. Latimer bade his wife's guests good-night, standing on the rug before the fire. Marie accompanied them across the room, holding the portiere aside for them, with her own hand. As she returned to the fireside, where her husband was seated with an open magazine in his hand, she said: "Let us go to bed, Rodger, I know it is early, but I'm tired to death."

The next morning as Mr. Latimer came from the stable, where he had been examining a saddle horse sent him for trial, he stepped from the dining-room, into a small room that opened from the library also, that contained a few books, a writing table, a lounge, and an easy chair. Mrs. Latimer had christened this room Mr. Latimer's study. "Here you can be alone whenever you wish to write or read by yourself," she had said as they were looking at it one day, when making their first tour of the house. When he seated himself at the table to write some letters, he was not aware that any one was in the adjoining library, from which he was separated simply by a curtain in the doorway. Mrs. Therbert had come in a few moments before, and was waiting the entrance of Mrs. Latimer, who soon entered.

"I'm delighted to see you, dear Charlotte," she said, "but you're late, it's nearly eleven, I've been expecting you for an hour."

"I intended to be here earlier, but I really did not know how late it was, we can get through by luncheon. Does Mr. Latimer lunch at home? Lucas never does, and I'm glad of it, it is all I can do to endure the noise of the children. Will comes home from kindergarten just before luncheon, and it does seem as though he would drive me crazy. But here is our old list of last winter, and it needs revising. You know who we had as well as

18 Rodger Latimer's Mistake.

I do, for Mrs. White always told us that she consulted you about everything, and that you did all of the business for her."

"What changes do you think we better make in the list?" asked Mrs. Latimer.

"I'll tell you what I think," replied Mrs. Therbert. "I don't know as you will agree with me, but we have too many girls down there."

"That's just what I think, we need more men, I said so to Harriet last winter."

"You see the trouble last winter was," said Mrs. Therbert, "that we invited some girls because we wished for their brothers."

"Well," said Mrs. Latimer, "let us strike the girls' names right off."

"Will the brothers come?" asked Mrs. Therbert. "Now here is Mr. Lingral, he is a splendid fellow, and a fine dancer, we can't afford to lose him; but what of his sister? will he come if we drop her?"

"Yes, he'll come fast enough, leave him to me," said Mrs. Latimer.

"Oh, Marie," replied Mrs. Therbert, "he can't resist you, can he, I wish I had your eyes, dear."

"Nonsense, Charlotte, I don't know why you should wish to be in any way different from what you are; your card is always full, the young men flock around you. I never saw you sit a dance through."

"I do usually have a good time; that's true," said Mrs. Therbert.

"You married ladies always had a better time than the girls, and now that I have joined your ranks, I don't intend to take a back seat," said Mrs. Latimer.

"Marie! how much attention you always received, Lucas said he never saw you look as well as you did last night. What a glorious winter you are going to have! I declare, I envy you; I was rallying Colonel Moran the other day about his attention to Miss Montford, and he quite resented it. He said that no man of appreciative taste could be won by the girls, from the married ladies of Clinton. I wont tell you what he said particularly about you, it would make you too vain."

"Colonel Moran is charming," said Mrs. Latimer. "I saw a great deal of him when we were in Saratoga, and in Newport I was out with him every day. He is simply delightful, he has such an enchanting way of devoting himself to you."

"He told me you were the most beautiful woman in Newport," said Mrs. Therbert.

"That was very good of him. He certainly was very kind to me there, and made my time pass delightfully; but now this list, Charlotte."

"Let us go over it name by name, and see who to strike off, and then we will see if we can't think of some new men. Do you know of any?"

"Yes, there are two I know of. How many balls shall we have?"

"We ought to have four," said Mrs. Therbert, "or three, and a german; say Marie, wont Mr. Latimer lead our german?"

"Certainly he will," replied Mrs. Latimer.

"I thought that he meant what he said last night, when he refused, he looked so determined," said Mrs. Therbert.

"It don't make any difference what he said, he will do it, I can persuade him," replied Mrs. Latimer.

"It would be dreadful if you couldn't persuade him, he is such a fine dancer; we couldn't get any one who would do it half so well. Suppose I talk to him about it some time when I see him, a man will do so much more for any other woman than he will for his wife."

"I can manage Rodger, perfectly, don't have any anxiety about the german, Charlotte. By the way, have you seen Grey Whitridge since his return, or hasn't he returned yet?"

"Yes, he came day before yesterday, and I never saw him looking better. We had quite a talk at the theater, it was a miserable play, but we can't expect anything good at this season; I was glad you weren't there. I wouldn't have gone, only there was nothing going on, and I could not bear to stay home. Mr. Whitridge inquired for you the first thing; what should we do without him in society?"

"He is certainly a fascinating man," replied Mrs. Latimer. "I don't know any one who could take his place, he can do anything, he's so versatile."

"Yes, he is," said Mrs. Therbert, "but we *must* attend to this list." The ladies set themselves to work taking each name under consideration, and weighing carefully the social merits of each, but paying special attention to the claims of several new men, they had in their minds. By the time they had finished their consultation, Mr. Latimer—who never for one moment thought that his wife had a purpose, or a sentiment, that she wished to conceal from him, and to whom the idea never suggested itself, that she could have the slightest objection to his hearing every word spoken between her and her acquaintances—had a pretty definite understanding of the ambitions and purposes of the two ladies, at least as far as the dancing class was concerned.

Mr. Latimer's dreams of a quiet home life, evenings alone with his beautiful wife, were not realized. Although the social season had not begun, Mr. and Mrs. Latimer were never for an evening alone in their home. Either some of Mrs. Latimer's friends would drop in, or they were invited to some house, where Mrs. Latimer was anxious to go. There were several clubs, making their arrangements for the winter, of which the wealthy and beautiful Mrs. Latimer was considered as an indispensable member. One evening when Mr. and Mrs. Latimer were at Mrs. White's Mr. and Mrs. Lefarve came in.

"We have been to your house to see you," said Mrs. Lefarve to Mrs. Latimer, after greetings had been given and received between all present, "and your man said that you were here, so Mr. Lefarve suggested we follow you."

"I ought to have seen you before, Mrs. Latimer," said Mr. Lefarve, "but really I have not been able to find you at home, although I have fairly haunted your house. We are forming a Histrionic club, and we all feel that it will be incomplete unless you give us the benefit of your talent and experience."

"A Histrionic club!" exclaimed Mrs. White. "That is something new; it will be delightful. Do tell us all about it, Mr. Lefarve."

"It's a club for parlor theatricals. We shall play in our own home theaters first, but some of the ambitious members hope that we may become so proficient that the latter part of the season we may rent a small theater, and put our plays on the stage for charitable purposes."

"Oh, it will be lovely! Mrs. Latimer," cried Mrs. Lefarve. "You must join us. We can't make a success without you; we specially count on you and Mr. Whitridge."

"I shall be delighted to become a member," replied

Mrs. Latimer, as her eyes sparkled with pleasure, "but I fear I can bring neither talent or experience to aid you."

"We shall be sure of both if you will join us," replied Mr. Lefarve, and he continued, turning to Mr. Latimer, "Surely we can count on you, Mr. Latimer?"

"I fear not," said Mr. Latimer. "I have no admiration of parlor theatricals, and certainly have no talent that could be utilized that way."

"Now, Rodger, that's not handsome," exclaimed Mrs. White, "you ought to join on Marie's account, even if you don't like them; it will be so much pleasanter for her."

"Really, Harriet," said Mr. Latimer in reply to Mrs. White, "I don't see where Marie is to find time for another club; it seems to me that she already has engagements enough to occupy every hour between this and next May."

Mr. White burst into a good-natured laugh. "You don't know these women as well as I do, Rodger," he said. "I've had ten years' experience; they will do more things and go to more places than you have any idea of. It would kill most men to do what these society women do. Marie'll find time; if she can't, Harriet here will help her."

"James, you ought to be ashamed to talk so; what will Mr. Lefarve think of you?" said Mrs. White, laughingly.

"Mr. Lefarve knows every word of it's true. Three engagements a day are nothing for you and Mrs. Lefarve," said Mr. White. "Rodger may not be able to find time, but Marie will, for every club, and opera, and ball that comes along. No use saying anything, Rodger; we shall have to fall into line. It's a doleful prospect, think of the number of stupid dinners and jams we shall have to go to before Lent, think of the tubs of things we shall have to eat!" Mr. White laid his hand on his stomach with a wry face that set them all laughing. "And the dances are the worst. Harriet and Marie dragged me out last winter, and then told me how rude I was to sit and talk with the men instead of dancing. I was kept dancing until I thought I should drop dead. I told them one night to take as an excuse that I was dead, and couldn't go. You'll reap the result, Rodger, of your folly in getting married before spring. It makes every bone in my body ache to think of what I've got to go through. Join the club graciously, Rodger, you'll have to do it in the end, you've mortgaged yourself."

"What a ridiculous tirade, James," said Mrs. White. "Any one would suppose you didn't like society."

"And I don't," broke in Mr. White.

"And were forced against your will to go," continued Mrs. White, not noticing his interruption, "when the truth is you are always ready to go—"

"Never! never!" exclaimed Mr. White.

"Well, Rodger,' said Mrs. White, turning to Mr. Latimer, "I hope *you* will not be influenced by James' talk, and will join the club with Marie."

Mr. Latimer's eyes were fixed upon his wife's face, on which he saw an expression as she gazed steadily at him, that arrested the assertion that he could not possibly do so, that was on his lips, and caused him to reply that he would be most happy to do anything that Mrs. Latimer desired.

As he entered his bedroom some hours afterward he threw himself in an easy chair before the fire and drew a small rocking-chair close to his side, as he said:

"Come, love, and sit here awhile; I wish to talk with you."

"Why, Rodger, it's past twelve," said Mrs. Latimer, as she stood by the bureau taking the pins from her hair. "It's time we were asleep."

"No matter what time it is Marie, I wish to talk with you for a few minutes," said Mr. Latimer, in a decisive tone, which his wife had never heard from him before when addressing her. She turned her head and looked at him, as he sat with his back toward her, hesitated a moment, then shook her long hair down over her shoulders and crossed the room, and took the low chair he had placed for her. She did not look at him, but gazed straight into the fire. He turned his head and regarded her intently for a moment, then he reached his arm behind her chair, and passed his hand down the length of. her beautiful hair, that hung over the back of the chair.

"How beautiful you are to-night, love, in that white dress, you look as you did at the theater the first night I fell in love with you," he said with a smile, as he again passed his hand the length of her hair. He looked into her face, but her eyes were not raised to his, nor did she return any recognition of his caress. After a few moments' silence, he asked:

"Do you really intend to join that Histrionic club, Marie?"

"Why certainly I do, Rodger, I think that's a strange question to ask me, after the talk that you heard between Mr. Lefarve and myself at Harriet's."

"And you expect to be an active member, and take part in the plays?" asked Mr. Latimer.

"Most certainly I do, if I join," replied Mrs. Latimer.

"But Marie, you know I dislike theatricals, I wish you would not join the club." Mrs. Latimer made no reply, and he continued, "I cannot take part in those—worse than nonsensical things."

"You need not join if you do not choose to," said Mrs. Latimer.

"Will you join if I do not?" he asked.

"Yes," she said, without a moment's hesitation, in a decided tone. There was a long silence. She was thinking, "I may as well make a stand now as any time, and have it over, once for all." He was thinking of the time the winter before, when he had requested her to leave the play, that these same people were putting upon the stage in Mrs. Von Stein's theater, and the sweet way in which she then yielded to his wishes. An awful chasm seemed opening before him, out of which a terrible specter arose. With an intuition quick as a woman's, his mind leaped to the conclusion, "She never loved me!" then immediately came the recoil—"She is angry, patience, it will be all right."

"Do you mean, Marie," he said in a gentle voice, "that you will join that club, and take part in those theatricals, if I request you not to?"

"There is no use in our quarreling, Rodger," she replied in a hard, determined tone, "but do you think you have any right to keep me from joining the club?"

"It's not a question of right, my wife, I hope that question will never be raised between us; that it will grieve me to have you do so, should be sufficient."

"But it will deprive me of great pleasure not to join," said Mrs. Latimer, "and why should I give up this pleasure, simply on account of a whim on your part?"

An angry flush rose to Mr. Latimer's brow; he opened his lips to speak, then closed them again, as the hot blood receded before an expression of pain. "It is not a whim, Marie, but a settled conviction, a long standing dislike of that form of amusement," he said in a slow, measured way.

"Well, and you think that I should conform my life to your narrow views." Again the hot blood surged into Mr. Latimer's face. "Seems to me we should each be our own judge of what we wish to do, and do it, without interfering with each other."

"We might do this," replied Mr. Latimer, "if we held no personal relation to each other, but do you think husband and wife can live happily together in that way?"

"I don't see why they can't, it seems to me the most reasonable way to live," said Mrs. Latimer, "it's the way James and Harriet live, and I am sure they are happy, he never interferes with her." Mr. Latimer knew that few women made greater effort to conform to their husband's notions and wishes, than did Mrs. White, but he did not care just then to correct his wife's assertion. "I am sure," she continued, "we shall not be happy if we are constantly finding fault with each other, and preventing each other from doing those things that we each wish to do, and find happiness in doing. We have done very well thus far, why shouldn't we keep on as we have begun. We have been very happy until now."

"Marie, listen to me a moment," said Mr. Latimer in a grave voice, "how have we lived since we were married? I'm not finding fault, but what has our life been? simply one of excitement and society. How little we have seen of each other; it was all right, we had to take a wedding trip I suppose; and we chose to make the round of those noisy watering places. You are a beautiful woman, and naturally attracted attention; I was glad to see that you enjoyed yourself, I was happy in seeing you happy; but I soon grew tired of living in a crowd, I wanted my wife to myself. I had married a woman that I loved, and it was not enough for me to stand one side, and see her dancing and walking and driving with other men; but that seemed the only possible way then, and so I consoled myself with the thought that when we were settled in our own home, it would all be changed. But how has it been, since we have been settled in this house? in the six weeks that we have been keeping house, we have not had two evenings to ourselves, and in those, you were so tired out, you had to go to bed. Now do you call this a happy life?"

"Yes, I do," replied Mrs. Latimer, "I think we've had a beautiful life since we were married. I would like to go back and live it all over again."

"Two thousand years of such a life wouldn't amount to anything," said Mr. Latimer.

"How can you say such a thing, Rodger, you have had everything to make you happy."

"Have I? I don't think so. It must be, Marie, that our ideas of happiness differ somewhat, and it would be unfortunate if that were so."

"I don't know that my ideas on the subject are at all peculiar," said Mrs. Latimer, "that they are at all different from other people's, it seems a very simple question."

"A question of what? balls, and dinners, and operas, and theatricals?" asked Mr. Latimer in a sarcastic tone.

"Yes, and the balls, and dinners, and operas, and theatricals of which you speak so contemptuously, are all delightful things, and add a great deal to life. I'm sure life is very stupid without them," said Mrs. Latimer.

"Well Marie, what of the home life?"

"We have a beautiful home, and I can't see why we cannot be happy in it, I'm sure I am."

"You are in it very little, my dear; not in it at all, I might say, without some of your friends around you. We are scarcely through breakfast, before some one is here, and then we do not have an hour to ourselves until bedtime."

"What do you wish, Rodger? you complain about my friends coming here to see me, and about my going to their houses to see them, and dislike the dancing class, and the Histrionic club; what would you wish me to do?"

"No, Marie, I am very glad to have you see your friends here, and see them in their own homes, but I do not like to have people in our house so much that we have no life together; to the extent that the privacy of home is utterly destroyed."

"What do you wish to do, and have me do?" asked Mrs. Latimer, "sit stupidly around this house doing nothing?"

Mr. Latimer was fast losing his patience, but controlled himself well as he replied: "I would like it, if we could drive together sometimes, and have half of our evenings say, alone together for reading."

"I'm sure we do drive pleasant days," said Mrs Latimer.

"Yes, in your fashionable hour, taking our place in the procession with hundreds behind us. That s no pleasure compared to a drive alone with each other, in the morning, in the quiet park."

"I cannot see," said Mrs. Latimer, "what pleasure you find wandering around that park alone, and in the woods beyond. There is some excitement in going in the driving hour; and as to our having our evenings alone, what should we do? It's natural for people to love society. I'm sure I would like to please you, Rodger, but you know we would find such evenings dull. I don't like books, and I do like society." Mrs. Latimer's voice was kind, almost pathetic, as she said this, and the tone touched her husband's heart. He placed his arm around her shoulders, resting his hand on the soft dark hair as it enveloped her, and strove to draw her toward him. "My love, I know you wish to please me," he said, "and you know that I love you dearly, don't let us waste our lives on society, when we might find such happiness in each other." But Marie withstood the pressure of his hand, and retained her bolt upright position. She neither turned her head toward his, that was bent low near her, nor in any way showed that she was aware of his warmth of feeling. After a few moments of silence, Mr. Latimer raised his hand from her shoulder, and as he laid it on the arm of his chair, said in a voice, low toned with emotion:

"We do not seem to think quite alike about these matters, so all we can do, is to harmonize our action the best we can."

"I do not understand you, Rodger, what do you mean?"

"That we must decide upon some consistent course of conduct, and adhere to it. I suppose that each of us may have to give up our wishes somewhat."

"I don't know what there is to decide, our life is decided for us by the position we are in, and I am sure I do not expect you to sacrifice your wishes to me, and I don't see what there is that I can possibly give up." Mrs. Latimer crossed her slippered feet before the fire and clasped her jeweled hands in her lap.

"You spoke of the dancing class a few moments ago," said Mr. Latimer. "I was gratified that your sister and. Mrs. Edmunds wished you to be one of the patronesses, it is really a compliment to you, and I shall be glad to attend the dances with you, but Marie, you must not expect me to lead your german."

"I think it would be very unkind of you to refuse, Rodger, and your doing so would place me in a very unpleasant position, for I have assured Mrs. Edmunds and Mrs. Therbert that you would lead it."

"Why did you do that?" asked Mr. Latimer; "you

remember I declined, the very first evening that Mrs. Therbert spoke of it."

"I didn't suppose that you were serious in what you said."

"Do I usually speak without a purpose, and not mean what I say?"

"I knew that you were perfectly willing to lead the german at Mrs. Richmond's last winter," said Mrs. Latimer, "and every one said that your figures were beautiful; how did I know that you had changed your mind, and did not wish to lead this one?"

"Only because I said that I did not," replied Mr. Latimer, as he leaned his head back wearily against his chair. "I was pleased to lead that german last winter, but it don't take long to satisfy a man with that sort of thing. Last winter seems ten years off."

"I'm sure Rodger, that you will not refuse, now that the matter has gone so far."

"No, I presume that I shall not," he replied in a hard, dry tone, "but Marie, let us understand plainly about these theatricals."

"What is there to understand? I have promised to join the club, there is not the least harm in it, and there is a great deal of pleasure in it; you need not join it, if you do not choose."

"If I decline to join that club, Marie, will you become a member, and take part in these plays?"

"I have said that I would, and I don't see why I should not," replied Mrs. Latimer.

"As a matter of course, that settles the question for me. As much as I dislike the whole thing, I shall join the club; I never shall be an active member." Mr. Latimer did not see the smile that curled the corners of his wife's mouth, as he bravely made this assertion, "but I have too

great a regard for you, and for my dignity as your husband, to have my young wife going to those rehearsals
without the protecting presence of her husband." Marie
was silent, and after a moment Mr. Latimer continued:
" It seems that our life is decided for us, I have very little
to say about mine." Then turning suddenly toward his
wife, as he leaned forward resting one hand on his knee,
he said:

" Do you know, Marie, what all of this leads to? we are
casting from us the holiest thing on earth; and that is a
home. You and I ought to weave about ourselves a
perfect life, from the love we have for each other, our
books, and the leisure we have for reading, and the
friends we could bring around us; and we would grow to
love the same things, and would go on through life, loving each other better every year, and being happier every
year. But don't you see that if we lead the life that you
seem to be marking out, we shall only eat and sleep in
this house, it will be full of people half of the time, and
the other half we shall be in a crowd; men and women
will come between us, our interests will be different, and
our aims different; God only knows what the end will be.
It seems a hollow, superficial life to me. So different
from what I dreamed my home would be," he added,
impetuously, as he rose to his feet, and rested one hand
on the mantel, as he gazed into the fire. Marie said
nothing, but kept her eyes steadily fixed on the toes of
her slippers. Mr. Latimer looked down at her, but the
expression, that was half anger and half pain, did not
soften as he gazed upon her face. After awhile she said
in an indifferent tone:

"Have you anything more that you wish to say, Rodger?"
There was a moment's hesitation on his part, then he
replied in a tone equally indifferent:

" No."

She quietly rose from her chair, and as quietly moved about the room preparing for bed. Mr. Latimer's eyes followed her movements for a few minutes, as he stood with his back to the fire, then he re-seated himself in the large chair, and leaning his head back, closed his eyes.

As Mrs. Latimer settled herself in bed, she said: " It's late, Rodger, are you not coming to bed?"

" After a little," he replied in a tone of unnatural constraint, " I presume I shall not disturb you, if I sit here awhile."

CHAPTER XXV.

As the winter advanced, the stream of society became a maelstrom. It was a rapid whirl of dinners, balls, receptions, operas and theaters; a bewildering kaleidoscopic view of beautiful women, flashing jewels, choice costumes, and lovely flowers, under brilliant lights, moving to rare music. And everywhere the central figure was the beautiful Mrs. Latimer. Her personal beauty, the richness of her dress, and her elaborate entertainments, were the talk of all of her friends. She never seemed to weary, but filled several engagements every day with perennial freshness, and unflagging gayety. She became the fashion, and therefore was carried on the shoulders of society. While she was intoxicated by her elevation, and every day added to the zest of the enjoyment, she kept her balance and conducted herself with the caution of an old society expert. Every move on the social board was made with shrewdness. The capital of her own good looks, and her husband's wealth, she used to such advantage, that her popularity steadily increased, and she was constantly surrounded by a crowd of admiring men and women, who fed her vanity by the most fulsome flattery. The mature women, who for years had been the accepted authority in Clinton society, did not quite like to pay court to so young a woman, but found it necessary to do so, as she could draw from them at any time, the men they most desired to grace their dinners, or give attraction to their dancing rooms. The girls, who were looking out from under the wings of their chaperones, thought Mrs. Latimer the most fortunate being in the universe. The old men feared that she was going too fast, while the younger men all agreed with Grey Whitridge, who declared one day at his club, "that he feared he had been a fool for permitting Rodger Latimer to carry off Marie Edwards," adding: "By Jove! she has the figure of a Venus."

Mr. Latimer was spoken of as a most devoted husband, so much in love with his wife that he could not bear to have her out of his sight, and was held up as a model for imitation, by pleasure-loving wives, when their weary husbands intimated that it would be well to send "regrets" to certain invitations, the acceptance of which would necessitate unusually late hours. "Look at Mr. Latimer," said one lady, "he goes everywhere with his wife, and how agreeable and pleasant he always is." And this was the impression that Mr. Latimer wished to produce. He had not been deaf to remarks, made among men at the clubs, regarding some women, who were frequently seen in society unattended by their husbands, and he had a morbid fear of such things being said of his wife. He determined, that at all hazards the public should see nothing to talk about in his domestic matters. He found himself in a very unsettled state of mind. His castle in the air—of four walls of a home shutting out the world, and shutting in himself and the beautiful Marie— had fallen with a crash. In place of a quiet life with a beautiful woman whom he loved, he found himself dragged from one place to another, and forced every day to meet people with whom he had nothing in common, and even those that he positively disliked. His early life as a conscientious student, had developed habits of regularity and industry, and being naturally a reflecting man, he had learned to love books. Possessing such habits and tastes, the ceaseless round of dances, card parties, dinners and operas, acted on him as nervous irritants. All regular habits were broken up, he never knew at what time he would be able to go to bed, and with some difficulty kept track of the places where his evenings were to be passed. He would have divided his time mostly between his clubs and his library, had it not been that he stood too much in fear of public opinion, to leave his wife dependent for an escort upon her many gentlemen friends, who stood ready to do her bidding. He would, at times, sit with Mr. White through a quiet evening, when Mrs. White and Marie were at the theater, but usually he claimed a place in her box, and was somewhere in the background of all of her parties and balls. As the winter wore on, he became impressed with the idea, that his wife would willingly dispense with his presence at many places of gaiety.

"Do not go out this evening, Rodger, if you are not feeling well," she said to him one evening immediately after dinner, when for the first time for weeks, they had dined at their own table alone. "Mrs. Edmunds is to stop here. I can go in her carriage, if you prefer to remain at home."

"Who will be in the carriage?" asked Mr. Latimer.

After a moment's hesitation, Marie replied: "Mr. Edmunds and Colonel Moran are to be with her, I believe; I can go down with them, and they can leave me here as they return, it won't be a block out of their way, you know."

"I prefer going with you," Mr. Latimer replied; "I'll order the carriage round. Perhaps you better put on your wraps," he added, as he touched the bell for the carriage.

"Very well," said Mrs. Latimer, "do as you like; you know it is Modjeska in Odette to-night. I know you don't like Odette, and it's not very pleasant for me to feel that you are making a martyr of yourself on my account."

"There is no reason for you to say that I'm making a martyr of myself, Marie, I'm doing exactly what I wish to."

"Which is to persevere in your **espionage**," said Marie, spitefully.

"Mrs. Latimer, that **is an unbecoming speech for you** to make," said Mr. **Latimer, as his lips drew in rigid** lines. "Do you wish to **go in society** without me?"

Mrs. Latimer was standing beside a table selecting from a vase of roses, those she **wished** to wear, **and as she** twined the stems together, she replied:

"It's unpleasant to be shadowed by **one's husband to** that extent that remarks are made about it, **especially, as** I know that more than half **of** the time you **go for no** other purpose **than** to be near me."

"It **has come** to a pretty pass, if the fact of a husband **accompanying** his wife to a place of amusement gives **cause** for remark," **said Mr.** Latimer, "and shows that in such society, there is reason that she should be thus accompanied. If I do go, just to be **near** you, it's a precaution for which you should feel thankful. I should think a woman could see Odette, with full as much sense of propriety if seated by her husband, as when surrounded by her gentlemen friends."

Mrs. Latimer made no reply, **and Mr.** Latimer seriously thought, for a moment, of asserting his authority, and declaring that they would both stay at home; but the prospect of an evening alone together in their present moods was not very inviting, and then he felt that Marie would not quietly submit to such a requirement. So he rose, as a maid entered, and announced that the carriage was at the door. "It's time to go," he said.

"We better wait until the Edmunds come," said Mrs. Latimer, without looking up from her roses.

"No," replied Mr. Latimer, "we will go on. "Standish can tell them we have gone, and they can follow us."

Mrs. Latimer went up stairs for her cloak, Mr. Latimer

stepped into the hall, put on his overcoat and returned, hat in hand, to the library, to wait her coming, where he sat gloomily watching the clock. Fifteen minutes had passed, when he heard voices in the hall. He found on going into the hall, that the butler had admitted Colonel Moran, who had his eyes fixed upon Mrs. Latimer, as she was descending the stairs.

"This is very kind, Colonel Moran," she said, as she came toward him in her queenly beauty, "but Mr. Latimer is feeling better, and has decided to go with us, our carriage is waiting, we will immediately follow you. Ask Mrs. Edmunds to please wait for us in the foyer, if you reach the opera house first."

Not a word was spoken between Mr. and Mrs. Latimer as they sat side by side during the two mile drive from their home to the opera house. Mr. Latimer discovered, when inside the house, that two boxes had been taken by some one, that were being rapidly filled by ten or twelve people. Mrs. Edmunds and Mrs. Therbert seemed to be seating the company, and he took the chair designated. He observed that Marie was not in the box with him, but was beside Colonel Moran in the next box. Mrs. Therbert seated herself by his side, and engrossingly appropriated him with her sprightly talk until the curtain rose. He disliked Odette exceedingly, and paid little or no attention to the stage. When the play was over, as the crowd emerged from the building, he became in some way separated from Mrs. Latimer and her friends, and waited outside on the sidewalk, amid the jostling crowd, looking eagerly for his wife until he felt sure, so long a time had elapsed since he left the house, that she must have gone on to the carriage, which was some little distance from the entrance, where he had ordered it to remain for them. As he approached the carriage, the coachman told him that Mrs. Latimer bade him say that she would drive home with Mrs. Edmunds. When he reached home he went immediately to his room, and on his way he passed Mrs. Latimer's maid in the upper hall, and said to her: "Mrs. Latimer has not come in."

"I know it, sir," she replied, "she directed me to sit up and let her in; she said she was going to a supper after the theater."

The next day near noon, Mr. Latimer was lounging in the little room called his study. He rarely occupied it for any purpose whatever, so rarely that no one would have thought of looking for him there. Once in this room he had overheard a conversation between his wife and Mrs. Therbert, as they were seated in the library, and he was fated this morning to repeat the experience. As he lay with his eyes closed, seriously weighing in his mind the advantages and disadvantages of going into his law office as an active partner, in order to escape the weariness of his idle life, the voice of Mrs. Therbert fell on his ear.

"Ask Mrs. Latimer," she said to the butler, "if I shall go to her room." As she was speaking Mrs. Latimer entered.

"This is very sweet of you to stop for me, Charlotte," she said, "in ten minutes more I should have been on my way to your house. Sit down, my dear, we needn't go for half an hour yet."

"How prettily you have your neck arranged, Marie, that is very becoming to you; why didn't you wear that dress last night? I believe it is even more becoming than that blue," said Mrs. Therbert.

"Do you think so?" asked Mrs. Latimer. "Colonel Moran said last night that I ought always to wear blue."

"Wasn't that a complete supper? Mr. Edmunds always does everything perfectly," said Mrs. Therbert.

"We had just the right number, two men apiece," said Mrs. Latimer. "How much pleasanter that makes it, than the same number of men and women."

"Yes, for us," said Mrs. Therbert; "but I wonder if the men like it as well."

"I'm sure they do; either you or I, Charlotte, can entertain two men."

"Better say that it takes two men to entertain us," said Mrs. Therbert, with a laugh. "Who did you come home with?"

"With Mrs. Edmunds, Colonel Moran and Mr. Whitridge. We drove to Mrs. Edmunds' first, and then Colonel Moran and Mr. Whitridge brought me home. How did you go home?"

"I'm almost ashamed to tell you, Marie; I don't know how it happened, but I went in Mrs. Edmunds' carriage, alone with Mr. Edmunds. I think that the arrangement was that Mr. Barstow was to go with us, but some way no one got into the carriage, and we drove off alone."

"Why, that was strange," said Mrs. Latimer. "Where did Mr. Barstow go?"

"I don't know. Don't you ever tell Lucas that Mrs. Edmunds was not in that carriage, he wouldn't like it. Did Mr. Latimer say anything about your staying to the supper?"

"No," replied Mrs. Latimer.

"I don't think Lucas liked my going without him."

"I presume not," said Mrs. Latimer. "I think it makes any man half cross to have his wife go off and have a good time without him. Not that he objects to the place, or people she is with, but he don't like to be left out. Was Mr. Therbert awake when you reached home?"

"Yes, and he was cross as a bear, but I don't blame him much, he had a dreadful time getting home. Did you know that it rained a little soon after the theater closed?"

"No, but it was a nasty night."

"You see," said Mrs. Therbert, "we went down in Mr. Whitridge's carriage. He dined with us. Then Mrs. Edmunds and Mr. Barstow, Mr. Whitridge and I went to the Bellevue in Mr. Whitridge's carriage. I thought Lucas would find Mr. Latimer and come up with him, but he didn't come across him, and the carriages were all gone and he couldn't find a cab, and so he took the street cars, and he had that two blocks and a half to walk, and it rained a little, and he had no umbrella. It didn't look quite right, Marie, say what you like, for a woman to go off to a theater supper, and then go home in a carriage alone with another man, and her husband walk home in the rain. Don't you ever let him know that Mrs. Edmunds wasn't in the carriage, for I told him the Edmund's brought me home."

"Why didn't he have his own carriage there for him?"

"We went down with Mr. Whitridge," said Mrs. Therbert; "his carriage was at our house for him, and he invited us to go with him."

"Well, I don't suppose Mr. Therbert thinks it is his wife's business to arrange for his return home from a theater," said Mrs. Latimer.

"No, of course not, but it was unfortunate all around. He was not right good-natured when he left the house this morning; the children noticed it."

Mrs. Latimer rose from the sofa where she had been sitting beside her friend, and stepped to a table near by and took from a jar a dozen or more of roses. She wound some tissue paper around the wet stems, and gave them to Mrs. Therbert.

"There, give him those, Charlotte; we'll leave them at

your house as we go by, and to-night give them to him, and tell him I sent them to him. You must keep your husband in good humor."

The conversation continued some time longer between the two ladies, who after a little went off together to a luncheon. Mr. Latimer had distinctly heard every word that had been said, and he was surprised that the artifice and management which had been disclosed on the part of his wife did not affect him more seriously than it did. He was aware that his strongest feeling regarding her was the desire that she should conduct herself in society in a way that would be consistent with the dignity of a married woman; and he congratulated himself upon the caution which she seemed to possess, and the determination which he thought she evinced, of not going beyond a certain line, which line—as society went—was a long way from the gossiper's target. As he reflected on his entire freedom from jealousy regarding her, he saw a more forbidding specter waiting by his side to accompany him through life, than the one that rose before him on the evening, when, by the fireside in his bedroom they had their first disagreement as to their home and social life. That evening it was a terrible specter that arose, as he thought, "She never loved me," but as he calmly reflected on her conduct in the clear noonday as he lay on the lounge in his study, the specter evoked by the thought, "I never loved her," was a ghastly thing, that cast a shadow forward the length of his life.

CHAPTER XXVI.

Two weeks after the incidents recorded in the last chapter, Mr. Latimer entered his office where the Mead Brothers were busily at work, and where the presence of a law student and an office boy, gave quite a business aspect to the place. As he entered the room, the elder of the brothers, who happened to be looking that way through the open door of an inner room, came forward to meet him.

"Good-morning, Mr. Latimer," he said, as he extended his hand; "we're very glad to see you here."

"I've only dropped in to see how the old room looks; don't let me disturb you, I wish to sit here for half an hour."

"Come into my office; it's at your disposal," said Mr. Mead.

"No, I thank you," replied Mr. Latimer; "I prefer to sit here."

He stepped to the window, and seated himself where he could look into the street, over which his eye had frequently wandered when he was sole occupant of that office, a poor young man, waiting for clients. It did not seem possible that he was the same man, who, in gloomy discontent, used to stand at that window, gazing into the street below. He vividly remembered the ambition, anger and mortification that then filled his heart, only it did not seem that it was he. He thought of himself as though he had been another man, and he criticised and berated that other man for his ignorance of life, and folly in thinking, that all desirable good lay in the possession of wealth, or could be encompassed through wealth. He remembered his envy of Grey Whitridge, and compared it with the contempt with which he now regarded him. He remembered the bewildering beauty that then enveloped the society women, whom he was fortunate enough to see in the houses of wealth, surrounded by the halo cast by gold, and he wondered where the beauty of Mrs. Therbert, Mrs. Richmond and Mrs. Lefarve had fled. He remembered how the witchery of dancing feet and regal feasts then turned his head; and he fairly groaned in spirit to think what sounding brass and tinkling cymbals the whole thing was to him now, a weight and burden to be borne. He could not believe that less than one year and a half had elapsed. How could a man change so much in so short a time! It was as though he had leaped from youth to age. He had passed in a few months, from a gnawing hunger to the nausea of satiety. A few months since, his heart would have bounded with delight, at the thought of leading a german in the home of a millionaire, now he felt like laying a rawhide over the shoulders of any man, who would dare to ask him to do so stupid a thing. What a little thing it seemed when once done! When he was outside the charmed circle, he was gloomy and unhappy; now that he was inside, standing at the very center, was he less gloomy and unhappy? He ought to be happy; possessed of an assured income, and of a wife who was said to be the most beautiful woman in the city; possessed also of leisure, and a large circle of friends; yet he was as restless and unhappy as a man could be. It was true he had not exhausted the capabilities of wealth, that there were some pleasures lying in wait for him, that money could buy, that he had not tasted. Mr. Whitridge and Mr. Barstow, and several other club friends, had invited him to the delectable pleasures of late suppers, and their after kindred gratifications; but his nature revolted from that species of pleasure. He left his chair, and walked slowly down the room in front of the rows of law books on the shelves, looking at them closely, and at times standing still in front of them, lost in thought. Yes, he ought to be there studying, it would be much pleasanter than going to the balls and dinners that he was compelled to; books were more to him than society, the training of his youth, and habits of his manhood had unfitted him for the idle dissipations that wealth seemed to entail; should he pick up his knowledge of law again, and enter earnestly into its practice, and come regularly to his office? He turned to the table where the law student was at work, and glanced over the paper that he was copying, then he entered Mr. Mead's room, and made inquiries regarding the business of the office, the number and character of the suits on hand. He listened attentively to all Mr. Mead said, and came to quite an accurate conclusion as to the character of the work that awaited him, should he resume practice. It seemed very uninviting, an uninspiring drudgery: to undertake it for the mere love of it, was impossible. He wondered at the enthusiasm with which Mr. Mead entered into a recital of several cases that were pending, and at his evident gratification, as he stated the aggregate amount earned by the office during the last six months. It seemed to Mr. Latimer a pitiful sum of money, for so much work. He felt that the incentive to labor was lacking in his life.

After lingering an hour in the office he went over to his club, where he lunched with half a dozen acquaintances, some of whom were possessed of inherited wealth, and some were active business and professional men, who had earned every dollar of their large fortunes. As he observed the superior health, intellectual activity and cheerful animation which the latter possessed over the former, he questioned if his uncle's legacy to him had been an unmixed blessing. He feared that he had permitted his wealth to place him in an unnatural position, and paralyze the best faculties of his being. He felt that he was a man of splendid health, stalwart and vigorous; but this physical strength was given to dancing and carrying a cane; that his mind was well stored and naturally active, but it had little employment outside of settling the momentous question of clothes and assisting in the selection of French parlor theatricals; that his sympathies and moral sense allied him to all humanity, but practically his sole interest centered in a circle of women who wore good clothes, and men who followed in their wake. He sat in the reading-room for several hours during the afternoon engaged in moral reflections, which ended in his going home to dress for the dancing class ball, which ball was to close the season before Lent, and was to be a splendid affair, the last ecstatic reel of the members of the dancing class before they sat down in penitential sackcloth and ashes to weep over their sins.

If Mr. Latimer had hoped in his ignorance of society's ways of wearing sackcloth, that he was to have a forty-days' rest, he speedily found out his mistake by discovering the special adaptation of the Histrionic club to the needs of the elite penitents. He soon learned that parties and public dances were to be foregone, and that the self-denying spirit required the sacrifice af operas and theaters, demanding that theatricals be relegated to private theaters, and that all dancing should be impromptu in drawing-rooms and at the rehearsals of the Histrionic club.

Mrs. Latimer had informed her husband several times with an icy dignity of manner that it was not necessary for him to escort her to all of the rehearsals held by the club, and frequently he did not know when or where they were held until after her return from them accompanied by some of her gentlemen friends and Mrs. Lefarve or Mrs. Therbert, usually Mrs. Therbert. The association of Mr. and Mrs. Latimer with each other since the unpleasant scene between them on the night of Modjeska's Odette had been conducted with conventional politeness. They were rarely alone together, unless when wearily undressing for bed at a late hour, or in the presence of the servants at the breakfast table. Even their Sundays were not passed with each other, for some one always dined with them, and it was not an unusual occurrence for three or four persons to come in for the evening, and remain until midnight.

There did seem to be a prospect of their passing one evening by their own fireside late in February. The day was the anniversary of Mr. and Mrs. White's marriage, which Mrs. White declared should be celebrated by a family dinner at an earlier hour than usual, so that the children could dine with them. A six o'clock dinner was ordered, at which there were no guests beside Mr. and Mrs. Latimer At nine o'clock the children were taken to the nursery, and soon after Mrs. Latimer announced that she must return home. Mr. Latimer was surprised that she wished to return so early, as she had said to him on their way to Mrs. White's that she had no other engagement for the evening, and he could not imagine that she wished to pass hours alone with him. On entering the library they found Mrs. Therbert sitting by the fire waiting their return.

"You see I have taken possession," she said, as she rose to greet them.

"Yes, and you are an angel for coming," exclaimed Mrs. Latimer, as she fondly kissed her.

Usually when any of Mrs. Latimer's lady friends came in, unaccompanied by their husbands, Mr. Latimer withdrew to his own room, and passed the time with his books, and such hours were most enjoyed by him of any that the winter brought him. But to-night he purposely staid in the library, taking up a magazine to read, so as not to be a check on the conversation of the ladies. For the past few days, he had been thinking much of the unfortunate state of affairs between Mrs. Latimer and himself, and of how little, after all, he really knew of her most intimate society friends. He had been thinking of Marie's comparative youth, her great desire for praise and adulation, which was fed and inflamed by the flattery forced upon her from all sides, of what seemed to him, her insane love of dress, and inordinate fondness of gentlemen's attentions. He questioned whether he had acted wisely in giving her an unrestricted bank account of her own, and blamed himself, that he had not insisted on accompanying her to every one of the Histrionic rehearsals; and he remembered, as he went over it as accurately as he could, that not more than one-half of the time had he been with her to these rehearsals. The result of these reflections had been, that he had made up his mind to identify himself more closely than ever, with his wife's society life, especially the informal part of it, of which he had really known but little. And another thing that he determined to do, was to break up the intimacy between Marie and Mrs. Therbert, whom he had come to regard as a woman of little principle, a thoroughly scheming, selfish one, who had no honest affection for his wife, whom she was constantly flattering and petting, for purposes of her own. In keeping with these determinations, he remained in the library, instead of going, as usual, to his own room; a proceeding which evidently discomfited both ladies, and which he plainly saw was making Marie angry. In fact, Mrs. Latimer wondered at his behavior in staying, and was revolving in her own mind, whether or not, it would do to take Mrs. Therbert to some other room. She did not wish to do quite so pointed a thing, and yet there were matters in connection with their forthcoming play that she wished to canvass with Mrs. Therbert, and of which she desired her husband to know nothing. For half an hour the conversation went on in a desultory sort of way, regarding some society matters in which neither of the ladies were evidently interested, and their gaiety of spirits was obviously assumed. But after awhile, Mrs. Therbert, who had glanced frequently from husband to wife, as though unable to understand this new state of affairs, and evidently feeling that something unusual was taking place, had taken place, or was going to take place, seemed to have made up her mind as to what she herself would do under the circumstances; turned the conversation abruptly from the subject on which Mrs. Latimer was speaking, by saying:

"Mr. Lefarve was to see me immediately after dinner, about that Medora dress of yours, and he wished me to ask you, if you hadn't better take cardinal instead of blue. He rather wishes for the blue for his own coat. Now what do you think about it? if it is changed we must do it soon, for so many other changes will have to be made in colors, if that is changed. I know Colonel Moran likes you best in blue, but Mr. Lefarve thinks the change better be made."

"I don't know as I care anything about it, Charlotte, don't let us talk of it to-night," said Mrs. Latimer, fixing her eyes upon Mrs. Therbert with a significant expression which Mrs. Therbert failed to see, owing to the way the light fell upon Mrs. Latimer; or for some reason known to herself, did not choose to heed.

Mrs. Therbert broke into a laugh. "You don't care!" she said, "well, you *are* a strange woman, Marie Latimer; I'm poorly paid for coming out in the cold to see you about the matter."

"Why, my dear Charlotte! don't say so, indeed—"

"Here I've been doing my best to keep that blue for you," said Mrs. Therbert, interrupting Mrs. Latimer in a most discourteous manner, "somewhat, to be sure, to please Mr. Whitridge and Colonel Moran, for they both declare that you ought to wear the blue, that it is so very becoming to you; but more to please you, and then you say you don't know, or care anything about it!"

"I meant I didn't care to decide to-night, Charlotte. I do care to do whatever you wish me to—"

"I have no wish, or opinion about it," interrupted Mrs. Therbert half angrily.

"Come, Charlotte," said Mrs. Latimer, who was anxious to appease her friend, "don't be so hard on me. I know it's very kind of you to come out to-night, and that you are very unselfish, I do care, as a matter of course I care for everything that relates to our play—"

Mrs. Latimer was interrupted by the entrance of her butler, who approached her with a large bunch of Marechal Niel roses, bound together by a narrow ribbon, to which was attached a card.

"How did these come, Standish?" she asked, as she took them from the tray.

"A man just left them at the door," the butler replied.

20 Rodger Latimer's Mistake.

"How lovely they are!" exclaimed Mrs. Therbert.   "I adore Marechal Niels; who sent **them, Marie?**"

Mrs. Latimer had detached the card from the ribbon, and after reading what was written thereon, she slipped it in the belt of her dress.   As she raised the roses to her face, she said in reply to Mrs. Therbert's question: "A friend of mine."

"I wish I had a dozen such friends," said Mrs. Therbert, as she reached her hand for the flowers, "these are the finest I've seen this winter."

"Now about that dress, Charlotte," said Mrs. Latimer, as she resigned her flowers into the outstretched hand, "perhaps we better not give up the blue, but I'll do as you think best. I don't see why we should give up a color that exactly pleases us, to Mr. Lefarve, but as I said, I'll do as you say about it."

"How queer you talk to-night, Marie.   I've nothing to do with that costume, it's nothing to me, either the blue or the cardinal.   Of course I wish to see you look your best, and take more interest in your appearance than I do in Mr. Lefarve's, but if you and Colonel Moran and Mr. Whitridge are satisfied, the rest of us ought to be."

"Well then," said Mrs. Latimer, as she took her flowers from Mrs. Therbert's lap, "I'll keep the blue, and if you cannot satisfy Mr. Lefarve regarding it, I'll talk the matter over with him.   Now tell me about Mrs. Black, Harriet said she heard that you had received a letter from her; is she in Algiers or Spain?"

Before Mrs. Therbert could reply to this question, they were again interrupted by the entrance of the butler, who brought a note to Mrs. Latimer, which, after breaking the seal that securely fastened it, she read attentively.   As she finished reading it, she placed it in her belt beside the card.   She did not look at her husband, but turned to Mrs.

Therbert, and vivaciously resumed the conversation with her, by asking several questions regarding Mrs. Black and her winter abroad. Mr. Latimer's thoughts took a new direction, that led him into a field of speculation—that of society flirtations—that was neither pleasant to himself, nor complimentary to his wife. It was nearly eleven o'clock, when Mr. Therbert, returning home from some public meeting, came in for his wife. He was both tired and cold, and could not be persuaded to remain longer than for Mrs. Therbert to gather her wraps around her. Mrs. Latimer accompanied her into the hall, and after an affectionate parting from her, returned to the library fireside, where Mr. Latimer was sitting, holding in his hand the roses which she had laid on the table as she passed down the room with Mrs. Therbert.

"These are beautiful flowers, Marie," he said, "who sent them to you?"

"A friend of mine," Mrs. Latimer replied, as she rested one hand on the corner of the mantel, and placed her foot on the fender.

"Yes, I suppose so," replied Mr. Latimer, "but which one of your many friends?"

"I don't know, Rodger, as it's of any importance to you, which one of the many, as you are pleased to designate them," replied Mrs. Latimer, who was ill-natured because she had been disappointed in her evening with Mrs. Therbert. The truth was, she did not wish her husband to know anything of the character or costume in which she was to appear the next week in their long talked of play, that was then to have its first presentation, so she had not dared to speak of any one of the several items that she had wished to talk over with Mrs. Therbert.

"It's of importance to me that my wife courteously answer any question that I may ask," said Mr. Latimer, with severe dignity. Mrs. Latimer looked morosely into the fire, and said nothing. Mr. Latimer regarded her in silence for a moment, and then said:

"I wish to know who sent these flowers to you."

As she remained silent, his face flushed with anger. At first he had cared very little who the person was that paid his wife the attention of sending her roses, but her persistent refusal to tell him, angered him, and also excited his curiosity regarding the donor. The authoritative tone of her husband's voice, aroused all of the feminine resistance within Mrs. Latimer, and she continued her silence. After a few moments Mr. Latimer asked:

"From whom was that note that Standish handed you?"

Mrs. Latimer raised her eyes, and fixed them full upon her husband's face, in a defiant stare, as she sneeringly said:

"Would my lord like to know also, who sent the letter I received yesterday?"

Instantly there was a reaction in Mr. Latimer's heart. His blood fell to zero, and the momentary sense of keen suffering occasioned by his wife's mad injustice, which had, as she spoke, immediately taken the place of the anger that had filled his heart, gave way quickly to cool contempt. Could that be his wife? had that flushed face, with its swollen lips, and fiery eyes, ever been beautiful in his sight? They looked into each other's eyes for an instant, then Mr. Latimer rose to his feet, and quietly laid the roses which he had retained in his hand, on a chair directly in front of the fire; after which he slowly walked the length of the room to the hall door. As he was passing through the doorway, he stopped, with his back to the library, holding the portiere aside with his hand, and without turning his head, said, in a voice held steady by force of will, and in a tone lower than his usual intonations:

"I shall occupy the north room to-night," dropped the curtain, and passed up the stairs.

Mrs. Latimer was too angry to care for consequences. She took the flowers from the chair where her husband had placed them, and held them to her face as though to inhale their fragrance. After a little she took the note from her belt, and read it several times over. As she read it, the expression of her face changed, the anger and resentment that had almost transformed her features, as she gave her stinging retort to her husband, was replaced by a look of complete satisfaction and happiness. The muscles of her face relaxed, her eyes grew gentle and dreamy, and a smile of pleasurable excitement parted her lips. After reading the note half a dozen times, she sat motionless, gazing in the smoldering fire for half an hour.

Then she leaned down low over the ashes, and with the poker raked up all of the live coals, which she gathered into a heap, over which she held the note between her thumb and finger. But just as she was going to lay it on the coals, she seemed to have changed her mind, for she rose, thrust the note into the bosom of her dress, and passed out of the library, up stairs to her room with a flush upon her face, and a light of happy expectancy in her eyes.

CHAPTER XXVII

Four weeks from that evening Mr. Latimer sat alone in a desolate home. The March wind came down from the north, like leashed lions, the carriages rattled over the hard pavement of the street, as though horses and drivers were hastening before the wild blast; but Mr. Latimer, sitting in the solitude of his chamber, heeded the storm as little, as did the dead mistress of the house, lying in her cold beauty in the drawing-room below. She was wrapped about in soft folds of white, silky woolen, surrounded by white flowers. There were flowers everywhere; on the mantel, on tables, on the piano, and all over the coffin that rested on a low bier in the center of the room, which seemed full of orchids, lilies of the valley, snowdrops, camellias, and white roses. The marble face was uncovered, and the head was turned a little to one side on its pillow. There came a dim light from the side gas jets, that cast into the silent room the softness of moonlight. Over this scene of icy beauty, reigned a deathly stillness, in strange contrast with the raging storm without.

It had been a backward spring, full of the sharp winds and sudden changes incident to the lake region, and Mrs. Latimer took a severe cold one evening, by standing in a current of air on the stage, during the presentation of a play by the Histrionic club, in the costume her character demanded, which costume was composed of very thin fabrics. Her cold took the form of pneumonia, that rapidly assumed a severe type, and in a few days placed her beyond human skill. All of her society friends would have gathered in sympathy close around her husband, after her decease, had they been permitted by him to have done so; but he shut himself away in the solitude of his own chamber, to which he admitted no one beside his servant, and Mrs. White, when he was forced to respond to some of her questions, regarding his wishes, in connection with the burial. Mrs. White tried to persuade him to look upon the face of his dead wife, but he would not.

"Let me alone, Harriet," he said, "let me think of her as she was, a beautiful, living woman. I would rather not carry in my memory a dead face."

"But Rodger," Mrs. White persisted, "you've no idea how beautiful the dear girl looks, so peaceful and happy."

Mr. Latimer begged to be left to himself, reiterating that it was better he should not see her. But that night, as he sat gazing vacantly into the fire, he suddenly started from his chair, as though a new thought had struck him, and went into the hall, and stood outside of his open door. It was past midnight, and not the slightest sound was to be heard. He supposed there were people up, somewhere in the house, but he did not know who was there, nor in which room they were. After listening a moment, he closed his door and passed slowly down the stairs, and across the deserted lower hall, and stood outside of the parlor door. He placed his hand on the knob, then turned his head to listen. Not a sound reached his ear, it was as silent as though he was the only living thing in the house. He opened the door, passed in, and quickly closed it behind him. He stood still and looked around the room, and at last let his eye rest upon the mass of white flowers in the center; all the impression he received was of an area of beautiful flowers, a mass of bouquets. He looked up and down the room, into the shadowy corners, and at the yellow gas jets turned so low, they gave forth only a weird light; stepped to the jet nearest to him, turned it up full head, then walked to the bier, and gazed at the white face embedded in white flowers. He stood immovable, looking upon the face of the woman he had called wife. No cry arose to his lips, no tears came into his eyes. His face had upon it a solemnity equal to that of the dead, and a sadness only living faces wear. He did not think of his wedding day, or of the blissful weeks that preceded it, nor of the disappointments that had come to him, from time to time, regarding his home life during the winter that was past, or of anything pertaining to himself, his life with Marie, or what the future held for him. Just now death seemed the only reality in all the world. Death, coming like a sharp blow in the middle of life, and cutting off one-half of it at a stroke. His mind was engrossed with the strong workings of nature, the impotence of human will, and human love, before physical law; the mastery of the material over the spiritual. With his eyes fixed immovably upon the unconscious face before him, he said to himself: "This cannot be an end, there is nothing here to suggest, or indicate an end, but there is a suggestion of a somewhere else." For a long time he gazed silently upon the white face amid the flowers, then he slowly left the room, without turning off the light with which he had flooded it. As he closed the door, it was with a wonder in his mind, that he did not suffer more. He reproached himself, because his wife's death had not occasioned him greater sorrow; he was shocked, to think that he could pass through such an experience without excruciating anguish, and with so little sense of personal loss. Shocked, to feel that the death of his wife had affected his mind more than his heart, had been the cause of awakening his intellect to new reflections of the deepest significance, rather than of wringing his heart with the anguish of separation.

The immediate practical results in Mr. Latimer's life. of Mrs. Latimer's death were, the closing of the house on Huron avenue, and his withdrawal from society, and close application to the business of his law office. He studied to make himself thoroughly familiar with the affairs of the office, giving the most diligent attention to both the technical forms, and legal principles. He soon became much interested in his profession, and not a long time passed before he began to reap the reward of his labor, in the delightful mental excitement that filled his days. The energies of his mind awoke in full force, and at times he possessed the exquisite pleasure that comes from intellectual creation. As the summer advanced he persuaded his two partners to go off for a vacation, leaving whatever business there was to be done in the office at that season, entirely with him. He neither knew or cared to know, where his old society friends were, he only wished to be left undisturbed at his work.

CHAPTER XXVIII

We shall have to go back a little in the season to Margaret McVey. It was early in May, that Miss Sargent was sitting at her desk engaged in making out her annual reports to several societies for which she was secretary, when Margaret, who was such a frequent visitor at the house that her coming and going was scarcely more noticed than that of its mistress; entered the library so noiselessly that before Miss Sargent knew that she was there, she had her arms around her neck, and was kissing her.

"Why my dear, how like a fairy you come," said Miss Sargent, "you must have had an early breakfast."

"Yes, I did have an early breakfast, for I didn't sleep much last night. Aunt Helen, are you very busy with that writing?"

"Not at all," said Miss Sargent, opening a drawer in the desk, into which she swept all of her papers, with a stroke of her hand. "These reports are nearly done, and I don't need them for several weeks yet. Now what is it, dear? for I know by the tone of your voice, that you have something of more than usual importance to say to me." Miss Sargent rose from her desk as she was speaking, and seated herself in a large chair, and Margaret dropped on a hassock at her feet, and rested her arm across Miss Sargent's knees.

"I want to go to Europe, Aunt Helen," said Margaret as she looked up in Miss Sargent's face.

"To Europe, Margaret!"

"Yes, to Europe. Aunt Helen, you remember that you proposed it last spring, I felt then that I could not go, it would have been a going away from everything, but now, I feel I must go, I can't stay here any longer."

"Well dear, I presume that you are right," said Miss Sargent, "you usually are, although I don't quite understand it. But it shall be as you wish, be sure of that, whether I or any one beside yourself understands it: but why this sudden start?"

"I wish that I could make you understand it, Aunt Helen," said Margaret, as she laid her head on Miss Sargent's knee.

"If you really wish to, why can't you dear, am I so dull of comprehension?"

"No, no," said Margaret, reaching out her hand to clasp one of Miss Sargent's, "but it is hardly natural that you and I should think alike on some subjects."

"Why not natural, Margaret, because I'm so very old?"

"Oh no, you're not old, that is, not old in your feelings."

"Well then, is it because you think that you have had some experiences in life that I cannot understand, that I cannot share?" Margaret clung in silence to the hand she held, and pressed it to her face. "Perhaps Margaret it might be well for us to talk freely upon this subject if we can," continued Miss Sargent, after a few moments' silence, "we are very much to each other, you are more to me than any one living, and while I fully appreciate the sacredness of the individual personality, and understand that our greatest sorrows can be shared by no one, and that the greatest changes in our characters are wrought out in solitude; yet my darling, this is a subject on which we might, and perhaps ought to talk freely, without the least reserve. And if we could for once put all reserve aside, and speak freely, it might be a comfort to us both. You never would let me tell you dear, how I suffered with you, but I did suffer, in tears and bitter indignation. The thought of your sorrow makes me weep even now; I know you are happier, or at least, less sorrowful, than you were a year ago, I know that some sort of comfort has come to you; and I know —and oh! Margaret! how I rejoice in it—I know how nobly you have borne this terrible grief, and how elevating upon your character its effect has been." By this time both women were quietly weeping, Miss Sargent could see the tears dropping from Margaret's eyelashes, upon her half-averted face. After a little Miss Sargent continued:

"I sent you all of the papers that contained anything regarding"—should she say Marie? or Rodger's wife? or Mrs. Latimer? After a slight hesitation she said, "regarding Marie's death. I have not seen Rodger since the evening of the funeral. John and I called late that evening at his house, and when the man told us that Mr. Latimer saw no one John insisted on sending our cards to him; I did not think it best, but on the whole I was glad afterward. Rodger came down to the library, and thanked us for sending our names to him, and said he would have regretted not seeing us, but admitted that he did not wish to see any of his society friends. He looked in good health, and had a sad dignity of manner that was very impressive. We invited him to return with us for the night, but he said he preferred remaining where he was. We were not there more than a quarter of an hour; he went to the outside door with us when we left, and as I extended my hand to say good-night, he took it in both of his, and looked in my face as though he was going to say something; but if he had intended to, he changed his mind, for he relinquished my hand with a pressure, and bade me good-night. The next

Saturday I sent him an invitation to dinner Sunday, and in the note I told him, I hoped he would consider our house his home, and come informally, whenever he chose, as he used to years ago; and that he must command me whenever I could be of any comfort, or service to him. He did not come to dinner, but wrote an appreciative answer, thanking me for my kindness, but said in his present state of mind it was much better for him to be alone. That is all I have known of him. I haven't seen him since; John says he is hard at work in his office, and he don't hear of his being out at all, only in his saddle, he is out on his horse for hours every evening."

While Miss Sargent was speaking, Margaret seemed to scarcely breathe, for fear of losing a word that she said. She did not stir, but sat perfectly still with her head in Miss Sargent's lap. After a little she broke the silence:

"Where does he live?" she asked.

"He closed the house on Huron avenue," said Miss Sargent, "you know he rented it furnished, and has rooms at the Hotel Normandie, I understand." Another long silence followed.

"Aunt Helen?" Margaret said at last.

"Yes dear, what is it?" But as Margaret relapsed into silence again, Miss Sargent said, "Ask me anything, Margaret; were I in your place there would be many things that I would like to know, and I will be glad to tell you anything, if I only knew what you cared to know." As Miss Sargent spoke, she gently pressed her hand on the head that lay on her knee. After another silence of several minutes, Margaret spoke hesitatingly in a low voice, and in broken sentences:

"I wish—I knew—how—they lived together; how—much he really thought of her. It's impossible to stop

Mrs. Herman talking, I have had to listen to much that was painful to me: she says—they—adored each other—that he was—very proud of her—and that she worshiped him—do you know any thing about it?"

"Nothing, darling, but what I have inferred. She was a society woman, very fond of dress, and they say after her marriage she dressed richly, extravagantly so, but in good taste. You know I don't go out much, and I rarely saw either of them after their marriage. I met them occasionally at dinners, and saw her a few times at the theater, and then she was always surrounded by gentlemen. Rodger always seemed to me, in some way, like an attendant in the background. I have heard that he was perfectly infatuated with her beauty from the first. You know that Rodger and I have been great friends ever since he was a boy, and I think I understand his nature; and I don't believe he ever loved her. Perhaps he did experience what men call an infatuation, though how that could have been, is past my comprehension. I saw very little of them, but I never saw any evidence of affection between them. I know something of human nature, and I don't believe he ever loved her. I think he made a mistake, and that he soon discovered it, but was man enough to abide by his decision. He had the reputation of being a devoted husband, but there was no evidence, that I could see, that her death occasioned him any great sorrow. That man John and I saw, on the evening following his wife's funeral, was not deeply suffering. He was sad and thoughtful, but he was neither heart broken nor desolate."

After a little Margaret asked: "Was she so very beautiful?"

"I never thought her beautiful," replied Miss Sargent, "she certainly had a fine figure, and there was a sort of statuesque appearance about her, that was rather imposing. They say that men thought her eyes beautiful, they were not beautiful to me, they were simply large, and well colored. What expression she might have thrown into them, for the sake of affecting her gentlemen friends, I can't say, but I never saw much expression of any kind in them. She did have beautiful hair, it was abundant, and a lovely color. I did not regard her as a woman of much mind, and I know she was not a cultivated woman. I should have said that she was the last type of woman that would have attracted Rodger; for he certainly is a man of thought, and we used to think him a man of large heart, and of straightforward character."

Miss Sargent ceased speaking, but Margaret neither stirred nor spoke, and Miss Sargent leaned her head against the back of her chair, and silence reigned in the room. After awhile she resumed the subject:

"One thing more, Margaret," she said, " Rodger and I never, when we have met, have referred to the past in any way, neither to you or Edgewood; or to our trips abroad together. Only once did he refer to your father, and that was in a letter that I received last summer, when we were at Mackinaw. In that letter he mentioned both you and your Aunt Deborah in connection with your father. I did not think best to show you the letter then, would you like to see it now?"

"Yes, very much," replied Margaret, raising her head from Miss Sargent's knee.

Miss Sargent went to her desk, and took from a drawer the letter referred to, and placed it in Margaret's hand, after which she resumed the writing laid aside on Margaret's entrance. Margaret read Rodger's letter, sitting on the hassock, with her back to Miss Sargent. She read it through very rapidly at first, and then turned back, and read it very slowly; going over some sentences several times. Among these was the sentence, in which he said: "I seem to be waking from a delirium;" and the one where he spoke of the old Edgewood home as being: "A hallowed spot, apart from the heat and strife of ordinary life;" and where he said: "I know that I had forfeited my right to a place beside him, and it adds to the poignancy of my grief this morning to feel that that was so." When she had gone over the letter many times, she leaned her head against the arm of the large chair, where Miss Sargent had been sitting, and closed her eyes. For nearly an hour Miss Sargent's pen sped over the pages, and Margaret sat in motionless thought. Then she rose, and with the open letter in her hand, went and knelt by Miss Sargent's side.

"You never can know, Aunt Helen, how much good you have done me this morning," she said in a calm voice, as she leaned her head upon Miss Sargent's shoulder.

"I'm very glad, dear," replied Miss Sargent, as she placed her hand under Margaret's chin, which she raised, so that she could look into the girl's face. It was a pale face, with eyes that held a sad story, but just then, a very calm face, with an expression of contentment on it.

"I cannot tell you now, Aunt Helen, but after a little I will, just what you have done for me to-day. May I keep this letter of Rodger's? I would like to have it." She spoke the name without a tremor of voice, and it was the first time that Miss Sargent had heard it from her lips for nearly two years.

"Certainly, Margaret, but—" Miss Sargent hesitated, looking anxiously into Margaret's face.

"Don't fear, Aunt Helen, I think I know what your caution would be, but I do not need it. Now let us talk about going to Europe, I'm very anxious to go, and soon."

"Well, dear, we'll talk it over with John after luncheon," replied Miss Sargent.

The plans were easily consummated for an indefinite residence abroad for Margaret and Miss Sargent. Miss Bond was included in their first plan, but she positively refused to leave home.

"I would die of fear before I got half way across that ocean," she declared, "and then I can't leave this kindergarten. Don't talk to me of Rome and the Alps, I don't care to see them; I know I couldn't be one-half as happy anywhere as here with these children, and then Mrs. Bray will need me more than ever, if you are away. If you have no objections, Margaret, suppose we have Mrs. Bray and Eloise come into the house, as soon as you leave, give up their boarding place, I mean, and come here and live with me until you return. We will close your rooms, both your bedroom and Sans Souci, and Mrs. Bray can have the next room to mine. She and Eloise would be company for me, and then when I go East in July, they can stay right on here if they choose, and I'll be back by the first of September, in time to can the fruit, and make jelly and pickles, and have the house ready for the opening of the school by the first of October."

So it was arranged, and in June Miss Sargent and Margaret sailed "for the other side," as Aunt Deborah always designated Europe. Miss Sargent went directly to Paris, believing that Margaret's low spirits would be improved by the most decided change possible from the secluded, eventless life she had led the past winter. The result confirmed her judgment. Margaret gradually became interested in the people and scenes around her, and she seemed taking hold of life again. But she wearied of the noise and confusion of Paris, and after a few weeks there, said one day to Miss Sargent:

"Haven't we had enough of this city, Aunt Helen? Suppose we go to Switzerland?"

"Where in Switzerland shall it be, Margaret?" asked Miss Sargent, glad to go anywhere Margaret might wish.

"Wherever you like. Lucerne? Interlaken? Chamouny?" queried Margaret.

"Suppose we go to Lucerne first," said Miss Sargent, "stay there as long as we choose, then creep up to Chamouny, loitering on the way as we like?"

"I have always thought that I would like to spend an entire summer in Chamouny," said Margaret. "I know I should never tire of staying there."

"Well, then, we'll go straight there now," replied Miss Sargent.

"No, I like your plan of sauntering from place to place. If you really don't care, suppose we go directly to Lucerne."

In a few days they were established in Lucerne, where they found a party of pleasant English people, with whom the time passed by so pleasantly in excursions among the mountains, and over the lake, that before they realized how rapidly the summer was going, they were told that it was too late in the season, for either a pleasant or safe journey to Chamouny. They then turned southward, and drifted through Milan, Venice, Genoa and Florence, in the most delightful leisurely way, and late in December took up their residence for the winter in Rome. Here they found several old acquaintances from Clinton, who were there for the winter, and soon were surrounded by friends.

Margaret had never been in Rome before, and its architecture and art seemed to arouse a new life within her. She cared little for any of the people who surrounded them, but spent her time in the picture galleries, and out of doors, being as much alone as was possible.

Rodger Latimer's betrayal of Margaret was her first, her only sorrow, and when overwhelmed by the flood, no thought of the sorrows of others arose in her mind for months. That is of the present, every day sufferings of the human family. But when she visited the Leek street mission kindergarten, the physical and moral degradation which she saw there, the disease, pain and crime, were to her a revelation of the universality of suffering. Her after knowledge of Mrs. Bray's sad life, deepened the impression received in the mission school, and she soon came to regard herself as one of thousands, and her sorrows as part of the common experience of humanity. While this knowledge did not assuage her grief, it quieted the clamorous cries of her heart, and led her thought from the little point of her own personality, to general experiences; and from the law of individual happiness, to the larger law of the well being of the race. During the first few weeks of her sojourn in Rome, she passed through a religious transition that wrought a greater change in her, than had the experience that brought her out of the narrow limitations of a selfish, personal sorrow. Of all the attractions of Rome, St. Peter's was the greatest to Margaret. Her esthetical nature was strongly wrought upon by the music and pictures of the great cathedral, by the mystic altar ceremonies, the mysterious gloom of the vast nave through which floated the peculiar odor of incense, and which seemed thronged with shadowy presences from the remote past. She attended religious services there every day, and as she knelt in worship beside the devout Romanists who were murmuring their prayers, surrounded by pictured and sculptured apostles and martyrs, grouped around their Incarnate Lord; she felt that her religious faith, through all her previous life, had been as narrow and selfish as her sympathies and ideas of suffering had once been. Here was symbolized the faith of many ages, the very air was full of the devotion of centuries to one God; sin and sorrow were everywhere present, but everywhere triumphed over by repentance and exultation. There came to her a new realization of the omnipresence of the Infinite, and there sprung up within her a faith in a universal love that filled all time, and stretched across the world enfolding every human being in a compassionate tenderness. Before this faith, nationalities and creeds vanished, cold forms shriveled into nothingness, and questioning doubts were dumb. Love was supreme, and trust in God, the universal law that brought universal peace.

With great wisdom, Miss Sargent kept her hands off Margaret's soul through this transition period. She read the girl aright, and trusted fully the pure instinct of her nature and her well balanced mind. But she was distressed that Margaret had gained neither health or flesh, by all of the changes of climate and scenery through which she had passed; nor was she the only one who regarded Margaret with anxiety. The slight, pale girl, dressed in deep black, was a familiar figure to those who frequented the picture galleries and the cathedral; and many a woman turned to look after her as she passed, with an expression of sympathy and solicitude on her face. Whenever her health was referred to in her presence, Margaret insisted that she was well, perfectly so. This declaration of Margaret's did not at all assure Miss Sargent, but she plainly saw that nothing could be done for Margaret, in any special way, but that she must continue to rely on pleasant and healthy surroundings, as she had done since leaving home.

The months passed rapidly and as the spring advanced, Miss Sargent and Margaret spent many pleasant hours planning a tour for the summer and autumn. One day as they were thus engaged, a servant brought in a package of letters. There were several for Margaret that brought her news from home, and told her all about the success of Mrs. Bray's kindergarten, and the happiness that Mrs. Bray and Miss Bond daily found in their association with their little children. Margaret was so thoroughly occupied she did not observe, that as Miss Sargent glanced over her letters, she quickly raised her eyes from one she held in her hand, to Margaret's face, and immediately went to her own room. When Margaret had finished reading her last letter, she seated herself at a table and commenced writing replies, and here Miss Sargent found her an hour after. She laid her hand on Margaret's shoulder, who looked up with an expression of startled apprehension, into the solemn face that leaned over her. There were tears on the eyelashes, and the cheeks were wet.

"Here is a letter from Rodger," said Miss Sargent in a grave voice, full of emotion. "He left it to my judgment, Margaret, whether or not to give it to you. You surely ought to have it. I'm going to my room to do some writing, and I'll leave it with you."

She placed the letter in Margaret's hand, and left the room.

CHAPTER XXIX

We left Mr. Latimer steadily at work in midsummer in his office. There was little business at that season of the year, but being alone in the office, he found himself sufficiently occupied through the business hours of the day, and when these were closed he usually mounted his horse and roamed through the deserted park, or wandered aimlessly around the surrounding country. Frequently he would take his dinner at the Park club house, and sometimes at some suburban restaurant, miles from the city. His object seemed to be to get away from people and be alone, either in the woods or on the lake shore. The night would often find him far from home, and frequently at midnight he would be riding slowly through the silent streets, between the converging rows of gas lights, that reached away in silent brilliancy toward his hotel. His life was one of almost absolute solitude. His manner was as grave as that of a sorrowing man of sixty, and as to the real life back of the silent lips and serious mien, no one knew anything. It might be one of pensive sorrow, of deep regret, of stern self-reproach, of chaotic hopes, or one of simply calm endurance. After seeing a suitable stone placed at his wife's grave, and arranging for flowers to be laid thereon every Sabbath morning, he went no more to the cemetery. Whether the past or the future possessed his thoughts, no one could tell. His face did not show a discontent, but rather a growing restfulness, as the summer passed into autumn.

One day late in September, he took his dinner at sunset at a road-house on what was called the Edgewood road, two-thirds of the way from Clinton to Edgewood. After dining, when he mounted his horse at the door, he sat still in the saddle a few moments, as though undecided where to go, then turned his horse toward Edgewood. But whatever his wish, or determination, may have been, after going straight ahead a few rods, he turned his horse around, and cantered back to the city. The next day he did not go to his office after his luncheon, but took his horse at his hotel, and rode directly to Edgewood. When he reached the village, he was surprised to see so little change in the place. It seemed to him, that the changes in the material world should have kept pace, somewhat, with the volcanic changes he felt there had been in his life, since last he was in these quiet streets. As he counted the months, he was surprised, and almost angry, to find that it was about two years since he was there last. Ten years, yes, twenty, ought not to have changed him so much, as he said to himself, he was changed. The college year had not opened, and the quiet of the summer vacation pervaded the village. He rode slowly through several of the principal streets, scarcely seeing man or woman. After a little he drew rein before Professor McVey's house, dismounted, tied his horse to a ring fastened to one of the elm trees, and went up the gravel walk. As he stepped onto the front piazza, George, the coachman, who was mowing the lawn, came toward him. For a moment neither recognized the other, then Mr. Latimer spoke: "Why, George, I am glad to see you again, how do you do?"

"I am very well, sir," George replied, taking Mr. Latimer's proffered hand, as he whisked his hat from his head, "and welcome back to the old house, sir."

"You've had some sad changes, George, since I was here."

"Yes, sir, the old master's gone, and it was a sad day for us all, when he went."

"Miss Bond has gone East, I understand, and Miss McVey is in Europe, is there any one in the house?"

"No, sir, none but me and my wife. I'm married, sir, I am," said the man with a happy grin, "and my wife is the cook. We are taking care of the place."

"Married are you, George? Well, that was a good thing for you to do, but can you tell me if I can look at some books in Professor McVey's library? Are the books in the same old place, or has the house been changed?"

"Not changed at all, only for the little ones, sir, the master's room is all there. I'll go round and open the door for you. It's like seeing a man come to his own home, to see you back again."

George unlocked the front door from within, and as Mr. Latimer stepped into the hall, he opened the library door for him to enter, and leaving the front door open to admit the fresh air into the close smelling hall, he went back to his mowing. "Changed only for the little ones," thought Mr. Latimer, as he hung his hat on the rack; "what could he mean?" Then he stepped back a little, and stopped midway between the open library door and the parlor door, that stood ajar. He pushed the parlor door open and looked in. A sacrilegious change seemed to have been made in that room. None of the pretty chairs that used to be there, met his eye; the sofa, small tables, books, curtains, scarfs, cushions, everything that he once thought made the room a charming parlor, for a beautiful girl, were gone. The same carpet was still on the floor, and his heart beat faster, as his eyes rested on Margaret's piano, that he had never seen out of her own room before. On the piano was a cover, embroidered by her own hands; how often he had watched the delicate fingers, as they stitched in that border of goldenrod. That piano cover had been Margaret's work for odd moments, for many months. Frequently Rodger had taken it from her lap and laid it one side, when he wished her to walk, or ride with him; and once when he thought her eyes rested too exclusively upon it, as he was sitting by her, he placed his hand over the stem she was stitching, and watched with delight her efforts to remove it with her own small fingers. It all came back to him; and how when she found it impossible to remove his hand, she slightly pricked each of his fingers with her needle; and the half-frightened, half-ashamed look, that came into her face, with a rush of color, when she saw that she had drawn blood with her needle point. How beautiful she looked that day! and how carefully she nursed the wounded finger for him! Now the folds of the cover hung motionless, and each spray of goldenrod seemed a silent accuser. He turned from the room, only glancing at the row of tables placed against the wall, and the double row of small chairs that were near them, and crossed the hall into the study. Here nothing was changed, all was just as it used to be. The chairs were in their old places, Professor McVey's large one, near the corner of the fireplace, with the table, holding a student lamp, and covered with books, by its side; and Margaret's little rocking chair not far off, by a round table. He closed the door, shutting himself into the room, and seated himself on the sofa. The books were arranged in their old order on the shelves, and the entire room seemed in readiness for the entrance of its master. The thought that he might come in at the door, seat himself in his chair, and take up a magazine, and begin reading, seemed much more natural to Rodger Latimer, than that he was lying in Oakwood cemetery. The personality of Professor McVey was very distinct to Rodger; it stood out in the clear, deep-cut lines of a living man, with nothing of the mistiness, or vagueness of death connected with it. He sat alone in the silence of that room for an hour; the memories of the past rapidly awakening, and accumulating, until he was completely possessed by them. As he looked at the books Professor McVey used to handle, a keen appreciation of the guileless nature of the man came over him. "How different," he thought, "from the people with whom I have lived during the past two years;" then looking around the library—"There was nothing sordid or selfish, or vulgar here; how he loved his books! he lived with the great dead, and no guile could find place in his mind. Simple old man! pure as a saint! how Margaret loved him! and how he loved her! Dear, darling Margaret! how *I* loved her." He suddenly rose, as a wave of feeling swept over him, rocking his soul to and fro, in an agony for Margaret's presence. He crossed the room to the door that opened into her Sans-Souci. He stood irresolute; he longed to enter her room; it was as though she were on the other side of the door waiting for him. He turned the knob, and swung the door back, the folds of the portiere hung straight and still before him. There was not a sound in the house, not a sound reached his ear from the yard, or the street; a silence like that of death was around him. Before he opened the door, it seemed as though Margaret, alive, well and happy as of old, was waiting him on the other side; now, as he stood before that motionless curtain, utter silence in the room beyond, it seemed as though Margaret, dead, was lying just the other side of the curtain. He could not raise it, and pass within; it was like invading a tomb. He dropped upon his knees, and laying hold of the curtain with both of his hands, he buried his face in its folds. Once he had a right to enter that room, not now; he had forfeited it forever, and by the wrong done had lost the love of her he had always loved. He saw it all now. Fool! fool! And for what? Never was so rich a heritage bartered for so meager a mess of pottage. In this house there had been the purity of Eden. No breath of murky air ever entered its portals; never a whisper that might not have been spoken on the housetop; never was there a look here that a saint might not have faced. Oh! Margaret! Margaret! angel in purity, woman in love! Never had her hand felt an unhallowed touch, no man's lips beside his own and her father's had ever touched her face, to another man she had never given a thought. Unlawful sentiment would have crept ashamed from her presence; and no love of adulation could ever have tempted her to step from the pedestal of her womanly dignity. If he could only cast his soul at her feet, and put the hem of her garment to his lips! He groaned aloud, and pressed the folds of the curtain which he held in his hands, hard against his face, as visions of the home he once called his own passed before him, followed by the vision of the home he might have had. The loss seemed too bitter, his fate unnaturally hard. How long he knelt there he did not know. When he rose to his feet he felt weak and exhausted, he stood for a few moments with bowed head close to the motionless portiere; then closed the door softly upon it and left the house, mounted his horse and turned toward the city. He had thought on his way out how he would walk through the orchard, sit on the south piazza under the vines, and visit the stable and lay his hand upon the neck of Margaret's horse; but he had not calculated on the flood of memories that overwhelmed him as soon as he stepped into the house, the sense of Margaret's presence, and of the great wrong he had done her, accompanied with the conviction that he had blighted his own life by the committal of that wrong, which seized him as he stood before the curtain that divided him from her room. On his way back he thought the situation all over, and determined to accept in a manly way the result of his action, by devoting himself to his profession and doing what good he could in the world with his money and with any legal influence he might gain. But when did youth ever accept a situation opposed to its desires until baffled on every side and defeated in every conceivable plan to change the situation! Although Mr. Latimer worked assiduously in his office through the autumn and winter months, he found time, as soon as his elastic nature began to recover its tone from the shock occasioned by the conviction that Margaret was lost to him forever, to turn over in his mind all of the possibilities of the case. He planned and rejected a great many imaginary courses of action and their results. He proposed schemes to himself and abandoned them as soon as they were ready to be put into execution; and he was at times flushed with the hope natural to his sanguine temperament, and then chilled with the despair that was just as natural to his sensitive organization. He could learn nothing regarding Margaret from Judge Sargent, beyond the simple fact that she had been with his sister in Rome during the winter. The judge knew nothing of his sister's plans for the spring or summer. At last Rodger determined to write to Miss Sargent. He dared not write to Margaret, and he felt he had no right to go unbidden into her presence. The remembrance of Miss Sargent's unvarying kindness to him, and of the almost romantic interest that she evinced in Margaret and himself during the summer they all passed together in Lausanne, added to the strong love that he knew she felt for Margaret, gave him courage to address her. At any rate, be the result what it might, it was doing no wrong to Margaret for him to write to Miss Sargent, who he felt sure would be both wise and full of tender appreciation of all concerned in any action that she might take. As soon as he came to this decision, he put it into execution, and sent the following letter to Miss Sargent:

My Dear Friend:

Do not be offended, I beg of you, that I address you on a subject, that perhaps you may think, I ought not to have the temerity to ever speak of to any one. I acknowledge that I feel like a culprit before a judge, and tremble in fear of the sentence that you may pass against me. But whatever the result may be, I must tell you all there is in my heart, and entreat that you will hear me, with what patience you can. When I think of the old acquaintance there was between yourself and my father and mother, and the many delightful days I have passed with you in the house of our dear Professor McVey, and those delightful summers that we four passed together in Europe: I feel that I can, with some confidence, tell you every thought of my heart; with the hope that you may read my actions of the past two years, in the light of the knowledge that you must have gained of the man, both of his weakness, and of what worth he may have possessed. Then when I think of your character, crystallized into uncompromising honesty, and your high moral standard, that does not admit of the least deviation in feeling, or intention; remembering, at the same time, your tender love for Margaret, I feel that it is hopeless to expect from you, anything but condemnation, and perhaps what seems to me in my extremity, a severe, unmerited, condemnation. I wish that you could know every feeling of my heart, and every thought of my mind, from the August of two years ago, when I left Edgewood with a love for Margaret, as great and unselfish, as I can conceive it possible for a man to feel for a woman; until last August, when I was fully recovered from a delirium, and the bitter disappointment following it, to find the love for Margaret as strong as ever in my heart, combined with a reverence for her nature, ten-fold greater than I had ever felt during the years of our engagement. Could you follow each step of that strange delirium, or fancy, or passion, perhaps, with your knowledge of psychology and of the human heart, you might be able to analyze it from its desire, to its last bitter regret. But I say frankly to you, that I do not now understand it. I do not wish to say one word in extenuation of my conduct, I have no such word to utter. It was an experience I cannot respect, and out of which I am blind to see, that any good can come to any one. I think I was the only sufferer, and very thankful I am, to be

able to believe this.   It was just that I should bear the natural retribution, as I was the transgressor against principle.   Perhaps my eyes have
been opened to a clearer, and deeper, vision by the experience of
these two years, but be that as it may, I know that Margaret has so risen
in my judgment, by conscious and unconscious, comparison with the
women I have met, that I regard her as the most perfect woman, in every
respect, that I have ever known.   I used to say this, years ago, but then
it was more a matter of feeling, an unconscious recognition of her worth,
through the instinct of love, which sometimes gives more of a negative,
than a positive judgment.   Now I know, I painfully realize, under the
fear that I have lost her forever, what it is in her nature, that is of such
priceless value.   I can give you no idea of the reverence that I feel for
her.   I am glad that she has never lived in the atmosphere created by
some women, who are called good women, that I know, or did know, a
year ago.   I am glad that the simple majesty of her nature, was never
vitiated by their trivialities, to use the kindest possible language.   As I
have awakened to an accurate knowledge of her worth, so have I become
conscious that I have always loved her, and never loved any woman beside her.   My eyes fill with tears, as I think of the gentle, happy girl of
three years ago.   Oh! why was I left to such blindness! Margaret must
have suffered; I see it now, I felt it last September, as I knelt outside of
her door, in the old house at Edgewood.   She must have suffered, and
through my act!   So constant, and trustful, and loyal! think of her
loyalty!   I know, that never in one thought, or in one moment's sentiment, did her heart turn from me; and I have learned that this loyalty
of nature is of the greatest value; nor did the possibility of such a
moment's disloyalty of sentiment exist in her.   My love for her was so
interwoven with my very being, by our association during our years of
childhood, and years of maturing thought, that I was not aware of its
power.   I have come to know that that little woman is more to me than
all in the universe beside; she is inextricably entwined around my life,
and her praise and appreciation have come to be my only professional
ambition.   My money is valueless to me because it cannot gratify her
tastes, and pass through her hands to the needy.   As for a home, I shall
go without one to my last day, unless I can have one created by her
presence.   I cannot imagine a fireside as belonging to me, where she is
not.   I do often dream of one, beside which she sits, of a home made
blessed by her presence.   I have dreamed of late, of the possibility of
gaining her forgiveness; and of picking up the threads of my life, which
I so heedlessly broke, and of placing them in her hands—her little
woman's hands—to weave together into a beautiful home life.   Margaret

must regard me with a sort of horror, as a moral bandit. I cannot see how she can have for me, any other sentiment than that of contempt. It would be just if she should forbid me ever to come into her presence again, but then I am conscious of possessing some worth, and some truth. I dealt with her falsely, and treated her cruelly; but I am neither false, or cruel. I do not understand how I could have wronged her so wickedly, it seemed so natural, so easy then; and seems so monstrous now. I do not ask Margaret to forgive me, to love me; but I do beg of her to permit me to be with her. Not as a lover; no word of love shall pass my lips, or be expressed by eye, or touch; only let me be with her; let us read, and talk and walk together, as we three used to years ago I wish Margaret to know the Rodger of to-day, as thoroughly as she thought she knew the Rodger of three years ago. I wish to live my life, and thought, out unreservedly before her. I would like to have our lives run close together, through consecutive days and weeks; so th t she might see the man under various circumstances, and in various moods; and judge him for herself. I wish to stand with uncovered heart, befo e her woman's eyes; stand long, with the searching light of her honest nature thrown upon me. I would like her to follow to its inciting motive, every action of my life, if she can thread such an inscrutable labyrinth. I know how miserably weak I have been, how false to principle in that one lamentable instance but I can trust Margaret to deal gently and show mercy. Could she permit me this probation, then I would accept, without a word of remonstrance, her command to leave her, and never come into her presence again; should it be, that her old love was dead, past all possible resurrection. I am not ashamed to admit that such a sentence would banish me to a life of loneliness, but I could not complain, as it would be my own hand that had hewed out the road to the desert. I think, my dear Miss Sargent, that you understand my heart, and see what I am hoping that you can do for me. I dare not address Margaret. I have no right to do so. But can you not approach her in my behalf? Make what use of this letter your judgment may dictate. If Margaret will permit me to go to her, please send me a cablegram to that effect. One word will be enough. I shall not misunderstand it. You may smile and think me impetuous, but more than life is at stake, and since I have been inspired with a slight hope, I find this uncertainty almost unendurable.

A few lines expressive of personal obligation and containing good wishes, closed the letter that Mr. Latimer sent to the address he had obtained from Judge Sargent. Immediately after mailing it, he went to a steamship agent, and with him calculated the probable time that must elapse before he would receive a reply. He then engaged his passage in what they thought would be the first outgoing steamer, after the cablegram would reach him. The few weeks that followed were weeks of feverish anxiety, of alternating hope and fear. Rodger could not concentrate his mind upon his office business, nor could he read or sleep. He held himself strictly to business hours, his other waking hours were passed mostly in the saddle. He rode long and far, often until both horse and rider were tired out. As the time approached when he might reasonably expect some message from Miss Sargent, he found his strength of will inadequate to the control of his feelings, and he was thrown into the greatest despondency, his mind being filled with sad forebodings. What hope he might have had when he wrote to Miss Sargent had so nearly died out, that when at last a messenger boy stood before him with a foreign dispatch, he felt it was his sentence of death, or banishment. He sent the boy from the room and locked the door; his limbs trembled beneath him, and he seated himself in the nearest chair, as he held the cablegram in his hand. His heart beat violently, he felt dizzy, and the room seemed to rock around him. It was several moments before he could master himself sufficiently to open the envelope; and even when he held the folded sheet in his hand, he did not dare turn his eyes to it. At last when he did read the message, the words, " Come to Baden," overcame him, and as he exclaimed, " Thank God!" he dropped his head on his clasped hands on a table near by.

CHAPTER XXX

It was toward the evening of a pleasant day in the last of May, that Miss Sargent was sitting on the piazza of a hotel in Baden, resting after a long walk. She was sitting close to an open window talking with Margaret, who was seated in the reception room within, her crossed arms resting on the window sill. It was early in the season and they were enjoying the quiet of the hotel, that did not contain more than half a dozen guests beside themselves: who like them, were wise enough to keep in advance of the annual swarm of tourists through Switzerland and Germany, in order to enjoy the clean rooms and the service of the goodly number of servants who were waiting the rush of travelers. The arrival of carriages from the station was anxiously watched every day, for fear that a large party of noisy people from somewhere might invade their quiet home life. There was another thought in the mind of both Margaret and Miss Sargent, whenever a carriage approached the house, for both knew that Mr. Latimer had had time to reach them; and although they did not speak upon the subject, each was expecting him daily. As a carriage drew up to the piazza that May evening, the eyes of both were turned toward it, and as a man stepped out, they immediately recognized the tall form and broad shoulders of Rodger Latimer. He saw Miss Sargent, but did not see Margaret, who had risen to her feet and retreated behind the window curtain. As he came toward Miss Sargent with uncovered head, she rose to meet him, and extended both of her hands in cordial welcome. He took them in his with a close grasp, as though to express his affectionate gratitude to her, by the pressure he gave. She turned to the window, and said:

" Margaret, Rodger has come."

Margaret immediately stepped partially in view and extended her hand, which Rodger held for scarcely an instant, as she quickly withdrew it as soon as she felt the touch of his. For one moment they looked into each other's eyes, and it would have been difficult to tell which face was the paler; then her eyelids drooped so low the lashes seemed to lie on the white cheeks. For half a minute Rodger gazed on the slight figure draped in black, the thin, pale face, the well remembered soft curling hair lying across the white forehead, then he turned abruptly and walked quickly away across the carriage road and the lawn, up a hill, and plunged into a grove, where he threw himself down upon the ground at the roots of a tree. He was not prepared for the change that he saw in Margaret. And it seemed to him that he was responsible for it all, even to the emblem of mourning that enveloped her. When he last saw her, she was a merry girl, all gladness and beauty, the embodiment of happiness and health, floating about in delicate colors and fleecy white, decked in ribbons and flowers, with a song on her lips. and a world of love in her eyes. He pulled his hat down low over his face as a vision of the girl he had looked upon a few moments ago rose before him. The large sad eyes, the wasted figure clothed in black, the pitiful mouth, and the cold touch of the thin hand, struck an agony of remorse to his soul. He had broken her heart, he said to himself, he had ruined her health, he had clothed her body in black. It was in vain he reminded himself that she was wearing conventional mourning for her father, that Professor McVey was dead, and that would account for her black clothes, and partially account for her sadness. He could not calm himself, he could not forgive himself.

For an hour he sat there alone under the trees, a victim of his imagination and conscience, then he rose and walked slowly back to the hotel, and went straight to his room.   The necessary occupation of unpacking his trunk, taking a bath and dressing for dinner, changed somewhat the current of his thoughts.   And after dinner, which he took alone in the great dining-room, as the usual table d' hote had been served some time before, he started in search of Margaret and Miss Sargent, in a calm, though rather depressed, state of mind.   He found them in their cosy parlor, Miss Sargent reading aloud by a shaded lamp, and Margaret lounging on a sofa near by.   Both rose at his entrance, and Miss Sargent turned a large chair toward the table, in which he seated himself, on her invitation.

"Now tell us all about John, and Clinton," said Miss Sargent, as soon as he was seated.   "When did you see him last ?"

"The day I left the city, but he would give me no message to you; he said he wrote so frequently there was nothing left to say.   I drove to your home on my way to the depot."

"Rather out of your way."

"Yes, about two miles," replied Rodger, "but I thought you would like the latest news, and I can assure you that your brother never looked in better health.   It was a cold afternoon that I was there, and he had a blazing fire, which he was enjoying with his usual satisfaction."

"I don't know what John will do when July comes," said Miss Sargent, "his occupation will be gone.   You know he usually goes up to Lake Superior in August, and I tell him he only goes because a fire is a necessity up there, in the evenings, the year around.   He would not come with you ?"

"I knew better than to ask him."

"Yes, I suppose so." As there was no reply made to this remark of Miss Sargent's, and as she feared an awkward silence, she asked abruptly, simply for the sake of saying something: "Don't you think we have a pretty room here, Rodger?"

"You have indeed," replied Mr. Latimer, looking around the room. "That is an unusually fine engraving," he added, rising and crossing the room to look at a picture on the wall. As he stood before it, Miss Sargent spoke to Margaret:

"Do you know, dear, where that last 'London Times' is?"

"I think it is in my room, would you like it?" said Margaret.

It was the first time that Rodger had heard her voice, and the sound lashed him like a whip; he winced and shrank from it. It was so pathetically sweet, so patient, so emotionless and measured in its tones.

"This is my doing also," he said to himself.

"Yes, if you please," replied Miss Sargent to Margaret, "I would like to see what Rodger will think of that art criticism."

Margaret went into an adjoining room and returned with the paper, which she gave to Miss Sargent, who said:

"Will you read this to us, Rodger? Margaret began it this morning, but we gave it up for a walk."

"Certainly I will," said Mr. Latimer, turning from the wall.

Miss Sargent's heart was touched with sympathy, as she noticed the distressed look upon his face. She was doing the best she could for the young people, but she began to feel as though she had two combustibles on her hands, which were being brought together over a powder magazine. Those two hearts were evidently charged to the brim, and a word, or tone, might be the spark to set fire to the hoarded powder. Mr. Latimer read the article designated; it was a long one, and he was a good reader, and soon all three were interested in the matter under consideration. When he finished reading he and Miss Sargent entered into a lively discussion of the subject. Margaret said nothing, but both Mr. Latimer and Miss Sargent included her in the conversation by turning frequently toward her, and directly addressing her. She evinced her interest in all that was said by looking back and forth from one to the other, as each was speaking, and in this way she and Rodger frequently looked into each other's eyes, though Margaret withdrew her gaze the moment that it encountered Rodger's.

It was late when Mr. Latimer rose to go, and the good-nights were formal. Miss Sargent asked him if he would take breakfast with them at eight o'clock the next morning and walk with them afterward, which invitation he gladly accepted.

The next morning after breakfast, when Mr. Latimer was equipped for the walk over hills and rocks, he went to Miss Sargent's parlor for the two ladies. He found Miss Sargent with her stick in her hand, tying her hat on before a mirror. Margaret was standing beside a table, absently turning the leaves of a magazine. He asked: "Are you not going to walk with us, Margery?" Margaret returned no answer. She could not speak, she could not even raise her eyes; she was so overwhelmed with the memories that old name brought out of their graves. She quickly turned, and slipped into her room, the door of which was near by. Both Mr. Latimer and Miss Sargent supposed Margaret had gone for her hat, but as she did not return, Miss Sargent said: "I wonder what has become of Margaret; she is usually ready before I am. I'll go and see what's the matter." She found Margaret sitting in a chair in the middle of the room convulsed with weeping.

"Why, Margaret, my child!" she exclaimed, as she pressed Margaret's head against her side as she stood by her. "What has hurt you? was it the old name, dear?"

"Yes, yes, oh! Aunt Helen, I cannot bear it! All of my old happiness and all of the misery has come back to me so, I cannot bear it!"

Miss Sargent soothed her as best she could. "I don't know, Margaret," she said, "as you could hope to meet him without this rush of memories at first, I'm thankful it did not come yesterday. It will pass, dear, and then you can meet him with more calmness I know it is very hard, shall I tell him that he better go off somewhere for a while and come back in a few weeks, or meet us in Chamouny?"

"No, no! I would not have him leave for the world."

Miss Sargent smiled as she laid her hand gently on the head that rested against her. "I am sure he will do just as you wish, Margaret," she said, "he may not have suffered as you have, but his face plainly shows that he has been having a sad time of it."

"Go and take your walk, Aunt Helen. I shall not be able to go out this morning, perhaps not to-day. Don't keep Rodger waiting any longer; he will think strange of it. Leave me alone; it will be better, I'll get over this."

Miss Sargent thought a moment, then said· "Perhaps it will be best, yes, we'll go and walk. But remember, dear, in all of your grief that Rodger has the worst of it. You have always done right; he is the one who has wronged another. I'd rather, a thousand times, be in your place than his."

"Aunt Helen," said Margaret, raising her pinched, tear-blotted face, "if Rodger says anything, don't blame him too much, don't be too hard on him."

"You can trust me, darling. You know I always liked him, and I think he is acting nobly now; doing the best any man could possibly do." Miss Sargent went to Mr. Latimer, who raised inquiring eyes to her face, as she came alone from Margaret's room. She only said: "We will have to go without Margaret this morning, Rodger; it is best, perhaps, that she be alone for a few hours, but I am quite sure she will go with us to-morrow."

Mr. Latimer picked up his hat from the floor, beside his chair, and followed Miss Sargent from the room, without saying a word. He walked in silence where she led the way, but hardly heard the sound of her voice as she spoke to him. She did not talk much as they went up the hillside, and they traversed two miles or more, in comparative silence; for he scarcely uttered a word in reply to anything she said. At last she ceased in her attempts to keep up any conversation. After a long while Rodger spoke:

"Pardon me, Miss Sargent, if I speak of myself, but this uncertainty is becoming more than I can bear. My presence here evidently causes Margaret pain. I must not stay, if it makes her suffer, I have caused her sorrow enough, already. Do you think she can ever forgive me?"

"I'm glad that you have spoken of her, Rodger, but I hardly know what to say to you; you must be patient and self-forgetting, for awhile."

"Don't misunderstand me, I pray; I could wait a century, if I were sure of her love in the end, or sure that I could make her happy; but it seems as though my presence tortured her."

"No, it does not."

"How do you know?"

"I asked her this morning, when I was in her room just before we left, if I should ask you to go away for awhile."

"What did she say; please give me her own words."

"She said, No, no, I would not have him leave. Remember, Rodger, what the dear girl has suffered. It's natural your coming should bring up all of the past, and that the remembrance of the happiness that you and she once had together, and of all her sorrow that followed, should sweep over her with irresistible force. Don't make too much of this; it had to come, but in a few days it will pass away, and then you and she can begin a new acquaintance."

"I don't wish a new acquaintance, I want the old one, of three years ago."

"That you can never have again. After such experiences as you and Margaret have gone through, the old life is impossible."

"Is her heart dead toward me?"

"Dead!" exclaimed Miss Sargent in a voice that startled Mr. Latimer, and which immediately give him great comfort, he turned and looked at her, and met a smile of calm assurance. They walked on in silence for a little, then Mr. Latimer, looking far away across the country, said in a solemn tone:

"What a fearful thing it is, not to do right. I see plainly enough now, that I was utterly in the wrong. I must have been mad, blind. I cannot understand how it could have appeared to me as it did at the time, I seemed to have been whirled off my feet, and to have been carried away by a force outside of myself. Poor Margaret, I don't see how she can possibly forgive me."

"You must not use that word, Rodger, Margaret has never felt the least unforgivingness toward you."

"Do you think she can possibly love me again? has she any of the old love in her heart toward me?"

"I must not tell you what I think. Isn't it enough that she said you might come, and stay with her?"

"Yes, it is; it's all I can hope for, more than I deserve. But please tell me, Miss Sargent, did she read the letter I wrote to you? did you have to persuade her to permit me to come?"

"No, I did not persuade her at all. I didn't say one word to influence her. I would not take that responsibility: I wouldn't dare to. I gave her your letter the day I received it, and she took it to her room, and was there alone for two hours; then she went off and walked alone for another two hours; when she returned, she said to me, 'Aunt Helen, you may telegraph Rodger to come, if you think it would be best:' I told her I had no judgment to give, that I dared not have any; that it was a matter her own heart and judgment should decide. Only, I said to her, that she ought to fully understand all that was involved in such permission."

"And she gave that permission?"

"Yes."

After several moments of silence, Rodger said: "I never addressed her by any other name than Margery, as you know; no one beside me ever called her Margery; when I spoke the name to-day, you saw how quickly she left me; shall I continue to call her by the dear old name, or shall I change it to Margaret or Miss McVey? I would like to do whatever would be most agreeable to her"

"Undoubtedly the old name was the cause of the tears in which I found her, but I believe it would hurt her if you used any other. But, Rodger, follow your heart; an honest heart rarely makes a mistake."

"If I followed my heart," Mr. Latimer said, with a sad smile, "I should burst through all the barriers, and take Margery in my arms and tell her how much I love her, and hold her there forever."

There was not much more talk between the two. Rodger seemed revolving something in his mind, and Miss Sargent left him undisturbed in his cogitations. They strolled over the hills, through the groves, and back to the *Conversationhaus;* where in one of the booths, Mr. Latimer purchased several pretty trifles, which, with some beautiful leaves he had gathered on his walk, he placed on Margaret's lap, as they found her, on their return, sitting on a bench under the trees, waiting for them.

"You missed a delightful walk, Margery," he said, as he laid the leaves and curiosities on her knee, "but judging from what I have seen of Miss Sargent's pedestrian enthusiasm, this morning, it's a loss easily made up. I feel sure that there will not be a ruin, castle, hill or spring, that we shall not visit; and on foot too, during the next few weeks." Then turning to Miss Sargent, he continued, "I'm as hungry as a wolf, do you take luncheon, or are you living on two meals a day?"

"No, we take a bite at noon, but we have nothing at this hour that will satisfy a wolf, I forewarn you. I didn't think it was so late," continued Miss Sargent, looking at her watch, "it's two o'clock."

"May I join you in the dining-room, after I have washed off some of this dirt?" asked Mr. Latimer, looking at his large white hands.

CHAPTER XXXI.

After the awkward reserve of the first few days had worn off, the three old friends dropped into the informal relations which they had held years before; and as soon as the first excitement of meeting Rodger was over, Margaret not only surprised herself, but Miss Sargent also, by the calmness of feeling, and naturalness of manner, that became habitual to her. Mr. Latimer's life immediately became one of devotion to the comfort and pleasure of the two ladies; and so perfectly were his arrangements made, their results seemed only those that would naturally come from the care of competent servants, belonging to a well managed hotel. Did they wish to make an excursion, the carriage, or donkeys, were of the best, and at the door on the minute. Did a rain come up when they were in the forest, or on the mountains, umbrellas and water-proofs were brought out from some hiding place to protect them. Were they miles from the hotel at noon, an ample luncheon always met them. The number of magazines and papers that usually lay on their sitting-room table, was doubled, and their bill of fare was noticeably improved, by the addition of rare game and choice fruits.

They lived out of doors most of the time, usually leaving the house soon after breakfast, and not returning until driven home by the approaching darkness. Margaret was specially fond of this out of door life; and she was always ready to go in the morning, and never ready to return at night. They spent days in the pine woods, and at the old castle: and made excursions up and down the valley, and through the forests, but their favorite place for riding, reading, and lounging, was among the rocks on the Battert. Miss Sargent said that she must draw the line somewhere, and declared that it should be at donkeys. There was nothing she would not drive in, no place that she would not go, that could be reached on foot, or in a wheeled vehicle; but when it came to going on donkeys, Rodger and Margaret must go without her. At first, Margaret hesitated about going off alone with Rodger, even for a short ride, but as Miss Sargent seemed to look at it as a matter of course that she would go, and Rodger appeared to regard it in the same light, her hesitancy vanished, and it soon came about that she and Rodger would be off together for hours on their donkeys. At such times Rodger gave her the same thoughtful care, that always characterized his manner toward herself and Miss Sargent, but in no wise was his manner different toward her when alone, from what it was when Miss Sargent accompanied them. If he took hold of the bridle of her donkey with a reverent hand, as though the beast was carrying an angel over rough ways, she was not aware of the devotion involved in the simple act; nor did she know the force of will that held the hand steady, that placed her foot in the stirrup. She never saw the intensity of passion that at times overflowed his eyes as they were fixed upon her face, as they walked under the trees in the forest, for on the slightest motion of her head toward him, his eyes were withdrawn; and when they again looked into hers, they were as free from tumultuous passion as her own. Rodger never spoke a word, gave a glance, or permitted himself a tone of voice, that could recall the past, or that would lead Margaret to

infer, that he even thought of holding any other relation to her, than that of the friend he then was.
When they first began to go out alone together, Margaret feared he might take advantage of the situation
and declare his love. Then as soon as his calm manner reassured her, with the inconsequence of a girl,
she wondered if he really did love her, as much as he
had said in his letter to Miss Sargent. His association with Margaret had come to be one of such informal confidence, he was constantly on the alert not
to mar it, or to startle her sense of security. The
three lived together as members of the same family;
always taking their meals together, meeting early in
the morning, and separating late at night. If Mr. Latimer was ready for breakfast first, and he usually was,
he would take a book and sit on a bench that was
under a tree in front of Miss Sargent's bedroom window, and read, until she called to him from the window
that she and Margaret were ready. They read aloud
to each other all sorts of books; novels, science, and
philosophy, and freely exchanged the various opinions,
the book in hand chanced to awaken in their minds.
During these frequent conversations, Rodger became
aware that the range of Margaret's thought had enlarged in the last three years, especially on religious
subjects. He once felt that he knew every corner and
angle of her mind, could analyze her every thought,
trace it back to its source, and forward to its result
on her character; but he found her much changed, and
at times, her thought was elusive, and escaped his
grasp. He felt this almost painfully one day, as they
were sitting on a rocky hillside together, Miss Sargent having sent them off alone, excusing herself on
the score of some writing to do. Rodger had been

reading an hour to Margaret, when he laid the book aside, and stretching himself on the ground beside her, rested his head on his hand that was supported by his elbow. "This is a beautiful world," he said as his eyes roved up and down, and across, the hillside, the plain, the woods, and distant mountains.

"Yes," replied Margaret, "this is a beautiful world, a wonderful world. I think, Rodger, that my early association with books, and bookish men, led me to over-estimate the world of ideas, the mental; and to under estimate matter. See how matter is tossed up into forms of beauty all around us. I can easily understand how some heathen have worshiped nature."

"I don't know," said Rodger, "this matter of worship is not very plain to me. I believe I really like the services in those great Catholic cathedrals better than any other. Their symbols are so engrossing, they capture the senses so completely, that one feels religous whether he is or not."

"I know that is so," said Margaret, "I have felt it. In St. Peter's, last winter, I was perfectly permeated and possessed by the influence of the ceremonies, the pictures, and the music. It all did me great good then, but it was because of—" she hesitated, Rodger's eyes were on her face, but her hesitancy was but for a moment—"my peculiar mental condition. I needed something to help me over a chasm, back to my religious faith."

Rodger dropped his eyes to the ground and commenced to scrape the moss off a small stone near him with his thumb nail. "And I found just what I needed in that great temple," continued Margaret; "but, Rodger, you soon outgrow that spectacular sort of effect that surrounds you there, and turn even from St. Peter's, for a more immediate sense of God. You soon get beyond all of that color, and line, and sound."

"But that color, and line, and sound, are just what I need," rejoined Rodger, "as a help to me. There is something tangible in that music, and the kneeling people, and the praying priest. I believe I'd make a pretty good Catholic."

"I could much easier be a Quaker than a Catholic," said Margaret. "I find a tendency in my nature to do away with forms, and days, and seasons. Such things are no great helps."

"You don't need external helps," replied Rodger. "You are better than I am, Margery. Perhaps your belief in a supreme being, and in moral responsibility, isn't stronger than mine. Let me read you a few lines I have here," continued Rodger, sitting up and taking out his pocketbook, from which he took a bit of folded newspaper. "I heard Horace Kent make a speech last spring, and one thought of his impressed me so strongly, I cut it out of the paper the next morning and have carried it ever since. Let me read it to you: 'It is when you come to those moral principles that touch the welfare of humanity, that the world accepts no compromise; and his stature is alone great, who puts himself in line with those fundamental principles of justice and liberty which we may call providential. I say providential, because all circumstances, all events, all times, of peace and war, of action and reaction, carry them forward to their ultimate destination, and we may therefore reverently say, that they are in the special keeping and hands of Him, who created this world from a perfect purpose, and to a perfect end.'"

"Let me see that," said Margaret, as Rodger ceased reading. He placed the slip in her outstretched hand. She read it several times over to herself, then read it aloud—"'Created this world from a perfect purpose, to a perfect end.' That is beautifully said; why isn't the whole of everything there? Was this a political speech, or was it at one of your bar dinners?"

"No, it was at a meeting to indorse Gladstone's Home Rule. The entire speech was an eloquent one, full of wisdom; but no thought in it struck me as forcibly as this. For days after hearing it, I kept repeating to myself, 'From a perfect purpose, to a perfect end.' Now I have as strong faith as you, in such a doctrine as this; in a personal good providence, but that is all a matter of the intellect. You. and some few others that I have known in my life, seem to possess a something else, that I know nothing of."

"And it is just this something else," pursued Margaret, "that is the most desirable of all knowledge, or experience. You think me fanatical, don't you?"

"No, I do not, but I am frank to say, Margery, I don't understand you; and I am equally frank to admit, that you, and some others I know, do possess something before which I bow my head. A something I do not possess. Your father had it—I knew him well—but there was one part of his nature, one part of his life, that I could not enter. I was shut out of it by my ignorance. I recognized the presence of this something, and could see its influence on his life. I could not call it superstition, and it was the farthest removed from fanaticism. You would call it religious faith, I suppose." Margaret turned her head and looked into the distance. Rodger observed her sad face, and was distressed. He put out one of his hands, and held it a few inches above one of her, that lay on the folds of her dress, that rested on the ground between them. "Pardon me, Margery, have I hurt you?" he said.

"Oh, no," she replied, turning toward him, as she drew her hand away from under his that had not touched hers.

"It is very pleasant to hear you speak of dear papa. I know you and he loved each other. I think of him every day. How good he was! what a beautiful life he lived!"

"Indeed, his was a beautiful life," assented Rodger, "and I'm beginning to see of late, that there are a great many beautiful things in this world. I'm beginning to believe, in a vague sort of way, that this world is going on very well, in spite of all the wrong doing and suffering we know there is in it. It does seem, at times, like a dreadful botch; I cannot understand the means to the end, but I am beginning to have faith in the ultimate outcome of it all." As Margatet was about to reply, the laugh of a child diverted their attention. It came from a little child that was tottering among the stones, followed by its nurse, some way below them, to one side.

"That must be a stupid girl," said Rodger, looking at the child, "why don't she keep a child of that age on the grass, instead of bringing it up here among the stones."

"Children are wonderful creatures," said Margaret, gazing after the child.

"Why, Margery, one would suppose from your decisive tone, that you knew a great deal about children. I did not know you ever saw any, beside that little diabolical philosopher next door to you, that Novalis Herman."

"Novalis is a dreadful child, but I am thankful to say, I know many other children beside Novalis. You don't know anything of my kindergarten experience, do you?"

"No, tell me what you mean," said Rodger, "your kindergarten experience?"

"Yes, my kindergarten. It's a beautiful thing, Rodger, to live with little children." Then she went on and related to him her visit to the Leek Street Mission Kindergarten, her meeting with Mrs. Bray, and her organization of a kindergarten for her in the Edgewood home

23

parlor. Rodger's face grew very **serious,** as she proceeded in her narration, and **from time to time he asked her a** question or two, **her answers to which enabled him** to come to an accurate conclusion **regarding the** whole affair. He fully understood her benevolence toward the friendless, destitute woman; and something of Margaret's isolation from society at that time, and her need of occupation. Margaret finished her recital by saying: "I can't tell you, Rodger, what a blessing dear Mrs. Bray and those children were to Auntie Deb **and** me, that winter."

That winter! It all **rushed into** Mr. Latimer's mind. **He** cast his eyes **to the ground a** moment, then raised **them** to Margaret's face. When Margaret commenced to speak of her kindergarten she did **not** think of the possible effect, recalling so consecutively **the events of** those months of loneliness and sorrow, might have upon herself; and was frightened to feel how completely she was mastered by the memories she had called up. Involuntarily she turned her white face full upon Rodger. His heart was full, but he dared not open his lips to speak without her permission. Her hand lay within two feet of him, but he dared not touch it. A gulf seemed to have suddenly yawned between them, over which they leaned with white faces staring into each other's eyes. Just when Margaret felt that she could not endure the situation a moment longer, a loud cry of terror brought them both to their feet. They turned in the direction of the cry. The child they had observed a few moments before had evidently lost its footing while wandering over the stones, and had rolled down the hillside a short distance into a scraggy bush, where it was held suspended by its clothes. The nurse, who was a tall, brawny woman, could have easily rescued the child from its perilous situation, as she was only a few rods above it; but she seemed bereft of her senses, and stood clasping and unclasping her hands as she screamed at the top of her voice. Rodger could see from where he stood that the child's limbs and, perhaps, life, depended upon the toughness of the fabric of which its little dress was made, which was caught in the bush and held the child dangling over a ravine. He sprang around the side of a rock, near which he and Margaret had been sitting, and dashed down and across the mountain side toward the child, leaping and springing from bowlder to bowlder like a deer. The distance was not great, and scarcely a minute had elapsed before he reached the child, which he took from its perilous position, and placed in the arms of the nurse. Margaret stood on the jutting rock watching him, and when he turned to come back she waved her handkerchief to him, which he answered by taking off his broad-brimmed hat and swinging it around his head. He did not place it on his head again, but kept it in his hand as he leaped across narrow crevices and sprang from rock to rock. Margaret went to meet him. The cry of terror from the nurse, the danger of the child, and Rodger's rapid rush to the rescue, had wrought her up to quite a pitch of excitement, and as Rodger brought himself to a sudden standstill in front of her, she reached out both of her hands to him in welcome.

"Well, done, Rodger," she exclaimed. "You have saved a life!"

Rodger took the extended hands in his own, and raised first one and then the other to his lips with courtly grace.

"I ought to have done something to merit such a welcome as this," he said.

"I'm sure you did do something," replied Margaret,

withdrawing her hands from his clasp. "If you hadn't been here the child would have fallen and been killed."

"I don't know as it would have been killed if it had fallen; and if the nurse had not seen that some one was near by, she might have taken it out of the bush herself. She's a stupid creature."

"Why, Rodger, how you ran. I never saw a hunter or a guide make better time, or spring more lightly," said Margaret, glancing up and down his stalwart frame, as they were walking homeward. "Where did you gain such agility?"

"Have you forgotten that I ranked as a good scholar in college?" said Rodger, with a smile. "Perhaps you don't know how much of my reputation was won by my muscle."

"Won't we have a splendid story to tell Aunt Helen," said Margaret, clapping her hands in glee. And she made a splendid story out of it half an hour afterward, as they were sitting together under the trees.

CHAPTER XXXII.

Early in July Margaret proposed that they go to Chamouny, reminding Miss Sargent of a promise she had given the summer before, when their tarrying so long in Lucerne had broken up their plan of visiting Chamouny that season; her promise that the next summer they would go early to Chamouny and stay there as long as Margaret wished.

"Yes, we'll go," said Miss Sargent, in reply to Margaret's suggestion, "and we'll stay until Christmas, if you say so."

They reached Chamouny as much in advance of the army of tourists as they had Baden six weeks before, and this gave them a choice of rooms. They took four on the second floor of the hotel they selected, all of which opened upon a piazza that commanded a beautiful view of the surrounding mountains, and the valley. Margaret's delight was unbounded as she stood on the piazza and looked over the scene spread out before her. It was difficult for her to stay indoors long enough to unpack her trunks and assist Miss Sargent in the arrangement of their parlor, for which room Miss Sargent had contrived to get an extra supply of easy chairs, lounges, writing tables and bookshelves.

"I see we shall make a long stay here, Margaret," she said, "and we had better make our surroundings as home-like as possible."

The second day after their arrival, the three were in their sitting-room gathered around a heap of books on the floor that a servant had just emptied there, from a box which he had unnailed on the piazza. Mr. Latimer was on one knee, sorting the books, which he handed to Margaret, who placed them on the shelves or tables, according to her taste. Miss Sargent stood by looking at Rodger as he matched the volumes before handing them to Margaret. Some of these books came from Miss Sargent's library in Clinton, some from Professor McVey's in Edgewood, some they had picked up in the various places they had visited, and a few Mr. Latimer had brought over in his trunk. As he was assorting these books, one that he took from the floor had an oldtime look about it that arrested his attention. He turned to the fly leaf and read Professor McVey's name in his well-remembered handwriting; and again, as on the hillside at Baden, the past overwhelmed him. His first thought was, as his eye rested on Professor McVey's writing, "What must that revered dead man have thought of him? what must have been his abhorrence, his contempt, his grief over the sufferings of his idolized daughter—and the bitterness of it? no reparation could be made him." He raised his eyes to Margaret who was standing at the bookshelves across the room, her back toward him, with an impulse to fall at her feet, entreating the comfort of forgiveness. There was no ardent passion in his eye now, no demand or importuning for love; his face was that of a self-convicted culprit, from which all color and almost all natural expression had been driven by the throes of remorse. He had risen to his feet and was standing with the book in hand, as Miss Sargent turned toward him. The pale face and compressed lips touched her heart instantly, she glanced at the fly-leaf of the book he held, stepped to his side, took his disengaged hand between her own with a sympathetic pressure, as she looked in his face with an expression of confidence and affection. He drew his hand from hers, laid the book on the pile on the floor, and quietly left the room without Margaret being aware that anything unusual had happened. He would have suffered less that day had he known that his old friend had never changed in thought or feeling toward him, so adroitly had Margaret managed to shield her father from any sorrowing he might have had for her sake, had he known that Rodger had committed an act by which he had forfeited all the respect and affection he had felt for the son of his dear friend. They saw no more of Rodger until evening, when he joined them as they were sitting on the piazza, listening to the tinkling of the sheep bells as the flocks were coming home down the valley, and to the jodelling of some one off on the mountain side. He said little as they sat there together an hour or so before going to bed, and Margaret didn't notice his silence, so absorbed was she in the beauty of the country around her. But she was deeply touched the next day by a new element in his manner toward her; a sort of fatherly solicitude that was different from anything she had ever seen in him before, and which at times brought tears to her eyes, so full was it of brooding tenderness. As soon as their rooms were arranged to their liking, they settled down to a regular routine of daily life that had little variety in it. They lived out of doors as much in Chamouny as they had in Baden. Their days were passed in climbing mountains, creeping over glaciers, or wandering through forests; and if the day was fair they invariably lunched away from the hotel, on some crag on the mountain side, beside some gurgling brook in the forest, or on some sunny knoll in the valley. There were always books in the baskets that followed them, and usually one beside, in Rodger's pocket. But wherever their days were spent, their evenings were invariably passed at home, in their parlor if it chanced to rain, with books, letter-writing and music; for their room contained a piano for Margaret, and Rodger was more than a fair player on the violin. When the weather was clear, they sat hour after hour on the piazza during the evenings, with Mont Blanc and the wonderful glacier of that range in full view, as long as the daylight lasted. Margaret frequently began her day by watching the sun rise over the mountains. Her room was a corner one, that had a south and an east window, and from the east window she would watch the deepening color of the sky, the coming of the sun as it touched Mont Blanc, and then the lesser mountains, and then the glacier; when the sunshine reached the grass of the hotel yard, she would go back to bed and sleep until called by Miss Sargent to get ready for breakfast.

A wonderful change was taking place in Margaret, as these happy weeks glided by. Gradually her health was established, and with restored health, came back the fair flesh, and delicate color; the brightness of eye, and elasticity of step. Miss Sargent and Mr. Latimer beheld the beautiful miracle that was being wrought out before their eyes, with feelings akin to awe; but Margaret did not realize when her heart once more rested in confidence on her lover, that every drop of blood in her veins, every nerve, and the very tissues of her body, partook of a new power: and that, in the atmosphere of happiness that enveloped her, her being was blossoming out to the fullness of its beauty. Poor Rodger was half the time in a delirium of love, and half the time depressed by fear and humility. As he saw Margaret's obvious happiness, and her restoration to perfect health, he could not doubt that she loved him; but why did she hold herself so aloof, he asked himself; never by glance, or gesture, by a touch of finger tips, or tone of voice, grant him permission to speak his love. Margaret had no idea how sorely she tried him by her archness and pretty ways. If at times her charms assailed his self-control, and for the instant he turned toward her with an impetuous movement, or a face flushing and paling with emotion, that moment, with a mental bound, she was beyond his touch: and while she had not moved from his side, she had thrown, by manner and expression, a barrier between, that he dared not cross; and before which his pulses cooled, and his heart turned sick with hope deferred. Nothing could be kinder than Margaret's manner: and Rodger was flattered and made entirely happy for the time being, by her evident happiness in his society, as they strolled through the woods, and walked over the mountains together. But the heart of the young man, at times, beat impatiently, and demanded a recognized position; a closer relation than this of serene friendship. But he never for a moment forgot that he had written to Miss Sargent that he would speak no word of love to Margaret unbidden: and he held himself to this promise with such patience and calmness as he was able; ever looking for a tacit permission from Margaret to speak. One evening he thought his probation was closing. He and Margaret had taken a long walk that afternoon, and on their return were sitting on the piazza with Miss Sargent. Rodger was smoking, and Margaret was sitting a little way off looking at the mountains. For some time Miss Sargent had been regarding Mr. Latimer with a fixed gaze; she broke the silence by saying:

"I would like to know, Rodger, how much truth there is in a story that our landlord told me about you this afternoon."

"I'll be glad to inform you, my dear Madam, if I

know anything about it," replied Rodger; "what was the story?"

"Why, it was about a young man here of the name of Jerome, a young American, who's traveling with a company of young men; the landlord said he had consumption, and couldn't live, and was destitute of money, and that you were paying his bills; how much truth is there in this story, Rodger?"

For a few moments Mr. Latimer was silent. Margaret came and sat down beside Miss Sargent, who spoke again:

"Is there any such young man here? what do you know of him?"

"This is all I know," said Rodger. "Sometime last week, I was sitting around the corner, on the piazza, smoking; it was a dark night, and I was alone, and I supposed everybody was asleep on this hall. The window of the corner room was open, but there was no light in it. After awhile two men commenced to talk in the room. The very first sentence arrested my attention: it was something like this: 'To think that I must die for want of a few hundred dollars.' So I sat still, and listened to the conversation, and learned that the speaker was from Philadelphia, a clerk in a store there, that his father and mother had died of consumption, that he had a sister teaching in the public schools, and that his health had been failing for some time; and that some physician had told him that his only chance was to take a sea voyage, and to spend some time in a mountainous region. The trip—as a matter of course—had cost more than he had expected, and his money was getting low; but what was worse, some physician here in the house had examined his lungs, and advised him to go home and stay there, but told him that he could not live through the winter under any circumstances, as one lung was gone, and the other was considerably affected. His friend, who I found out afterward was a theological student, gave him sound financial advice, and orthodox spiritual comfort, but did not seem to possess much else toward helping him out of his troubles. The next morning I got hold of all the facts I could; it is one of those sad cases every one meets with in summer traveling."

"You need not say in summer traveling, Rodger," said Miss Sargent, "a few years ago I was in Jacksonville in January, and one morning as I came out from breakfast, there was a man reclining on the piazza steps, thin as a skeleton, pale, and coughing hard enough to shake his bones apart. I sat down by him, and learned that a few moments before he had come from the depot, and had given his last cent to the driver for his hack fare. He was evidently near death, but through the advice of some thoughtless or incompetent physician, he had paid out his last cent to get to Florida, expecting when there, to obtain some light employment that would pay for his board."

As she ceased speaking a moment, Margaret asked, "What did you do with him, Aunt Helen?"

"Took care of him, as a matter of course. We got a pleasant room for him, that opened into a garden full of roses, and a nurse, and we fed him, and petted him, and read to him whenever he wished us to."

"Well?" said Margaret, as Miss Sargent again ceased speaking.

"Yes, I suppose it was well," answered Miss Sargent in a grave voice, "he only lived three weeks, and he was buried under a magnolia tree. It was his wish. He said those last weeks of his life had been the happiest he had ever known; and he wished to lie under a warm sod. A singular idea, wasn't it? But he told me he had hardly been warm for two years. What did you do for this young Jerome, Rodger, is he here yet?"

"Oh, yes, you must have seen him, he sits at the table next to ours; he wears a gray suit, has black hair and black eyes."

"Have you seen him, and talked with him yourself?"

"Yes."

"Has he any property at home? Can he recover? How long is he to stay here?"

"No, he has no property at home; he cannot recover; so a physician in the house tells me, a great man from Zurich: as to his stay here, he leaves to-morrow, I believe." As Mr. Latimer said this he struck a match, lighted his cigar that had gone out, and smoked in silence.

"Come, Rodger," said Miss Sargent, "you need not expect to escape me in this way. I want to know all about the young man's needs, and what you've done for him; what plans you have made for him, and if there is anything that I can do, in seeing that he has proper clothing, or in supplying him with needed money."

"Suppose I answer your last question first, my dear friend. There is nothing you can do in supplying him with needed money, for he doesn't need any. As to clothing, I went through his trunk in a real motherly way, to his last flannel shirt. As to his plans, I don't know anything about sick men, or their needs, but my Zurich doctor helped me out, and we have a beautiful plan reaching, he, the doctor says, far beyond the young fellow's life."

"What is it? What are you and the doctor going to do?"

"We are *not* going to place him in the Home for Friendless Women, or in an orphan asylum," said Mr. Latimer, with affected seriousness.

"That is well," replied Miss Sargent, with like seriousness, "I have had a great many necessitous cases to look after myself, and from the experience I have gained, I should say that you and the great Zurich doctor had done very well, so far. I suppose that neither of you advised the young man to jump off Mont Blanc for exercise, or swim back home for the good effect of a salt water bath."

" No, we did not."

"Now, as Margaret and I know what you and Doctor Zurich did *not* do, please tell us what you *did* plan to do."

Rodger dropped his tone of mock gravity, as he replied: "We planned for the young man to go home, reaching there by the last of September. His sister is to get a substitute to hold the place in the public school for her, and go with her brother to the Gulf climate, somewhere, and stay until, well, until he don't need her attention any longer. The doctor says he cannot possibly live beyond February, but that he will not suffer much, and that he and his sister will have a charming time through the early winter in that Southern climate. Think of a doctor's talking that way of a man who is to die in a few weeks! But let us go in to dinner, he added," rising to his feet. "I hope we shall have a clear night to see Mont Blanc."

"I hope so, too," said Margaret, as she slipped her hand in Miss Sargent's, as they started for the dining-room; "but every moonlight night clouds up so, or the mist rises over the mountains, I begin to be afraid we sha'n't see Mont Blanc by moonlight, after all."

Mr. Latimer pointed out young Jerome to Miss Sargent, as they were seated at the table.

"What do you think of him?" asked Rodger.

"I don't think it shows any remarkable knowledge in

your Zurich doctor, to see that a man in his condition cannot live long. I am glad you are smoothing his way, Rodger; and now where are those birds you promised us for dinner?"

Immediately after dinner, Miss Sargent tarried in their parlor to receive a gentleman from New York, who had sent his card to her. As he entered the room, Margaret withdrew to the piazza, where Mr. Latimer found her soon after, leaning on the railing gazing at the mountains as their outlines were merging into the dusky horizon, and at the stars as they came out in the sky above. As he stood beside her, she turned her head toward him and said:

"Aunt Helen and I have been talking about you, Rodger; she says as a matter of course, your Zurich doctor does no more for Mr. Jerome, than to give his professional opinion without charging anything, and that it is you who planned that his sister should go south and take care of him. I think that it is very beautiful in you to do so much for a poor, friendless young man."

"You overrate what I have done, Margery."

"It's a great deal," she replied, "think what a difference it will make to Mr. Jerome, all the difference there is between suffering and comfort."

"It may be a great deal to him. I can see that it will be; I'm speaking of my part in it; it's a little thing for me to do."

"A little thing!" exclaimed Margaret.

"Yes, a little thing, Margery. I make no exertion, only write one letter to a Clinton banker; and I give up nothing, all that I give to Jerome is simply from the overflow of my income."

"But how many beautiful things you might have purchased for yourself with that money."

"There are no beautiful things that I wish for, and if there were, there's money enough left to buy them. It's very pleasant to hear nice things said about you, Margery, if you deserve them; but there really is no value to be attached to what I've done for Jerome. You simply can't see a man suffer, if it is in your power to relieve him."

"I suppose you'll admit that a generous heart is of value?"

"Yes, of the very greatest."

"Many would never have thought of assisting Mr. Jerome, the idea of it would never have occurred to them. It takes a generous nature to do a generous act; it is the heart that suggests to the head."

"So it does, but the generous act of one man may require no sacrifice on his part of time, inclination, or anything whatever; while that of another, may require great self-denial. To illustrate: I know a young woman, who had it in her heart to assist a needy woman—and the needy woman was very needy and helpless—and this young woman gave her time and money, and social influence, to gather a band of pupils; and then, as though that were not enough for her to do, in order to make her plan successful, she opened her own home, and turned her parlor into a schoolroom; and gave up her mornings to a troup of little children and their teacher; and did it all with such sweetness and womanly tact, that the object of her sympathy never dreamed of the sacrifices made, but was brought to believe that she gave as much as she received." Mr. Latimer ceased speaking, and looked away from Margaret, off into the night. All of the time he had been speaking, Margaret had not changed her position of leaning with crossed arms on the railing; but as he ceased, she raised herself and stood by his side. Her heart was beating fast, and as he turned his head

toward her, she pressed her left hand on her breast. The
light from the parlor shone through **the** door **full** upon
her. Her eyes had the **old** time wide-open, luminous
look in them, her lips were slightly parted, **and the** wind
stirred the fluffy hair above her brow. Rodger's heart
ached with the intensity **of its love, as** he looked at her.
He extended his hand, **and she laid** her right one in it,
palm to palm. Every drop of **blood in** his veins rushed
on in ecstasy as he tightly clasped **it; his time** had come!
It was but for a moment, though, **for** Margaret quickly
withdrew her hand, turned with a **half-frightened** air, and
passed rapidly into the parlor, where she ran into Miss
Sargent's arms, who, after bidding good-night **to** her
guest, was just then going out on the piazza **to** join
Rodger and Margaret.

"You're not going in as early as this, are you dear?"
said Miss Sargent, as she passed her arm about Margaret
and turned her back; "I want to tell you and Rodger of
a beautiful man that we are to see to-morrow. Did you
ever hear of Doctor Brunson, Rodger? Charles Brunson?" she asked, as she seated herself and Margaret on a
lounge, not far from Mr. Latimer.

"Charles Brunson? No, I do not recall any such
man," said Rodger.

"I've met him only a few times myself; he was at
Mackinaw last summer, Margaret, when we were there,
but perhaps you do not remember him."

Margaret said she did not; and Rodger inquired who
he was.

"He's a wonderful man," Miss Sargent replied, "he is
thoroughly educated, and has traveled all over the world.
He inherited a fortune, not a large one, but his income is
more than sufficient for his wants, and there never was a
man who did so much good with so little money. He is

a preacher, but he has no special church under his charge; he preaches wherever he finds a vacant pulpit, wherever there seems to be a demand for him at that time. He is always doing good to some one. I don't believe there's a man in America, who has befriended as many young men and women; there is no end of the sewing machines and type-writers, that he has assisted dependent girls to buy; or of the young men he has helped to positions. And then his correspondence is something wonderful; he's constantly receiving letters from all over the country, from people who're in trouble, asking for advice, and for pecuniary assistance, and for all sorts of things. He answers all of these letters himself, and keeps up a regular correspondence with a large number of young people, for the purpose of giving direction to their mental and moral development."

"And was it this Francis de Sales you had in the parlor just now?" asked Rodger.

"Yes, he's to preach in the English church to-morrow morning, and we'll go and hear him. He's a beautiful speaker."

The next morning they went to the English church and listened to a sermon from Doctor Brunson, on Peter's denial of Christ, the thought of which, was the brotherhood of man. Although the sermon did not contain a single denunciation of any of the methods of conducting business at the present day, of any of the existing social codes, or customs, the principles evolved from Christ's life and teachings, were presented in so simple and practical a manner, that the mere statement was a terrible rebuke, and a fearful denunciation, of nearly all the relations held between man and man in this Christian era, world over, be they monetary, or social; ecclesiastical, or political.

24 Rodger Latimer's Mistake.

CHAPTER XXXIII

Very early the next morning Margaret was wakened out of a deep sleep by a tapping at her piazza door. She opened her eyes upon a room full of moonlight, and lay very still listening When the rapping was repeated she sprang from her bed and went to the door.

"Who's there?" she asked.

"It's me, Margaret, Aunt Helen," replied Miss Sargent's well-known voice. Margaret immediately admitted her.

"I woke up a few moments ago," said Miss Sargent, "and the moonlight was so bright in my room I stepped out on the piazza to look at the mountains. They are beautiful, Margaret. You can see Mont Blanc almost as clearly as in daylight. Get on your clothes and wrap up warm. It isn't three o'clock yet, but you might wait six months for such a view, and then not get it. You have spoken so frequently of wishing to see Mont Blanc by moonlight that I was afraid you might be disappointed if I didn't call you."

Margaret was hastily putting on her clothes. "Indeed I should have been," she said, as she drew the curling pins from her front hair, passed a comb through her bangs, and then tied a soft, white woolen scarf about her head and ears. No cry of delight passed her lips as she stood without and looked upon the scene before her. Its holy calm silenced human speech. The moon was at the full and shone through an atmosphere as clear as diamond. It was three-quarters over its night's journey and hung in the southwest large and bright. The air was free from moisture, and perfectly still. The heavens were nearly bare of stars. Right in front of Margaret stood Mont Blanc, rising aloft above the lesser mountains that seemed like subjects grouped around their king. There stood the monarch, not leaning against the sky, as it so often appeared to in the day, but standing out in space, with an immensity of night back of it and above it, towering in its mighty strength far up from earth into the heavens, where it rested in eternal calm.

"Rodger must not lose this," said Miss Sargent, after she and Margaret had stood side by side for some time gazing in silence on the scene. She turned and passed down the piazza toward his room, which was the other side of their sitting-room, being the last of their four rooms. In a moment she returned and drew a chair close to Margaret, who had seated herself in her absence, but was still gazing in rapt attention on the glorious panorama before her. Soon Rodger came toward them with a large shawl hanging from his shoulders, and a Turkish smoking cap on his head.

"Good-morning, Miss McVey," he said in an airy tone, as he came to Margaret's side, opposite to Miss Sargent. Margaret did not return his salutation in words, but turning her head looked up to him as he stood beside her, with a smile of kind greeting. Immediately he caught her mood, and after gazing a moment at her face radiant with the intensity of her emotion, he looked off into the night and up to the majestic mountain. The smile left his lips, he crossed his arms on his breast, and stood in motionless silence. For half an hour no word was spoken, then Miss Sargent said:

"I think I must go in, Margaret, I would like to stay, but I dare not sit longer in this night air."

"May I stay?" asked Margaret, as Miss Sargent rose to go.

"Certainly, my dear, by all means.   Rodger will stay with you, won't you, Rodger?"

" I shall be glad to," said Mr. Latimer, "if Margery will permit me, we ought not to lose this scene; we never shall see anything like it again."

As Miss Sargent went to her room she looked to the northeast and noticed a line of daylight along the horizon, and the gray of morning above it, softly mingling with the moonlight of the night.

Mr. Latimer seated himself in a chair by Margaret's side.   For a long time he was fully possessed by the solemn beauty of the surpunding scene, but after awhile he began to feel the presence of the woman he loved. Margaret gazed at Mont Blanc and he gazed at her. She was not thinking of Rodger at all, and he saw she was not, nor was she thinking of herself.   She was lost in a revery that had no beginning, and led nowhere.   But he felt content to gaze in silence on the enraptured face; the fluffy hair that had escaped from the fleecy head covering, the far-seeing eyes, and the delicate curves of the slightly closed lips.   Something of the definiteness of daylight was surrounding them, though they knew it not, and yet the light retained a little of the dreamy mistiness of moonlight.   Rodger sat very quiet, hoping that Margaret would turn to him, and after awhile she did.   As her eyes rested on his face, she read in every lineament the entreaty of his heart.   He had not spoken a word since Miss Sargent left them, and he was absolutely unable to utter a commonplace sentence, as Margaret turned toward him, nor did he strive to conceal the passionate pleadings of his love.   There was a downward flutter of her eyelids, a moment's hesitation, then she raised her eyes again to his face, and read every word written thereon. Instantly there came a rush of color over her neck and brow, and as Rodger saw the red wave surging up, he trembled from head to foot. Margaret quailed and dropped her eyes, then turned them to the mountains an instant, and then immediately back to his face. He sat motionless as marble, only his white face pleading before her. The entire nature of the girl; reason, will, and feeling, bowed in obedience to the immutable law of love, and as she leaned affectionately toward him, he dropped upon one knee beside her chair, and clasped both arms around her, and held her to his breast. For a long time nothing was said, neither could speak. After the first ecstatic sense of possession—that tumultuous joy that follows the meeting of heart with heart—had subsided somewhat, so that consecutive thought was re-established, the mind of each turned to the past. Margaret remembered, as though thinking of an unpleasant dream, all of her months of sorrow and loneliness, all of her bitterness of soul, and the dread she had felt of the years that awaited her in middle life, and old age, should she be unfortunate enough to live to old age. And now as she felt Rodger's heart beating beneath her head, his cheek pressed to her brow, and his arms around her; she was ashamed, that in her hours of suffering, and apparent desolation, she had exclaimed against God, and questioned His love and goodness. Humbly she prayed for forgiveness, and a faith founded on a belief in the immutable justice and goodness of a Supreme Being.

Margaret gained the calmness of thought long before Rodger did, and his confession was not to heaven, as hers had been. He thought of the last time he held Margaret in his arms, as his promised wife, on the little piazza of the Edgewood home, and then, how he had called another woman wife. Oh! the bitter waters he had wrung out for Margaret to drink! The years passed before him, what they had been to him, what they must have been to her; could she forgive it? was it possible that she could love him without accusation and recrimination? He raised his head from hers, upon which it had been resting, and as he tightened the clasp of his arms around her, he cried:

"Oh! Margery, my love! my only love! can you ever forgive me? Peter denied Christ three times, and Christ forgave him; can you forgive me?"

"Hush! Rodger, don't speak in that way," she replied, and as she spoke, she raised her hand and laid it with a soft pressure on the side of his face. How well he remembered the sweet caress! The touch was light, but no words could have meant as much. It told him of complete forgiveness, of a perfect re-establishment of the old relation between her and himself. The reaction shook him with tremendous power, and he burst into tears, and sobbed like a woman, as he bowed his head again upon Margaret's. She wept with him, and comforted him, as only a gentle woman can comfort the man she loves, when he suffers.

"And you are sure, darling, that you love me as much as you used to?" he asked, after she had soothed him into peace, and they had both become calm.

"Very sure, Rodger, and with an unalterable love, for this is based on a positive knowledge of your character."

"You ought to have known me well," said Rodger, "in those years, when we lived so much together."

"In those years I never thought about knowing you, I only loved you," she replied.

Rodger caught the little hand that was wandering in light touches from his cheek to his brow and hair, and pressed it to his lips. He kissed the warm palm, and each dainty finger. Then he took her other hand, the left one, and looked at it. It wore no ring. He held it in one of his own and passed the other gently over it, as he seemed lost in thought. After a little he took a small box from his inside coat pocket, and from the box took a ring, which he placed in Margaret's hand for her to look at.

"It's the old ring, Margery," he said, in a very sad voice, scarcely above a whisper. "I came across it accidentally, more than a year ago. Since last September I have always carried it about me. May I put it on your finger again?"

She smiled as she gave it back to him without saying a word, and he placed it on the finger which it had encircled for more than a year, in the happy, careless past. He did not look at her as he placed it there, but looked at the hand with the ring on that he held in his own. After a few minutes he said, without raising his eyes:

"It's an old fashioned setting, Margery, we'll have it reset."

"No, I like it better as it is, I shall never have it changed."

He raised his eyes to the girlish face so full of happiness, and placing his arm around her shoulder, drew her to him and kissed her lips with as unselfish a devotion as a doting mother might have kissed the child of her life. Why was it, in obedience to what mental law, that just then, as he leaned over the maiden he loved, the image of Marie Edwards rose before him?

"Just now, my darling," he said, as he raised his head, "a thought of Marie came to me; shall I tell you of her? as near as I can, how I came to marry her, how I thought I loved her? As near as I can, I say, Margery, for I don't think it possible to give a very clear account of the relation."

"Yes, Rodger," replied Margaret, as she raised her

head from Mr. Latimer's arm; "I would like to have you tell me all about Marie, but not now, sometime tell me all you can, everything."

"I am glad to hear you say so, my darling love. You and I must have nothing from each other. There must be nothing we cannot speak of. I'm sure that I am not only willing, but anxious, to lay my life bare before you, with all of its weaknesses and mistakes. I don't want to have a skeleton in our home."

"You are right, Rodger," said Margaret, "there must not be any locked up rooms in our hearts that we cannot enter together, nothing hidden away that we fear to stumble upon. There must not be anything to be avoided between us. Sometime tell me all about Marie, and all about your married life with her." She spoke as calmly as though speaking of some one who was a stranger to them both. "I could not bear to live with you, haunted by the fear that some chance word of mine might be like a spark to a magazine of memories. We don't want any ground whereon either of us might chance to step, to return a hollow sound, and I'm afraid this might be the case, if we do not, with the most perfect frankness, go over with each other all of the experiences of our lives during the years of our separation, since that August when I last saw you in Edgewood."

Her words deeply affected Mr. Latimer. "Do you know what you are asking, my dearest, my darling?" he said.

"Yes, perfectly," she replied, as she held both of his hands close, as though to quiet his great agitation. "In doing this, we may perhaps give ourselves some sad hours, but after all, will there not be more of happiness than sadness in them? And, Rodger," she continued, looking him in the face, "can you not go over every inch of the way, holding my hand in yours?"

"Every inch of it, Margery," he replied, confidently returning her gaze. "But it is not my telling you all about myself, everything in my life to the last detail, during these three years; for I really believe that with my arm around you, darling, you knowing how completely I love you; you could bear, perhaps, to hear all about my infatuation and merited disappointment, for you never did me wrong; but, Margery, it's different with me, I cruelly wronged you; and while I see the force of what you say, and I know that it is best, and I can understand the sweet serenity that will bless our married life, when as husband and wife we sit at our own fireside with our lives fully known to each other—and I know it must be so, and I would not have it otherwise—yet, Margery, you will have to be patient with me, and tell me very gently, of those dark days I brought to you."

"O Rodger, you don't quite know me yet," said Margaret, "believe me, when I say that I never knew how much there was in life until this morning, and just now, I would not, if I could, change the past. But don't let us talk of it now, it will come along naturally in its place, as we live together. Shall we go to Aunt Helen?"

They both rose to their feet. They had not noticed the lapse of time as they had been talking, they had not seen the moonlight on the mountain side fade out before the dawn, its yellow light give place to the purplish hue of the morning clouds. It was night, when they sat down there together, with the silence of three years between their hearts, but it was full day as they stood side by side, Rodger holding in his hand Margaret's hand, that wore the old betrothal ring. Before going in to see Miss Sargent, they waited a few minutes to see the sunrise. It touched the top of Mont Blanc, then passed swiftly from peak to peak of the lower mountains down whose snowy sides the light quickly came, gilding with brightness the myriads of crags and rocks, and falling at last upon the meadows below in a golden sheen.

Rodger took off his cap, and stood with bared head, as he turned his eyes from the mighty mountains, to the slight girl by his side, who stood in a radiance of sunlight, looking into the coming day.

THE END.

www.ingramcontent.com/pod-product-compliance
Lightning Source LLC
Chambersburg PA
CBHW021708110726
47902CB00005B/1108